THE DEEP END

A NOVEL

THE DEEP ENID

A NOVEL

TYLER TORK

CASTLE
PRESS

an imprint of

THE OGHMA PRESS

OGHMA
CREATIVE MEDIA

Bentonville, Arkansas • Los Angeles, California
www.oghmacreative.com

Library of Congress Cataloging-in-Publication Data

Names: Tork, Tyler, author.
Title: The Deep End/Tyler Tork
Description: First Edition. | Bentonville: Castle, 2020.
Identifiers: LCCN: 2019952069 | ISBN: 978-1-63373-536-1 (hardcover) |
ISBN: 978-1-63373-537-8 (trade paperback) | ISBN: 978-1-63373-538-5 (eBook)
Subjects: | BISAC: FICTION/Fantasy / Contemporary | FICTION/Science Fiction/Steampunk |
FICTION/Fantasy/Urban
LC record available at: https://lccn.loc.gov/2019952069

Castle Press trade paperback edition November, 2022

Cover Illustrator and Designer: Dylan Hale
Interior Designer: Casey W. Cowan
Editor: Gordon Bonnet

Published by Castle Press, an imprint of The Oghma Press, a subsidiary of The Oghma Book Group.

CLORA

THE LAST THING YOU WANT when trying to manage an overloaded tray is a bunch of people blocking the hallway. "Make way!" Clora called. "Don't make Miss Marlee's breakfast late."

"She's gone mad," said old Jitennes, the floor maid. "Screaming like a lunatic, then crying. I wouldn't go in there."

"Of course you must go in." Marlee's clerk Bylamar, immaculate in a pleated velvet tunic, poked a folded paper in Clora's direction. "She has a full schedule."

Clora ignored the paper, dodging between them and two other maids, using the implied threat of hot cocoa and pastries to break a path. "I'll tell her. Anni, the door, please."

"She locked it," Anni mumbled.

Clora thrust the tray into Anni's hands, and reached into her pocket for the ring of three keys she had the honor to carry—one for her own room, one for Marlee's, and one for Marlee's wardrobe. She held the door open with her hip while retrieving the tray and backing into the room.

"Get out! I said I need to be alone!" Marlee was seated on the bed, covers clenched in her fists, wild-eyed.

Clora recognized this mood. A calm demeanor was the way to remain unscathed. "Ah, miss, but you've also said on no account is breakfast to be delayed. So I'll just set it down before I go. Where would you like it?"

"I don't—I don't know. The usual spot?"

Was the inside table or the balcony more usual? For fair weather, the balcony, Clora decided. The floor maid had already opened the curtains, so she bumped the handle with her elbow and maneuvered the tray outside.

Marlee followed Clora out, walking to the railing and looking out across the river. "Holy cow!"

Clora followed her gaze, but saw nothing to explain Marlee's astonishment or the reference to cattle. The city was much as usual, the weather tower and the huge Perlmite dome poking up through the brown fog of industry, the dirigible masts by the bay with a couple of airships docked at each, the glider launch ramp built up the side of one of the hills surrounding the city. With a distant clatter, a mail glider trundled up the ramp, accelerating until it leapt into the sky in a cloud of steam. Clora glanced at the watch pinned to her sleeve. Right on time.

"I guess I'm not in Cleveland anymore." Marlee seemed to be speaking to herself. Then she turned to look at the food Clora set out on the wrought-iron table. "That's far too much. Stupid girl."

"Mister Digriz is joining you this morning." Clora tried for a patient tone. "As you told me yesterday."

Now Marlee seemed embarrassed. What was going on? Maybe Clora hadn't seen this mood before, after all. "Sorry. I, uh, can't deal with him now. I can't see anyone. I have such a terrible headache."

"After the way I hear you carried on last night, I can't say I'm surprised." Clora tucked the tray under her arm. "I'll just send in Miss Yrenn, then."

"What part of 'can't see anyone' is unclear to you?"

"You mean to remain in your robe all day?"

Clora's incredulity must have registered, through whatever mental fog Marlee was in. "Uh, no. Of course not."

"Who is to dress you, if not Miss Yrenn? I certainly can't, or she would tan my hide for boots."

"Well, I seem to have enough boots. She can come after breakfast. But no one else." Marlee looked out over the bay again, twisting a napkin into a tight coil. "Dismissed."

MARLEE

MARLEE SAT. SHE STILL HAD no idea where she was or what had happened to her, but the initial panic was subsiding, and she was definitely ready for breakfast. She reached for a plate, disturbed again to see that brown, short-fingered hand.

Her heart was still racing. She was freaked, of course. Super freaked. But at the same time, her mind was ticking over like a computer, weighing courses of action.

Her first instinct had been to hide what happened. Logic told her that was still a good choice. Everybody here already knew her. If she told them she wasn't who they thought she was, and had no memory of them, they might help her. Or they might throw her in an asylum. Or believe her and still do nothing to help. She could always confess later. But the cat, once released from the bag, could not be reinserted.

Picking up a round bun, she walked into the bedroom, standing before the mirror. The image in the tarnished reflection was totally unlike her—a short, pudgy woman in a white linen nightgown, dark-skinned, with frizzy white hair. She looked older, maybe late twenties. And fat! She touched the round chin, the pale eyebrows, the heavy breasts, and was filled with a sense of unreality. This couldn't be happening. But trying to wake up wasn't working, so any hope this was just an unusually realistic dream was fast fading.

She was nowhere on Earth. Not in the past, unless the history books just somehow failed to mention an age of dirigibles and steam-powered glider launchers. Not in the future, unless things had taken a very strange turn. And everyone here was dark-skinned and white-haired like her, except the girl who'd brought breakfast, whose hair was pale orange. But she looked to be only in her mid-teens. Perhaps she too would go white before long.

The bun turned out to be filled with spicy ground meat. Chewing, she looked around the room. It was large, with a plaster ceiling sculpted into swooping curves and streamlined winged creatures, painted in the center to resemble a cloudy sky. The shiny-metallic green wallpaper was covered in fuzzy raised patterns of vines and flowers, and heavy wooden furniture was carved with beast faces and clawed feet.

Under a window sat a roll-top desk, closed. A few drawers in front turned out to contain pens, stationery, several dark-red square candles, a box of straight pins, a small knife. The stationery had a shield-shaped crest with a picture of a dragon clutching a sphere, above the words, *"Ai verdaro Marlee Forossi."*

So, her first name was still Marlee. But why? It was an unusual name, and if—as it seemed—she'd been thrown into some other world, it seemed long odds she'd end up with the same name. It's not like this was a version of herself from another dimension. They looked nothing alike.

A small metal plate on the roll-top turned out to be a latch, revealing dozens of labeled niches stuffed with paper, and a collection of thin books bound in colored leather. Possibly something useful there, something to look at after breakfast.

A man was now seated at a table at another balcony on the same floor. He saw her and nodded, an acknowledgment a fencer might give another fencer. Someone she was supposed to know. She nodded back, and sat.

How had she gotten here?

Her memories were muddled. She wasn't sure of their sequence, and none felt recent. Maybe the last thing was a party at Alpha Sigma Alpha— she wasn't a member, but Stacey invited her. There'd been a beer-drinking competition, and she participated in that, but how had it ended?

She poured from a sturdy ceramic teapot, into her cup. The liquid was dark brown and opaque, not tea or coffee. Cocoa? A sip, and she set it down. Maybe it was cocoa, but it was horribly bitter. She took a bite of sticky bun to chase down the taste, and continued reviewing her recollections.

CLORA

WHEN CLORA RETURNED. MARLEE HAD her chair back from the table, scowling at the floor. She'd eaten more than half the food.

"I want to make a change. Don't bring me pastries anymore. Fruit, yogurt, dry toast, a hard-boiled egg. Less food."

Clora paused in her dish clearing. "What's yogurt?"

"All right, cheese then. You know what cheese is?"

"Yes, miss. And by toast, do you mean toasted bread? What do you mean by dry?"

"No butter."

"Very well, miss. Miss Yrenn is ready for you."

"Fine. But nobody else after that."

In the hallway, Clora gave Yrenn the nod, then paused beside a wing-back chair. Bylamar looked up from the papers in his lap, peering over his spectacles. Mr. Digriz, leaning against the opposite wall, straightened up too. "You needn't either of you wait. She isn't seeing anyone."

"Surely that doesn't include me," Bylamar said, while Digriz helped himself to a couple of sausage rolls and a podfruit from the tray.

"She's in a mood. She was out so late, I thought she'd have a bad head, but she barely tasted her remedy." Clora pointed her chin at a cup of thick green liquid on the tray. "I don't know what the matter is."

Bylamar sighed and pulled out his pocket watch. "Remind her we have a full day." He again held out the folded sheet. "Please give her this schedule."

"Does it look like I have a free hand? I'll take it when I come back."

When she did return, Marlee was seated sideways at her vanity while Miss Yrenn, a huge, tall black-skinned woman with a gravelly voice, stood behind her with one knee planted in the middle of Marlee's back, yanking savagely at the corset laces.

"Hello," Marlee complained. "Does a person get to breathe?"

Miss Yrenn gave a booming laugh. "Beauty is your duty."

"Can't I be beautiful in a looser dress?"

"No. Clora, girl, hand me those pins."

"Clora," Marlee muttered. She picked up Bylamar's page from the vanity. "What's this?"

"Your schedule. Bylamar says hurry, or you'll be late meeting your grandfather. Mister Digriz is still waiting, too."

"Bylamar?" Marlee scanned the paper. "I can't do all this. I need time alone." She threw the paper down. "I'm not saying it again."

"Arms up!"

"Shall I tell them you're indisposed?"

"Yes. All day."

Clora opened the door to pass this on, then shut it on Bylamar's protest. Digriz, still helping to support the wall, just looked amused.

"Arms down!" Miss Yrenn waggled a ruffled underskirt. "Here, step in." Marlee stepped inside.

Miss Yrenn waited a moment, then glared at her, and jerked her head. "No fooling around."

Marlee turned halfway, and Miss Yrenn tied the skirt. "I spoke to the Misses Hrootsi, about your clothes for court."

"Court?"

Miss Yrenn fluffed the underskirt's ruffles. "They have trouble finding enough matching garnet beads for the yellow silk, and wished to know whether glass will suffice. I told her no."

"All right."

"We want everything perfect for your grandfather's investiture. Turn."

Marlee turned. "His... sure, of course. Whatever you think best."

"After all, you will be a Highlady. There's a standard to maintain. Face front."

Clora watched Miss Yrenn fasten the buttons of the dark red dress. There was something off about Marlee today, some distraction. Something big was going on, and Clora meant to figure out what.

MARLEE

ALONE AT LAST. MARLEE FIRST found and made use of the bathroom attached to her room. She should've gone earlier, but the corset made it more urgent.

She'd let herself be dressed and her hair done, hoping to change into something more comfortable after Yrenn left. But while the dress was designed to make solo toilet usage possible, she wouldn't be able to undress alone without scattering little buttons all over the floor. The corset actually wasn't unpleasant, though. It was comfortably snug, familiar.

Which was all the weirder. Though she didn't remember anything about this place or people, everything seemed familiar. It felt natural to snap orders to the maid, as if she'd been doing it all her life. Though apparently not even she would dare snap at Miss Yrenn.

She was still sorting through memories. As she retied her underthings and smoothed the layers of her dress, she pictured her mom as she'd last seen her, hurriedly applying makeup, late for a book club meeting. Her dad, who called every Saturday morning even with nothing particular to say—not that she cared what he'd been doing with his new girlfriend anyway. Her boyfriend Bobby, her girlfriends, her team on QuestZone.... What was going on back home? Was she missing? Unconscious? Or, horrid thought, did the previous inhabitant of this body swap places with her? Was she even now busy making a shambles of Marlee's life?

Whatever the situation, everybody must be worried about her. And she had projects due for school, the big Econ paper. At least, she didn't remember turning it in. It was pretty minor in the grand scheme, but it bugged her. She'd started it late, and meant to make a big push to finish.

Well. Enough time mooning about. She'd better find clues before more people barged in on her. Her eye fell first on Bylamar's schedule. It was on heavy paper, written in a tidy squarish script. The top right corner said, *"2 Cavy 687,"* presumably the date.

The obvious place to start was the desk. Perhaps there was a diary. But first, on impulse, she opened the stationery drawer, uncapped a pen, and drew a few squiggles on a sheet of thick, cream-colored paper. The pen wrote smoothly, the line black and crisp. Nice.

She signed her name, or tried to. "Marlee Feldman," she wrote. But her fingers didn't want to form her usual rounded letters. They tried to go all spiky and angular, ending as an unreadable mess.

This was more upsetting than anything else, or maybe it was the last straw on top of everything else. She tried again, with no better result, then again, drawing each letter carefully. Which approximated her signature, but looked like an obvious forgery. She gave a little sob, stood up, knocking over the chair, and threw the pen against the wall.

She paced for a couple of minutes, then wiped her face on her sleeve and returned to the desk, opening the roll top.

The little niches were each neatly labeled. Some labels looked like names, others read *"horses"*, *"royals"*, *"rates"*, *"rents"*, *"contracts"*, and *"ideas."* There was also a built-in machine with a crank handle and two horizontal rollers, a few gummy cubes, a magnifying lens, blank metal disks, a roll of string, a squat silver salt-shaker....

The books first. There were three, each with a metal latch that opened to her touch. Two were ledgers, filled with columns of names and numbers. The last was the hoped-for journal, unfortunately only a quarter full. She flipped to the last non-blank page.

Wineday, 30 Elabolon 687: cloudy, hot, it began. If today was 2 Cavy, this couldn't be yesterday's entry. Damn! She'd hoped for something about the day before.

She read on.

Gaddis reports new foal looks promising. Of course he would say so. Must go out next week. If she's no better than the last one, Gaddis is out.

Dined with D.C. He's bought a patent for a new brewing process, wants funding. How much can beer actually be improved? Ask Rob.

S. Lallis has signed an unwise contract with Father. A lovely little scheme. I've tied up the salt pork suppliers so he can't meet the contract. The only way he can raise money to pay the penalty is to sell shares, at a discount since Digriz is putting out the word that Lallis' company is in trouble. Which, technically, is true, even though we're the ones causing it. So we buy up shares on the cheap and collect a penalty besides. Quite pleased I thought of it.

Jeyne has a new floozy he wants me to meet. Doubtless another gold-digger, but that's not my problem. Might be entertaining.

"Marlee," Marlee muttered, "you are a piece of work." At least here were a couple of clues. Digriz was spreading rumors on her behalf, so he must be an employee. Rob was someone who answered questions, perhaps another employee. And she raised horses, or someone raised them for her. She licked her finger and flipped back, skimming.

Cousin Neidra has turned up in a little town thirty miles away. Dirty, ragged, lying in a hay-stack, quite mad. They had to put her away. A shame, since she's been one of Father's backers. My uncles are the obvious beneficiaries. Not Kosimo's style, I think. He'd just have her killed. So, likely Freddan.

Must find out how he did it—and in only four days, since the locals saw her a week before she was identified. Might come in handy. Ask Rob.

Could the same thing that happened to her, have happened to Neidra? If so, Neidra might well appear insane—or whoever was in her body might actually have flipped out. It would be something to look into, once she learned enough to avoid being locked away herself. And it confirmed her opinion that revealing her plight might be a bad idea. There was no hint anyone was doing anything to help poor cousin Neidra, just that she'd been "put away" somewhere. Doubtless her fate would be the same, if she were discovered. She turned back another page.

CLORA

CLORA RAPPED ON THE DOOR with the side of her shoe, then slipped inside with a stack of linens in her arms.

Miss Forossi was at her desk, absorbed in her papers, her journal lying open beside them. Clora licked her lips. She'd been offered plenty of money by more than one person for a look at that journal, but Marlee was careful never to leave the desk open, and nobody else could unseal it without destroying it, and maybe themselves as well. But she could watch for opportunities.

"And I thought my family was dysfunctional."

"Pardon, miss?"

Marlee looked up. "Clora, do you have a family?"

"You know I do. My ma and two brothers. Ovid works in your stables."

"That's right. Tell me, do you and your brothers ever try to kill each other?"

Clora laughed. She set the clean sheets on the bedstand and started to strip the bed. "Not since we were little."

"Nor kidnap each other's friends to use for leverage?"

Clora gave her a sideways look. Marlee didn't seem angry anymore, at least. "Not sure I know what that is."

"That's what I thought." Marlee walked to the window.

Clora bundled up the sheets. "You and your brother get on pretty well."

"Well, yes. As long as our interests align, apparently. It's nice to know there's somebody who doesn't want me dead."

Clora unwrapped a pillow cover and fluffed the pillow. "Bylamar is unhappy you missed your meeting with Mister Josip. He said you best really be ill."

Marlee turned back around, and a flash of annoyance crossed her face. "Don't you have things to do?"

Clora got busy and finished the sheets, checked the water pitcher and the small candy bowl on a side table, which needed refilling.

"You can take those away."

"Miss?"

"The candy. Get rid of it."

"But you just ate some." Three wax-paper wrappers lay near the bowl.

"Exactly."

Clora picked up the bowl and loose wrappers, dropped them into a pocket. "Will there be anything else?"

"No. Wait, yes. I'd like to talk with Rob as soon as possible."

"Rob?"

"Yes, I ask him things all the time. I have a science question."

"Do you mean Doctor Entersoe?"

"Um, sure. Just send him to me here."

"Won't you go to the laboratory?"

"Are you arguing with me?"

"Miss, no!"

"I thought the deal was I tell you what I want and you do it."

"You said as soon as possible. I could send a page to fetch him, but he won't come until it suits him. So the quickest way is to go to him, as usual."

"Can't you just call... no, I guess not." She paused. "Okay, here's the deal. You're going with me."

"Okay?" Was it a foreign word?

"Yes. I need you to carry—" Marlee looked around. "—that pitcher. To show Rob."

"Yes, miss." Clora threw the old sheets onto the bed and picked up the pitcher, one of Marlee's special dish set, painted with purple lilies, nearly full of water. Marlee held the door and followed her out, turning to lock up while Clora waited with the heavy pitcher in her arms.

"Marlee! Wait!" Lady Elga hurried down the hall toward them, baby Josip over her shoulder.

Marlee stiffened, but turned from her door, smiling at Elga. Clora adjusted her grip on the heavy pitcher, expecting a long wait.

"Good morning!" Elga said. "I was just coming to see you. I heard you were ill."

"Uh, hey, you. I'm better now, but don't tell anyone. I'm enjoying the time off."

"Oh. We were looking forward to taking care of you, weren't we, duckie?" This addressed to the baby. "Say boo to auntie, darling."

The baby looked at Marlee, wide-eyed, then gave a goofy grin. "Boo!"

"Eek!" Marlee cowered back.

The baby laughed, and Elga bounced him. "Did you like the Divine Quanz?"

"Um, yes, lovely."

"Because yesterday at tea, it sounded like you were only going so you could sit in the box with some Duke's son, and expected to hate it."

"It was better than I expected."

"And how was Lord Whatever?"

"About like I expected. Look, I'd love to stay and chat, but I have eighteen things to do, and I'm afraid my girl's arms might fall off."

The woman waved her free hand. "I know, you only have time for us on your sabbath." She rubbed noses with the baby. "Everyone's busy. Mommy and little Josip will just have to entertain each other." She walked on, clucking to the baby.

"Take the back way," Marlee whispered. "I don't want to meet anyone else."

They walked down the hall, past polished wood and paintings, past old Kzan shuffling down the hall with a basket of green glow rods, replacing those in the wall sconces with bright, freshly shaken ones. Clora ducked into a side passage used by servants, and took the stairs carefully, a little water sloshing onto her sleeve from the pitcher.

They emerged onto a brick path winding through perfect lawns, past tall, sculpted shrubs, statuary, and flowers arranged in patterns. Three gardeners were out, but no family members were in sight.

Dr. Entersoe worked in a one-story building set well away from the main house. It was made of soot-stained brick and concrete, with tall windows that levered out. Marlee opened doors for her until they came to one with a frosted glass pane lettered, *"Laboratory B"*.

Marlee took the pitcher. "Thanks. I'll take it from here."

Clora strolled back to the main house, enjoying the sunshine, thinking. It hadn't escaped her notice that as they walked to the engineering building, whenever they came to a branch in the path, Marlee happened to be a little behind Clora, forcing her to choose the path.

Almost as if Marlee didn't know the way.

Downstairs, in the kitchen, she found Mr. Digriz leaning over a table, talking with an undercook as she chopped onions. He looked up as she approached. "Any news?"

"Any reward?"

Digriz solemnly handed over a ten-centime coin. Clora dropped it into her pocket. "You can find Miss Marlee at the engineering building. I didn't tell you."

MARLEE

MARLEE HESITATED OUTSIDE THE LABORATORY. It occurred to her, too late, if there were more than one man inside, she wouldn't know which one was Rob.

Well, waiting here wouldn't help. She went in.

Fortunately, there was only one person, at the far end. His tweed tunic was hung over a chair, his puffy sleeves pushed back to work on something inside a wooden console. He scowled. "I'll be a minute. Don't touch anything."

She set the pitcher on the nearest clear counter space. The tables were crowded, above and below, with boxes and sacks, stacks of books and loose papers, microscopes and glassware, dirty machinery. The place smelled like dust and oil and burning. A small bin on one table held a collection of cracked rubber rings. She took one out and handled it, the crumbly material staining her fingertips.

"In what sense is that not touching anything?"

"What happened to your rubber rings?"

He threaded his way to her. If she tried to come to him, her skirts would probably have knocked over a bunch of things on the floor under the tables. "Those aren't rubbers. That's elastrin. It's expensive, so when they get rotten, we collect them and melt them down for reuse. They make excellent seals, but don't last long. What did you want? I'm busy."

They certainly looked and felt like rubber. Marlee tried to remember what she knew about it. "They're made from tree sap, right?"

"You astound me. Did you read a book?"

"I learned about it in seven—um, from a traveler."

"What do you want? What's the pitcher for?"

She dropped the ring back into the bin and wiped her fingers on her dress. "I'll get to that." Or maybe, hopefully, he would forget about it. "First, I've been thinking about my cousin Neidra—remember her? I'm starting to think maybe someone did something that swapped her mind with someone from... somewhere else. Have you heard of a way to do that? And would you know how to switch them back?" Who knew whether that really was what'd happened to Neidra, but it was an excuse to ask what she wanted to know for herself.

"Not offhand, but that's not my area. I do chemistry and aetherics. You must consult a psychist for this sort of thing. You keep coming to me with these odd questions. Science is a specialized endeavor these days."

"Well, you were close by."

"It pays to go straight to the expert, even if they're less convenient. I think Sedon Harrick is the best man in town for that sort of question. Was there anything else?"

"I don't know. Do we have any open windows? I mean," she hurried on, "do you have any updates on anything I've asked earlier?"

"Let me consult my notes." He walked back to his desk. "You know, I'm not your personal research service. I work for your father, not you."

"I asked him once. He said, 'Good old Rob works for the family. Ask him whatever you like.'"

"He never calls me Rob."

"I'm paraphrasing."

"Let's see." Rob flipped back through a notebook. "You asked me to check your dishes for detection of deekree fish venom, but I think I already told you they were fine. Just because it comes from a gland in an otherwise edible fish, doesn't matter. Poison is poison. Is that why you brought the pitcher? Did you want to test it?"

"Yes. That's right."

"Well, I can't. I don't keep exotic poisons on hand. I told you that already too. Besides, it's not necessary to test every individual poison. The little bit of your hair or blood or whatever the maker put in, ties into the spell. Anything that would harm you will trip the alarm, even something that wouldn't hurt anyone else. Say, something you were allergic to." Rob closed the notebook and threw it onto his desk. "And if you want more detail, once again I'll have to refer you, this time to a wizard. When it comes to detection spells, I hear good things about Ferrina Greenbough."

She owned special personalized poison-detecting dishes? Given what she'd read about the family, it shouldn't surprise her. Still, it was a reminder of the seriousness of her situation. People might be trying to kill her, and she didn't even know who to watch out for. Probably some of her own relatives were on that list.

"Anything else?" Rob's tone softened a little, and he looked almost sympathetic—which for some reason was even more annoying than his previous condescending manner. She must not be controlling her expression well.

"Not now. But I have something for you." She'd remembered something else from seventh grade science class. "When you melt down your rub—your elastrin, try throwing in a little sulfur. That should make it last longer."

Rob smiled tolerantly. "Chemistry advice from a banker?"

Marlee's eyes narrowed, and Rob took a little step back. "Maybe you don't know everything. Try it and see." She picked up her pitcher, turned and walked out. A metal stand clattered to the floor behind her, knocked over by the dramatic sweep of her skirts.

She shut the door and leaned against the rough wall, a little short of breath. She'd gotten so angry, it'd been hard to keep from smashing that smug bastard on the head with a random flask. Even now, she wanted to go back in there and kick his tweedy ass with her pointed shoes. She walked down the hall to give herself time to cool off.

Marlee—other Marlee—was worried someone might be trying to poison her. Given what she'd read, it seemed all too likely. She was the sort of person who probably needed killing.

And poison wasn't the only option. What if someone snuck into her room at night with a dagger? Clobbered her in the hallway? If she died here, she might wake up back home. But what if she just... died? Her heart raced, but her mind still ticked over, coldly strategizing. She'd have to learn as much as possible about any plots against her.

Marlee walked past more closed doors, past sour smells and a "chunking" sound. What if she went to her brother—Petro, wasn't it?—and confessed all? He probably wouldn't kill her. He'd want his real sister back. But he wouldn't care about getting her back home. Everything she'd read suggested nobody in her new family would care about that.

A tall, green-skinned man in a stained white coat came out of a door ahead, saw her, and stepped aside. She nodded to him absently as she passed. Green? It didn't look like makeup.

Whoever caused Marlee's situation might know how to fix it. But why would they? This might be exactly what they'd wanted. If they didn't already know their plan worked, she'd like to keep it that way.

She stopped at a doorway into a room containing tall racks of glass tanks filled with something pink and blobby. Two women moved along the rows, drawing a little reddish liquid from a valve on each tank, before pouring a clear liquid into the open top. The contents of the tank being serviced quivered, crowding away from the glass. Marlee made a face, and moved on.

The house, or palace, whatever you called it, was full of people who'd expect her to recognize them. Even if she hid in her room, people might barge in with questions she couldn't answer. She should stay away until she'd learned enough to disguise her ignorance. Just go away and figure things out, leaving some excuse.

She came to a place where the hallway broadened out, the green tube-lights barely illuminating a stack of rusty metal barrels in front of a sturdy wooden door that opened upward, like a garage door. She stopped there, meditatively pushing a chunk of wood with her shoe.

She had to get into town. She could see the expert Rob recommended, Harrick. Figure out what had been done to her. Learn enough to keep the deception going.

It was the start of a plan, anyway. She returned to the entrance door, where there'd been a few children in uniforms lounging on a bench. There were still three of them, waiting side by side just inside the door. Marlee addressed the largest, who looked about ten years old. "You. I need a message carried. Can you do that?"

He stood to attention, silver buttons flashing in the sun. "Of course, miss!"

"Do you have any paper?"

The boy produced a flat case containing a stack of odd-shaped papers, a pencil, and a dark candle like those in her desk. Marlee scrawled a quick note, folded it, and handed it over. "This is for Clora, a maid in the main house. You know how to find her?"

The boy hesitated, glanced at the note. "Won't you seal and address it?"

There hadn't been any adhesive on the paper, though she'd seen how to fold it into its own envelope. And she wasn't certain how to spell the girl's name. "Just take it to her, please."

The boy shrugged, gave a little salute, and sped out the door. Marlee followed, hoping to find a secluded spot to wait for Clora to show up.

"There you are."

Marlee jumped, turning to see who'd spoken. Seated on a decorative boulder beside the entrance was a tall, slender, man. He wore a green tunic with thin black stripes, a bit of lace at the neck and cuffs, and a scalloped edge hanging over sharply creased black pants. Unlike most other people she'd seen here, he was light-skinned, with long brown hair held back with a silver band. "Sorry to startle you. When I heard you were up and about, I thought we might have our meeting, after all."

Right. Who was this? Bylamar's schedule listed several meetings. This couldn't be her grandfather, but that was all she could rule out. "It's not really convenient."

He stood. "We can talk as we walk to wherever you're bound."

Marlee sighed. By sending the note, she'd committed herself to wait here. She sat on the bench, signaling the man to do the same.

"So." He sat, careful of his clothing. "Why did you want to see me?"

Good question. She looked out across the perfect lawn for a few seconds. "I think you know," she said, hoping he did.

This made him visibly nervous. "I'm not sure what you mean."

Marlee raised one eyebrow.

"Is this about my meeting with Freddan?"

"Good guess."

He was silent, looking at her.

"Trying to come up with a story?"

He laughed, running a finger under his collar. "Trying to figure out how you heard about it so quickly. I was going to tell you, of course. He sent for me. I couldn't very well refuse. If for no other reason, he bought up all my markers."

Markers? Presumably he wasn't talking about pens. "Why should he want you?"

"Why should he not? I'm a useful fellow, as you've said yourself. He had a job for me."

Marlee waited.

"Oh, all right. It's about Jane."

"What about her?"

"Her?" He looked confused. "I'm talking about your cousin."

Apparently her was the wrong word for this cousin. Then she remembered a note from the journal. "Oh, right. Jeyne. What about him, then?"

But now the man no longer seemed nervous, and was looking at her curiously. Best to cut that short right away. "Look, I've still got a headache and I'm not in the best mood. Get to the point."

He shrugged. "Nothing to concern us. Just an unsuitable romance Freddan wants me to learn more about, break up if necessary."

"If necessary?"

"If he seems set on doing anything silly, like marrying the girl. It won't affect my work for you."

So this was an employee. All right. "And what's up with that?"

"What's up?" He glanced upward.

"I mean what's going on with our... stuff?"

"Ah. Well, it's slow work. They have a loose organization, so I talk to a lot of different people. Extra funding would help."

Marlee sensed she was being served up a little bullshit. "No doubt. I'll think about it."

"What about at your end? Can you get the key, or will we need the child?"

Questions. She didn't like them. "I don't know yet."

"Please find out soon. Next Wineday's our best chance. If we wait a week, we might not have time to finish everything before your trip."

Was he talking about her trip to court? Or was she due to travel somewhere else? And what sort of scheme was she involved in? A key? A child? How could she get more information without giving away how much she didn't know? "What else is happening?"

"Nothing new since last time... oh, Howarth's out of the way for another year or more. His regiment shipped off to the Salaties, according to his mother's maid."

"Hm." The man was starting to annoy her. Any time she spent with him was just that much more chance to make mistakes and arouse his suspicions. "All right, I think you'd better go now. I've got a lot to do. I'll let you know about the, the child."

"Right, then." He stood. "I'll make sure everything's ready, in case."

"You do that."

CLORA

VII

THE NOTE WAS UNSEALED. AND barely recognizable as Marlee's handwriting. It demanded Clora come in person with transportation—not specifying what sort. To say nothing to anyone. To bring money, and meet her on the drive beside the engineering building, immediately.

Well, she couldn't leave without talking to someone, could she? Didn't Marlee have any notion how the household operated? An under-housemaid couldn't order a carriage, grab money, and leave, not if she hoped to keep her position and stay out of jail. She slapped the note against her leg, undecided, then went to the head steward, Ronall Greaves.

Greaves perused the sheet in silence, holding it with the tips of his fingers. He peered down at her. "You're certain this was intended for you?"

"The boy who gave it to me was certain."

"You are assigned to Miss Marlee personally, are you not?"

He knew that very well. A retort sprang to mind, but she simply nodded.

He handed the note back. "Then you are excused to obey her orders. Instruct Hanny to do anything you were supposed to be doing." He flicked his hand at her. "Go."

"She says bring money. I don't have what she would call money, and I'm sure not supposed to touch hers."

Greaves pointed to the note. "I'd say this authorizes you to fetch her purse to her."

"And what about her bodyguards?"

"It doesn't mention them. Perhaps she sent for them separately."

After requesting a carriage and driver, Clora went to Marlee's room, finding the purse and pulling together a few other necessary items. As long as she was there, she also looked around. The roll-top was shut, the journal presumably inside. She checked the drawer just in case. No books, but a sheet of stationery had been scribbled on, crumpled and thrown back into the drawer. Clora smoothed the paper, read it, then re-crumpled and replaced it. Why was Marlee practicing a different signature? She'd heard rumors that Marlee was in some kind of trouble with old Josip. Could she be planning to flee and assume a different identity?

Fifteen minutes later, the carriage crunched to a stop on the gravel drive outside the engineering building, and Clora leaned out to look around.

Miss Marlee came out from behind a large bush and hurried to the carriage, pushing Clora inside and crowding in. "I told you to come alone."

"Without a driver, we wouldn't get far. Miss."

"Well, fine. Tell him to go into town. To a library."

In Clora's experience, a library was a room in someone's house, so this was a puzzling request. "Whose library?"

"A public library." Marlee looked at her expectantly, but Clora shook her head. "All right, a bookstore."

"Fillerner's?" That was only bookstore she'd heard of, and she knew it was popular in Miss Marlee's set.

"Any big one."

Clora stuck her head out the window to instruct the driver. The dynamo hummed, and Clora grabbed a handle as the vehicle lurched forward.

So, she was to have an Adventure! She'd been afraid once she delivered the carriage, Miss Marlee would send her away. Everyone know Marlee had intrigues, so when she'd been sent for to serve her, Clora dreamed she would get to participate in some. But Miss Marlee, as Clora should've realized, was as forthcoming about her schemes as a turtle.

Until now.

Her mistress sat in the facing seat, looking out the window with apparent interest as they passed out the gates and started downhill. Miss Marlee's hair was disarranged, there were smudges on her dress, and a scuff on her shoe. As per usual. She got Marlee's attention by tapping her knee with a hairbrush, then handed her the brush and a mirror.

"Thanks." After a few moments, Marlee returned them, looking tidier. Clora passed her a charmed cleaning cloth.

"Um." Marlee turned the cloth over in her hands.

"Right here." Clora pointed to her own skirt to show the position of dark smudges where Marlee had apparently wiped her fingers.

Marlee made a tentative dab at a stain, then scrubbed with unnecessary vigor until it was gone. "Did I miss anything?"

"No, miss. I can't do anything for the shoes just now. Sorry, miss."

"No problem." Marlee's nose wrinkled as they rumbled out onto the bridge and a breeze brought them a whiff of town. Clora sniffed, but it was just the usual—smoke, horse manure, people, something acidic from the tin works. Nothing to pull such a face over.

Fillerner's was some distance, far from the markets and factories on the river bank, among the more expensive tailors, wig-makers, confectioners and physicians on the High Street. Clora hadn't been to this part of town, or in fact, any part except the market just across the river. Since moving to the big house, she'd been allowed out only on errands for the kitchen.

There was quite a contrast between the River Market and the High Street. Most people here were beautifully dressed, or at least tidy. There were few horses, and little manure in the street. Instead, most traffic was steam carriages puffing out smoke, and a few of the newer steamless carriages like theirs. They passed a cafe with tables spilling out onto the pavement, women with parasols having tea and watching the passersby.

"Oh God," Marlee moaned, looking out at the diners. "I missed lunch. I could just about kill and eat something raw right now."

What was lunch? "Shall I have your driver stop here?" She reached for the window.

"No, I don't want to be eating where people can come up and—and talk to me. You can go out and bring me back a sandwich while I'm at the bookstore."

A sandwich must be some fancy foreign concoction they served at these cafes. But Clora didn't get to find out, because when Marlee walked into the bookstore, three clerks immediately bustled over, showing her to a cozy little room, bringing a plate of sliced meats, quail eggs, and cheese, and a red wine from the Giolur valley before even asking what books she wanted to see. Clora followed, bemused, and took a chair in the corner, beside the small fireplace.

The clerks fluffed the chair cushions, shook the desk lights brighter, and hurried off after books on Marlee's long list of subjects. "They certainly know how to treat a customer," Marlee commented after they'd gone.

Clora raised an eyebrow. "They know how to treat someone from the big house."

"They know who I am?"

Clora snorted.

A clerk hurried in and deposited a stack of books on the table, pointed out the bell to ring if anything more was required, and left. Marlee took one thick volume from the stack, fingered the tooled-leather cover, and flipped through the pages. "This might take a while."

Clora pulled a much-folded gazette from her bag and opened it to the latest story of Lord Grah's adventures, prepared, as servants must be, to wait as long as needed. Marlee read, humming a little. Twice, clerks deposited more books.

When Marlee next set a book aside, Clora took advantage of the pause to speak. "Ah, miss?"

"Hm?"

"Are you planning to read all that here?"

"Not all. This one's no good."

"There are such a lot of them, miss. It might be better to choose the ones you like and take them away."

"Take them away? Buy them, you mean?" Marlee eyed the stack. "They look expensive. How much money did you bring?"

"Just your purse, but surely your credit is good here?"

"Oh, well, I suppose. Okay, good idea. Sure, I'll sort out the ones I want. Will you tell the driver I'll be ready to leave soon?"

"Yes, miss." Clora stood, brushed down her skirts and headed for the door. At the back of the store, she walked down a hallway past offices, to the cobblestone back lot, where their carriage waited along with two others. The three drivers sat around a weathered wooden table, playing cards. Their driver, Kraik, looked up as she approached, tipping back his shiny hat with his thumb to expose greasy bangs.

"Fifteen minutes," Clora said.

"And then where?"

"She didn't say." Clora turned to go back in.

"Wait a bit. What's up with her awfulness today? They say she's behaving odd."

Clora had formed a theory, a rather fantastic one. But it wasn't one to give away for the asking. "She had a night of it, and was cranky this morning 'cause of her head, so she skipped all her appointments. And now she's studying something. Probably some new way to make money."

Back to the reading room. Marlee had created two stacks, the shorter one presumably books she wanted to keep. There were a few more yet to look at.

The plate from before had been removed. Too bad—Clora'd wondered whether Marlee ate the quail eggs. Normally a favorite, it'd been surprising to see them left to the end, but what she was thinking now might explain it.

But if she was right, what should she do about it? Duty required her to report it to a family member. But what if she reported it to someone who preferred it kept quiet? Clora didn't want to be in the position of being inconvenient to anyone in the family. Such people tended to vanish. She supposed she could wait until a group of them were assembled. That should be safe. Or send old Josip an anonymous note. That wouldn't get her a reward, however.

More to the point, that would be the end of the affair, when it was barely begun. Sitting before her now, sipping tea, was a real Adventure, like in the stories she read, the sort of excitement she dreamed of. Would Kassie Helger, Master Spy, simply call the police if she found a criminal? Would Lord Grah run and tell tales? No. Her heroes would jump in and root out the whole plot. And in the case of Lord Grah, at least, figure out how to turn it to their advantage.

Was there an advantage to be had here?

Anyone would know playing around with the Forossis was dangerous. They'd not hesitate to dispose of anyone who seemed a danger to them.

But several things about the situation just didn't make sense.

One more test, Clora decided.

She dug into her handbag for a little enameled metal box. She hesitated for a moment more, then walked over to set it beside Marlee. Marlee tensed a little, but didn't look up.

"Time for your medicine, miss."

"Ah, right." Marlee picked up the box and pried the lid open—to reveal a jumble of straight pins of the type used to attach documents. She looked up at Clora, expressionless.

"It's amazing how you look just like her. Even knowing, I can't see a difference." Clora tried for a cool tone. "I never thought a disguise spell could be so perfect."

Marlee snapped the box shut. "What are you talking about?"

"You're not the real Miss Marlee. But you puzzle me. If you're a spy, you're a poor one, because you left it a little late to do your lessons. And you use language below your station, and all those foreign words, lunch and yoggert and so forth. What country are you from? But then you got the accent perfect, and you copy her handwriting pretty well, too." Clora nodded toward the woman's notes, which looked like the real thing.

"You're insane. No one would believe you."

"No? What did you have for supper last night?"

The mantel clock ticked away several seconds.

"What was the name of your cat that a horse trampled year before last? What's the horse's name?"

More seconds passed. A clerk looked into the window, and Marlee motioned him away. "What do you want?"

There was only one way the impostor would avoid detection long enough to do Clora any good. "I'll help you. You need someone to tell you the things you don't know."

"And what do you get out of that?"

"A promotion. You'll need me close by. Make me your companion."

"My—"

"To keep you company. You never—I mean, Miss Marlee never had one before, but I think now you'll want one."

Clora had known Marlee forever, and through necessity, could tell when she was about to start laying waste to all in the vicinity. This woman's jaw tightened, and the first two fingers of her right hand began a rapid drumming on the table. Clora had a flash of doubt. How could she have learned this mannerism, and so little else? For that matter, it suddenly occurred to her, how had she opened the desk in her bedroom without blowing her hand off?

The woman took a deep breath, put her hands in her lap and closed her eyes.

Clora watched, apprehensive.

"Fine." The woman's eyes opened. "But won't the family wonder why you suddenly got promoted?"

Clora started breathing again. "I expect they'll think you've took me as a lover."

"They'll what?"

"Everybody knows you don't like men. I mean, Miss Marlee doesn't." Clora edged her chair back a little. "Begging pardon, miss."

"That's what 'companion' means here?"

"Not generally. That's what folks will think you mean."

"Well. Okay. But aren't you a little young?"

"I'm sixteen. My younger cousin got married last year."

"All right. I'm not... not that way. I've got a boyfriend back... back home." Marlee paced the short length of the room.

"Where is home?"

A hard look. "Why should I answer your questions? You just show me what I need to know, and we'll be fine."

"So it's a deal?"

The woman set her teeth, and smiled. "It's a deal. The first thing I'll need is a place to hide out and study."

"Why not your apartment in town?"

"I have an apartment?"

"So I heard. I haven't gone there."

"Where?"

Clora shrugged. "I expect the driver knows."

"Still, it would look funny, wouldn't it, if he doesn't know and I can't tell him how to get there."

"If he doesn't know, I'll suggest Jossen House, instead. That's a nice hotel."

Marlee—it would be just as well to think of her by that name—thought about it. "All right, that seems safe. Clever plan." She looked at the clock. "The driver must be waiting by now."

"He'll wait. There's something else." Clora shifted uncomfortably in her chair. "Two things, really."

Marlee waited.

"What'd you do with her? With Marlee, I mean?"

"Why is that your business?"

Clora wanted some reassurance Marlee was well, mainly because she'd known her so long. But a cool-headed conspirator wouldn't admit that. "If she comes back, and finds out I helped you, it'll go bad for me."

"Fair enough." Marlee pointed to herself. "She's here. At least, this is her body, I guess, but she's not in it. I don't know how I got here."

Clora looked closely at Marlee. She'd never heard of such a spell, but her knowledge of magic mostly came from what she read in stories, and that was probably exaggerated for drama. This was even more implausible than the spells in stories. Yet, it might explain some things. "So where's the real Marlee, then? Is she in your body?"

Marlee looked cross. "How should I know?"

"So she could come back."

"Maybe. I hope we'll swap back. If we do, she'll be grateful to you for helping keep her body safe. You know what her family's like. If I'm locked up in a lunatic asylum, Freddan or someone will find it easy to arrange an accident for me. From what I've read, I can't imagine why any of them would want her back." Marlee waited a few seconds, then added impatiently, "You said there were two things. What was the other one?"

"You have to write a letter, miss, for the driver to take to the house. We have to do it here, so we can send him right off when he drops us."

"All right." Marlee looked at the pad she'd been making notes on. "I guess I want nicer paper than this to write a letter." She opened the door and beckoned to a clerk hovering nearby. "I need some blank stationery."

Within a short time, it was provided, and Marlee sat to write. "How do I explain why I'm staying away?"

"You're figuring out a new way to make money. They'll like that. But say it fancy."

"Dear Bylamar, I've learned of a new business opportunity," Marlee said as she wrote, "and must stay in town several days to research it. Cancel all my appointments."

"That's just how she would say it."

Marlee turned the paper around. "How's the handwriting?"

"Good enough." Clora gave her a curious look. "How'd you learn her writing so fast?"

"Apparently my hand knows how to write, not my head. If I just don't think about it, it works." Marlee picked up the pen again. "I've decided I need a companion, and am appointing Clora.... Spell it?"

Clora spelled her full name. "He'll have to talk to the head steward to set it up—"

Marlee waved her to silence. "...to that post. I rely on you to arrange the details."

"Ooh, excellent. There's a proper attitude."

"Is there anything we need them to send?"

"Miss Yrenn?"

Marlee shuddered. "No."

"But have her send some clothes. More money? Course, you can always go down to your bank for some."

"That's right, we have a bank, don't we?" Marlee sounded pleased.

"Oh, and your guards. She never goes to town without them."

"I have guards?"

"Usually two at a time, in shifts."

Marlee picked up the pen, and in a few more minutes they wrote the rest of the letter. "Now for the tricky part." Marlee picked up a blank sheet, took a breath, and dashed off a signature. She held it up to look at. "That feels unfinished."

"Miss Marlee always does a sort of squiggle underneath. It starts here and crosses itself—"

"Right, right, I've seen it on her copies of her letters." Marlee picked up the pen again. After a couple of tries, she got the back-and-forth loopy motion down. Then she signed the letter.

Clora pressed it onto the blotter, folded it, and showed Marlee how to light the sealing wax stick by poking the wick into the little hole in her seal ring.

Whatever did they do with letters where she came from? Clora let three drops fall onto the letter.

"Okay." Marlee stamped her fist down, leaving the ring's impress on the wax. A little off-center, but it would do. She scrawled "Bylamar" across the outside. "Send it off."

"Okay." Clora gave her a mischievous grin.

Marlee looked at her suspiciously. "That's not a word here, is it?"

Clora shook her head.

"Crap. It won't be easy to quit saying it."

Kraik knew where the apartment was, a short drive through the fashionable part of town. Marlee seemed pensive, staring out the window without seeming to see the passing sights. When Kraik pulled over beside a tall brick building and got out to open the carriage door, Marlee handed him the letter. "See this gets delivered immediately."

"I'll just wait until you're safe inside."

"You'll leave now. Yes, right now." Marlee waited until he was gone. "All right. How do we get in?"

Clora pulled out a bunch of keys from Marlee's handbag, but there was no keyhole here, nor any handle. Marlee pushed, and it didn't move. Clora stood on tiptoe to peer through a high window at an ascending flight of carpeted steps. She stepped back, swinging the parcel of books by her side, to look the whole thing over. "I don't know."

"Fat lot of help you are so far."

Clora looked around the entry alcove for any switches or cords. "Think it's a magic lock?"

"Sure, I guess I just say 'Open Sesame' and it opens."

The door clicked, and swung toward them. Clora scrambled out of its way. They looked at each other.

"Voice lock." Marlee's laugh was shaky. "Come on, then."

EDSGAR DIGRIZ

JEYNE HAD DELAYED HIM SO he almost missed his train. The man was a menace to health and sanity. Though at least, associating with him tended to be profitable, since neither he nor most of his friends had any notion of remembering which cards had already been played. And he still hadn't met this peasant girl of his.

There was a bump as the train caught the overhead rail and lifted off the track. A fat man walking in the aisle stumbled and caught himself against the back of Digriz's seat, cursing.

"Sir!" said the man in the facing seats. "Language!" The boy he was traveling with, who looked to be about six, stared with fascination and a little glee at the cursing passenger.

"Sorry." He bumbled past, holding the overhead bar against the swaying of the carriage.

Digriz looked out the grimy window as they rolled past the first wizard-built support tower, an irregular, curved column of brown crystals that burst from the ground like a huge finger curled over the train. They picked up speed and passed another, and another.

The idiot child was staring at him now, and when the boy was undeterred by his patented icy glance, Digriz picked up his newspaper and opened it between them.

He could not, however, pay attention to the news. His mind was on his meeting with Marlee. She'd seemed distracted, distant. Had something changed between them? His business with Freddan couldn't be that big a deal, could it? She had to recognize the necessity.

This was a bad time for her to start acting strangely. With the completion of the current plan, he'd have enough to pay off every debt and a good bit left over. He had several excellent investments lined up. A fellow with his ear to the ground found opportunities, but one needed capital to take advantage of them.

They needed to go over the final details, but she'd barely mentioned it before shooing him off. Could she have changed her mind about going forward? She hadn't explained her reasons for doing this in the first place, but a fellow who talked to fellows could build up a pretty good picture. She was in a bind, and had to do something. Could she have a new plan that didn't require him? She knew he'd set things in motion he couldn't easily call off. Timing was crucial, and it was all he could manage to keep that unruly crowd from taking action on their own instead of awaiting his guidance. Surely, if she were changing the plan, she'd say so!

Wouldn't she?

With a sigh, he folded the paper and set it down again. The man across from him was asleep. The boy knelt on the bench, face against the window, looking down at the passing scenery with evident fascination.

He was a local, with brown skin and red hair that would turn yellow by the time he was old enough to join the army. The boy took a handful of nuts from a basket his father had bought from the snack cart. He gave Digriz a shy glance. "Cows," he pointed out, displaying a blinding grasp of the obvious.

Digriz looked at the passing scenery. "Those are racing cattle. Their owner breeds them to be fleet of foot. Fast," Digriz added when the child gave him a blank stare. "The fastest cattle come from right here around Corilan. The cattle in the Shizi Valley are faster, but they're cross-bred with antelope, so they aren't allowed to race. It wouldn't be fair."

"That's not true, is it?"

"I swear it is. You can bet your schoolmates, if they don't believe it."

"You're so pale. Are you sick?"

"Thank you for your solicitous inquiry. Yes, I am sick. It's highly contagious, and I expect you and your father will also fall ill. You'll probably die painfully."

"That's not true."

"No, really I'm Dwillikan. Everyone is pale where I come from."

"Want a nut?" The boy held his hand out, displaying a few damp almonds glued to his palm by some blue substance.

"Tempting, but no, thank you. I've already eaten."

"Where are you going?"

"To check on a boy. He's about your age, actually."

"Is it me?"

"That depends. Are you an orphan?"

"No. This is my da."

"Then not you."

The boy's father had slumped to one side, and it seemed tantalizingly possible he would fall into the aisle. Unfortunately, he jerked awake instead, and rubbed his face. He looked at Digriz, then at his son, who was swinging his feet. "Geri, are you bothering this man?"

"No, sir." Geri looked out the window again. "Da, see those cows?"

The man looked out the window. "Yes. Black and white." The talent for stating the obvious clearly had been inherited.

"Those are racing cows."

"What?"

Digriz stood and took his hat from the rack. "If you'll excuse me, my stop is coming up." He gave a little bow and hurried out.

He stopped in the smoking car, negotiating his way between tightly spaced padded chairs to grab a spot in the corner. His third-class ticket didn't entitle him to be here, but he'd found conductors never checked up on anyone well-dressed. He took out a slim silver case—a present from Marlee—and chose a dark, spicy Trennish cigarette. He twirled the tip against the ignition spot on the back of the case, took a puff to help it catch, and returned to his newspaper.

DIGRIZ STEPPED ONTO THE ELEVATED platform, and down the steps to the dusty main street. He took his time, pausing to look into shop windows. A thin gold watch on a fine chain caught his eye. He pulled out his own ticker, a beat-up steel model which had been through the wars—literally, since it was a hand-me-down from his father, the Colonel. He jogged the old watch in his hand, considering the price label next to the one in the window, then reluctantly put it away. Not today, but soon. It could be had for less in the city, anyway. This was the shop's one ridiculously expensive item that they never expected to sell, to make their other prices look reasonable by comparison.

A few doors on, he reached his goal, the carpentry shop. He stepped in to the sharp scent of shaved wood. Sunlight from the front windows lit a display of wooden toys, some polished, some brightly painted, but the main part of the store was full of furniture, mostly unfinished.

"I'll be with you in a minute, sir!" a woman called from the back.

"No hurry." Digriz paused over a small table whose surface was inlaid with a klamat board in three different colors of wood, varnished to a high gloss. He ran his fingers over the smooth surface.

The woman walked up at his side. She was a foreigner, brown but dark-haired, with a Ijolais accent. "It's a fine piece sir, for only thirty-five. It was commissioned, but not picked up, so we're letting it go for the original price less the deposit."

"A fair price, but I have no place for it. The ideal spot in my apartment is already occupied by the little table you sold me when I was last here."

"Oh, sir, so it is! I didn't know you without the mustache. Are you still happy with that table?"

"Delighted. But I've marked this one, and if I should move to larger quarters, I may write to inquire whether it's still available."

"Let's hope so! Are you here on business, then?"

"Alas, I have no business in this life but to be a burden to my father, which he feels I can do best at a considerable distance from him. No, I just like to get out from time to time. The country is clean, and the people one meets are friendlier and refreshingly honest."

"That's so, I shouldn't like to live in the city."

"So I'm afraid I only wandered aimlessly in to say hello, with no notion to buy."

"You're most welcome. You were so kind to my boy, sir, when you were here last. He still speaks of the gentleman who can make wonderful animals out of paper. He'll be sorry to have missed you."

"He's away?"

"He started school this last month. It's hard for a lad who loves the outdoors as he does, but it'll be winter soon enough in any case."

"But everyone's well? You, your husband, the boy, all doing fine?"

"Raddel has a bit of a cough, nothing serious. And yourself?"

"Fine, fine. How is the school here?"

"Lord Willett sponsors it, sir, and he's found a good teacher. That strict, she is."

Digriz recalled his own school days with a repressed shudder. "I'm sure he'll do well. He seems a bright child."

After another five minutes of conversation, Digriz escaped to the street, asked a carter for directions to the school, and stopped there only long enough to look through the window to confirm the boy was in fact there, in the front row, being drilled in his letters.

He'd grown a bit, losing most of his baby fat, and his red hair was cut short, a style popular with his age-mates. But it was definitely him. Digriz turned away from the window and wandered back toward the train station, sucking on his front teeth.

As he approached the hostelry, a short, plump woman came out with an empty basket hung on her arm, walking briskly toward him. When she recognized him, she stopped. She seemed surprised, but not nervous—not as if she'd been contacted by Marlee and told to keep a secret from him, for instance.

"Eddie!"

"Jennet. I was just coming to see you."

"You didn't tell me you was coming."

"I didn't know myself until this morning."

"Is something wrong?"

"Not that I know of. Anything wrong here?"

"No. I just sent you a report four days ago." A flash of annoyance came into her eyes. "Are you checking up on me?"

He was, but no point in saying so. "No, I had business further up the line and thought I'd stop in."

"Ah." She smiled a wicked little smile. "How long a stop was you thinking to make?"

"Not as long as I'd like. Work awaits. But I can stay for a few hours."

"Oh, sure, you'd have me drop everything in the middle of the day! If you make me lose my job, who do you think will capture the child when you're ready?"

"Steady on!"

"Ah, no one can hear. I'm no idiot. And who's to go to market for tonight's dinner?"

Digriz shrugged.

Jennet looked away, then smiled again. "All right. I'll be as quick at the market as I can, and for the rest, well, Kalli owes me a favor. Want to help?"

"At the market? My physician has advised me to avoid dirt, noise, and flies, so I'd best not."

"Right. Well, go in and have Kalli draw you a pint, and I'll be along in a bit." As she walked away, her hips gave a little twitch. Digriz smiled.

CLORA

THE APARTMENT WAS A MARVEL of modern decor. A flight of narrow stairs led to a large room running across the back of the building, the back wall and ceiling all windows, big panes of smoked glass in a steel lattice. The sun shone on the painted brick of the inside wall, but didn't heat the place up much. Clora set the parcel of books on a beautiful table, a simple swoop of pale wood. There wasn't a single clawed foot, finial or carving in evidence anywhere.

"This is more like it." Marlee sank down on a chaise whose thick red cushions rested on a burnished metal frame. "I'm exhausted. I've been on edge all day that I'd run into someone I was supposed to know. Safe now." She beckoned. "Come get me out of this horrible dress. If there's nothing comfortable to wear, I'll lounge around in my underwear."

"Won't you look around the place?"

"I can't. It would require getting up. Tell me what you find. If there's a bathroom, I could get up for that. And food. They didn't feed me much of anything."

Clora leaned over her and started to undo buttons on the back of her dress. Her fingers paused as the fabric opened to reveal a small scar just above the shoulder blade. She'd seen that scar many times when Miss Marlee was in her nightgown—knew how she'd gotten it, in fact.

Clora had a moment's doubt. Could this possibly be Marlee still, playing some game? It would be easy enough to pretend to forget, to make up some foreign-sounding words. But why work so hard just to fool her maid? And then give in and send that letter?

"Is there a problem?"

"Just thinking." Clora quickly finished the buttons, and started on the corset laces. "If you won't move, you can anyhow study." She reached into the pocket of her dress, threw a loose stack of papers onto the chaise.

One fluttered off the edge, and Marlee grabbed it. "What's this?"

"Newspaper drawings of most everyone important in town."

"But this is terrific! How did you do this? *When* did you do it?"

"Took them off a tack board in the back of the bookstore. I expect they put them there to train the staff to recognize important visitors. Stand up now." Clora helped her out of the dress, careful to avoid rumpling it further. This Marlee was just as hard on her clothes as the other. She took the dress with her to explore the apartment.

There were four other rooms. A small but modern kitchen, with built-in labeled bins for flour and beans and so on, all empty. That made sense. Miss Marlee came here alone, and would hardly cook for herself. There were some of Miss Marlee's special dishes in a cabinet, and a drawer labeled for cooking utensils contained a collection of restaurant menus. A large bathroom had lots of pink marble and an east-facing window above the deep tub. A small bedroom with a single bed and a window, and a long bedroom with a wide bed but no window. She guessed the smaller room would be hers.

The large bedroom had no wardrobe, but contained that modern innovation, a clothes closet, where she hung the dress. It needed ironing, but would take another wearing before washing.

Marlee looked up when Clora returned with the menus. "Oh, take-out? Excellent." She flipped through the stack. "What are you in the mood for?"

This was the first time Clora could remember anyone asking what she was in the mood to eat. One ate what was available, or what Cook chose to make for the servants. She could easily get used to being asked.

She looked over Marlee's shoulder, but didn't recognize the names. Most seemed to be written in foreign. "What's Beef Gorzune?"

"You're asking me? You're the local expert. I suppose it involves beef."

Clora didn't feel ready for anything with not a single word she recognized, but this had at least one honest ingredient. "I could try it."

"Then I'll get something from the same place. What's bluefish?"

"They're not really blue, and not really fish. I don't know why they call it that. They're this big, with shells."

"Do I like them?"

It was a strange way to ask, but Clora understood. "I don't know whether you like them especially, but you eat 'em."

"I'll have that. Can you find the place?"

Clora found it—a fancy establishment four blocks away. The doorman wouldn't admit her in her servant dress, but when she explained her errand, sent her around back to the kitchen door.

Back at the apartment, she banged on the street door until Marlee came down in a bathrobe to let her in, looking cross. "We have to figure out how to get it to open for you." Marlee's silk-clad behind led the way up the stairs. "Tomorrow, let's send for whoever makes these voice locks. Unless you happened to see some instructions when you were looking around?"

"No. Another thing we have to do tomorrow is shop for better clothes for me. I can't be your companion in the dresses I have."

Marlee had set places at a small table at the far end of the glass gallery, including a bottle of wine and two glasses. Clora unpacked covered dishes from the basket, and Marlee picked up a cover. "It smells all right." Chunks of meat in a thick sauce with onions, mushrooms and a side of a purple root vegetable. "This must be yours. Oh my god, what's this in mine? Bugs?"

"Those are bluefish."

"When you said they had shells, I thought you meant like shrimp or crab, not beetles." Marlee looked over at Clora's food.

Clora pulled her plate a little closer. "I can't eat those things," she lied, "if you're thinking to trade. I come out in spots. You've eaten 'em plenty of times, and they're not bugs, they're from the sea. And, too, don't say 'bugs.'"

"It's not a word?"

"It's a word, but it's common."

"Insects, then." Marlee picked up a bluefish and looked it in the eye. They both seemed morose. A drop of orange sauce fell onto the table. "All right. If she ate them, I'd better learn how. I found a cabinet full of wine. Is this a good one?"

Clora shrugged. "I drink beer." She took a bite. The meat was tasty, but a little too spicy. "Miss Marlee loves wine. She knows all about the different kinds."

"Oh, good, another subject to study." Marlee peeled the lead seal off the bottle and picked up a corkscrew. "Sorry, there's no beer. I guess you break these open and eat the insides?"

Clora nodded and reached for a bluefish. "I'll show you."

"This is cozy. How long can we stay, do you think, without anyone thinking it strange?"

Clora cracked the shell open. "I don't know. Not more than a few days."

"What's this trip to the capital Miss Yrenn was talking about?"

"That's more than a week away. Your grandfather, Josip, is being made a Count at the annual Honors ceremony. You, I mean Miss Marlee, she's been planning the trip for weeks."

"So it would look funny if I stayed home."

"It would be odd. You've always wanted to meet the King. What's your plan?"

Marlee scraped bluefish meat from the shell with a spoon, and sniffed it. "For now, read. And I want to see a Doctor Harrick as soon as I can. How do I get in touch for an appointment? I don't know where his office is."

"There's a city directory on that shelf. The afternoon post is in a couple hours, but the answer wouldn't come until morning. If you're in a hurry, I noticed a messenger service down the block. The sign is a red circle with yellow lightning. You can have them wait for an answer."

Marlee took a bite, chewing slowly. "Great. But you go. I have to study." She swallowed. "This isn't bad if I close my eyes and pretend they're not bu—insects."

MARLEE

THE SCENE CAME THROUGH IN patches and flashes, vague impressions. A curve of red neon, glowing blue letters. Wet street shining in the white light of a streetlamp, seen through a rain-speckled window. A face she recognized—Judy, from her floor of the dorm—laughing, pushing her hair back over her ear. A young Hispanic man sitting at the bar, his features lit by the glow of a smartphone.

Then Bobby, her Bobby. He looked past her, listening, nodding. He'd always listened well. Now she could see only his hands, picking up a glass half an inch to turn it on his coaster, finger drawing a triangle in water on the table. She wanted to see more, see his face again, but she wasn't in control.

The hand pulled away, and her vision followed it. There he was again, glancing at his phone. He looked away, spoke, stood, picking up a light jacket. Without transition, she was looking at him through glass, partly blocked by notices taped in the window. He hunched over his phone, hand covering his other ear. She recognized the place now, a little pizza restaurant near campus. He was in the entryway, squeezing over to let someone by.

He shut the phone off and leaned his head against the glass, eyes closed. The door opened again and a couple pushed past. Bobby shrugged into his jacket and walked into the night. Another jump to Judy's face, looking out through the window, surprised and a little offended. A guy sitting next to her was turned away, laughing and talking to someone else.

The scene spun away, and Marlee opened her eyes to darkness and a faint coppery taste. The room was pitch black, and she was panicked, short of breath. Where was she?

Oh. Her apartment in Corilan.

She got up, felt her way across the room, polished boards cool under her feet. She'd always hated waking in the dark, and doing it in an unfamiliar room was worse. She found the bathroom, and sat on the edge of the big tub, moonlight striping the floor through the barred window.

It must be about four. She'd stayed up late reading, long after Clora excused herself and went to bed. There was so much to learn, and the list only grew longer. She'd filled both sides of two sheets with questions, and would visit the bookstore again tomorrow. It was harder than she'd ever studied for any class, but then, the stakes were higher.

There was still no hint of dawn in the sky. Maybe she could finish that geography book before breakfast.

THE PSYCHIST'S CONSULTING ROOM WAS large and dark, with just one small window and a single light bar in a ceiling fixture. Street sounds were muffled, and the place smelled of roses and some resinous herb.

There was no desk. Dr. Harrick was tall, bald, and narrow, in a dark silk tunic with slits showing flashes of yellow underneath. He walked to his chair and stood waiting for Marlee to sit. She smoothed her wide skirts. She'd decided the full Forossi presence was called for, so she'd had Clora dress her in her nicest things, rather than the more casual garb she'd found in the closet.

"To begin," Marlee said, "This must be completely confidential. Nobody can even know I've been here."

"Certainly, but there's no shame in —"

"Shame isn't the point. Your word."

"Of course." Harrick crossed his legs. "If anyone asks, you haven't been here. My consultations are always confidential."

"Good." Marlee looked down, weighing her next words. She didn't doubt the doctor's intention of keeping matters private, but her family had ways of persuading people, so caution was still a good idea. Besides, she didn't want the doctor think she was crazy. "I don't believe you've examined my cousin Neidra?"

"If I had, I wouldn't be at liberty to say. One has, of course, read of the case in the papers."

"Of course. I visited her recently, and she seems to remember places and events from another life, in another world." This was a lie. She had no reason to think their situations were the same, just wanted a pretext to ask her questions about herself.

Harrick picked up a pair of half-glasses from a small table and tapped it on his knee. "In some cases of amnesia or psychosis, the patient makes up elaborate false histories. One's mind wants to fill in the gaps with something."

"Yes, but.... She was very convincing. Let's suppose, just for argument, that these are real memories. Say her mind was somehow swapped with someone from a different world."

"Well." Harrick opened the stem of his glasses and started to bring it to his mouth, then noticed what he was doing and set the glasses aside. "There are other worlds. Armin Goodenagh proved that. We don't know much about them, though. Certain drugs can cast the spirit free to roam among the planes, but they're dangerous even with proper training, and it's hard to bring back any coherent impressions. The visions are dreamlike, inconsistent."

Her own dream of the night before—had it been a vision? But she hadn't taken any drugs yesterday, at least not that she knew of. "The drugs are dangerous, you say. Dangerous how?"

"The wandering spirit might fail to return, resulting in a body with life but no mind. They can relearn, but it wouldn't be the same person. Over time, you might say, the body grows a new spirit."

"What if someone from another... plane, swapped places with them? Could that be what happened to Neidra?"

Harrick shifted uncomfortably. "There are a few cases in the literature where the subject awoke with the belief that they were someone else, but there's controversy whether these are true cases of transmigration." He leaned forward. "The drugs are rare and expensive. Why would your cousin's captors use them? They had her for at least a few days, didn't they? I'd have to examine her, but it seems more likely she was broken by torture and perhaps more conventional drugs during that time. Sorry, I don't mean to be insensitive about your relative."

Marlee waved this away. "You obviously don't know my family if you think that would bother me. All right. I hear you think it's unlikely, but suppose she did get swapped somehow. Would there be some way to swap her back?"

Dr. Harrick leaned back, looked up at a corner, and tapped steepled forefingers on his chin. "As I said, nobody's even sure that can happen. I doubt there's been much research on the subject. I suppose it's reasonable that the original, ah, inhabitant of the body might retain some connection to it, so if you could evict the outsider, Neidra might return. If you continue to administer the drug, you might vacate the body for her return. But after such a delay...."

This wasn't helpful. They now were discussing ways to get rid of the intruder, and she was the intruder. She didn't want to be gotten rid of, she wanted to go home.

If this world's Marlee was camping out in her body, how could she knock her loose to regain possession? Was there a way to phrase the question without revealing her real interest? "But if they've swapped bodies, and the original Neidra is living in—"

"Young lady, you keep talking about a swap, and I don't see why you think that likely. Why would you assume there was a, ah, usable body at the other end?"

"What? Why wouldn't there be?" Marlee's fingers tightened on the chair arm. That was her body he was talking about.

"Unless that other body was also taking some similar drug, the more likely cause of a spirit being set free to roam are severe brain damage or death."

Marlee stared at him, a cold chill of horror creeping down her spine. "There's—um. Aren't there other ways that could happen?" She thought back to the party. "Getting very drunk, for instance?"

"It could be different in different worlds, of course. You might ask Miss Neidra whether, where she comes from, alcohol can do that."

"All right, but that can't be.... Look, let's just suppose —"

"We're teetering on a high stack of suppositions already."

Marlee's voice rose a notch. "I'm paying for this. Can't you just answer my questions?"

"Of course. I only want to make sure you're not wasting your time and money on a plan with no chance of success."

"They're mine to waste."

"True enough. Pray, proceed."

"Suppose... Nevermind supposing. We need to know more. We might need to tell someone at the other end how to send Neidra back." She held up a finger. "Don't tell me there might not be another end. Who could help us with this?"

"I would have to research the question—"

"Fine, do that."

"—and speak with your cousin."

Unless she had the fantastic luck that Neidra's problem really was the same as hers, that would spell an end to the deception. But that was in the future. "I'll set it up. We'll go together."

Harrick picked up a little leather notebook from the table and flipped through the pages. "How far away is she? I'm free tomorrow afternoon."

"Too soon for me. I want you to do that research first."

"I always begin by interviewing the patient. If the problem isn't what you think it is, we'd be—"

"—wasting my money, yes, I know. Let go of that, o—all right? We're doing this my way. Assume I'm right. How long do you need to learn enough to be of some use?"

"Perhaps two weeks. I need to read papers, write letters...."

"Too long. Do it faster."

"Miss Forossi, you're not my only client."

Marlee reached into her purse for a stiff bank envelope, untied the string closure, and pulled out a few large bills. "How much for me to be your only client, and how soon can you finish that research?"

Harrick blinked, put his glasses on, took them off again. "Perhaps four days. If I use the air mail...."

"Do it, whatever. How much?"

Harrick flipped through pages, then looked up. "Thrice my usual rates, plus expenses. That would be—"

"Fine." Marlee held out two bills.

Harrick leaned forward and took one. "This should cover the first ten days. If we're done before then, I'll return the balance." He folded the bill and tucked it into an inside pocket of his tunic. "Of course, still, the first thing I'll do when I talk with your cousin, is to test whether her recollections are invented."

"Yes, I got that." Her memories were too complete, too detailed, to be an elaborate fiction. Weren't they? But this whole situation was ridiculous. Marlee bit the inside of her lip. "How would you tell?"

"I'll look for inconsistencies, see whether she knows anything she couldn't have learned here—things that haven't been discovered here. I would still be able to help if her memories are false. In fact, that would be simpler. I would also find out the last thing she remembers from her other life, and ask whether she recalls experiencing any of the side effects of the drugs, in the few days after she, er, came to this world."

"What side effects would those be?"

"It depends on the drug. Most of them stay in the body for a few days, so the subject might experience additional visions or strange dreams."

Could last night's dream have been a true vision of home? Was that coppery taste when she woke one of the side effects? "I'll want a list of those."

"A list of...."

"The different drugs, their side effects, and where in town someone might buy them."

Harrick looked a little alarmed. "I wouldn't advise—"

Marlee waved him down. "I don't want to use them. I just want to find out who bought some."

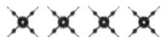

MARLEE SAILED BY CLORA IN the hallway, and the girl packed away her ubiquitous gazette to hurry after. As they left the psychist's house, her two guards took up station behind them. They were large men, heavily armored in dinged-up plate mail, conical shields strapped to their massive forearms.

Marlee scowled at the ground, and didn't talk. She probably wasn't supposed to be friendly with the guards, and she was in no mood to talk, anyway.

The fact she had the same first name was suspicious. Nobody could've arranged it on purpose—nobody knew how, and anyway why would they bother? And she wasn't behaving much like herself, not the self she remembered. How could she be sure she was really sane Marlee Feldman, not crazy Marlee Forossi? She needed a test. Something that hadn't been discovered here, like Harrick suggested.

Like, what?

EDSGAR

XI

JEYNE WAS IN A GOOD mood. Digriz made sure of it by sitting to his right at the card table all night and discarding the cards Jeyne needed, making him win a little money despite poor play. Digriz lost more than a little, but planned to claim that as expenses when he reported to Freddan.

Feeling expansive to his less fortunate friend, Jeyne offered to treat Digriz to breakfast at a place that would easily cost more than his night's winnings. Digriz accepted. Keeping him in sight and in a good mood was the point, after all.

They sat at a window overlooking the street, watching dawn creep over the hills. Digriz had an omelet with sage, goat cheese and earthy-tasting bog mushrooms, but no coffee—it was nearly bedtime. Jeyne, who knew no fear, held a large mug of coffee in one hand, a sausage roll in the other. He brushed crumbs from his stained silk shirt, sprawled back, tipping his chair dangerously, and stared at the ceiling. His long legs stretched out, silver boot-tips tapping together. "Ah, gods, that was fun, Eddie. But Alyssa will be steamed. I was supposed to go to her show."

Digriz reached for the salt. "She'll have to understand you're your own man." He brandished the shaker, spilling a few grains. "You're not letting a woman boss you, are you?"

"Zeus, no! It's just she's so much more—pleasant—to be around when I've done something to please her."

"Once she sees she can't bend you round her fingers, she'll be pleasant enough, believe me! The hope of marrying well above her station will keep her in line."

Jeyne dropped his chair to the floor, looking embarrassed. "You don't know her, Eddie. She's not like that."

"All women are like that."

"You have to meet her, then you'll see. She won't even accept expensive gifts from me."

Digriz waved at a waiter, who with the uncanny gift of waiters everywhere managed not to see them even in the otherwise empty room. "She's holding out for the big score."

"Tonight is their last at the Crooked Dog. You have to come."

"Don't you want to see the Divine Quanz?"

"No, I fuckin' do not want to see the Divine Quanz, if it means I miss Alyssa." He looked around, irritated, at the waiter. "Are you blind?" he called out. "Don't you see my friend waving at you like a floodin' lunatic?"

The waiter gave a little start and strolled toward them. Digriz turned to the window to hide a smile, looking down at a few early pedestrians. As one passed through the green circle cast by a street light, he leaned forward for a better look. "Say, who's that? I think I know her."

Jeyne looked. "Oh, yes, Clora something. Marlee's maid."

"You're right." Digriz turned to the waiter, who'd stopped by their table to goggle at him, fishlike. "Asidel tea. Thanks. I didn't know her, so nicely turned out. Is she borrowing her mistress' clothes?"

"They'd hardly fit, she's such a little thing. Ah, I forgot. She's Marlee's companion now, so-called, so I imagine Marlee's bought her some nice things. They're spending a little time in Marlee's apartment. Took off without notice, didn't even take along her bodyguards at first."

Digriz's lips pressed together. Were they, indeed, taking a holiday just when things were getting hot, and not even sending him word? He'd been calling at the big house twice a day and being told Miss Marlee was out, but it hadn't occurred to him to take it literally. He'd been worried it meant she didn't want to see him.

Down on the street, the former maid crossed another pool of green light. "We have to call on them, don't you think? Since they're up?"

Jeyne grimaced. "Oh, I don't know. I'm for bed."

"You've just had a pint of strong coffee. Come, let's finish here, and go wish them well. It's at least eleven hours before we have to be at the Crooked Dog. There's time enough for sleep."

"It's true I haven't seen her in a while. But don't rush. She won't be up yet. The girl's just going to the market up the road. We'll meet her on the way home. Finish your breakfast."

The girl looked around apprehensively when they came up behind her, Jeyne's hard-soled boots clopping on the pavement. She relaxed only a little when she saw who it was. "Morning, gents."

Digriz raised his hat. "Fair greetings to you, miss, and congratulations on your... promotion."

Jeyne bowed. "We mean to call on your mistress."

Clora looked him over. "You're in a state. Maybe you should call later."

"No time! I'm abed before long. But I have to remind her, she must come and meet Alyssa later. You too, of course."

"Thanks, I'll tell her. But you can't see her now. You put us in a cleft, showing up at a mealtime when there's only enough for two." She hefted her market basket. "I'm not even sure she's awake."

"We've eaten," Digriz said. "If she won't see us, we'll just escort you to the door."

Clora looked as if she'd like to send them rolling, but she nodded and walked on, the two of them on either side of her.

"What's she doing?" Digriz asked. "I've missed her these last few days, and I expect Bylamar has missed her greatly, too."

"She's been busy, some business thing she doesn't explain to me." She walked a little faster.

A minute's brisk stroll brought them to a sooty, three-story brick building. Two guards came to attention as they approached, nodding to Jeyne. The little sharp-featured one, whom Digriz hadn't met before, looked suspiciously at him, hand going to his belt. He was unshaven and a little cross-looking.

Jeyne craned his head back. "The light's on in the bath."

"I'll just announce you," Clora said.

"No need. We'll show ourselves in. Open!" Jeyne said, and the door swung open.

"Here!" Clora reached for his sleeve, but he slipped past her. Digriz tried to go also, but the little guard grabbed his arm.

"I'm with him." Digriz pointed up the stairs.

"That's true," Clora sighed. "Let him in." She passed Digriz her basket and hurried up the stairs.

Jeyne dropped his brocade jacket across the back of a chair. "Is that her singing?"

"Must be. Sounds too good to be a cylinder." Digriz left the basket on a convenient table. Clora disappeared through a doorway.

"Never known her to sing before."

"She must be happy." Digriz looked dubiously after Clora.

"She's not half bad. What language is it, can you tell?" Jeyne prodded the chaise cushions, then sat.

Digriz shrugged. The singing stopped, and Clora returned. "She'll be out in a bit. Can I get you gentlemen anything? No? Then excuse me, I have breakfast to make."

Digriz knelt before a low bookcase against the back wall, and ran a finger over the row of books. Histories, geography, politics, *The Modern Factory* by Lenepold, *Principles of Magic* in two volumes, Kimilan on finance, theology....

"Books? That's new since I was here last."

"Studying." Digriz nodded. "If there's anything calculated to make her even more dangerous, this is it."

Marlee came out, hair still damp, wearing a loose beaded cotton shirt and baggy black satin pants tied with a wide red sash, edged at the bottom with dangling copper disks.

"Ho, coz," said Jeyne. "There's a nice get-up. It'll cause a stir in the town."

"This is just something comfortable for around the house. I had Fernie's run it up."

"Did you tell them where you intended to wear it?" Digriz asked.

"No, what business is that of theirs? I just sketched what I wanted. They added the bangles and things on their own."

"They'll make more. We'll be seeing it in the arty cafes within a week," Jeyne said. "Got a Boraggan look to it—people go for that sort of thing these days, and now they can advertise, 'As worn by.' You should wear it when you come out with me tonight to hear Alyssa perform. You haven't forgotten? Chalula will be there."

"I hope you gentlemen don't mind if I go ahead and eat. Of course. What time will you come for me?"

"Around seven." Jeyne stood. "If you'll excuse me for a moment, I've had rather a lot of coffee."

"Among other things," Digriz said.

Clora set out plates for herself and Marlee. Bread and jam, a crumbly cheese, a teapot. "Will that do, miss?"

Marlee opened the teapot to sniff. "Yes, thanks. Sit, eat."

Digriz sat. "Actually, if I could have a word in private?"

"Oh?" Marlee looked at him, brows knit. "I suppose." She motioned with her head at Clora, who picked up her plate and left.

"This little holiday must have your family in an uproar. May I?" He pointed to the cheese.

Marlee pushed the plate toward him. "Help yourself. Mother sends admonishing notes, and Bylamar comes by to pester me, but everyone else has been mercifully silent. I think that's how they express their displeasure. Much my favorite way."

"Quite." Digriz broke off a small piece of cheese and sniffed it. Geffindell—delightful. He cut off a wedge. "You would've heard from me too, had you bothered to tell me where you were going."

"Oh dear, did I forget to send a note? It was a sudden decision."

Digriz lowered his voice. "And what of our plan?"

"Don't worry about that."

"Don't worry? You spoke to Karina already? You have the key?"

"No, I've been thinking you should talk to her."

"I? Are you mad? I can't be connected with that end of things."

"No, I suppose not." Marlee swirled her tea and leaned back, looking pensive. "The truth is, I've been reluctant to do it. I need your advice on how to put it to her."

What in Hades was the matter with the woman? "It's a simple piece of extortion, such as you've probably been doing since you were three."

"I worry about how she'll react. What if she doesn't do what we want?"

"She visits that boy, despite the danger. She cares about him. Once we have him, she'll give up the key."

"Yes, if she believes we'd harm him." Marlee frowned at the door. "What happened to Jeyne?"

"I expect he's in the kitchen, trying to pry information from your servant. Doubtless they're starved for gossip about you back home. Anyway, Karina will believe the threat. After all, it's you."

"Won't she wonder what we'll do with the key? Put yourself in her place. What would you think we were planning?"

Digriz put a dab of jam on his cheese, and took a tiny bite. "Smuggling something. Who cares? She'd never guess the real plan."

"If you could—" Marlee began, but then Jeyne returned.

"Just take care of it," Digriz whispered, "and get me the key. Quickly. I'll take it from there."

"Hey, coz." Jeyne leaned over the table, tasting a crumb of cheese. "I've asked your girl to set up my room. It'll save time if I don't have to go home." He paused at Marlee's look. "That's all right, isn't it? After all, that's why I pay part of the rent."

"Of course."

Jeyne nodded. "I'll just write Willet a note to send a fresh outfit." He crossed to the desk. "What do you think, for tonight? The teal?"

"Why not?"

MARLEE

COMING BACK UPSTAIRS FROM LETTING Digriz out, Marlee found Clora hovering at the top. "Is he asleep?" Marlee asked.

Clora nodded. "Is he gone?"

"Yes." Marlee went to the table and piled dishes onto the tray. "I don't know whether he suspects. Why did you let them in?"

"I didn't ever! The door opened for Jeyne. By the way, you don't have to say 'sesame,' just 'open.'"

"I like to say 'sesame.' Well, at least the mystery of the closet full of men's clothes is solved."

"Why'd you agree to go out with them?"

"The way he said it, it sounded like I'd already agreed. I sort of remember reading something about it in the journal, too."

"You're not ready. I think you should have a headache and stay home."

"I have to get out there. Whoever did this to me, they'll be watching for me to act strange. The longer I hide, the stranger it looks, don't you think? Four days is already too long."

"Are you real sure someone did it? It couldn't just have happened?"

"Based on what the doc said, I'm sure someone dosed me with, what was it? Kokoleaba. His list mentioned a coppery taste as a side effect. And I dreamed about home again last night." This one had been brief, and without vision. Her mother's voice, talking about work, about Aunt Helen's birthday party coming up on the weekend, about the dog's hip dysplasia, but without pausing for a response, and with a false brightness. Marlee frowned. When was Helen's birthday, anyway? Sometime in January—the 21st? The 23rd? But the last thing she remembered was the sorority party on December 16th. She couldn't have been gone that long, surely. She'd been here only a few days.

Marlee picked up the tray and headed for the kitchen.

Clora followed. "What was it you sang in the bath? They wondered what language it was."

"Something from home. What language? English."

"None of us understood it."

"Seriously, come on." Marlee sang the first line, softly. "If you were mine again, I'd never let you go." And she noticed that while she knew what the line meant, the sounds weren't regular words. "Oh." She put her hand to her throat. "Excuse me." She turned and hurried out, down the short hallway to her room, vision blurring.

She shut her door and leaned against it, breath coming in gulps. She'd been coping with all the changes. She no longer woke in panic in the darkness, gasping for air and unable to remember where she was. She'd been getting used to the food and lack of Internet. But this fresh loss found her unprepared.

Whatever language she'd been speaking for most of a week now, wasn't English. Even when she thought she was saying "English," it was really the name of whatever they spoke here. The language she'd grown up with was gone, except whatever bits she could reconstruct from songs she'd memorized. Though why bother, since nobody else could speak it?

There was a soft knock on the door. "Miss, are you well?"

"Go away."

A pause, then retreating footsteps. Marlee sat on the bed, then flumped back and drew a pillow over her face. Dr. Harrick had sent her a note to drop by tomorrow morning—what was the earliest she could go? She was ready to go home. Meanwhile, there was a whole day of torture to get through.

She threw the pillow across the room, knocking over a small china dog. She checked herself in the mirror—it was still disconcerting to see a stranger's brown face staring back. She brushed her hair, corrected her makeup, and went to the kitchen, where Clora was washing up.

"Put on your going out clothes."

Clora set a wet dish in the rack, and looked at her warily.

"Now."

CLORA

✕↕↕↕

CLORA WAS WORRIED. MARLEE HADN'T rehearsed or picked up a book all day. She'd been running from shop to market to cafe, drinking more Rhenian red wine than seemed wise. She'd brought another two bottles home with all the groceries and other supplies Clora was hauling upstairs.

Marlee took the one item she was carrying, a cloth-covered basket from the baker's, into the kitchen, humming brightly with brittle cheer. "Just bring all the food in here."

Clora found her searching the cabinets.

"I need a big kettle."

Clora set her packages on the table and opened a cabinet. "Here."

"With an open top."

"You need a saucepan." Clora opened a different cabinet.

"The middle one. Half full with water and make it boil."

Clora closed her eyes, considered telling her to jump it, then sighed and took the saucepan to the faucet. "Is this really more important than studying?"

"This is proof I'm not crazy, for when I see Harrick tomorrow."

"Does Harrick need that?"

"No, I do. I used to make this with my dad, but nobody here knows about it. If you want me to study you can get a book and read to me while I work. Wait, where's the corkscrew?"

"I don't think you should have any more."

Marlee gave her a dirty look.

"In a few hours, we go out with two people who know you well. You're not ready, and if you're drunk you'll slip for sure."

"If I slip, they'll think it's because I'm drunk. Perfick—perfect excuse."

"Then you be careful to be a lot less drunk than you seem. If you mess up, you take me down too. If I decide you'll fail anyway, I'll turn you in myself and hope for a reward."

Marlee's silence now made Clora start to fidget. That had perhaps been a mistake. "I'll bear it in mind," Marlee said at last. "Now go. I'll call you once things are underway, and you can read to me from the *Principles of Magic* book."

Clora picked up the illustrated gazette she'd bought at the stationers, nodded, and left. She settled on the chaise in the back room, and distracted herself from her worries by flipping first to the serial. At the end of last week's installment, the heroine, Kitrie Maine, was in considerable peril. The balehounds had detected her trying to sneak into the mansion of the possibly evil but undeniably handsome wizard, and chased her off the grounds, into the forest, and up a tree, around whose base they now slavered. Night was coming, and with it the poisonous bats she'd been warned about. And Fenz Darkmoor, who could ordinarily be relied upon to rescue her, was himself a prisoner in the wizard's basement, perhaps about to be subjected to cruel experiments that would leave him horribly altered. Clora smoothed the page, arranged the cushions more comfortably, and began.

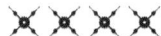

THE PAGES CLORA READ TO Marlee from *Principles of Magic* had been interesting subject matter, but seemed to have been written to disguise meaning rather than clarify it. They'd both quickly tired of it and switched to a volume of banking law, which proved even worse. Marlee finally declared she couldn't attend to two things at once, and chased Clora out of the kitchen.

A couple of hours later, Clora had finished her gazette—the heroine escaped but managed to get into new trouble—the newspaper's gossip page— marking certain items for Marlee's attention—and the court news, and was partway through a piece about the war in the Kovhlee, of special interest because a second cousin was participating. A door opened, to reveal Jeyne in his nightclothes, blinking in the evening light coming through the back windows. He ran a hand through his disheveled hair. "What time is it?"

Clora pointed to the tall clock beside the stairwell.

"My head hurts. Is there any wine?"

"Miss Marlee is cooking with it. She might even be putting some in the food."

"She cooks?"

"Only the one dish, I think."

"It smells good."

Clora was noticing the smell. It was intriguing, tomato-ey and spicy and garlicky and toasted-cheesy. And it was a while since they'd eaten, so she was ready to sample it. She set her paper aside. "Let's see whether it's ready."

Marlee was asleep in the kitchen chair, several loose papers and a half-empty wine glass on the work table before her. The kitchen was a mess. If there was any pot or pan or knife not dirty, Clora couldn't spot it. She eased around the table to peek in the oven, while Jeyne found the wine glasses and helped himself from the bottle.

"What is it?" he said.

"She hasn't said. They're like giant tarts."

Jeyne nudged Marlee, who woke with a start. "I think your thing is starting to burn."

"Shit! Yes, take them out. Careful, the topping might be slidy."

Clora used a rag to pull out the two racks, keeping them level as she deposited them on the table. Jeyne came around to look, and Marlee leaned forward. The bread around the edge was just a little overdone in spots, but the cheese was nicely browned and bubbly. Other ingredients peeked out from beneath the cheese—mushrooms, spicy sausage, chunks of onion. "What is it?"

"A new invention." Marlee lifted an edge to look underneath. "I will name it... pizza."

EDSGAR

XIV

DIGRIZ ARRIVED DURING DINNER AND was given two wedges of the new dish. "The crust rose too much," Marlee said, "and the cheese isn't right. But I can fix that. This is more or less what I had in mind."

"It's tasty." Jeyne wiped a dab of sauce from his chin. "Is this the business idea you're researching?"

"Why, um... yes."

Digriz reached for another piece. "That could work. Not in your usual line, though, is it? Thought you were more interested in shipping and finance. You'd run a restaurant?"

"Of course not. I'll own a restaurant. I can hire someone to run it."

Jeyne swallowed and held up a finger. "Mm. You must be thinking of me."

"Am I?"

"Of course! Haven't I told you dozens of times I could run this or that restaurant better than they're doing?"

"I, uh, thought that was just talk."

"It would get Daddy to stop bothering me to do something useful."

"I wouldn't hire him," Digriz said, "unless it doesn't matter whether the place makes any money."

"Hey!" Jeyne looked a little miffed.

"Actually, it doesn't matter much. The first one would be just to test the waters." Marlee tapped her fingernails on the table. "He'd bring in the high-class trade, wouldn't you think?"

"Certainly, he's a famous diner. Known for his good taste."

Jeyne spread his hands. "Am I part of this conversation?" he appealed to Clora, who tried to hide a smile behind her napkin.

"Nobody's stopping you from talking." Marlee turned to Digriz. "Do you know someone else who could mind the business end of things?"

"Actually, I do."

"I can floodin' well do it myself!"

Marlee and Digriz looked at each other.

"He doesn't want an assistant," Digriz said.

"It's a lot of work to run a restaurant," Marlee said. "But he doesn't mind work."

"He loves work. Ordering dishes and napkins, making sure they don't run out of salt, hiring cleaners, checking the spelling in the advertisements—"

"All right, all right." Jeyne crossed his arms. "Of course I'll need a helper to take care of minor details."

"Exactly. An underling." Marlee stood to collect dirty plates. "You set the tone, greet important guests, plan the décor, choose the beer—"

"Ah! Good call!" Jeyne said. "Beer would be the perfect accompaniment."

"Then it's settled." Marlee walked toward the kitchen, weaving slightly. "Your first job is, find a location." She bumped the door open with her butt. "Near the University is good. Students love this stuff. Will love, I mean."

"Leave the dishes," Jeyne called after her. "We should go."

"Oh, don't worry." There was a ring from the front doorbell, and Clora stood. "There was never any danger she would do dishes."

Jeyne left to adjust his attire. Digriz picked up the gazette from the chaise, flipped through it. At the bottom of the stairwell, Clora's voice rose, so he went to the top of the stair and leaned over. She had the chain on, and was speaking through the crack in the door.

"I tell you, she's not available. No, she's busy." Clora paused, but Digriz couldn't make out what the person outside was saying. "I'll tell her when she gets back. I'm sure she'll call on you in the morning. Yes, I know, but she really will this time. I'll tell her it's important."

Digriz ducked back as Clora closed the door, and by the time she reached the top, was arranged innocently on a chair. She stopped at the table to pick up a few dishes, glaring at him. "Do you always listen to conversations that don't concern you?"

"How am I to know whether they concern me if I don't listen? Was that Bylamar?"

"Yes, he's so persistent."

"I'd pass that message on if I were you. I can understand you want to protect Marlee from people who might try to reason with her about you, but her grandfather wants to talk with her about the death of her Uncle Benin. Word is that he suspects her, and is furious she skipped their meeting the other day."

Clora set the dishes down. "He suspects her of killing him? But I heard about that. He died in a riding accident."

"Apparently Josip doesn't think it was an accident. She was on the scene, and he believes she had reason. I mention this because you two are close, and because you'd hear about it when you got back to the big house in any case. Listen, Clora, I'm concerned. Marlee seems not herself recently."

"Oh? I wouldn't say so."

"There's no point in pretending. I can see you've noticed, too. She's distracted, absent-minded. It's unlike her. She's behaving oddly. Cooking, singing.... Reading. Is something worrying her? She's as important to me as she is to you." Probably for similarly practical reasons. "If there's something I can do, tell me."

"I'm sure she knows she can—" Clora began, then a door opened and Jeyne came bowling out, resplendent in teal satin with maroon accents, Marlee following in her jangling Boraggan outfit.

Jeyne stared at Clora. "By Jove. Aren't you ready? We should be gone."

"Bide a moment." Clora left, and Jeyne flopped into the chair across the table, looking at the clock.

Digriz, annoyed at the interruption, sat up and straightened his ties. "I'll be interested to see whether your friend is a decent musician." He'd already been planning ways to compliment the woman in a subtly backhanded way that would cause festering doubts. Let Jeyne believe others found her second-rate and were just too polite to tell him so, and he might start to see her in a different light.

MARLEE

IT'D RAINED, AND THE AIR smelled clean. The streets were crowded with foot and carriage traffic. The occasional powered bicycle hummed past. Most people, seeing two large, alert, armored bodyguards following the four, gave them a wide berth.

Clora, excited at her first ever show, was a distance ahead, chatting with Jeyne, asking questions. Marlee tried to stay close enough to overhear, but Digriz's hand on her arm drew her gently back. She scowled at him, and the bodyguard looked a question at her.

"A word," Digriz murmured.

Marlee flipped her fingers at the guard, and he dropped back a few steps. "What?"

"When will you speak with Karina?"

"What a pest you are! I'll see her tomorrow."

"At what time?" At her impatient huff, he added, "Look, you're the one who wanted this. If you have another way to deal with the Josip problem, say so and we'll call it off."

"I don't know. Fourteen-ish."

"Ish?"

"Around fourteen o'clock. If it changes I'll send a note."

"I'll be ready."

Clora had taken Jeyne's arm and was talking to him about dogs, about which she apparently knew a little.

Marlee thought of the lecture Clora had given her earlier, and bit her lip.

"What is it with you and her?" Digriz asked. "You usually go for someone a bit... more experienced."

His eyes glittered at her in the gathering dark. He observed altogether too much. Still, he might be some help. "She's useful at the moment. But she might become a danger."

"You could have her killed. She hasn't anyone powerful to avenge her."

Oh. "I'd rather an option that's a little less final."

"Just to keep her in line. I see. Any family?"

"Hm? Oh, two brothers. One works at my stables. Ovid."

"Easy enough. I could arrange some evidence against him, to be discovered if she gives trouble. Give you copies to show her at need."

"Evidence? Of what?"

"Oh, theft, assault.... Would you want him hanged, or just several years in jail?"

"Jail should be enough."

"Fine. Seventy crowns, and consider it taken care of."

"Seventy!"

"All right, fifty. I'll have to hire help."

Marlee didn't yet have a good handle on the value of money in general, much less the going rates for frame-ups. Should she should try to bargain him down further? They apparently had a regular business relationship, so he probably wouldn't quote her an outrageously high price to start. She nodded. "He can't know about it. If he wrote to her...."

"I understand. It's a surprise, to be used at need."

The Crooked Dog was built on two levels, a carpeted raised section surrounding a wooden floor. Tables crowded around the edges of the lower level, leaving the space before the stage clear. The room was already full, but a tiny cute man in a suit met them at the door and showed them to their reserved table. "Most honored, thank you sir," he murmured, and hurried away to aim a waiter in their direction.

A few people were on stage, setting up stands and musical instruments. Jeyne pointed. "That's Alyssa, at the *zoukis.*"

The *zoukis* resembled a monster xylophone, with curved rows of gleaming brass bars, hanging bells, and four padded hammers. Alyssa was dwarfed by the contraption—thin, pale and freckled, with straight brown hair, she wore a shimmery gown of dark green—or so it looked in the dim tubelight. Another foreigner, tuning a round-bodied guitar, might have been her brother. The third, waiting with a double-barreled flute in his lap, looked like a local.

Marlee took a chair facing the wall. Her bodyguards leaned against that wall, looking around the room. The cones of light from overhead left their faces in shadow.

Four guards took turns watching her, two at a time, in six-hour shifts. So far, watching was all they'd had to do. They didn't say much, and she hadn't asked their names, still unsure whether she was supposed to know them.

"Ma'am?"

Marlee looked around to find the waiter looking at her. "Whatever he's having." She pointed at Jeyne. Clora frowned at her, but she ignored it, focusing instead on a bowl of salted nuts on their table.

She didn't want to look at Clora. Who did the girl think she was, to threaten her? But was siccing Digriz on her brother going a bit too far? It's not like any harm would come to him so long as Clora didn't turn on her. It would just be insurance, and pretty harmless. The girl left her no choice. Clora'd made it clear she was in it for her own advantage, and it'd been silly to expect anything else.

Behind her, the music started up. She shifted her chair to get a better view. It was a bright little tune, mostly on the flute. Jeyne's girlfriend came in with a quick run of notes, two hammers in each hand. She hit a couple of wrong notes, but made up for it in enthusiasm.

"She's still learning this instrument," Jeyne leaned over to tell her. "But see how she goes at it!"

Digriz seemed to have overheard—he made a sour face. What was that about? The music was pretty good. "She seems to be enjoying herself."

"That's just it. She enjoys whatever she does. See, the audience likes it, too. She wrote this piece."

Marlee had a sip from her glass. Smoky, peppery, strong. "It's a nice tune."

And danceable. People on the lower level were moving onto the dance floor in two long rows of couples, merging into a lively dance involving flinging people around and changing partners. A couple at the end a row waited to rejoin, the woman in a full blue skirt with sequins and a poufy butt-pad, the man in a striped black and gray tunic which made him look even taller and skinnier than he was. The music came around again, and they swept into the figure, the man lurching above the crowd.

"Will you and Clora dance?" Jeyne asked.

Apparently, she was supposed to know that complex step. Perhaps, like her handwriting, it would come once she tried, but perhaps not. "Why don't you take Clora out yourself?"

Clora looked wistful. "I don't know the dance."

"It's dead simple. That couple in red know what they're doing. Step in, step out, twirl about, join hands with the other couple, rat-a-tat, rat-a-tat— the only tricky part—then kick, step, kick. Women switch partners—right arm, see? Twirl, cross, the up couple make an arch, down pass through, and repeat with the next couple."

"That doesn't sound simple at all, but I guess I could try. Let me watch a few more times."

Marlee watched, too, and practiced the tricky kick step under the table quietly. Her foot bumped Clora's foot, doing the same thing, and Clora flashed her a conspiratorial smile.

The song ended before Clora got confident enough to join, and a slow number started up.

"A sweeve." Digriz held out his hand to Clora. "You can do this, I'm sure."

Jeyne and Marlee watched the two move out onto the floor. "She's more than I expected," Jeyne said. "Clora, I mean. Clever. Asks good questions. Laughs in the right places. I can see why you like her."

Marlee should set him straight about their relationship... but no, people were supposed to think that. "She's great." She looked around. "Where's that waiter? I want another of these."

After the slow piece, was another fast one with people in rows. Digriz and Clora stayed on the dance floor, and though Clora hesitated a bit, Digriz was a good leader, and they got through it with fewer missteps than some. Jeyne peered around in the gloom trying to identify other people at the high tables, hoping some of the better crowd had turned out for the show, but there seemed to be nobody of consequence besides themselves.

Before the next piece, the guitarist came to the front. "This is our last show here, and we've arranged a special treat. You've all heard of Chalula, the Gawandapar. She's here for a week starting tomorrow, but she's agreed to sing a few songs with us tonight." He sounded pleased, and a wave of finger-snapping from the audience showed they too liked the idea. A door opened behind the stage while he was still talking, and a figure moved into the light. "Here she is, please welcome Chalula!" The man stepped back, leaving the dark-swathed figure alone on stage.

There was more snapping, and several people in the room stood. Marlee, however, felt rooted to the spot. The way this woman moved, the shape revealed by the clingy black robe....

Chalula swept back the hood from her head, and stood looking at the audience. Her skin was black as night, her face angular, with a high forehead. Marlee made a little involuntary noise. The singer's black hair was swept back, sparkling with wedges of white—glass? Ivory? And then she threw back her arms and sang in a velvety, resonant voice.

Jeyne swore under his breath and pushed his chair back from the table. Marlee had spilled her drink, some of which flew in Jeyne's direction. "Sorry. Did I get you?"

"Only a little." Jeyne dabbed at his knee with a napkin.

"Okay."

"What?"

Marlee arrested her eyes' drift back to the stage. "Nothing, sorry. Can you get me another of these?"

"I don't know that you should have another."

Not only did she need another, she desperately wanted to be alone for a minute. "Do you know what real pain is?"

"I'm not sure."

"Want to find out?"

Jeyne picked up her glass and stood. "I'll be right back."

"Don't rush."

Alone, Marlee studied the singer again. She certainly did not want to

get the woman alone somewhere and get her out of that slinky robe. Their
eyes met again during an instrumental part, and Chalula gave a quirky little
smile. Marlee looked away, feeling heat rise in her face.

It was no use. This day was just one unending disaster. And now Clora
and Digriz were returning, and she had to pretend nothing was wrong.
Clora was flushed, laughing, a little perspiration on her brow.

"Having fun?" Marlee said.

Digriz pulled a chair out for Clora. "They're a lively band. And while
Jeyne's girl is no beauty, she certainly has a spark. I can see I have my—"
he glanced at Clora, who was occupied with looking around at the other
tables—"I can see why he finds her interesting."

Oh! This must be the inappropriate match Uncle Freddan hired Digriz
to disentangle her cousin from. And she was attractive in a way, though too
skinny for Marlee's own taste.

"Gah!" Marlee pushed her chair back. "I need a—I'll be back."

She hurried away, looking behind when the guards fell into step after
her. "You can't follow where I'm going." They didn't answer, but when she
found the door marked "Ladies," didn't follow her in.

The restroom was a bit primitive, and smelled, but it had a little cast-
iron sink and a scratched and speckled mirror. Marlee steadied herself on
the sink, splashed cold water on her face, then remembered that was a dumb
move. Sure enough, the mirror showed her eye shadow was running—it was
only charcoal from a burnt matchstick. Makeup here was primitive at best,
but at least she had a spare match in her pocket.

Miss Yrenn had done her makeup that first day. Clora showed her how
to make up her new face before she went out again, and now she did her
own, though it was difficult to make a straight line at the moment.

Face fixed, she started pacing the little room. Who did this Chalula
woman think she was, to give her such looks? Marlee would have to pretend
to like it, play along—that would be in character. But she wouldn't like
it. Not a bit.

Her Bobby—so far away. What was he was doing now? Did he think
she'd gone insane? Was her body in a looney bin, drooling, vacant? She
shuddered. That idiot doctor thought she'd died or had brain damage,

but he didn't know what he was talking about. She shouldn't have given him all that money when he clearly didn't know his stuff. He'd better have something good for her in the morning.

By the time she emerged, there were three women waiting at the door. The first one glared as she passed. No-one had knocked or tried the door—the guards must have discouraged them.

The manager was on stage saying the band would take a short break. Marlee arrived at the table just as Clora and Jeyne walked up together. The musicians on stage set down their instruments and dispersed, Alyssa and Chalula walking toward them.

"Oh, crap," Marlee muttered, and finished her drink in one long gulp.

"May we?" Alyssa said, but Jeyne had already stood to borrow extra chairs from adjacent tables. Chalula sat beside Marlee, and Alyssa sat near Jeyne, looking curiously at Clora and Digriz. "Who are your friends?"

Jeyne pointed. "You recognize my cousin Marlee, I imagine. Her companion, Clora, and my friend Digriz."

"Call me Eddie."

"Mister Digriz. I've heard of you from Jeyne." Alyssa's voice sounded cool. "And of course, everyone knows Marlee."

"We're honored you came to our little show." Chalula had a charming accent, not evident in her singing.

Marlee looked at her empty glass. "Jeyne wouldn't take no for an answer."

"And this is a lovely outfit." Chalula brushed the metal disks on Marlee's sleeve. "Boraggan, I think?"

"Sort of." Marlee's arm tingled where Chalula touched it, and her face felt hot. She played with the glass. Wouldn't someone yell "Fire" or something, to get her out of this?

"Darling," Jeyne said, "Marlee wants me to run a restaurant for her."

"That would be just your sort of thing, wouldn't it?" Alyssa sounded dubious. She probably had no illusions about her sweetie's organizational talents.

Well, it didn't matter what she thought. Marlee wouldn't be around long enough for the restaurant to go broke anyway. She'd find some way to get home. She let the conversation go on without her, her gaze straying. Chalula's arm lay beside hers, beaded with tiny drops of sweat. Marlee reached for the bowl of nuts to have an excuse to set her own arm farther away, where she couldn't feel the woman's heat. Then a leg brushed hers, a slow movement, obviously deliberate. It was an electric shock up her spine. Marlee sat up straight, then stood, her chair scraping against the floor, and suddenly everyone was looking at her. "I—I've got to go. Not feeling well."

"Not surprised, coz. I did warn you about that stuff." Jeyne stood. "I'll see you home. Shall I call a carriage?"

"No, no, you stay for the rest of the show. I've got..." She waved her hand at her guards. "I'd prefer to walk."

Jeyne hesitated, looked at the nearest guard. "All right, I suppose you're safe enough with Rojais. You'll go straight home, yes?"

That made two of her guards whose names she knew. Rojais, she rehearsed internally while collecting her things and turning down an insincere offer on Clora's part to accompany her. The girl clearly loved the dancing, and Marlee needed anything but conversation at the moment.

Rojais preceded her out the door, looked around, then stood aside to let her out. The other guard followed. Dark had fallen, the street was mostly empty, and the green streetlights were misted in wispy, acrid-smelling fog. Tannery. She was getting to know the smells of the city. She started for home.

She'd have to go back to the big house tomorrow. Bylamar was likely to pop a blood vessel if she stayed away longer, and her father and grandfather had both sent insistent notes in the most recent packet of papers. She didn't feel apprehensive at the moment. Even drunk, she'd done fine tonight. Clora was a worry-wart. She could handle her liquor, and she would be okay—er, all right—at the big house.

Then things started happening. Rojais stepped up beside her, his arm rising smoothly, the disk of his hand-shield blocking her view. There was a loud clang, and his hand jerked toward her face. She stumbled back, confused. There was a distant, flat crack, and Rojais stepped in front of her while someone grabbed her roughly and pulled her back—the other guard. A second clang, a shower of sparks from the metal pan on Rojais's shoulder, a ping from the stone wall beside her. Now Rojais was backing up, following her and the other guard toward the corner they'd just rounded. Something buzzed past her cheek, followed by a third crack. Then they were around the corner.

"Someone's shooting at me!" And how stupid that must sound. Rojais had somehow managed to block two shots, and get her behind cover, before she even knew what was happening. "How did you—" Her question was drowned out as Rojais raised his forearm to his lips and blew into a tube that was soldered to his armor, producing a piercing whistle.

The guards crowded her against the wall, facing outward. Marlee looked around wildly for attacks from other directions, in the gaps between them, but there were just a few people on the street running away. Feet pounded toward them from the direction of the Crooked Dog. She tensed, but as the runner passed under a streetlight she recognized the pointed helmet and brass-on-black uniform—a policeman. Another officer arrived from around the corner, and Rojais spoke to them both, low-voiced, sending them after the would-be assassin. Then he hustled her back the way they'd come, one large hand on the small of her back, staying between her and the street.

"I don't want to go back there. Take me home!"

"Don't be an idiot. When people are shooting, you get off the street."

"Am I hearing you right? You're calling me an idiot?"

"You know better than this, Miss." The big man's voice was tight with worry and frustration. "The last few days, you've paid no attention to security. You go out without your special dishware or your gun, you sit outside at cafes, you don't give us notice where you're going. We were supposed to be relieved an hour ago, but our replacements wouldn't know where to find us, would they? Now my dose is wearing off. You saw how late I was stopping those bullets."

Late? He hadn't even seemed to be hurrying. And what did he mean about his dose? But it seemed a bad time to argue when he had a fresh dent in his shield that would've been a hole in her head otherwise. Anyway, he had a point. "I'm sorry, Rojais. You're right, I've been distracted."

He shot her a narrow look, then leaned forward to check out an alley. "You say I'm right?"

"Yeah. If I make any more mistakes, say so."

"Huh." Rojais seemed to relax slightly. They reached the Crooked Dog, and he crowded through the doorway with her. "Messenger," he told the doorman. "Now."

CLORA

XVI

PEOPLE NOTICED, OF COURSE, WHEN Marlee returned so soon after leaving. The band's break wasn't even over yet, so there was plenty of attention to spare for sudden arrivals of prominent persons. Clora could tell something was wrong. Marlee stood near the doorway, stock still, face expressionless, left thumb rubbing her index finger. One guard spoke to a busboy.

Clora stood, but the guard pushed the boy toward the door, and the two of them started for the table. The other guard stayed at the door.

"I'm feeling better now." Marlee smiled at Digriz as he stood and pulled out her chair for her. "I guess I just needed some air." Her voice seemed overly bright. A waiter followed her to the table, and when he suggested another Pepper Mill, she shook her head. "Tonic water."

The waiter looked confused. "Tonic...?"

"She wants water." Drunk or not, Clora had best find a way to snap Marlee out of it before she made a major thumb-in-eye.

Chalula leaned toward Marlee. "Eddie tells me you sing."

Marlee shot Digriz a poisoned glance. "He overheard me in the bath, and he's been giving me a hard time about it."

"He says you have a lovely voice."

Digriz leaned in. "I think you should go on stage and sing something. The crowd would love it."

Marlee smiled sweetly. "And I think I'll stab you with my little knife."

The guitar player was trying to get their attention from the stage. Thank the gods! Clora nudged Alyssa and pointed.

"Break's over." Alyssa stood and gave Jeyne a quick peck on the cheek. "Walk me home after?"

"Without a doubt."

Chalula stood and smoothed her gown. "I hoped to speak with you," she told Marlee.

"Just at the moment, I have enough problems."

Chalula inclined her head. "I'll be in town two more weeks, should you find you have the attention to spare. I'm at the River Inn."

Marlee looked annoyed. "It's not true what they—what?" Marlee looked down at Clora's hand, clamped around her forearm.

"Dance with me," Clora said.

"What, now?"

"Now."

Marlee glanced at her guard, then shrugged. Clora half-dragged her down to the dance floor, noticing a slight trembling in Marlee's hand. They stopped at the edge, waiting for the music to start, and Clora put her arm around Marlee's waist. She leaned her head close. "What's going on? Pull it together."

"I might be a little tipsy. It's just everything. Well, someone tried to kill me, but that was just the finishing touch."

"What? Who tried to kill you?"

"I don't know. A sniper. So we came back in. Rojais sent for more guards."

"Then you only have to hold it together until they arrive."

"And then there's that thing with wossit, Aunt Karina."

"What thing?"

"I supposedly have some plan with Digriz to, to apply some leverage to get her to give us something."

"What's leverage? Blackmail?"

"Maybe."

"So if you don't want to, don't do it. Aren't you the boss?"

"Sure, but it's a plan from before, and there's a reason for it, so I'm afraid to just drop it. It's supposed to solve some problem with Josip. If we don't do it, I still have the problem with Josip, plus Digriz'll want to know why I'm changing my mind." The music was starting, soft and slow. "What if I can't dance?" Marlee whispered.

"People will just think you drank too much, which happens to be true."

Marlee took a deep breath, closed her eyes, swayed a little in time to the music, then took Clora's hand and moved onto the floor. After a couple of tentative steps, she tightened her grip and her tread grew more certain, steering Clora around the floor among the other couples.

"Ow," said Clora.

"Sorry."

The dance was a slow one, and Clora pulled Marlee closer. Marlee took a ragged breath and clung to her. "I can't do this anymore," she whispered. "It's too hard. I don't have to explain to them. I can just go. They won't guess. I'll live on my horse farm and figure out how to get home."

"And the problem with Josip?"

"What do I care? It's some family politics thing. I've got plenty money of my own. Who needs them?"

Clora bit her lip. She would have to tell what she knew, but not on the dance floor. She patted Marlee's back.

When the music stopped, two more of Marlee's guards and a policeman were waiting. Marlee ran to them, pulling Clora along by the hand, and the men fell into formation around her. Clora waved goodbye to a surprised-looking Jeyne and Digriz.

Too bad they had to leave early. Digriz was an agreeable companion, with manners and dash. She could envision him as the hero in a serial, going out and getting things done.

They were rushed out the door into a waiting carriage with drawn curtains. Clora caught a glimpse of a nervous-looking policeman in the driver's seat up top, looking very young in a helmet a size too large for him. The carriage shook as the guards got onto the standrails. The other policeman followed them in and sat beside Clora, opposite Marlee. He reached up and flicked on the ceiling light.

Marlee's hands came off the pale leather seat and joined in her lap, knuckles pale. "Did you catch them?"

The policeman shook his head. "Our men are canvassing the area for witnesses." He kept his eyes on the floor, and Clora was amused and a little delighted that she was now being treated as an important person, not to be looked at directly. The carriage started moving, and Clora put her hand on the wall as they bumped through a pothole.

When they finally stopped, Clora leaned across to wake Marlee while the policeman climbed out. Marlee seemed unsteady, so Clora let her go first, prepared to grab her sash if she should start to fall.

They were back at the big house, under the archway at the carriage door, and as they stood straightening their clothes, the door banged open and a woman in a robe and nightgown hurried out. "Your mother," Clora whispered. "Tam."

"My baby!" Tam threw her arms around Marlee. "Did they hurt you?"

"I'm fine, mother. They missed." Marlee hugged Tam awkwardly.

Marlee's father, Severn, fully dressed with sword and all, came out next. Instead of going to Marlee, he looked at Rojais, just now getting down from the carriage. "Report."

The guard looked exhausted, but stood at attention. "I was escorting Miss Marlee to her apartment when I saw gunfire coming. I blocked two shots, let one pass because it was a miss. By then my partner had got her behind cover, so I summoned the constabulary to pursue while we got Miss Marlee to safety. At last report, they hadn't caught anyone."

"What do you mean you let one pass?" Tam pulled away from Marlee to glare at the guard.

"Because it was going to miss her, ma'am."

"Just by this mush!" Marlee showed the distance with her thumb and forefinger.

"Leave the man alone, you two," Severn snapped. "He did exactly right. There's more danger from ricochet in blocking a miss than letting it go by. And you!" He looked closely at Marlee. "You're a disgrace. You're drunk, and what's that outfit?"

Marlee drew herself upright, swaying slightly. "They'll be wearing it in all the smart cafes next week."

"It's barely decent. Trousers?"

"Pfft. Where's Petro? Doesn't he know the family should rally round when someone's tried to be assin, assassinated?"

"He's away," Severn said, "unlike you, doing something useful."

"Well excu-u-use me. I'll have you know I invented pizza today. How's that for useful?"

Clora pulled Marlee toward the door. "I'll get her to bed."

"I can walk." Marlee pulled her arm free and forged ahead. Clora gave an apologetic little bob, and ran after.

Clora saw Marlee settled in bed, then slipped out. The east wing's oldest maid awaited in the hall. "Follow me, miss, and I'll show you to your room." The maid's posture was as stiff as her voice.

"Oh Ferni, come on, it's me."

"Yes, miss. This way, please."

Clora followed the woman two doors down the hall. "It's been a weird few days."

"If miss wants to talk, she can be sure I'll listen attentive like. I know how to behave to those as been promoted over those who been working here much longer." Ferni pulled down the bedclothes. "I found an old nightgown for you. In the morning I'll send for your things from town, if you like. We didn't have enough notice to get a fire laid."

"It's okay. Oh, now she's got me doing it. I mean, I don't need a fire, thanks." Ferni didn't leave, though. Waiting for instructions. "Good night."

Clora changed into the nightgown that lay across the bed, and opened the wardrobe to hang up her dress. It was her best one, that she'd chosen for going out, and she didn't want to get it wrinkled. She'd have to wear it again tomorrow.

She sat on the bed, brushing her hair with a silver-handled brush from the vanity, and looked around her new chamber. It was nothing like as large or as nice as Marlee's of course, and its window overlooked the courtyard instead of the river. But it was much better than any room she'd had previously, and all hers.

It was disappointing, hurtful, that Ferni treated her like a stranger. She'd have to look up the three other girls she'd been sharing a room with—maybe they'd be happy for her. And more important, they'd have the latest gossip.

EDSGAR

XVII

THOUGH IT WAS HIS HABIT to avoid rising before ten if he could, it seemed best to avoid notice, so Digriz made an exception to catch a train so egregiously early that he could reach his destination, a small rural station, before dawn, carrying his powered cycle.

The roads cross country were rutted and overgrown, fallen into disuse since the railroad was laid. But motoring goggles, a stout cap, scarf and jacket mostly protected from lashing weeds and branches.

It was still early when Digriz topped a rise and stopped to get his bearings. The valley spread out before him, farm fields high with wheat and hops. The thread of a stream glowed orange in the dawn light, and the old mill's roof was just visible over some trees. He lowered his goggles and twisted the throttle, humming along the sheltered roads between the fields.

The mill was boarded up, but on one window in back, the boards were just for show. Digriz parked the cycle behind a bush, and scrambled up the sloping stone wall. He pulled the boards off the window in one piece, slipped inside, and repositioned the cover. He edged around the cracked millstone that almost filled the room, and up a set of stairs to a loft room taking up half the second floor. A hooded figure leaning against the wall looked up and raised two fingers in the sign that all was well.

Digriz leaned down to look at the face inside the hood. "Good makeup," he whispered. Jennet had used white and gray grease paint to turn her cheery round, brown features into the pale, gaunt visage of a

Hoosian. It wouldn't be convincing in full light, but was good enough to fool a small boy in a dim room.

Jennet smiled, pointed to the wall behind her with her thumb, then held her hands beside her head, eyes looking around wildly. Digriz nodded. The boy was pretending to sleep. "How many did you get, then?" he said loudly, with a Hoosian accent.

"Only one boy so far, Jormin."

"Quiet! If he hears our names, we'll have to kill him. We need him alive to get a good price from the captain."

"Sorry, Jor, uh, boss."

"Just be careful once he's awake."

"He's a good strong 'un."

Digriz smiled. When the boy showed up in a few days claiming to have been captured by Hoosian slavers, this far from their home waters, everyone would put it down to imagination. And if anyone did believe him, at least they'd have a misleading description of the kidnapper. He signaled her to follow him downstairs, where they could talk more freely. "Did you get away from the inn all right?" he whispered.

"I told them my grandmother was ill. How long do you think it'll take me to nurse her back to health?"

"A couple of days, three at most. I'll send word we have him, and await a reply." Digriz paused under the window. "Do you need anything?"

"The drug."

"Right." Digriz dug into his pocket and produced a small blue bottle. "Not more than three drops at a time, for a boy his size. What'll you tell him while he's under?"

"It's a fantastic adventure he'll remember, of pirates and sea-dragons and blue mers. I used to tell my little sisters stories at bedtime."

"Excellent."

"The other thing I need is my eight crowns."

"Soon enough. And there's a bonus this time. I found you another job."

"I meant it when I said this was the last one."

Digriz held up his hand. "Not that kind of job. This is honest work. I know someone in the city who needs a restaurant manager. You can do that, right?"

"Certainly!"

"There you go, then." Digriz jammed his boot into a crevice in the wall, boosted himself up to the window, and soon was out again in the sunlight.

The mill had been carefully chosen as their headquarters. This time of year, crops were mature enough not to need weeding, but not yet ready to harvest, so it was unlikely anyone would be out to bother them. And from here he could communicate with Marlee. He walked his cycle upstream to where a pair of overhead wires crossed the water, then pushed through the foliage to the nearest pole. Swinging his pack onto the ground, he pulled out the necessary equipment—a black wooden box with a tongue of paper protruding from the top, a pair of long, coiled wires, a small toolkit in a leather wallet, and climbing spikes. Strapping these to his boots, putting his extra-long belt around the pole and rebuckling it, he climbed.

Near the top, he looked around. Nobody in sight, and trees blocked the view in most directions anyway. He reached up carefully, stripped a bit of insulation from both wires, and clipped his own wires to them, releasing the coils to dangle.

Back on the ground, he hooked wires to contacts on the clacker box. He charged up the dynamo with a crank on the side, and fed in the paper message tape he'd punched out in advance, in the dot patterns of clacker code. Too bad he couldn't use a cipher, but the clacker companies refused to deliver encrypted messages. Still, Marlee would understand his simple message, and it wouldn't reveal anything to other eyes that came across it.

MARLEE

XVIII

AWAKENING FOR THE SECOND TIME in the big house, Marlee groaned. She hid her head under the covers, but blocking the harsh outdoor light did little to ease the pounding in her head.

"Drink this." Clora's voice was brisk and unsympathetic. Marlee peeked over the covers, watching the girl set a cup on the bedside table. "You'll feel better in a minute."

Marlee sat up. The stuff in the cup was green and sludgy, but didn't smell bad. She downed it in a few gulps. Not something she'd choose normally, but tolerable. "What were those things called that I was drinking last night?"

"Pepper Mill, I think they said." Clora got the desk chair and moved it up next to the bed.

"That's right. No more of those."

"It wasn't the type of drink at fault, but the quantity." Clora refilled the empty cup from the water pitcher. "Drink this. We only have a few minutes before everybody will come wanting to talk with you, so let's plan."

"Why are we here? I wanted to go to the apartment."

"The policeman said it wasn't safe."

"That green stuff helps. Why didn't you give me that last time?"

"I did. You didn't drink it because you didn't know what it was. Here, more water. Bylamar has your day planned out, so I might not see you again until night. What should I do?"

"Let me think. Oh God, what time is it?"

"Around eight. And don't swear to god, as if there was just one. Where are you going?"

Marlee swung her legs over the edge of the bed. "I have to send a message to Digriz not to... well, I have to send him a message."

"This is your blackmail plan to help with Josip?"

"I told you that? Didn't I tell you I'd decided not to do it? Why did you let me sleep?"

Clora gave her a squinty look. "I'll tell you why. First, it wasn't really a choice. Second, you didn't say you had to do something about it right away. Third, you might want to hear what else I know first."

"All right, what?"

"The problem with Josip is, he thinks you murdered your uncle Benin."

"He thinks *what?*"

"That somehow you arranged his death. Did you?"

"How the hell would I know?"

"Hell?"

Marlee rolled her eyes. "How in Hades would I know?"

"I thought maybe in your journal." Clora pointed to the writing desk.

"I did read something about the death, but no confessions. Would you bring it here? The red one."

"Sorry, the desk only opens for you."

Fine.

Marlee went to the desk, found the journal, and the entry she wanted.

Wednesday, 19 Moukion 687. Fair, cool

    Father has hired an Aakol mathematician for the laboratory. Rob claims they're barely more than primitives, but grudgingly admits their usefulness.

    Most shocking thing happened today! We were at a tea on the patio at Benin's, when Benin had a horrible accident. He was on horseback, his usual daily run, and didn't duck far enough under a low branch. We weren't watching him, but we all heard the thump. On seeing his horse run on without him and his legs sticking out from behind the trunk, we all jumped the railing and ran to his aid, but there was nothing to be done.

Clora handed the journal back. "I don't figure she was really that shocked."

"Why would they suspect me and not the others who were there?"

"Maybe you're the only one who had reason. Maybe they thought you might and the others would never."

"But how would I arrange for him to not duck? How could this not be an accident? According to this I was nowhere nearby."

"Maybe it's a lie. Maybe you had an accomplice hiding in the tree, and when Benin passed under, he brained him with a club, *whap!*"

"Well... maybe. But why would I draw attention to myself by having them do it while I was there?" Marlee held up a hand. "We could make theories all day. One of us should go there, find out as much as we can about what happened. Can you do that?"

Clora sat up a little straighter, hands in her lap. "I will investigate the crime and make a full report."

"Terrific."

Clora deflated a little. "But can I? I'd have to go to Benin's house. I can't just up and go wherever I want."

"Why not? You're not a servant anymore, you're my companion. Take some money and go. Tell people I sent you. I'll write a note you can show them, if you think it'll help."

"Yes."

Marlee opened the stationery drawer. "But what worries me is, what's Digriz doing meanwhile, and how is it supposed to help with this?"

"Maybe he's trying to prove you didn't do it. Maybe he's getting information about someone else who was there."

Marlee doubted it. Digriz seemed more of a specialist in the dirty tricks department. "No. Whatever he's up to, I'll tell him to call it off until I know what it's about. Send in Bylamar right away."

Clora left with the note, and a moment later Bylamar entered, brandishing a folded yellow paper. "This just came for you. I don't know what it refers to."

The paper bore a lightning logo and the printed legend, *"Speedy Messenger—Faster by Clacker,"* followed by a message handwritten in block letters.

TO: MARLEE FOROSSI, FOROSSI HOUSE, CORILAN
FROM: PORLOON & CHASE LTD, PILKER FORD
HAVE YOUR MERCHANDISE. PLEASE ADVISE DISPOSITION.

Marlee folded the paper and tapped it against her knee. She had a sinking feeling. If this was something Bylamar didn't know about, it must be from Digriz, so it must mean he'd already kidnapped some poor child on her behalf. She could write back and tell him to release the boy—but if it turned out he was doing something really essential, they wouldn't get another chance. After the boy was kidnapped once, whoever had charge of him would be vigilant. "It's private. If I get any more of these, bring them straight here and don't open them."

"Will there be a reply?"

"Not yet." Marlee needed an excuse to talk to Karina now. What did she know about her? Ah. Shipping. "I have to arrange transportation for this merchandise. When can I talk with Karina?"

"With all the things I've had to move around because of your absence, you're booked solid through Wineday."

"Oh, no no no. That's not how it'll be. Today, the earlier the better. Set it up now, then come back and talk about the rest of my schedule. No, I mean it. Go!" And she said to his back, "No more speeches or prize-givings. I'm not leaving home until they figure out who's trying to kill me. Oh, except I need to visit Neidra."

Bylamar halted. "Sorry?"

"I want to visit my poor sick cousin, as soon as possible." There was an easy solution to the problem of not knowing where the madwoman was being kept. This is what underlings were for. "Arrange the details."

The maid who brought in breakfast was unfamiliar. She seemed to be trying to walk quietly, and the glassware rattled a little on the tray.

"Oh, go set that on the balcony. I don't bite." The girl continued to walk slowly. Marlee was tempted to snap "Move!" but feared it would cause breakage. She missed Clora already.

At least this time breakfast wasn't the feast of her first morning. She spread fig preserves on her toast and looked out over the city. It was clear now, but clouds were rolling in from the sea, and the weather tower predicted rain later, if she was correctly interpreting the gray triangle midway up the pole. From the market across the river came the distant clatter of carts and shouts of vendors, and downstream, by the docks, two dirigibles clung to their masts, one disembarking passengers into an elevator, another loading freight by crane. A man, made tiny by distance, hopped onto the side of a large crate as it left the ground, grabbing a cable to hang from as it rose, turning ponderously. As it neared the top, two men leaned out of an opening in the dirigible's cabin to straighten it and haul it in. Marlee shivered. No way would she ever want to dangle over such a long drop.

"What do you want?"

Marlee jumped, and set her cup down sharply. The woman in the bedroom leaned forward, hand on the door frame, chin poking into the outdoors. She was tall, thin, about forty, wearing a severe green dress, her white hair in a coil. She stared at Marlee and shook her free hand in a hurry-up motion.

"Good morning, ah, Karina." Marlee decided to have a talk with the staff later about letting people barge in unannounced. She forced herself to smile. "Come sit, let's talk."

"I've things to do. I'm leaving for my office in two minutes, so let's not waste time in jibber-jabber. Bylamar said it was urgent."

Marlee took a moment to pour more chocolate. She'd expected time to prepare for this meeting, but this world didn't like to co-operate with her plans. "I know about the boy."

"What boy?"

"The one you visit. The one you're hiding. Have you heard from the people who're supposed to be watching him, today?"

Karina went still, lips pressed into a little straighter line. "I don't know what you mean."

"I believe he's gone missing." Marlee took a sip of chocolate and looked away. She hated doing this, but it was also disturbingly thrilling to exercise this kind of power. She watched the last load of dirigible passengers board the elevator, and waited.

"You're a monster."

"Don't worry, Auntie, he won't be harmed." Marlee turned to look at her. "He'll be returned once I have what I want."

"Which is what?" Karina's voice was tight.

"Your key."

"Key?"

"I want to do a little smuggling."

"Oh, that key. No."

"You'd get it back in a couple of days." Maybe.

"Out of the question."

Marlee shrugged. "It would be a shame if something happened to that boy." One nice thing about this place—all the old clichés were new again. "I wouldn't hurt him, of course. But my friends are impatient." She stirred her cup, the spoon scraping slowly against the side.

"You don't have him. You're lying."

"Go check. No rush. You can have, oh, until dinner."

Karina held her fists at her sides, glaring, then turned on her heel and strode out. Marlee let out her breath, picked up her cup. Hoped she'd done the right thing.

CLORA

✕ˑ✕

NOBODY TRIED TO STOP CLORA leaving the big house and commandeering a carriage and driver, though she felt terribly guilty doing it. Kraik was the driver she found, lying across the driver's bench of a carriage with one leg dangling over the edge, ankle bare between shoe and trouser leg. She stepped up and rapped it with the tip of her umbrella.

Kraik snorted and sat up, coughing. "Here, what for you whacking at me?"

"Thought you might like to work 'stead of napping."

"Shows what you know." He rubbed his ankle.

"Don't be a baby. That didn't hurt. Come on, I need to go to Benin's."

"I ain't a stop you."

Finally finding someone who didn't treat her differently than before, somehow wasn't the relief she'd expected. "Should I go tell Miss Marlee I can't find no-one down here willing to take me on her errand?"

"All right, don't get nasty. Get in." He swung to the ground and bent to disconnect the charging cable. "Which place of Benin's you want?"

"Where he died."

"That's a ways!"

Clora paused with the door open. "Best get on, then."

"But it's like to rain!"

"More reason to hurry."

"Fine for you." Kraik shut the door after her a little harder than necessary. "You being inside and all."

As the carriage rattled down the drive, Clora slid the window open, leaning her chin on the sill with a pleasant rush of anticipation. Here she was, out on her own, investigating a crime, like in the serials. It was important work. She would clear the reputations of the innocent and track the evildoers—though unlike her heroes, she'd content herself with identifying the evildoers, letting others do the actual capturing. Also, the reputation of the innocent—assuming Marlee was innocent in this case—was pretty well tarnished beforehand. Still, how many girls could say they'd detected a real mystery?

Plus, she was working on the same case with the dashing Mr. Digriz. Though he didn't know it, wherever he was, they were on the same team, both trying to discover the real killer of Benin Forossi, or to prove it really was an accident. He'd been patient with her countrified dancing skills, the night before, and funny and charming and maybe a bit dangerous. She could be his partner in future missions, perhaps, if she did well on this one.

The house where Benin died was well out of town. It did, indeed, start to rain before they got there, drumming on the roof and misting the windows. They left the city limits, passed through a couple of old-fashioned towns, bumping over uneven cobbles. Then they were really out in the country, passing fields and the occasional isolated house. Finally, they turned in through a gate in a tall stone wall, wheels crunching on the white shell driveway and splashing through fresh puddles. The house was red brick, with tapering salmon-colored corner stacks Clora thought were called Hesperan towers.

"You going in which door, then?" Kraik asked.

"Front." Clora had status now, and could call on the lady of the house. She even had calling cards, picked up yesterday, still smelling of fresh ink.

The carriage scraped to a halt near the front steps, and Clora sat looking up at the imposing carved wooden doors, rubbing the handle of her umbrella with a gloved thumb.

Kraik leaned over to look through the window at her, water dripping off the rim of his cap. "Was you getting out, then? Not that I mind sittin' here all cold and wet, but I do need to charge the wagon for the trip back. That would be in the garridge there, under the smoking chimney. Where I expect there's a warm fire."

"Take me around back."

"Eh, right." Kraik's head drew back out of sight. In a few seconds they passed under a brick arch, pulling up beside two other carriages under a domed ceiling.

As Clora stepped out, Kraik clambered down, wringing his cap out. The dye ran, leaving gray spots on the pale flagstones. "Cheap piece of...." He crammed it back onto his head. "Just you walk round that way. You'll see the door."

Clora found some servants at their ease in the kitchen, a large stone-floored room a half-level down from the back door. A tubby man in a server's vest stood up from the table and looked up at her.

"May I help you, mi—the gods, it's Clora!"

"Hello, Cousin Melkin." The Forossi country estates were all clustered fairly close together. Growing up in the Forossi stables, she had relatives belowstairs in several houses.

Melkin hung up her umbrella and helped her out of her jacket, looking puzzled. "I didn't recognize you at first in this getup."

"I've had a change of fortune."

Melkin scowled a little, perhaps making assumptions about the causes of her advancement, but the other servants came up, and he didn't speak. He hung the jacket, his lips pressed into a line.

One floor-maid was familiar from Clora's school. The other looked foreign, perhaps Ijolais. An older, iron-visaged woman wearing a silver housekeeper's key ring held back, but the two girls clustered around. An older boy remained at the table. He had the mottled brown-and-white hair of mixed ancestry. He gave her a long look, then bent his head back to his work, a tiny wood carving.

The girl she knew from school, Gerdal, distracted her from the boy by fingering the fabric of her sleeve. "This is tops. You marry a rich one?"

"I'm not married." Clora twisted her head to show her right ear—no ring. "I'm doing important work for the family. I thought I'd stop to see Melkin, and catch the latest news."

"Ooh, there has been a happening." The other maid's accent confirmed her Ijolais origin. "The master, he was killed, two weeks back."

"It was horrible," Gerdal said with relish. "Brains all over the place. Come have a cup and we'll tell about it."

Clora chatted with Melkin about the health of his mother, her aunt, until Gerdal returned with a fresh steaming cup for her. "You saw what happened?" Clora asked as the girl settled at the table.

"I was serving tea on the patio—me and Sjillan." Gerdal gestured at the Ijolais maid. "I don't think anybody saw it. There was a thud and we turned, and there he was, laying on the ground behind the tree. The horse had run on without him."

"Everybody was on the patio?"

"Yah. Lady Forossi—Wenda, that is, our mistress—and Miss Marlee, and Elga with little Josip, and Swen's fiancée as I forget her name...."

"Mindolin," Melkin said.

"... and another woman, older...."

"Lady Tahlia," Sjillan said. "This was asked by the men who came afterward. Also, they ask was anyone near the tree? Who ran there first? Did they touch him?"

"Who did run there first?"

"Lady Wenda," Gerdal said. "I never knew her to run that fast. But she touched naught. She shied back, and then we were all there, so nobody couldn't've done nothing to him. Anyway, he was plain dead already, no question about it."

"Miss Elga, she felt his arm," Sjillan touched her wrist. "Then I was sent for the house guards. They have ask us all about this for many hours."

"Sounds like an accident." Clora looked around the table. The boy with the carving was still studiously ignoring the huddle. "Why did they ask so many questions?"

"That was later," Gerdal said. "On the day, they just set a guard, and the police spoke with us a while, and they had a wotsit, magic guy."

"Forensic wizard." Melkin sipped from his cup. "From the University. He walked about the tree with his magic-sniffing pigs—"

"Three of them," Gerdal put in. "Little black ones. So precious!"

"... set up lenses and the like, made notes."

"What did he find out?"

"They didn't say," Gerdal said. "But we figured not much, 'cause they all went away and we had the funeral. But the next week, there they all was again, only twice as many, and took us each aside separate."

"So something happened meanwhile, to make them think there was foul play."

Sjillan shrugged. "They do not say, but they ask closely where each person is and who does what when."

"So where were they, then, and what did they do?"

Sjillan gave a large shrug. "As I say, I am sent off immediately. I do not see much."

"It was a madhouse," Gerdal said. "Lady Wenda, she fainted. Elga tried to calm her down, but Miss Mindolin, she screamed her head off, the fool thing, and little Josip got loose while Elga was helping her, and he started crying, so I scooped him up."

"And Marlee?"

Gerdal shrugged. "She hung back. I was busy, not watching everyone."

"The stable master said she brought the horse in," Melkin said.

"They didn't tell me that," Gerdal said. "She catched the poor beast, then. I guess it was spooked with all the blood and hollering."

"So if the horse was part of a trap, she might've..." But she was trying to clear Marlee. "Uh, noticed."

"Or she might've fixed it back before anyone got to see." The boy looked up at last from his carving, a little defiant, eyes the color of storm clouds and with the storm's turmoil behind them. He looked back down again immediately.

Thank you so much. "What's your name?"

"Unnentio."

"What's your first name?"

"Don't use it."

He looked like a stable boy. "Did you see the horse when she brought it in?"

He looked up at her again, curiously. "Why? You ain't just wondering."

Well, she'd known it couldn't last. "No, I've been asked to find out."

Gerdal's eyes widened. "You're a police now?"

Gerdal hadn't gotten significantly smarter since their school days. "No, I'm just helping one of the family."

"Go on!" Melkin said. "Which one?"

Clora hesitated. It wouldn't be a secret for long anyway, not with Kraik sitting around a stove with the grooms, giving them the news from the big house. "Miss Marlee. I want to show she had no part in it." She looked around the table. "Didn't anyone see or hear aught?"

Unnentio looked up again. "I heard the p'lice talk about the horse."

"What?" Sjillan said. "You never tell us this before."

Unnentio shrugged. "Nothin' to tell. That first day, the wizard man came in and cussed at the animal, then he told the head police there wasn't no mations about her."

"Mations?"

Melkin leaned in. "I think he means emanations."

"Oh, sure." Clora nodded. If magic has been used on the horse recently, there should still be some residue a wizard could detect. "Did he say anything else?"

Unnentio shook his head. "Not as I could hear. But Miss Marlee, she's good with horses."

The housekeeper had been busying herself with chores as they talked, but now returned to the table with a tray of bread and a pot of jam. "You think she could've made the mare jump? Without using magic? At just the right second, and from a ways away?"

"Might be. Don't know how."

Her attempt to clear Marlee wasn't going as well as she'd hoped. Clora reached for a slice of crusty brown bread and spread it with jam, welcoming the chance to think. The jam was kostaberry, golden and tart, with a little dark, strong buckwheat honey. "Oh, this is so good."

Melkin scooped out some for himself. "Cook makes more than we can use, when the berries are in season. I'll send back a couple jars with you for Miss Marlee."

"She's gone off sweets somewhat, but if she doesn't want them, I can find a use for them." She chewed, sipped tea, and thought. "Maybe I could see where it happened. If it won't disturb the Lady."

"Oh, you won't bother her," the housekeeper said. "She's took to her room, refusing visitors."

Eagerly, Gerdal and Sjillan led her upstairs through quiet halls and a glass-walled study done in rose satin, onto the patio. Though the rain had stopped, the slate tiles were still dark and shiny. "That there's the tree." Gerdal pointed.

It was an oak, just starting to turn color. Its long branches spread over the riding path. Clearly, it was impossible to hide in the tree. Though it hadn't yet begun to lose leaves for fall, the foliage was too sparse to conceal a lurking assassin. And though invisibility spells were common in the stories Clora read, she knew they didn't exist in real life.

"Which branch was it?" she asked. None of them looked low enough for even a tall man on a tall horse to brain himself on.

"Oh, they chop off the branch," Sjillan said. "The Lady orders it so. And the men who come, they take it away."

"They cut other branches as well," Gerdal said. "To bar any accident. The master always forbade anyone should touch them, but now he's gone, the Lady wanted them off."

Clora picked up her skirts and stepped over the low marble railing onto the wet yard. "Show me where it was."

The maids followed reluctantly, careful of their shoes in the wet grass. Sjillan pointed out where the branch had been, the cut end painted with tar.

Clora walked a little way, up and down the horse path, but any clues that might have been lying on the wood mulch were long gone now. She hadn't really expected the King's inspectors to have missed anything.

On the patio, Gerdal brushed off a chair to wait on. Sjillan, looking ill at ease, stood beside her.

"Show me where they sat, and what they were doing when... the accident happened." Clora took down all the details of how people had been disposed on the patio and in the house. Marlee would've had an easy view of the tree from where she sat, but so would a few others. Little Josip could probably be ruled out as a suspect since he was not yet two years old, but what could anyone have done from that distance, view or no view?

"Was anyone near the tree earlier?"

"Oh, yes," Sjillan said. "Everybody was."

"They played tockers on the lawn," Gerdal explained. "The leader ball ended up under that tree the one time, so they was all in there trying to hit it again. And they was around the yard and garden all day, doing this and that, and nobody keeping special track where they went."

Clora looked up again at the tree. "I wish I'd seen that branch before they cut it." How could someone have arranged for the branch to meet up with Benin's head? It seemed impossible, but the investigators must have some theory, or they wouldn't keep on with the case.

A device mounted on the branch to whack him as he passed? How could the killer remove it before someone spotted it, right above the path? Something to raise the ground as the horse approached? If non-magical it would be large and obvious, and if magical, they would've found it.

If the horse could be taught to jump at the right time, that could do it. But that took time. Marlee couldn't have come out here to train the horse for days on end, without anyone noticing.

"Actually," Gerdal said, "you can see the branch. I just thought, we got a pitcher."

The portrait gallery was dark, and Gerdal lit an oil lamp. "The master didn't hold with them green lights. Messes the colors."

The family's pedigree wasn't long, so only a few unlovely visages glowered down at them in the flickering light, from among the landscapes. They stood before a painting of a group of men on horseback, with dogs and rifles, on a lawn with forest in the background.

"This is by Tuban," Sjillan said. "The master was most proud with it. It was make in his own yard, see? Here is the tree."

Clora had already spotted it, and her finger traced the line of the lowest branch. It could have brained a rider who didn't duck. "Is this accurate?"

"Tuban, he very precise."

The boy, Unnentio, was gone from the kitchen when they returned. Clora stayed another hour, updating them on the latest from the big house—only fair after they'd told the only exciting news they'd had in years. She left with protracted goodbyes and a basket of food hooked over her arm.

Unnentio was waiting for her, leaning against the carriage house. He stood as she approached and gave a nervous little half-bow. "I got something else as I din't want the others to hear."

Clora's heart sped up a little. "All right."

"I din't tell the pleece. But as you work for Miss Marlee I can ask you. When she brung the horse back that day, she give me a quarter-crown and told me to brush her down real good."

"She said that?"

"Aye. Real good, she said. This here horse, she said, has had a hard day and would surely like a good brushing. And she give me a quarter-crown."

It was far more than a usual tip. One might assume Marlee was buying something more than just a horse-brushing. "What's your question, then?"

"When those men come back, I didn't say nothing to them. Question is, you got something to help me forget about it for good?"

Clora's eyes narrowed. "That's a dangerous game." In the stories, blackmailers always got their comeuppance.

The boy stood up a little straighter. "I ain't afraid of you people."

It was a little pitiful, really. The investigators would have it out of him eventually, assuming it was even the truth. Trying to buy his silence would only make it look like there was something to hide. "I might have something for you, but I want some talking in exchange."

"Yeah? What about?"

"What'd you do with the brush?"

Unnentio looked surprised. "Wash and hung it, like always."

"Where did you brush him?"

"In his stall."

"Where I used to work, we stripped the stalls every week."

"We do that here."

"So if there was something on the horse that you brushed off, it's long gone now." He opened his mouth to speak again, but Clora overrode him. "So talk now, and it's you against Miss Marlee. Even if they believe you, it ain't a crime to tip well. And then they ask, why didn't you say this before, the times they talked to you?"

Unnentio looked as if he would like to say more, but when Clora started walking again, he stepped out of her way. Only when she was safely past, heading for the carriage, did she let herself grin.

But the grin faded as she considered what she'd learned. The boy was probably telling the truth. If he'd wanted to make something up, he could've done better. Even if the proof had been destroyed, this certainly suggested Marlee had something to do with Benin's accident.

Still, how could she have done it? What could possibly have been on the horse to make it jump, that the wizard and the police had missed?

Well, she'd think about it on the way back. Right now, she'd best find her absent driver.

Marlee had been left alone long enough.

CLORA FOUND A NOTE ON Marlee's desk.

Meetings all day. No breaks. Bylamar is a beast. You're invited to formal tea with my parents at 1600. Not actually an invitation, more a command. Wear your best. Come to my room at 1530.—M

Clora's heart fell into her boots. Her former fellow servants' attitudes were hard to bear, but it was nothing to compare with what she anticipated from the family. They were unlikely to actually murder her, but these weren't people whose attention she wanted.

But she'd known she was putting herself in that position. Of course they'd want to know more about her. Just because it was inevitable, though, didn't make it pleasant.

She folded the note and stuffed it into a pocket, then went back to her room. There, she froze on finding the door, which she'd locked, standing open. Had someone searched her room? Might they still be in there? Clora's mind raced. Was there anything that would reveal any of Marlee's secrets if found? No, they never wrote things down. The only things in there were her own clothes, books and other personal possessions.

Standing back, she eased the door open. Then, seeing who was sitting in the wooden chair beneath her window, her apprehension was replaced with exasperation, and the breath she'd been holding came out as a sigh.

Her visitor looked up, smiled, and set down a newspaper. "There you are! I been waiting an endless time."

"Hello, mother."

"That's all you got to say after I come all this way?"

Clora entered, and shut the door. "How nice to see you, mother. I didn't expect you."

"I come in a great rush, with no time to write first. Ain't you gonna ask why?"

Clora plumped herself down onto the bed. "Why did you come, ma?"

"Well you may ask! I had a note in the morning post from my sister's boy about your goings-on in this place." Her mother sat on the bed, clapping her on the thigh. "Hoo, ain't this a comfy mattress! How is it I don't get the news about my girl from her own self? They taught you how to write in that school, you couldn't pick up a quill to let your ma know you were promoted?"

"Well, ma, you know Marlee. She could change her mind the next day. I thought I'd wait and see."

"You oughta written me at once, so I could advise you how to get her not to change her mind. What presents has she give you? Besides that fine dress? Any jewelry?"

"Ma, it's not what people think. I just help her out and keep her company." She patted the coverlet. "You see we don't share a bed."

"Still and all, a companion has to look good to make her mistress look good. There should be jewelry. What is she paying you? I'll speak to her. You know she always minded me."

Clora carefully avoided rolling her eyes. Besides her duties as head cook at Severn's ranch, her mother had sometimes supervised Marlee when she was growing up there. But as far back as Clora could recall, Marlee hadn't much minded anyone. "Feel free to try. I'm sure she remembers you fondly." Or at least, she would, once Clora had an opportunity to remind her. Thank Tyche they hadn't run into each other before Clora returned! "But it's not a good time to bother her. Someone tried to kill her last night."

"I saw in the paper. Poor girl! She'll want soothing. That's a chance for you to get in good with her."

"Yes, ma, I'm doing that. We've been away a few days, so she's busy. She won't have time for us until this evening, if then. How about we go down to the servants' quarters and you can visit?"

"Girl, that's a fine idea. I best talk with the cooks here about what new dishes the family likes. And catch up on news."

News meaning, of course, gossip. Well, it might keep her out of trouble.

MARLEE

GRANDFATHER JOSIP KEPT HER WAITING in the hallway outside his library. There didn't seem to be anyone else in there, so it was probably payback for skipping the earlier meeting. She couldn't sit. The whole day had been a series of narrowly escaped disasters, meeting after meeting of scrambling to figure out what was going on. She'd gotten many sharp looks from her brother Petro, and Severn was positively sarcastic.

It said a lot about this family that they seemed to be attributing her distraction to new love and hangover, rather than as a reaction to being shot at the night before. Though in fact, she found herself fairly unconcerned about her unknown assailant in the streets, at least compared with the threats in this house. Dreading the coming interview, she appreciated this brief respite.

As she stood looking up at a painting of a naval battle, a page boy hurried up, stopping at attention and holding out a folded paper in a self-important way.

Marlee smiled. They were so cute in their little blue uniforms and caps. She took the paper, recognizing Clora's handwriting on the outside.

Marlee,
  Saw your note.
  Guess who's here for a visit! My ma, Elinora. I know you'll be pleased, since she helped raise you, back at the ranch. I remember how you always used to call her Elli.

I'm taking her and her usual big plaid bag around the servant areas. If you need me, we'll probably be in the kitchens visiting with the other cooks. I know you're busy, but should you see her, please take a moment to greet her and ask after my brothers. She had a letter from Garvi recently.
Clora

Marlee folded the letter. "Thank you. No reply." Decent work. She was warned, told how to recognize the person she should recognize, and how to make it seem she knew her, but without being obvious, should the note reach the wrong hands.

The door into the library opened, and a thin, sour face peered out at her. This must be Josip. He crooked a finger, and turned away. Marlee followed, glancing around the room while his back was to her. It was large, luxurious. Thick wool carpet with an ornate pattern. Large stone fireplace, cold now, surrounded with relics of hunts—heads and antlers, and an etching of a younger Josip victorious over a large animal she didn't recognize. Before the fireplace, a spotted pelt might have come from a huge cat. The other walls held tall shelves packed with books, rolled-up charts in diamond-shaped holes, and a shelf of models—ships, dirigibles, and buildings.

Josip dropped into a padded leather armchair with a sigh. Marlee sat in a chair made out of animal horns, which was more comfortable than it looked, and waited. Waited for several interminable seconds, while he looked at her searchingly with keen gray eyes.

"I've always thought you were the brightest of the lot. The canniest."

A promising start. "Thank you."

"You might be the best choice to manage things when I'm gone."

"All right. Not anytime soon, I hope."

He ran his hand over his chin. "It would be a shame if I have to kill you."

Marlee paused, heart racing. "Um, I agree."

"Did you murder my son?"

"I don't know how that happened."

Josip stared at her for a long time. "Unfortunately, you're also the best liar I know."

"I learned from an expert. But I'm not lying now."

"You didn't actually say you didn't kill him."

"You think I did it, and forgot? It wasn't me."

Josip glanced at the side-table under the window, which for no apparent reason, had a log on it. He snapped his eyes back to her. Looking for a reaction. What... oh! Marlee stood, crossed to the window. The rough bark had a dark brown stain on it.

Josip levered himself out of his chair and limped over to stand beside her. "Yes, that's it. I'm keeping it always with me until I have justice."

"It must be terrible to lose a son that way. So suddenly."

He turned away, went to his chair. "When I find out who's responsible, there'll be another death. There'll be no question of a trial, you understand. I only require enough evidence to satisfy myself."

"I'd like to know, too. But why are you so sure it wasn't an accident?"

"I don't see why I should lay my cards on the table." He turned to look at her. "We both know you had reason to want him gone. I ask you again, did you kill Benin? Yes or no."

"No."

"No?"

"No, sir."

Josip turned away, looking tired. "Tell Bylamar to turn in your train ticket. You'll travel to the capital with me on the airship. Until this is resolved, I'm keeping you under my eye. We'll talk every day."

"As you like."

He sat up straighter, took a deep breath. "On to other business. I understand someone took a shot at you last night."

"Three shots."

"Floodin' anarchists. They catch anyone?"

"Not that I've heard. Are you sure it was anarchists? There are other folks who might be unhappy with me."

Josip scowled. "Someone's stirring them up, a new leader, calls himself Night Wind. But he's been too careful for the Seidos to identify. He talks to this person and that person, but somehow never to our spies. I'd almost think he had their names, except if he did, he'd do more than just avoid 'em. We don't even have a decent description, goes around in a mask. They took a shot at Count Morrienne, too, blew up his valet." Josip thumped his cane on the floor, twice. "Well, we'll get them. They can never resist bragging to their friends. What else do we have?" He reached for a paper on the side table. "I'm getting old," he grumbled. "Never used to need lists. Ah yes, the Julal Valley mining rights. Have you closed on that yet?"

Guessing time. "Um, no."

"Why not? I know you were busy with your new toy, but you didn't find time to pass by their office? We need to finish it before they come to their senses and raise their ask."

"I just... I feel uneasy about it."

"The reports came back clean." He scowled. "Never mind. If you have a bad feeling, there's probably a reason, even if we don't know what it is." He made a note. "Find out what you need to, but we need a decision before we leave. What about Masters Feenix and Hart? Do we invest in their scheme?"

Another total blank. "Sure."

Josip's brow wrinkled. "Really? I know you like gadgets, but we'll never make back the cost of laying the wires. Why should anyone use the things? The mail comes twice a day, and if you're in a hurry there's always the clacker. Who would pay so much to not even be able to see who they're talking to? Having a voice come out of a little box, that's not a satisfying conversation. What's so funny?"

"Oh, grandfather. I'm sorry. Yes, we should definitely invest in this. It'll be huge."

"Why? They're no use unless the people you want to talk with already have one. Why would anyone pay for a remote talker before there's anyone to talk to on it?"

"For status. To be the first one on their block. Trust me on this. The price of stuff like this always comes down quickly. Everyone will be able to afford it before long. And people love to talk. They'll pay for it."

Josip waved his hand. "Fine, fine. I still think we'll lose money, but you know more about these things than I, and you never win big without risk. It needs a better name, though. 'Remote talker' has no style."

"How about 'telephone'?"

Josip screwed up his mouth. "What does that even mean? It doesn't sound grand enough for a status item. I'll put Narlu on it. We'll need a prettier case for it, too." He scribbled on his list. "Now, about the Gosseyn Trading Company insurance bid...."

"IT WAS HORRIBLE." RETURNING TO her room, she'd run into Clora heading the same direction. She stepped around a maid carrying a stack of linens and hurried on down the hall, letting Clora catch up as best she could. She lowered her voice. "Nobody caught on, I think, but I got some mighty strange looks, and Severn read me the riot act about not paying attention and forgetting stuff."

"What's a riot act?"

"He made some harsh remarks. I have a plan, though. I told Bylamar to write a one-page summary of each deal we've got going."

"How did you explain that?"

"As part of my new system to keep my projects organized." Marlee pushed through into her room, and looked around to make sure it was empty. "Close the door. What'd you find out?"

As Marlee paced, Clora sat on the edge of the bed and gave a run-down of her activities, ending with her conversation with the groom.

By this time Marlee was seated at her desk, tapping her teeth with a pen. "So it looks like maybe she did have something to do with it."

"I been trying and trying to think how."

Marlee set the pen back in the drawer. "Is there something you can sprinkle on a horse to make it jump?"

"Just at the right second? Nothing I ever heard of."

"What if it was magic?"

"The police wizard checked the horse, remember? And Benin, and the path, the tree, everything. Magic leaves a trace. Even if the stable boy was telling the truth, you can't just wipe it off with a brush."

"What if the magic wasn't done to the horse? What if it was done to whatever was on the horse that got brushed off?"

"That could be what the police think, but if it was stuck well enough to the horse to lift him off the ground, how could it come off so easy? Maybe you just thought the horse deserved a good brushing. You always liked horses better than you liked people."

"What've you been doing since then?"

"I had to entertain my ma a while, then I asked around about the police captain on the case. Did you know he's getting all the reports from your guards now?"

"They write reports about me? Shit!" They'd been standing around in the waiting room all during Marlee's supposedly secret meeting with the psychist. Well, she had an excuse for that, if anyone asked. Thank god—the gods—for Neidra!

"I tried to find out where they keep the evidence," Clora continued, "but I don't suppose they'd let us look at it anyway."

Marlee grimaced. "I know where the bloody section of branch is."

"So it definitely was the branch that hit him? Anyway, that was all I had time for. Now about this tea with the family?"

"Yes. That. It's a regular thing, evidently, and since we're together, they expect you there, too."

"Can't you tell them I'm sick?"

"Listen, Clora. You don't want to give these people the idea you're afraid of them. Is that what you're wearing?"

"Ma picked it out. Don't you like it?"

"It's fine, just wondering." Marlee glanced at the clock. "Twenty minutes still? I'm starving. I'm going to invent lunch. It's right at the top of my list."

"Good. If you're that hungry, maybe you'll be on time for once."

"I'll meet you in the hallway in ten and you can show me the way. I need a little alone time."

Clora stood. "See you then."

Marlee locked the door behind Clora, then stood surveying the room. Alone at last! And with just time to try something that had occurred to her while being bored in a meeting. She stood in the middle of the room, closed her eyes, and tried to envision where the secrets were hidden.

It was no good. Things never came to her when she tried to remember them. She had to think about something else, sneak up on herself when she wasn't expecting it. She looked around, and spotted a pile of books on the bureau. Someone had fetched them from the apartment in town, but she had no bookshelf in the room, so they hadn't been put away like the rest of her things.

She stood some of them on top of her desk, with a stone vase and a heavy china dog as bookends. She flipped through a few, then paused over the last book, a thin, blue volume of poems everyone memorized in grade school. This one should be hidden, she decided arbitrarily. Someplace safe. She turned with it in her hand—to face a blank wall, other hand held out before her.

Ha! She walked over, keeping her hand out, and touched the wall, then ran her fingers over the wallpaper.

The wall seemed ordinary, solid when she rapped on it. She felt all around, but found no seams or hidden latches. Could there really be a hiding place here?

The door to the hallway rattled, and she moved quickly away from the wall. "Are you in there?" Clora called through the door. "We got to go."

"Come in here a second." Marlee unlocked the door. She didn't like to have someone else in on the secret, even Clora. She already knew so much. But if there was anything more to be found, she really needed to find it.

Clora looked down at the watch pinned to her sleeve. "We'll be late. I thought you were so hungry."

Marlee pulled her in and relocked the door. "I think there's a secret hiding place in this wall. You read those spy stories. How do these things open?"

"Lot of ways. What makes you think it's right there?"

"I tried to fool old Marlee into finding it for me." Marlee lifted the poetry book. "I decided I needed to hide something, to see where I would take it. I took it to that wall. How would Marlee want it to open?"

"I don't know. No, wait. She likes touch locks, like the desk and her journals. If it's forced open, boom!"

"So I touch the wall? Where? There's no little metal plate like on those other things."

Clora shrugged.

Marlee stood back, looked at the wall, and tried to imagine where she would press to open it.

Clora fidgeted. "You always make us late."

"Open the curtain. I need more light." Marlee leaned close to the wall, closing one eye to sight across the low ridges of fuzzy purple flocking.

"What are you doing?"

"She must've used this hiding place often. She had a lot to hide." Marlee moved her head. "She'll have touched the latch often."

Ha, there! Three spots in the fuzz were worn down, near where her hand had automatically gone before. She held her hand up. If she turned it so, three fingers matched the worn spots, the others coming down on areas too smooth to show wear.

Clora looked again at her watch. "If there even is a hiding pla... Oh."

A section of wall quietly swung out. The edges were irregular, following the areas of purple fuzz so the seam was disguised when it was shut. Marlee expected a small cupboard, but this was a reasonable sized shallow closet, shelves stacked with an untidy assortment of items. Several outfits hung from a short bar across one end—not regular clothing, but costumes. Disguises, including a leather tunic with steel plates, padded to bulk out the shoulders.

Marlee pulled out a flat box covered in red fabric. "I want to see what this stuff is."

Clora bit her lip. She looked again at her watch.

"All right." Marlee put the box back, pushed the hidden door, and it swung silently back into place. "Fine. Right after tea, then." She picked up her wooden case of poison-detecting dishes. "It's in the blue parlor. Know where that is?"

"Yes, but that's a big room for just a tea. Are you sure?"

"That's what Tam said."

A footman met them at the door to the blue parlor, opening it as they approached. Marlee stopped in the entrance, Clora bumping into her. It was a large room, but it had to be to accommodate everyone in it. The whole extended family must be there, including some she didn't recognize from the pictures she'd studied. But what really caught her eye....

"Are we going in?"

Marlee gave a little wave, held up one finger, and backed out, dragging

Clora a little ways down the hallway. "What the—what in Hades was that?" she whispered.

Clora looked bewildered. "What?"

"That, that thing. The giant lizard."

"Giant... oh, the Aakol. Or it might be an Hsaa, I guess. What about him?"

"It's a *giant fucking lizard.*" The footman looked at them curiously, then averted his eyes. She dragged Clora a little farther down the hall.

"It's not polite to call them lizards. How would you like it if he called you a monkey?"

"Why didn't you tell me about them?"

"Tell you what? I thought you knew."

"Why?"

"Because you read about them in the red geography book. Aakol, the desert tribes."

"I never... All right, but they could've had a picture, or a footnote saying, 'By the way, they're giant lizards.'"

"Everybody already knows that. Who else would live in a desert?"

"Well, certain things in that book are starting to make more sense now. What's it doing at tea?"

"What's he doing. The males have red throats. I guess he was invited."

"Why haven't I seen any before now? Out on the street or whatever?"

"They mostly don't live around here. They don't like our weather."

"Wait a minute. I remember. It was in her journal. There's a new Aakol in the lab."

Tam came out into the hallway, looking a little apprehensive. "Dear, are you coming in?"

"Yes, mother." She put her arm around Clora's shoulder and started for the door, leaning in to whisper. "There's an empty chair next to it. I am not sitting there."

"You never liked them."

"That hasn't changed."

Tam took Clora's hand. "I'm so glad you came. Did you have a pleasant excursion this morning?" She led the girl through the door, to a chair across the table from Severn and the Aakol.

As she was seated among a cluster of Marlee's cousins, Clora threw her a desperate look, but Marlee had her own problems. There was now no escaping the last open seat, beside the lizard. There was no place setting there, so it must have been intended for her all along. They knew she would supply her own dishes.

The Aakol stood as she approached, smoothing its satin tunic, a bright construction-worker orange that clashed horribly with its red throat. Her father looked up, but didn't stand. "Dear, I'm sure you remember Tertesk, our new mathematician."

Oh god, it was reaching out its... *paw*. She was expected to touch it. "Of course." She smiled and clasped the long fingers lightly. They were dry and cold, with little ridges.

"I am being honored by being here." Its voice—his voice—sounded entirely human, but seemed to come from the sides of his head. His mouth didn't move.

Marlee caught a fleeting smirk on her father's face. Of course. He'd invited the creature here just to test her, because that's what he did. That's what the whole damn family did.

"He's doing excellent work for us," Severn said. "Calculating flow patterns for our propeller designs."

Marlee sat in the chair Tertesk pulled out for her. "So you're here as a reward? Funny, I've never regarded meals with my family in that light. I would've taken the cash instead."

Tertesk hesitated, looked over at Severn, crinkling the fine skin beneath its eye. I know how to recognize when an Aakol is confused, Marlee realized.

"A joke," Severn explained. "No money was offered."

Tertesk nodded and sat.

Marlee was tempted to move her chair farther from the lizard man. She forced herself to keep it exactly midway between it and her other neighbor. Josip was across the table. The horrible old man gave a tiny smile and raised his cup. Point to her, she guessed, for being polite to the thing rather than pitching a fit. Well, fine, she needed all the credit she could get.

The room was even more elaborately decorated than her bedroom, the walls lined with blue granite columns, murals in the spaces between, a wall of windows giving light. Three long tables were arranged in a U shape, with everyone seated on the outside. A servant with a long white asymmetrical mustache walked into the inside space to set out serving dishes. Marlee checked what plates her father had set out, and chose the same from her case, before setting it on the floor behind her.

The other diners were busy serving themselves or talking. Besides Severn, a few others had their own dishware, different in decoration but of the same design. Josip, his children, and some of their children, including her brother Petro and cousin Swen. Jeyne, who waved from across the room, had normal dishes. He wasn't important enough to murder.

Lucky him.

Tertesk had special food, a collection of small plates containing what looked like dry sticks in different colors, a bowl of tiny yellow grains, a perfect gray hemisphere of something mushy. But he poured himself tea from the common pot. He gestured with the teapot. "Shall I pour for you?"

Not likely. "No, thanks, I'll have this." She chose a differently shaped pot at random. This turned out to be the bitter chocolate which she had begun to tolerate, though it was still much better with a big spoonful of sugar.

Clora, the center of attention on her side of the table, gave Marlee a desperate glance. "No, Miss Mindolin, I don't get it done any particular place." Clora touched her hair. "Salla cut it last week." Marlee didn't recognize the young woman Clora was talking to, but the name was familiar—someone's fiancée, maybe.

"The third floor maid?" Mindolin seemed surprised. "It's quite nice. What does she charge you? No doubt much more reasonable than the people uptown."

"We trade, miss." Clora looked uncomfortable. "I do hers, she does mine."

"But that's simply charming!" Mindolin cast a sly look in Marlee's direction. "It's so country. I envy those simple ways, I really do."

"I say," said the portly gentleman to Marlee's right. "Didn't you have a stallion in a race last week?"

"Eh?" Marlee had read about it in her journal. "Oh, yes, he ran. Didn't win. I was too busy to attend."

The man sighed. "I too, haven't been home for weeks. I have a good man who runs the barony for me, but between business and dear Karina's social events, it's hard to get out there myself."

Ahah. This was Karina's husband Torvig, Baron Bellado. Her first real baron. His picture from the bookshop's collection must have been drawn about fifteen years and fifty pounds ago.

"So I am not forgetting," Tertesk said, apropos of nothing, "Dr. Entersoe asked me to give you this." The lizard man held out a small black ball, which she took gingerly, trying to avoid touching him without being obvious about it.

"Sulfurized elastrin," he said. "He begs to know in more detail where you learned of it."

Marlee squeezed the ball—firm. She dropped it on the floor, then scooped it up on the rebound and handed it back, because no pockets. "I'll stop by the lab later."

"... and that's when I told him to drop it." The laugh came from Uncle Freddan, across the table. The woman beside him looked embarrassed, so she was probably his wife, whose name Marlee had forgotten.

Marlee took the excuse to study Freddan as she served herself two slices of, maybe, duck with plum glaze. Large, florid, loud. This was the man old Marlee suspected of driving Cousin Neidra mad. Perhaps the one who'd arranged whatever'd happened to Marlee. The man who was pressuring Digriz with markers, whatever those were.

He didn't look intelligent enough to be dangerous, but perhaps he had clever minions. She took a bite of duck. Yum. She reached for more slices from the platter.

"Excuse me, dear."

Marlee turned to find Karina leaning over her husband's shoulder.

"Marlee and I have some catching up to do."

Torvig nodded, patted his mouth with his napkin and stood, holding the chair out for her. Karina gave him a little nod of dismissal, waited for him to leave, then leaned close to Marlee to speak low. "Where is he?"

The boy, she meant. "He's safe. Do you have something for me?"

"I need it back by tomorrow evening."

Marlee suppressed a smile. "You'll get it back when I'm done with it."

"You know there's no way I can hide that it's missing. If I don't have it on Waterday, they'll change the codes, and it'll be useless to you. That's not in my control."

"Waterday morning early." That would give them two nights, hopefully long enough for whatever Digriz had in mind.

"Here, then." Something pressed into Marlee's leg, savagely hard. She reached below the table and took a flat object from Karina's fingers, bunching the chain that hung from it into her palm. Karina smiled and stood. "Breakfast Waterday, then!"

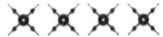

MARLEE LEFT THE TEA AS early as she thought could be excused without raising eyebrows, claiming she was behind on work, which was actually the truth. Clora, with no such excuse, gave a forlorn and accusing look as Marlee slipped out.

She hurried down the hall. She'd already written and sealed the message to Digriz on a blank clacker form—only one message, because there was only one thing she could possibly tell him, whatever Karina did. She soon found a page to carry it to the clacker room.

Now, to look through that secret closet!

But as she walked to her room, a doorway opened and someone came out—a short, wide woman, cheaply but respectably dressed for travel, in a blue sari-like garment and wide green sash. The usual white hair made her age hard to gauge, but she looked maybe late thirties or forty. Then Marlee noticed the large plaid bag slung over the woman's shoulder, and forced a grin. "Elli!"

Elinora's face lit up. "Lee-lee!" She stepped forward, arms open, and Marlee found herself the recipient of an enthusiastic hug.

Marlee overcame her surprise enough to give a firm hug back, then stepped away, hands on the woman's shoulders. Here, at least, was someone who wanted neither to kill her nor test her. A pleasant change. "Come into my room. What news from the ranch? Have you heard from..." Dammit, she'd forgotten the name. "... your son?"

"You know how it is in a war. Nothing for months, then fifteen letters at once with all the details cut out. Last I knew he was well. Lost a toe to the cold, but that happens. They're well back at home, 'cept for Hulder, who I reckon will finally go under the earth this year. Galdiflims, both lungs."

"Hm." Should she be much distressed at Hulder's impending demise? "How was the trip?"

"Oh, it was nothing. Fesdaranick—we been courting so he thinks he can tell me what to do. He said I shouldn't travel alone, but on the train it's full safe, not like the highway. Even if I do run into anyone set on mischief, I always got my rolling pin." She patted her plaid bag. "Had to clock a few ruffians in my time."

"It would be a foolish ruffian who risked your wrath."

"Foolish and unconscious, aye both. I hear you had a little holiday in town. You shoulda come to the ranch, both of you. The foals are beautiful."

"I wish I could've, but it wasn't really a holiday. I'm starting a restaurant and had to try recipes and talk with suppliers."

"Then you for sure shoulda sent for me! What manner of food?"

"Something new. Actually, we'll need a cook. Want the job?"

Elinora laughed. "Do you know how much work that is? No, I'm pleased with my situation, ten people to cook regular meals for and a girl to help. Taisie's coming along right fine, by the way. I left her in charge, and I reckon they won't starve though they may be glad to see me again, as they should be. I'll help you plan the restaurant, though. Ya fathom, it's hard to run a big kitchen. Just because you can make one of something, don't mean you can make thirty as good, or in a hurry. You've got to have a system."

"Super. I—I mean, excellent! You should talk to Jeyne, because he'll be managing it. Oh, and don't worry, we're finding someone else to do the actual work."

Elinora quit grimacing and nodded. "Right, then. He's a good lad, and knows restaurants, to be sure, but a bit..." She waved her fingers around. "Needs guiding. Needs a sharp wife."

"He has a prospect who might do, but his father doesn't like her."

"Then let's be sure to make the restaurant a bumpus, so he can do as he pleases. If you write out your receeps for me, I can start thinking about how to do it."

Marlee opened her desk. "I'm still experimenting with it. Maybe you can help with that, too."

EDSGAR

XXI

THE KNIFE FLIPPED THREE TIMES in flight, landing with a solid "thunk" in the tree trunk, in a straight line with the other three. Digriz smiled, walked over, and wiped each blade before sliding it into his vest-pocket sheath. He walked back to the throwing line and stood side-on to the target, flexing his fingers.

But when a shout came faintly through the woods, he sat and picked up his fishing rod, looking around to make sure everything was in place. Skillet drying on a rock, kettle on the little kerosene stove, two fish in a cage suspended in the stream, and remains of a third resting comfortably in his stomach along with fried parsley root and apple.

The man came around the bend in the path, shouting "Craesey!" Past middle age, weatherbeaten face, clothing simple and worn, probably a farmer. He stopped when he saw Digriz across the stream, and raised his battered straw hat. "Excuse me, sir, I'm looking for a young boy, so tall, a bit stout, large ears...."

"Sir, I have seen him."

"In truth? Half the town been out looking for him."

"An hour ago, no, nearer two. He stood just where you stand now, wielding a sturdy oaken sword, with which he defeated two pirates."

"Pirates, you say?"

"Mister Birch Senior, and Mister Birch Junior, there beside you. A pair of dirty slavers, he called them. The boy won easily, though I have to say the pirates didn't put up much of a fight. Hadn't got their land legs yet, I'd imagine."

"But sir, where is he now?"

"I'm sorry I didn't know he was missing, or I'd have escorted him home. I feared his battle was like to scare the fish, and asked him to vanquish elsewhere. He said something about tracking the vermin to their lair and scuttling their ship, and cut off through the wood in that direction." Digriz pointed away from the old mill.

The man took off his hat, revealing thinning white hair. He looked away through the trees. "Yonder is the old rock quarry."

"Is it? I'm not familiar with the area. Is there a lake in the quarry?"

"There is, sir."

"I imagine he's just gone for a swim, then, to sneak up on the pirate ship unawares."

The man jammed his hat back on. "This comes of teaching children to read. Our lord is a good man he, many ways. But this school he's gone do, is bound to make boys flighty. I say, what was that?"

Digriz tried to look puzzled. "Sorry?"

"There was just a noise, as like it was a bell."

Digriz had heard it, too. Of course, it would finally ring the minute anyone else turned up. He cupped his hand to his ear. "I don't hear it."

"Not now, I—"

"I do, however, hear my water boiling." Digriz reached for the kettle. "The call of the crested river sparrow is bell-like."

"This won't no bird, sir—"

"Do you suppose that boy will be all right at the quarry? He knows how to swim, I trust."

The farmer looked alarmed. "I do not know, sir. Excuse me." He took off briskly through the wood.

Digriz waited until he was sure the man was gone, then tore through the trees to bend over the portable clacker station. He tore off the curl of punched paper tape the machine extruded, laying it across the top of the machine. Referring to a chart embossed on a brass plate on the cover, he wrote the decoded letters on the bottom edge of the tape.

TO: PORLOON & CHASE LTD, PILKER FORD
FROM: MARLEE FOROSSI, FOROSSI HOUSE, CORILAN
MERCHANDISE NO LONGER REQUIRED. RETURN UNDAM-
AGED. MY REPRESENTATIVE WILL BRING OTHER ITEM TO-
NIGHT WHERE WE LAST MET, 2200.

Digriz let out a breath he hadn't been aware he was holding. He'd not been looking forward to having to send Jennet away and take care of the boy. He tugged the wires, and stepped back as the clips above pulled loose to let them fall in a tangle. He wound them up, thoughtful, stuffed them back into the box. What representative? What did she mean, where we last met? Probably her apartment, not the Crooked Dog, which would be too public on a Wineday, being packed with Dionysians worshiping in their usual way. It had to be the apartment. But why hadn't she just used the code word for one of their usual places?

Freeing the boy and getting away themselves might take an hour. If he hurried, there would just be time for a decent dinner at The Waves after he got back into town.

CLORA

XXII

ON HER WAY TO MARLEE'S room, Clora met her ma going the other way. Elinora waved a piece of paper. "No time to talk, I got a mission! Where's this clerk of Marlee's?"

"First floor, that end."

Marlee's door was locked—Clora opened it with her own key. Marlee stuck her head out from the secret closet. "Oh, it's you. Good."

Clora sat on the bed. "We have a few hours yet, but I've been thinking about what I should say to Digriz when I meet him."

"Oh, you're not going. I'll meet him myself."

"What? But you told him your representative would be there. I thought you meant me."

"At the time, I did, but I have a few things I need to talk with him about in person. Alone."

"You're going out without your guards? After last night?"

Marlee waved at the rack of clothing. "I'll go in disguise." She picked out a washerwoman's dress, and threw it onto the bed. "This one, I think."

Clora could only imagine what trouble Marlee could get into, wandering around on her own in an obvious disguise. "They'll not let you leave without an escort now."

"I'll evade them."

"You can't evade me. You're not ready to wander around on your own."

"You just want to see Digriz again. He's bad for you, girl." Marlee set a small jar of green powder back on a shelf, and stood perusing the shelves. "I'll be fine. I'll have my little pistol."

Oh, sweet Hera. "Yes, every washer woman carries a gold-chased Ginsdale. Folks won't wonder about that at all."

"Hidden, of course." Marlee took down a flat box and opened it. "What do you suppose these are?"

Clora stood up to look. The case contained about thirty thin curved slivers of ivory, each resting in its own groove. Two grooves were empty. She picked one out and held it to the light from the window.

"There's a line in the middle." Marlee held one by both ends, and pulled it apart. One half was a hollow tube, the other a metal point, glistening with a droplet of clear liquid.

"I'll guess you don't want to stick that into anyone you like," Clora said after a moment.

"Probably not." Marlee carefully fitted the pieces back together, and set it back in the box. "I'll bring a few along when we go out. Might come in handy. Do you think these grooves are supposed to tell what they are? See, there are seven different kinds. No chart, though." She took three at random, and pushed them into her hair. "Can you see them?"

Marlee was overconfident at the best of times, and going out armed with multiple weapons could only make that worse. One sliver was still visible, so Clora pushed it farther in. "If you're wearing that dress, you need the right attitude, too. You can't go about like a princess if you want folks to think you're a serf."

Marlee had already moved on, opening another box which turned out to contain a set of fine silk scarves in different mottled colors, each pulled through a matching enamel finger ring. "Ooh, this is fine." She drew a rust red one from its ring. "Why are they hidden? Look, there are weights sewn into the ends."

"Those hang down in your bosom so it stays without tying." Clora took the scarf and arranged it around her own neck, tucking in the weights. "I think green is better for you. This one—"

"Later. They are pretty, but I won't need them tonight. You want to come? Then order a carriage, have it stop by the side door so you can run inside for something you forgot, and I'll sneak into it. The gate guards are there to stop people coming in, right? Have you ever known them to search a carriage to make sure who's leaving?"

"No, that'll probably work. You'd get them in trouble, though, because I know Severn gave orders regarding you."

"That's unfortunate, but not my problem. If they don't catch me, they probably need the lesson." Marlee picked up the dress. "Why do you say this is a washer woman dress?"

"It just is. That's what they wear. See the strings on the sleeves, so you can tie them back?"

"Help me out of this. I'll put it on and you can show me how you think I should walk."

So Clora spent some time showing Marlee how to move and speak, and they experimented with makeup they found in the closet, to make her less recognizable. By then it was time for Clora to change her own clothes to something less showy. Her old servant dress would do. It was Wineday, a common enough servant half-holiday that there'd be plenty like her on the street.

But she paused in the hallway. Something was nagging at her. Why keep disguises and makeup in a secret closet where, after you put them on, you'd have to parade through the halls to get to a door, liable to run into anyone? Why not keep it at the apartment in town instead?

Might there be a secret way out of the house? In her stories, there were always secret passages and escape tunnels. There was a secret closet, so why not hidden passages? That one wall, at least, was clearly thick enough to accommodate it.

She turned back to face the door, hesitating. There was no-one else in sight. She pounded on Marlee's door. "Marlee!" she shouted. "They're coming for you! They're here! Run!"

Then she calmly unlocked the door, walking in to find Marlee wide-eyed, pressed against the wall a few feet down from the secret closet. "Not really," Clora said.

"Are you insane? You nearly gave me a heart attack." Her eyes were practically spitting sparks. "You think that's a joke?"

"Not a joke, a test. Why are you there instead of outside, jumping off the balcony?"

Marlee looked at the wall, then at Clora. Her expression moved from anger to thoughtfulness. "If I needed to escape, I'd do it here." She took a step back. "It's not even on the outside wall." She turned her back to the wall, closed her eyes. "I'm escaping," she murmured, barely audible. She turned again, one hand out at chest level, touched the wall, paused. And tapped the baseboard lightly with the toe of her shoe.

A narrow section of wall swung back.

Clora hurried over to look. This space was as deep as the closet, but contained only a wooden hatch in the floor, locked with a heavy iron bolt. Marlee looked around, and their eyes met.

"You didn't change clothes yet." Marlee grabbed a light rod from the bedside lamp. "Go. Hurry back. I'll go down there and make sure there's an exit."

When Clora returned, the room was empty and the hatch open. She grabbed a light herself, tucked it into her sash, and eased into the opening, feeling for rungs. After descending perhaps thirty feet, her boots touched hard floor.

Her light showed a short, narrow passage of rough planks, leading to a cross passage of brick. "Marlee?"

"Quiet." Marlee appeared from around the corner. "Climb back up and close that door."

"What if we can't open it from this side? Are you sure we can get out?"

"Yes. Go, hurry. Follow the outside wall this way and take the steps down." And she was gone again.

The narrow passage must run along the edge of the basement, Clora decided. The mortar on the outer side was rough, pushed out in spots, dirt embedded in it. The other wall was also brick, but more neatly dressed. There were pantries and firewood storage on the other side of it, she believed. This hadn't been constructed for Marlee—it was older than her. It had to have been included when the house was built.

Clora passed three other openings like the one to Marlee's room, ladders in each. Several rooms on higher floors must have access to this passage.

A shared escape tunnel, unknown even to the staff. Well, not all of them, because it'd been swept recently. But Clora hadn't heard of it.

Shadows clustered around, and she shook the wand brighter. Finally she came to a low archway cut through the outside wall, stairs leading down into darkness through a long passage which changed from brick walls to a rock tunnel midway down. Now there was a little air moving, a whiff of earth and forest. At the bottom of the stairs was a small round room, with a door standing open to the evening. Marlee's light, outside, cast a glow on pebbled ground. Clora stepped through the door, whose outside was disguised to merge into the surrounding rock face when shut.

They were in a little grove with a concrete bench. It would've had an excellent view of the town, similar to Marlee's bedroom balcony, except the view was blocked by a thick stand of pines. The bench was on a little ledge at the top of a long set of stone steps that curved around the slope. It was useless for scenery, and useless for resting. She could think of a reason people might still come up here, but probably there were more convenient places for a little privacy.

Marlee tried the bench. "What is this place?"

"I think it's the public park your family built below the house. People don't come here much. It's a little steep."

"And this bench is most uncomfortable." Marlee stood. "So we have a secret exit. Good. I still can't believe you did that to me, though. Wow."

"It's to get even for the times you got people in trouble, because you did as you pleased when they were supposed to be minding you. A few times it was me."

"That wasn't me, though."

"No? You sure seemed willing to let the gate guards be punished for your slipping past them. At least if you get out this way, they can't be blamed."

Marlee stood and dusted her skirts. "Just as well. We would've had a problem sneaking back in. This way, nobody needs to know we were gone."

Clora pulled the rocky door shut as far as she dared. There was probably a hidden catch on this side to open it, but once it latched they might not be able to find it in the dark. Well, nobody was likely to see it at night, back in the shadows of this niche, even if they came up here.

Marlee stood near the top of the stairs, looking down. "I guess this is the only way out."

"So why are you just standing there?"

"They're awfully steep."

They didn't seem that bad to Clora, and there was a nice solid-looking handrail on the open side. "They won't get any less steep after the moon sets."

Marlee took a deep breath. "Right." She grabbed the handrail firmly and started down.

MARLEE

XXIII

MARLEE EXPECTED THE STREETS TO be deserted, but there was traffic across the bridge, mostly boxy wagons pulled by turtle-shaped carts with the driver riding on top, and horse carts. The factories apparently worked all hours, pouring out smoke, and once across the river, the few streetlights were shrouded and dim. People were outlines, trudging from place to place, the occasional running footsteps of couriers dodging around them. There was a distant police whistle, and faint shouts.

They paused as a wagonload of coal turned ahead of them into an archway in a large stone building. The pavement vibrated beneath Marlee's feet from the deep roar of whatever machinery was inside.

Once away from the river, the factories turned to apartment houses and the occasional business. A school, stables, a large brick mansion behind a spike-topped fence. Traffic thinned out. After a couple more dark streets, they came to a well-lit block that seemed to have a party going on in every building. "Are these bars?" Marlee asked.

"And... other things."

"Why no signs?"

Clora shrugged. "Everybody knows where they are."

"They're doing a good business."

"Well, it's Wineday."

As they passed one doorway, it flew open, spilling out laughter and music—well, singing, anyway—and a man who staggered into Clora and bounced, fetching up against Marlee. Marlee, heart racing, grabbed the man's loose shirt front and pushed him against the wall, her other hand, she was surprised to find, holding a dagger against his chest.

Suddenly wide-eyed and sober, the man backed up flat against the wall. "Don't want no trouble."

Clora grabbed Marlee's wrist. "People are looking," she whispered. "Put that away and don't kill no-one."

Marlee glared at the clumsy idiot trying to merge with the wall. "No. It would delay us."

She shook off Clora's hand and stepped back, starting to put the knife away before realizing hers was still in its sheath, and noticing the empty sheath at the man's belt. She threw it clattering down the street, making a woman in a tight dress step aside.

Marlee walked backward for their first few steps away, keeping her hand on her own knife. "Hey," she whispered. "That woman's wearing lipstick. You said there was no such thing."

"What woman? Oh, her. That's lip *paint.* What would you do with a stick?"

"Never mind." They rounded a corner, and Marlee relaxed a little. "Where do I get some of this paint?"

Clora looked a little shocked. "I don't know. You wouldn't wear that stuff."

"Just watch me."

"No, you don't understand. She's a—she's not respectable."

As they passed under a light, Marlee looked hard at her. "Are you blushing?" Marlee grinned. "Come on, you can say it. What is she?"

"You know full well. Walk faster. We should go a few blocks out of our way to make sure no-one's following us. And for next time, that's not the best way to pass unnoticed."

"I know, sorry. Old Marlee took over for a second." Marlee watched Clora as they clopped along a dark street, wishing she'd worn better shoes, and thinking about another time the old Marlee had peeked out. She'd have to take Digriz aside, when they found him, and tell him to cancel the scheme against Clora's brother. She'd been a little drunk, that was the only excuse. All right, more than a little. Even sober, though, the idea of not having any kind of hold over Clora, who could so easily do her so much harm, gave Marlee butterflies in her stomach. She was still halfway inclined to let him do it.

How much of that was her, and how much was the influence of old Marlee? She'd never schemed to blackmail anyone before she came here. On the other hand, she wasn't sure what she'd have done in a similar situation back home. You just don't know, until it happens. Even people who aren't sharing someone else's head can surprise themselves.

Finally the streets started looking familiar, and Clora stopped them down the street from their apartment, backing into an alley. She looked at her watch. "Twenty-one forty-five. We made better time than I thought. Even with stopping to fight drunks."

"Let it go, okay?" Marlee looked around, but didn't see anyone. She took Karina's key out of her pocket, twisted the chain around her fingers, ran her thumb over the surface. It was a thick brass oval with a random pattern of bumps and indentations on the surface.

She sneaked a look at Clora's watch. Twenty-one forty-six. Hopefully, Digriz would be early. They were too exposed out here. She imagined snipers lurking on the rooftops, or someone coming up the alley behind them. "I want to wait inside. We can watch for him through the peephole."

"I don't know. I don't see anyone around, but there might be someone watching for you to come here. And the doorway's deep. What if they're hiding in there? Maybe this wasn't such a good place to meet."

Marlee was beginning to think the same, but it was annoying to have pointed out. "I couldn't think of anyplace else to tell him. But we're in disguise, and the fog's pretty thick. We'll stroll past on this side of the street, and when we're close enough to see nobody's hiding there, run across. If there is someone, we just walk on. Ready?"

Clora paused, then nodded. Marlee pulled her tiny gun from its sleeve holster and held it hidden in one hand, the other still gripping the key. They walked along at what seemed to Marlee a snail's pace, Clora repeating some gossip about Lord Somebody's wife that Marlee halfway listened to, nodding, while staying alert for any movement in the corner of her eye.

Finally certain the doorway alcove was empty, Marlee nudged Clora, and they pounded across the street. Nobody ran after them, but they crammed into the opening as if pursued. Marlee said, "Open! Open!" and the door swung out, oh so slowly.

Clora wasn't looking at the door, though—she was looking up. "What's th—look out!" She tried to drag Marlee out onto the street. Marlee stumbled, twisting, looking up herself to see the top of the door impact a pale globe hanging from the shadows above. There was a soft pop, and the globe exploded in a glare of blue light. Marlee's legs went out from under her, and she collapsed to the pavement, only Clora's grip on her arm saving her from a painful fall. But Clora couldn't hold her upright, and ended up staggering over her as she sank to the ground.

"Gods slag it!" Clora said. "How bad did it get you?"

What was that, Marlee wanted to ask, but couldn't speak. She couldn't feel her limbs, couldn't turn her head to watch as Clora stooped over her and came up with her gun, holding it awkwardly and scanning the street. "You've got to get up. It's a trap. They'll be coming for us."

There was no way Marlee could get up. She tried to move, but if she was succeeding, she couldn't tell. She could move her eyes, and shut them, and nothing else. She couldn't even panic properly.

"Shit!" Clora moved to Marlee's feet, bending. "Open!" She started dragging Marlee toward the door, but now Marlee could hear multiple running footsteps, approaching from the left. Too slow! Clora would never get her through the door in time. Run for help, you stupid girl. Finally Clora did, leaping over her with an anguished "Sorry!"

"Let her go. This is the one we want. Move her before the police arrive." Someone in a hooded robe stepped over her, and Marlee was hoisted up, her head flopping back to give her a close-up view of a knotted sash. She closed her eyes, hearing Clora yelling for help in the distance as she was hustled across the street and away.

EDSGAR

XXIV

DIGRIZ CHECKED HIS POCKET WATCH. Twenty-two oh-three. He beat again on Marlee's door, pulled the bell cord, then stepped back onto the sidewalk and looked up. The windows were dark. The place felt empty.

Maybe she'd meant to meet at the Crooked Dog after all. Or she was late. Not unusual, but she knew how crucial tonight was.

He took out his little notebook and pencil to leave a note, but a gleam caught his eye from the corner where wall met pavement. He looked closer, then reached down, incredulous, to pick up the chain with its brass pendant. This had to be the key he'd come for. But why was it lying on the sidewalk? Could Marlee have left it there expecting him to spot it? He very nearly hadn't. She'd been here, obviously, or her promised "representative".

That must be it. She'd sent someone with the key, and they got spooked for some reason, dropped the key, and fled. He pocketed the key and chuckled. That messenger would be having an interesting conversation with Marlee soon.

And now, he'd better run or he'd be late to his next appointment. He walked three blocks before picking up a cab to his apartment. It was in a significantly lower-rent district than Marlee's place, but he'd lavished money on the inside. He threw his jacket onto a blue velvet armchair, hung his cap on the amerite hat rack, closed the heavy, silver-threaded curtains. His sweaty traveling clothes went into the laundry bag, and he opened his wardrobe to lay out the clothes he'd need for the next part of the evening. Soft leather gloves, cape, soft-soled boots. Pale cotton shirt with the trademark black lace ruff of his alter ego. The mask, but before the mask, the spell. It was the only one he knew, and he'd paid plenty to learn it, but never regretted the cost. He stood before the mirror and spoke the twisty words, picturing the face he needed, forcing it over his features. His skin darkened, acne scars bloomed across his cheeks, his hair shortened, lightened, grew wavy. Nose shorter, eyes wider, darker, ears more prominent. He examined the result. Ears a bit larger, he thought, and it was so. There. He spoke the final words, and the new features settled into place with a hot prickling sensation. He put on the mask, tied the cape and flipped its hood up over his head.

"The Night Wind walks again," he said in his Night Wind voice.

The back stairs were empty, as was the alley. Nobody followed him as he moved away from the building, and he ran into no policemen. They didn't bother much with this part of town.

The technician waited, as arranged, near the fountain of the peeing boy. He looked nervous as a netwing, so it must be him. But still, the formalities must be observed. "Excuse me, sir," Digriz said. "Did you spy the cuff pin I lost here?"

The young idiot actually looked around on the ground for a few seconds, before recognizing the signal. "Oh, ah, I did, sir, a magpie took it." He stuck out his hand. "Joobal."

Digriz brushed fingers with him. "First mission?"

"I'm glad I can finally do my part for the cause." Joobal kept his voice low, but Digriz could hear the tremor of excitement in it. "And with the Night W—" He stopped speaking because Digriz's hand was over his mouth.

"Don't say my name out here."

Joobal nodded and made a repentant grimace.

Digriz suppressed a sigh and wiped his glove on his cloak. He himself must once have been that innocent, but he couldn't remember it. "Come along. The quicker done, the better."

The lad was tall, and his long strides kept putting him ahead of Digriz. He would notice and drop back for a little, then surge ahead again. It was like walking a poorly trained dog. "Do settle down."

"I'm excited to be working with the Forossis' thinking engine."

"Hsst!" Digriz made a chopping motion.

"Sorry."

In another few minutes they stood at the door of the dark edifice. A carved dragon arched over the doorway, one clawed forefoot clutching a sphere where it touched the sidewalk. Digriz felt for the slot beside the door, and inserted the key. There was a click, and the double doors swung open. Warm air rolled out, carrying the scent of machine oil.

One room took up most of the building's interior. Joobal tugged the cord beside the door, lighting a chandelier.

About a third of the room was set up as office, with maps and schedule boards on the wall, three desks, a tea urn and cups on a table. This area was enclosed in metal mesh—behind it, row on row of machinery filled the remaining space, identical brass cylinders and rods, extending back and upwards into the darkness. Racks of paper tape reels took up one side, to the high ceiling. Another bank held thousands of narrow drawers on chain drives.

Joobal led the way to the operation panel, pointing to a slot. "The key goes here."

Digriz slid it home. For a second, nothing happened. Then, a series of clicks. Something back in the machinery started to whir. The needles on a few dials leapt up, and there was a distant cough, followed by a thrum. Irregular clacking echoed through the room.

Joobal sat before a keyboard. "You may as well sit. It'll take a while to get up a head of steam. Meanwhile, tell me what you need so I can start punching up instructions."

"First, I need to find a particular airship. It's traveling from here to the capital, then back. It might be two different airships, in which case we're only interested in the one coming back, eight to twelve days from now. They'll have tried to hide it."

Joobal had threaded a paper tape into the punch, but now he paused. "How do you mean, hide it?"

"They won't want anyone to find out about the trip, including the people who work here."

Joobal gestured to the rows of drawers behind the mesh. "So it won't be in the records? How do you expect me to find it? I can only find things that are actually there."

"I don't know. Look for the airship-shaped hole in the records. You're the expert."

Joobal leaned back in his chair and contemplatively cracked each knuckle. The sound from the machinery was now a steady low rumble and hiss, slowly building in volume.

"All right." Joobal pursed his lips. "All right." He leaned over the code keyboard. "They still have to on-board supplies, they still have to have a crew, and pay them. They can't erase the whole history of a ship, because they'll be getting invoices...." He started to type, the hammers making little clacks as they punched holes in the tape.

Digriz watched for a minute, then went to the tea table and lit the water heater. He sniffed the bricks of tea, found a nice Lolly Dew Black, and scraped a generous amount into a pot. He took a pack of cards from his pocket and practiced second dealing and false shuffles until the water was hot.

Joobal had stopped clacking and was checking over his strip of punched paper. He glanced up as Digriz approached with a tray. "Do not bring liquid near this machinery."

Digriz set it on a nearby desk. "Will it take long?"

"Let's see." Joobal fed the tape into a slot, which grabbed and pulled it in. A ripple of movement ran down the rows of brass rods. Joobal spoke over the suddenly increased clatter and hiss. "Are you sure all this noise won't bring someone?"

"The building is soundproof. They usually have a guard here." Digriz spooned a little sugar into a cup. "But he was indisposed."

The chain drive on the drawers of cards jerked into motion, and a drawer slid out under a metal rack. About half the cards rose from the drawer, were snagged by the rack, and shifted to an empty drawer. Some of these rose out and were replaced in the original drawer. A new, full drawer dropped into position.

"This machine has fifteen enchanted registers," Joobal shouted. "Only the University at Decriaxen has more. That red cylinder is one. All the relays in this whole rack feed into that register."

Digriz could hardly care less about the workings of the machine. "How long will this take?"

"I'm not sure. I... ah, here we go." The few cards remaining in a drawer, fell out onto a belt which whirred into motion, dropping them into a little metal tray beside the tape punch. The noise died down.

Joobal picked up the cards and fanned them out to show the printing along the top, the random-seeming arrangement of round holes. "Let's see what's special about these three." He stuck one into a slot, and a tiny flip board above the console sprang into life, movement raining down its face as tiles dropped to display rows of symbols.

Joobal muttered to himself and unrolled a fresh length of instruction tape. "This will need a couple more passes."

"Very well." Digriz sipped his tea, and waited. And waited.

"Well, here we go!" Joobal held up two cards. "These two ships are scheduled to fly from Paroona to here at about the right day, and it shows them both as having more cargo space available than that kind of ship can actually carry."

"A mistake?"

"They don't make that kind of mistake much. This machine has to schedule shipments to meet contract deadlines and collect early delivery bonuses. If the machine thinks there's more room available than there really is, it'd be chaos."

"So what's it mean?"

"There's another ship flying that day, and it'll take the extra cargo. This one." Joobal held up a card. "This says the Pride of Fools is having maintenance then, but really it's the third ship."

"How do you know?" Digriz held up a hand. "Never mind. You're too eager to explain. Just figure out how we get one of our people on board for that trip."

"You mean as crew?"

"However you can. If you can control who they call as a substitute, I'll arrange for a crewman to fail to show up."

"Fail to show up? Will he be 'indisposed,' like the guard?" Joobal grinned.

Digriz didn't grin back. "Don't worry. He'll recover."

Joobal laughed. "You're like a walking plague. They should call you the Ill Wind."

These technical types tended to get overly familiar once they were in their element. He allowed a little frost into his voice. "Will we be done here by the time the staff arrive?"

Joobal flushed. "Sorry." He turned back to the console. A few minutes and two more runs of cards later, he shook his head. "I think this crew are a regular group. They've all worked for the company for years and have worked together a lot."

"So an outsider would stand out too much, and I'm sure they won't take extra passengers on this trip. Can we ship someone as cargo?"

"Like, in a crate?" Joobal scowled. "They don't let you specify which ship will take it, but if we time it right, and ask for delivery at a specific time, I think so."

"Fine. Figure out the details."

CLORA

✖ ✖ ⚥

CLORA TRIED TO GET COMFORTABLE on the hard bench in the guard station. The officer in charge quizzed her about what happened, then everybody bustled off to scour the streets, leaving her alone in her misery.

She looked up when the door banged open. The only other person in the room, an ancient sergeant too feeble to participate in the search, also glanced up, then pushed his work to one side and levered himself to his feet.

Severn Forossi stood in the door, face like a thunderstorm. He looked around at the empty desks, found Clora. He crossed the room in four long strides and took her arm, pulling her to her feet, two house guards following him in to take positions beside the door.

"What happened? Where is she?"

"You're hurting me. I don't know." She jerked her arm from his grasp. "I had to run."

Tam came up behind her husband, and laid her hand on his shoulder. "Dear, you're scaring her. Let me talk with her."

Severn stood there a moment longer, nostrils flaring, then stepped back and gestured Tam forward, turning away.

"We're worried, Clora," Tam sat, patting the bench beside her. "Please tell us everything."

Clora went through it all again. Severn paced, several times looking as if he would speak. Tam gave him warning glances, and he said nothing, until Clora wound up with, "... and then I ran away and yelled for the guards."

"You did well." Tam patted her knee. "Or you'd have been captured too, and we wouldn't have even this much. Don't you think she did well, dear?"

"Not really. Doing well would've been to keep her from sneaking out at night in the first place."

Tam raised an eyebrow. "I'm trying to recall any occasion where anyone was able to keep Marlee from doing what she pleased."

"The way to do it, is to alert her guards, so they can go with her."

Clora had been thinking that too, in a fine swelter of guilt and misery, so she couldn't reply. But Tam's hand rested on her wrist. "I'm sure this seemed best at the time. Severn, dear, Clora is Marlee's employee now, not ours. It would be disloyal to disobey, and if she did, next time Marlee would just go alone. At least this way she had someone with her."

"All very well, if there is a next time."

Tam stood, brushing off her bottom. "If they just wanted to kill her, they could've done that there. They needn't have risked dragging her off. We have time to find her."

The desk sergeant, who'd been standing by, spoke up. "We've sent a boy to fetch our on-call wizard, sir. Did you bring a sample as requested?"

Severn slapped his tunic to find the right pocket, and pulled out a tortoiseshell comb. "Will this do? It has hairs in it."

"Blood is best, but hair will do. Put it on this paper, please sir. The fewer people touch it, the better, is what magic folk always tell us. Thank you!" The old man set the paper on his desk. "And now, if you gentles will come with me, we have a comfortable sitting room through here."

Clora felt a flash of anger that she'd been just left on the hard bench instead of being shown to the sitting room herself. But when Tam gestured her to join them, Clora shook her head. She didn't think being in the same room with Severn would be wise at the moment. She did, however, help herself to a softer chair from behind a desk. The sergeant resumed his work without comment. The house guards just stood against the wall.

Clora moved the chair to the window, and leaned her elbows on the sill. A storm had blown in from the bay, rain now falling in slanting sheets. A man and boy hurried past outside, the man hugging a black leather bag to his chest, hunched against the weather beneath a shiny cape.

A moment later, the door burst open and the pair entered, shedding droplets on the stone floor. The boy pushed the door shut while the man shook water from his hair and hung up his cloak.

The cloak, Clora could now see, was edged with a narrow band of symbols. She sat up, interested. This must be the wizard. He looked around the room, keen, dark-eyed. He was orange-skinned, black-haired with a touch of grey, probably from the Fezec Archipelago, origin of many evil wizards in the stories Clora read. He spoke to the sergeant. "Has the missing one been found?" His accent confirmed Clora's guess about his homeland.

"They're still out looking."

"This is her friend?"

"Her hired companion."

He turned to Clora. "I am Kekkou. You shall assist me. This will make the magic stronger." He walked to the nearest desk, and cleared half the surface by pushing everything over to one side. A few papers fell to the floor. "Where is the sample?"

The sergeant pointed, and Kekkou picked the paper up by its edges.

"I'll fetch the father, sir."

"I wouldn't!" Clora said. "He'll just bother you and hurry you while you work."

"Abide here," Kekkou told the sergeant. He set the comb on the cleared desk, put his bag on a chair, and opened it. "You, girl, stand here. Take this."

A hemispherical glass bowl, threaded on its rim. Clora held it up with the fingertips of both hands while Kekkou tweezed hairs off the comb and put them in. The boy handed him vials from the bag, and Kekkou put little dry bits into the bowl, wiping the tweezers with a silk cloth in between. As he worked, he referred to a thin book bound in worn leather.

"I've never seen a spell done."

"M-hm. Do not breathe upon these things." Kekkou poured a heavy green oil over the other ingredients. He snapped his fingers over the bowl and a flame sprang up from the oil. Smoke poured from the concoction, and a sharp herb smell filled the room. "Be still now," the wizard warned. He waited a few seconds, then clapped another bowl on top, screwing them together.

The flame went out, gray smoke coiling within the globe. Kekkou took out a little paint pot, dipped a fine-tipped brush, and copied a row of symbols from his book onto the globe, drawing them along the seam between the hemispheres. Clora still held the globe, so he crowded behind her, reaching over her shoulder, for the last two marks.

As he finished the last symbol, the smoke in the globe drifted to one side. "There, it works. The girl lives, and is that way."

The sergeant stood. "Now may I fetch the father, sir?"

"Go." Kekkou took the globe from Clora, avoiding touching the paint, and blew on it. He noticed Clora still watching. "This is not part of the spell. The paint must dry before we take it into the rain."

"We really must hurry."

"We do." Severn stood in the archway. "We'll use my carriage."

Severn held the carriage door open himself as the wizard ran out from the guard station, shielding the globe with his cloak, Tam following. Clora didn't try to crowd in with them, but climbed up to sit beside the driver, shielding her face against the wind-driven rain. The carriage rocked as the guards took station on the sides. "Go!" Severn shouted through a window under the driver's seat. "Turn right up there!"

The carriage was a new model, and trundled along at a good clip. Not as fast as a horse at full gallop, but without the need to rest. But the turns Severn called out took them back across their own path twice. What was going on in there?

Finally Severn called a stop, and Clora bent to look through the window. Kekkou, looking angry, held the globe in one hand while he flipped through his book. There were now three or four little smoke clouds floating, merging and separating. "There is a blockage. A wizard helps them."

"Unblock it, then," Severn said.

"I would need something else of hers. An article of clothing, perhaps?"

"Hair is all they told us to bring," Tam said.

"I've got something!" Clora took the little pistol out from under her sash, and leaned over again to thrust it through the window opening.

Kekkou took it gingerly, in a fold of his cloak. "She has much contact with this?"

"Carries it everywhere."

"It may do." The wizard passed the cloak-wrapped gun to Tam, and reached for his bag.

"Here, now." Severn glared out at her. "You had her gun?"

"I told you that. She dropped it when she fell, and I didn't want to leave it on the ground."

"Why didn't you shoot them?"

It hadn't even occurred to her at the time, but she wasn't about to admit that. And truth was, even if she hadn't been too busy running away, she'd never used a gun and had no idea if she could hit someone. "I might've shot two of them. But the other four or five wouldn't have let me go in that case."

"Best pray to the gods that we find her unharmed." Severn turned to watch the wizard work.

Clora would've liked to keep watching also, but the position was awkward and, once Severn ordered the driver to start quartering the streets, unsteady, so she never learned how the gun would help. They kept driving as the rain came and went, then as the light grew and the streets began to fill with early traffic of vegetable carts and newspaper vendors. Kekkou called a stop, declaring the spell exhausted.

"Get out, then," Severn said. "Bylamar will no doubt have found a better wizard by now, and will have more people searching. Tell your captain I'll be in touch."

MARLEE

XXVI

SHE WAS HOPING THEY'D HAVE to carry her far, to give the city guards a chance to spot them. But they were out on the street just a few seconds before the change in sound told her they were indoors. She opened her eyes. It was dark, and the view still mostly of someone's stomach anyway. The numbness was wearing off, but she still couldn't move.

Not speaking, they carried her downstairs, down a hall, down more stairs, then more. How many levels of basement did this building have? The air grew cold and damp, the spaces more echoing, and there was a whiff of sewage.

Finally, a metal door clanged open and she was dropped onto a barely cushioned surface. The ceiling was stone, arched and groined, the top lost in shadows. Someone leaned over her, glow tube held back to keep their face unlit.

"Is she all right?"

"She'll be well. We have to get these clothes off her before she recovers." A sharp male voice.

It was nice to hear she'd recover from the paralysis, but it didn't improve her overall situation much. Whatever these people wanted, it probably didn't involve giving her an award and setting her free.

"Why are you all standing there? I said get the clothes off her. There's no telling what tricks she may have hidden in them."

"We'll need a woman for that, sir."

"Why, can't your clumsy fingers work the ties? Never mind. Find one, then. Tick tock!"

They left for a time, during which she tried to move any smallest part. She could move her eyes, and hold her breath, but that was of limited usefulness in getting free. Otherwise, not a twitch, but she did start to itch on her right side, then on her nose. A few minutes passed. Was it possible to be driven insane by unscratchable itches?

A door creaked open, and a pair of heads came into view—a hooded figure with a glow rod, and a young woman with curly yellow hair and fair skin. "Undress her." The hooded person had a man's voice. "Put these on her. Make sure she isn't hiding any weapons, and bring her clothes back out."

"Zeus, it's really her. How did you catch her? Did the Night Wind approve this?"

"It's not for him to say."

"So he doesn't know."

"Hurry and do this before the block wears off."

The blonde grabbed Marlee's shoulder and hauled her onto her side as the man walked away. Marlee's current garb was simple, without the tiny buttons or many layers of her regular clothes, and the woman needed mere seconds to undo the fastenings. Working them off her slack body was evidently much harder, involving a great deal of rolling her around and a certain amount of swearing. But finally they were all off. The cold underground air raised goose-pimples on Marlee's bare arms.

"Well." The blonde rolled Marlee onto her back on the scratchy mattress, and stood over her with a bundle of clothes over her arm. "It's obvious you're not hiding anything now. Can you hear me? I see you're looking at me."

Marlee blinked and, of course, said nothing.

"I expect they'll kill you for the crimes of your class. They've been talking about something like that. There'll be a trial, of course. We're not animals. But there's no doubt of your guilt." The woman looked off to the side. "He wanted me to put those on you, but that sounds like far too much work. You can dress yourself."

The blanket the woman threw over her was even rougher than the mattress on her bare skin. She itched in three new places before the door even closed. The footsteps receded, and Marlee was alone in the dark.

Despite the well-organized capture, she was clearly in the hands of amateurs. The men being shy to undress her, imagine! And that search had been far from thorough by, say, TSA standards. A few obvious hiding places on—well, in—her body hadn't been checked nor, more important, her hair. With any luck, the three little ivory slivers with their hidden loads of poison, or whatever, were still nestled in there.

And, as a new itch started up on her thigh, she decided who she'd like to test the first one on.

EDSGAR

XXVII

WHILE HE READ THE LETTER Digriz handed him, the man behind the gate ran his fingers backward through his beard, making the hairs stand out in all directions. He looked up narrowly at Digriz. "You are this Echeren, then?"

"I am."

"Happen Miss Marlee didn't tell us anything about this previous."

"But you have her letter there." It hardly even counted as a forgery, since Marlee would surely have written it for him herself, if he'd been able to meet with her last night. "Why don't you take me to the stable-master and let him decide?"

The old man looked him over again, and Digriz did his best to project the image of an honest, hard-working horse trainer. He'd taken care with his wardrobe to suggest a professional man of no great wealth, but some pride in his appearance. The clothes were of good quality, but not new.

"Eh, come along then." The man unlocked the gate. "I'm Gerraken. I keep the grounds."

"And fine grounds they are." Indeed, the shrubs were so symmetrical and the grass so even that the old man must have at least a couple of assistants.

Gerraken led him along a shell path, around a wing of the low white house. The rear of the property was considerably less landscaped. The even lawn led to two tidy barns, but beyond was pasture, light woods and riding trails, and a dirt track. They went to the nearer barn. "Oy, Gaddis,"

Gerraken shouted from just inside the doorway. Two boys looked up from oiling tack, and a short, round, weathered-looking man scowled down from a hay loft. Gerraken pointed. "This here man is sent by the missus to look at our horses."

Gaddis climbed down and walked over, brushing off his hands and giving Digriz the once over. "A foreigner? To what end? I don't need nobody to check my work."

Digriz nipped the letter from Gerraken's hand to pass to Gaddis. "I'm a racing expert." That much, at least, was approximately true. "Miss Forossi is considering whether she should sell any of her horses, or buy any new ones, to give her stable better racing form."

"The horses we raise here are fine racers."

"I believe Miss Forossi was disappointed with Hesterly's performance in last week's Great Cable, and would like an independent opinion. You will cooperate with your mistress' wishes, surely?"

"Tchah. Fine, suit yourself. Look around all you like. You, boy!" He pointed to one of the lads, who'd stopped cleaning leather to watch this exchange. "Go around with the foreigner and see he gets up to no mischief. And you, back to work. Do you think you're paid to gawp?"

"Actually, I'll need to do more than look around. I need to see the mounts' form. I'd like you to get someone to put them through their paces."

"You want what?"

"And I want to talk with someone who cares for them. Who mostly feeds them?" Digriz already knew the answer, having asked Clora about her brother's work the other night, in the guise of pleasant conversation.

Gaddis crossed his arms. "That'd be Ovid. Would there be anything else you'd be requiring?"

Digriz ignored the sarcasm in the man's tone. They would never be friends anyway. "Thank you for asking. It was a dry walk up from the station, so if the kitchen has any chilled juice or tea, I'd appreciate a pitcher and three glasses."

A young man arrived at the exercise yard a few minutes later with an amused expression on his face and a tray, which he set on a stump. "You're the expert, then?"

The lad was about nineteen, tall and muscled. This must be Ovid. Digriz could see the family resemblance.

"I know a few things." Digriz took the cloth off the pitcher and poured himself a glass, took a small sip. Tangleberry juice, cool and tart. He gestured to Ovid and his stable-boy chaperon, who was perched on the fence. "The other glasses are for you, if you like. Join me at the rail. What do you think of this mount?"

"That's Deever Dain." Ovid picked up a glass. "Two years. Good staying power, but fractious, and raises his hooves too high in a gallop. Oy, Will," he called to the rider. "Run him a couple times round."

"I see what you mean," Digriz said after the horse pounded past for the second time, raising a cloud of dust. "Sell or keep?"

"Oh, keep. We might be able to train him out of that, and for breeding he's solid enough."

There was no better way to flatter someone than to ask him for advice, so he sounded Ovid out about each horse, taking notes in a little notebook.

Actually, the lad had good horse sense. He'd been watching and noticing, and knew what made for a good racer, better than Digriz himself, who knew racing only as a spectator and bettor. If she didn't find it necessary to send him to jail, Marlee might do well to promote him to stable-master in place of dour Gaddis.

Three more horses were put through their paces before the bell rang for workman's tea. Compared to a town tea, this was a primitive affair. Served in the kitchen of the main house, it included quantities of brown bread, greasy sausage, and pickled beets. There were eight at table, plus a tired-looking young woman doing all the cooking.

All these were locals, curious about the stranger and about what his presence implied. Their questions kept him from quizzing Ovid as he'd intended, but there were more horses to see.

On the way back to the paddock, Ovid held up a hand, and Digriz stopped. "What?" Digriz asked. Ovid's gaze was fixed on the side of the path ahead of them.

"A coney," the stable boy said, just as Digriz spotted it himself. Ovid reached for his belt and drew a long knife. The rabbit held still, its black eye glittering at them from among the tall grass behind a board fence. Ovid held the knife by its tip, drew back and let fly.

The knife turned three times in midair, and would've hit dead on and point first, except the rabbit took fright at the last second and darted across the path, zigzagged across the yard, and vanished behind the barn. The stable boy laughed, but Ovid just retrieved his knife.

As the next horse was led out, Digriz stood quietly, working out his plan. He waited until the stable boy left them for the more interesting pastime of throwing sticks for a large black-and-white dog. "You're pretty good with that knife."

Ovid grinned. "I hit the target now and again."

"I wonder whether you're as good as I am."

Ovid's grin widened. "Happen you fancy a contest?"

"If I can use my own knife." Digriz opened his vest to display the set of three slim blades he always carried.

"Let me see one a them."

Digriz passed him a knife. Ovid touched the point, tested the balance. "Very fine. Better than my rough old thing, to be sure."

"If you don't think it's a fair contest...."

"Oh, I can take you, fancy knives or no. What stakes?"

"What say the knives themselves?"

"If you win, you get my knife, and if I win, I get your three?"

Digriz looked out over the exercise yard. He should at least pretend to pay attention to the horses. "Well, let's say if you win, we swap. These 'fancy' knives cost a bit more than yours." And either way, Digriz would get his hands on Ovid's knife.

"Done, but not here. Gaddis don't allow gaming."

A lack of witnesses suited Digriz perfectly. "I'm at the Thistle, in town. Come out when you're done work."

After he'd viewed all the horses, Digriz imposed on Gaddis once more, for a ride into town. There were none of the classy new powered vehicles out here, so a stable-boy took him in a curricle.

While shopping in the village for a sturdy leather sack, Digriz considered the list of people who'd done work for him before. There was only one who seemed right for this job. He stopped at the post office to send a note, which would go out on the 16:40 train.

In the taproom of the Thistle, Digriz ordered one glass of beer and prepared to make it last until Ovid showed up. He'd need a steady hand, so best not be the slightest bit drunk. He took a tiny sip and set it aside.

Digriz always carried a small book, not so much for something to read as to avoid being obvious when he eavesdropped on conversations. The Thistle was near the train station, and much of the taproom's custom were travelers awaiting a connection. Business people, king's men, soldiers... It was amazing the things people would say, as if there weren't another ear in the room. Things that were often interesting and, occasionally, useful. Digriz opened his book in the middle and pretended to read.

"... Mallets can't win without Simmi...."

"... the nose on that child? If Destrili's really her father, I'll...."

Time passed. Digriz finished his beer, and when the host started eyeing him for taking up a seat without buying, bought a birch beer to keep the man happy.

"... suppose we're due some rain yet before the frost...."

"... captured the Forossi bitch...."

Digriz froze in the middle of turning a page, then completed the motion. He shifted to get a look at the speaker, a marine officer with a bit of braid—Digriz'd never gotten the ranks straight—talking to a businessman.

The businessman leaned in. "Who did it, do they know?"

The officer shrugged and looked around conspiratorially—Digriz's eyes dropped back to his book. "Could be a family thing, you know? They say Freddan's been fighting her father for control of the shipping business. But they're claiming it's anarchists."

The words, "the Forossi bitch," might apply to a few people, but that comment narrowed it down to one. Digriz put the book away and stood, edging through the doorway past a group of Cybelians in their brown robes, and hurried to the station. The attendant was changing the schedule board for northbound trains, using a hooked pole to take down the 16:40. Digriz looked at his watch—just missed it, and the next wasn't until 19:12.

Damn, damn, damn! Digriz paced the platform, then ran down four stairs to the street, paused, headed toward the clacker office.

He was stopped by the realization that he didn't know where to send a message. If it was the rebels, anyone involved would be staying away from their homes. He'd have to go into the catacombs himself to find them. That unruly bunch wouldn't pay attention to a note anyway. Whatever authority the Night Wind possessed, would have to be exercised in person.

He might as well use the time to finish his business with Ovid. He divided his waiting time between doing more eavesdropping in the Thistle, and worrying about his chosen hireling for the second part of the Ovid project. Tanni "the Fist," as his nickname suggested, was prone to resolve conflicts without a lot of discussion. It shouldn't be a problem in this case, since he was also fleet enough to avoid a fight. That, and a height and build resembling Ovid's, were the main requirements for the job. What he had in mind was simple enough, Tanni should be able to manage.

He was on a bench outside when Ovid arrived. The hands on the city hall, down the block, stood at 18:30. This would have to be quick. Digriz stood. "It's too crowded in there to throw knives. There's a bit of woods out back."

"Suits. I shouldn't like word to get back to Gaddis in any case. Lead on."

Digriz led the young man around behind the inn and a short way into the forest, where he'd pinned a hand-drawn paper target to a smooth-barked tree. "Center counts three, then two, then one. If it's on the line, it's the lower score. We'll throw from behind this stick. First to fifteen wins. Agreed?"

Ovid gauged the distance. "Sure you can throw that far?"

Digriz grinned. "I'll manage."

Ovid stood behind the stick, weighed his shot, and let fly. The knife thunked home, a solid two. Digriz stepped up to the line, breathed in, and threw on the exhale. Dead center.

Ovid whistled. "Not bad!" He started over toward the tree to retrieve the knives.

"Lucky shot." Digriz sneaked a peek at his watch. He was starting to like this young man. It was a shame he'd have to beat him, and beat him soundly. He'd get the man's knife either way, but it would be better not to have him go around bragging he'd beaten the foreigner.

Ovid threw another two. Digriz stepped up to the line, glanced at the target, then deliberately looked Ovid in the eye as he whipped his arm down, hearing the thump. On the line for two points.

Ovid made no comment this time as he went for the knives. He was clearly shaken. On his next shot, Ovid released a touch early and hit at a slant, barely hanging on for one point. Digriz threw another bulls-eye.

They finished with Ovid five points down. Ovid looked at the two knives still stuck in the tree, then gave Digriz a stiff little bow and left without a word.

Digriz bowed to the retreating back, then crossed to the tree. He used gloves to remove Ovid's knife and put it into his new leather sack, looked again at his watch, and walked briskly toward the station.

CLORA

XXVIII

CLORA DREADED RETURNING TO THE big house. Bad enough to be viewed as Marlee's amusing temporary plaything. But now, to have helped her sneak out, to have failed to protect her, with her own future as uncertain as Marlee's... What if she were never found? Clora didn't imagine her own fate would be a happy one.

So she longed to go anywhere but back home with Severn and Tam, but if anyone had suspicions she was involved in the kidnapping, fleeing would surely cement them. She stayed atop the carriage as it rolled across the bridge and through the massive gates, which clanged shut behind it. Then she tried to avoid everyone on her way back to her rooms.

But when she opened her door, she found Karina seated near the window, waiting. She paused in the doorway.

Karina stood. "Come in and shut the door."

Again, there was nowhere else to go. Clora shut the door behind her and stopped a respectful distance away. "May I help you, ma'am?"

"Your mistress has something that belongs to me. I require its immediate return."

The key. Clora froze, mind in a whirl. What had happened to it? After the kidnapping, she hadn't given it another thought, too worried about Marlee's fate and her own. "I'm not sure what you mean."

"I think you do know." Karina took a step closer. "This whole abduction is a fake, isn't it? It's exactly the sort of thing she would do. This is her way of scooting off with my... with the item, leaving me to be disgraced."

Clora stepped back. "It looked real to me. If she set it up, she didn't tell me. And I don't know what she has of yours." Denying all knowledge of the key might be the only thing keeping her alive. Marlee had told her how adamant Karina was that it be returned before its absence could be discovered. Surely she wouldn't welcome learning anyone else was in on the secret. "You could come and search her rooms."

"I've done that. This room also."

"Then I don't know where it is." Not a lie. It must be with Marlee, and she didn't know where that was.

"So you won't object if I search your garments."

"Of course." Not that objecting would do any good anyway.

"Remove them, and place them on the bed."

Clora undressed, then while Karina felt through her old servant dress, she put on one of her new dresses.

Karina looked up at her, blue eyes like ice. "If she doesn't come back, I'd still better get my property by this time tomorrow. Understood? Or else I have other ways to find out what you know."

Clora's stomach clenched. She didn't want to discover what those other ways were.

"Understood?"

"I—I understand."

Karina gave a curt nod and left.

Clora sank down onto the bed. Marlee had something on Karina. That was how she'd gotten the key in the first place. But neither of them had given Clora the details, so she had nothing to hold over Karina in her own defense.

Clora rang for her breakfast. She might as well take advantage of her position while she could. While waiting, she paced the room.

Everything was going to ruin. Just yesterday she'd thought she was so smart, telling that stable boy he was playing a dangerous game. She should've listened to her own advice. She'd thought she could make a deal with the fake Marlee and get away with it. She'd been crazy, impulsive. If she'd gone to Freddan and told him about it, she'd have gotten a reasonable reward and been done with it.

Then she felt guilty at the thought. Old Marlee didn't deserve special consideration. She'd chosen to play her family's deadly games. But new Marlee hadn't done anything to merit betrayal.

The door opened, and the maid Gurthen came in with a tray. She looked around for a place to put it, and Clora pointed to the dresser. "Thanks,"

"Will that be all?" No "miss," and a hint of a surly tone. The staff, ever sensitive to subtle signals, must have figured out she was in disgrace.

Clora paused. To have any hope of saving herself at this point, she had to either save Marlee, or find that key, or at least find out Karina's secret. And there was one person who could possibly help with all three of those. "Has Mister Digriz been to the house this morning?"

"Who's that, then?"

"Tall foreign gentleman, thin, pale skin. A friend of Miss Marlee's."

"Oh, that one. No, he ain't been by."

Who would know how to find him? "Where is Mister Jeyne?"

"He's gone out."

"I have to see him right away. Can you find out where he's gone?"

Gurthen shrugged. "He left early. He was talking with Mister Bylamar last night."

Clora bolted most of her breakfast, then picked up the last roll to eat while hurrying downstairs. Bylamar's office was in a warren of small rooms for the family's staff, tucked behind the inner courtyard. There was a line when she arrived, three couriers and a city guard standing in the hallway, who eyed her silently as she breezed past. Another messenger waited at the desk as Bylamar wrote a note. He folded the paper with two quick, efficient movements, pinched a wad of clay from the stick on the corner of his desk, stamped it with his seal, and passed it to the messenger, who set off at a run. "What is it? I'm busy organizing the search."

"That's why I'm here. I think Marlee's friend, Digriz, might be able to help. Do you know where he is?"

"I, too, would like to speak with him. I dispatched a messenger to his residence, but he seems to be out."

"He and Jeyne have been going around together. They said you might know where Jeyne is."

"You mean to go and find him yourself?"

"Yes."

"Master Jeyne is in town, inspecting our properties in the University area. He means to start a restaurant. I gave him a list, and told him to begin at the Pigeon Street property, which I believe most suitable. I have a copy of the list." He turned his chair to the wall of shallow drawers behind him, opened one, and pulled out a flimsy sheet of onionskin copy paper. He pivoted again, fed the sheet into the rollers of his copier along with a second sheet of blank onionskin, and turned the crank until the papers fed out, catching them before they could fall. He passed the still-damp copy across the desk.

Like any second-generation copy, this one was faint, but it was readable. "If you see Mister Digriz, send him along to me. Go." He raised his voice to be heard out in the hallway. "Next!"

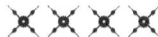

NUMBER 18. PIGEON STREET HAD a long street frontage and a wide lift door, raised to the top of an opening the height of two men. Jeyne was just inside, pointing and waving his hands as he talked with a stocky woman who stood with arms crossed, nodding. Jeyne glanced around as Clora rode up, then again, more closely, as she reined in and dropped to the pavement.

"Clora! I didn't think to see you today! Here, tell me what you think of this space. It's bigger than we need, but see, we can put a stage there, and a bar over here. Jennet, this is Clora, Marlee's friend."

Jennet's eyebrows lifted. "She has friends?"

Clora glanced around the cobwebbed, cavernous interior. The floor was wide, grimy planks, with steel columns at intervals. It seemed to be in use as a warehouse, with piles of crates along one side, but the space was mostly empty. She tried to envision it filled with University students, smoke and shouting. "It will do. You should add a big window on the street. But that's not why—"

"Say, isn't that Marlee's mare?"

Clora still held the reins, since there was no post here to tie them to. "Yes, this is Mist. She was the only one left. Everybody's out looking for her."

"Looking for the horse?"

"Looking for Marlee."

"She's missing?"

"You hadn't heard? That's why I'm here." As Clora told the previous night's events, Jeyne's expression grew alarmed.

"But this is horrible!"

"I'll say it is," Jennet said. "She's supposed to be financing this project."

Jeyne waved her off. "Don't worry about that. Father's so relieved I'm doing something useful, he'd probably put up the money if she doesn't. But don't they have any idea who took her?"

"Everyone seems sure it's anarchists. I hoped to find Digriz here. He knows a lot of people, I thought he could ask around."

"I think he's out of town," Jennet said. "He said he was running an errand for Marlee."

"Yeah, I know, but to do it, he needed a—something Marlee had for him. She never got to give it to him, so maybe he's still around, waiting for it."

"You could try his place," Jennet said. "But he's not there much."

Clora sighed. "All right. Where is it? If he's not there I'll leave him a note."

Jeyne started for the chain to roll down the big door. "I'll take you."

"Just a moment, mister." Jennet put her hands on her hips. "We have a lot of work to do."

"I have to help my cousin."

"What can you do that everyone else isn't already doing?"

"I don't know." Jeyne gestured helplessly. "I'll go down to the guard station and ask what they need. You do things without me. Find out about getting ovens built. Arrange for beer from Ferdik's and Swelt's. You know what we need." Spotting a cab on the next block, Jeyne waved at it and started running.

"If you see your father," Jennet called after him, "talk to him about money. Just in case. And we'll need that recipe. Which baker did she use?"

Clora scrambled up onto Mist, then twisted in the side saddle to answer. "The Wheat Sheaf, on Waycross." She kicked her heels and clattered off down the street.

MARLEE

XXIX

IN THE DREAM, MARLEE WAS in her usual seat in the third row, watching Professor McPhee get worked up about century-old events. McPhee paced before the whiteboard, hunched over, graying hair in a ponytail which bobbed hypnotically. Marlee had trouble paying attention to the lecture. She'd had too much fun the night before to manage well in an 8 AM class. Her head was still pulsing little jolts of dull pain with every heartbeat.

"So the British Navy knew to use lemon juice to prevent scurvy, before 1800. However, the highly trained scientists of the Scott expedition, in 1911, suffered greatly from it. How did the world forget how to treat scurvy?"

This was all familiar. Marlee remembered this class session. McPhee was about to pause, look around the room. And call on her. The woman had a killer instinct for picking out students who hadn't done the reading.

McPhee's eyes met hers. "Ms. Feldman?"

Marlee squirmed. "Um...."

Oh, come on. Not again! She'd done the reading after the class, of course. She knew the answer now. Come on! Say they didn't know about vitamin C.

"Um, they didn't know about vitamin C?"

They just knew lemon juice worked.

"They just knew lemon juice worked?"

Then the ships got faster.

"Ships got faster?"

McPhee smoothed an eyebrow. "Are you asking me? Or telling me?"

"Um, I'm not sure?"

"It's not a bad start. Say more."

This was too hard. And anyway, she was dreaming. This had already happened. It didn't matter if she answered correctly. She started to drift away as McPhee's gaze shifted to another student. "Mr. Wallace? Can you finish Ms. Feldman's answer?"

Marlee's eyes opened to a curved stone ceiling lit with steady, dim green light. Her head was still pounding a little, and there was a nasty sour taste in her mouth. She tried to move her fingers. Nothing.

She sighed. At the time, she'd rather have been anywhere but in that class, but now, she'd give anything to be back there. It'd been embarrassing, but at least she'd been at no risk of execution.

Funny how she'd known part of the answer, though. It'd happened just like in the dream. A lucky guess, barely avoiding total humiliation. It'd just come to her. It was weird that somehow during the dream she'd forgotten that, and had been expecting a total fail.

She tried to wiggle her toes. Nothing. She closed her eyes. If she couldn't do anything now, she could at least try to be well rested when a chance came.

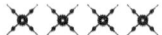

THE ABILITY TO MOVE RETURNED with an agonizing tingling, as if her whole body had been asleep and suddenly regained circulation. She sat up with a gasp, the rough blanket sliding to the floor, and shook out her arms, slapped at her thighs, until the sensation subsided.

Then she reached into her hair, feeling around... Nothing! She swore, checked again, then took the single glow tube from its wall bracket and inspected every inch of floor and mattress. Maybe at least one needle had waited to fall out until she was already in the cell. But all she found on the stone floor was dirt and several large roaches.

She sat on the hard cot—actually, a stone shelf with a terrible thin mattress—and buried her face in her hands. She'd really been counting on her secret weapon, planning, while she lay there helpless. That was her escape, and now escape was gone. She wondered whether, when they executed her, it would hurt much, and whether she would wake up back home. If only she could go home right now! But no matter how hard she wished, here she stayed, in the damp, cold stone chamber on the awful mattress.

She looked down at the little pile of clothes that had tumbled to the floor along with the blanket, which she'd shaken out and thrown aside in her search. She might as well get dressed, before anyone started spying on her through the waist-high slot in the door. The undergarments weren't like the ones she'd had, and took a moment to figure out, but soon she was dressed and warmer, anyway, if not feeling significantly better. She rattled the door. Solid. There was no keyhole, even if she had anything to pick the lock with, and even if she knew how to pick locks—at this point, it wouldn't surprise her much to find that she did. She looked through the slot, seeing fire-lit stone. The opening was too narrow for her wrist, but she scraped the back of her hand feeling around within reach of her fingers, finding only rough wood and nail heads.

A face loomed up on the other side, brown skin and shadowed eyes. Marlee gasped and pulled her hand back in.

"Up and about, then, are we?"

Marlee recognized the voice of the man who'd ordered her searched. "Let me out!" she snapped. "Or you'll be very sorry."

Soft laughter. "I don't think so."

"What do you want with me?"

"Justice."

"Listen. You've got to listen to me. You have the wrong person. I'm not who you think I am."

"Your family seem to think we have the right person. Such a to-do! I thought they'd be glad to be rid of you. I suppose it's the principle of the thing. They won't find you, though, not until we're done with you."

"Look, I have to... I need a toilet."

"You're so high and mighty you've forgotten how to use a chamber pot?"

"What are you talking about?"

"Right back there in the corner."

She'd wondered what the deep, chipped enamel bowl was for. "You've got to be... You expect me to go in there?"

The man laughed. "You can 'go' where you like, but I think you'll be happiest with the results that way."

"There's no paper in here."

The man moved away from the opening. "Improvise." He sounded bored.

Marlee's list of who she would like to stab with a poisoned needle, should she get her hands on one, underwent a revision in its ordering.

In the constant gloom, it was easy to lose track of time. Twice, food was pushed through the slot—roasted meat with too much fat, vegetables boiled far too long. No utensils, of course, and no napkin. Sleep was impossible, and she had nothing to do except pace and worry. Now and then she went to the door and listened at the slot. Sometimes there was movement out there. Someone was guarding her.

Since the only way she could get out would be to convince someone to open the door, she called out each time.

No answer.

The fourth or fifth time she tried, there was a rustle and a face came into view. A woman, not the same one who'd undressed her. "Who are you?" Marlee asked. "What's your name?"

"Ro—uh, they call me Lily."

"Lily, what does your group want? You're anarchists, right?" During her enforced stillness, Marlee had remembered where she'd heard the name "Night Wind" before.

"That's what they call us, but it's not true. We're not anarchists. Well, mostly not. We're against the monarchy and the system of privilege that lets a few families keep getting richer while everyone else works hard and stays poor." The woman—hardly more than a girl—spoke with a degree of earnestness that was almost painful.

"We're not so far apart. I think that's unfair too."

The girl snorted. "Yeah, surely. I know about the things you've done. You're not against the system. You're the worst part of it. And everybody knows you're crazy for the nobility."

That was what people thought of her? That shouldn't be any more embarrassing than everybody thinking she was a villain, but somehow it was. Wait, stay focused. She shifted from a squat to a kneeling position, wishing they'd given her a chair. "There's a certain romance to the old system. But it's not a good way to run a country. I'm in favor of democracy."

"See, that's what I think! That whole divine right thing is nonsense. What are the gods but a bunch of jealous, squabbling children with thunderbolts?" It sounded like Lily was quoting something from a speech. "They don't have the sense to choose good leaders."

"Exactly. You see, we're on the same side. If you'd just let me go, I'd work for the cause of democracy alongside you."

"Well, no." Lily sounded regretful. "I couldn't do that."

"Why not? Don't you think I'd do more good for your—for our cause—alive, not dead?"

"First, because I know you're just lying to save your skin. And second, you'll do us a lot of good dead. You're so famous that when we publish the transcript of your trial, everyone will want to read it, and then they'll see that our arguments are right and join us."

Marlee sighed. Having used the Internet, she didn't share Lily's optimism that people simply exposed to superior reasoning would be much influenced by it. But by the same token, reasoning with Lily about it seemed pointless. "Look, the Seedos already have spies in your organization."

"Seedos? You mean the Seidos?"

"Whatever. There are too many people in on this to keep it a secret. They'll find out where you're hiding me, and when they get here, probably any minute now, who will they find guarding me? You, that's who. It won't be pretty. I wouldn't want them to hurt you, because we're on the same team. But I don't think I could stop them."

"We know who your spies are. They only find out what we want them to know."

"Maybe. But they also know who you are. If you do this, don't you think they'll find out who was responsible?"

Lily was quiet for a time. "My real name is Rosette Valutin."

It seemed like a non sequitur, but also progress! "Thanks, Rosette. I know we can—"

"That name should mean something to you. Can you honestly tell me the name Valutin was so unimportant that you don't even recall?"

Of course I don't recall, you stupid cow, that was someone else! Marlee closed her eyes and took a deep breath. "Oh, you're that Valutin?"

"You drove my father to his death. My brother had to join the army to pay our debts and support us when you put us out of business. He lost an arm and a leg, and his peace of mind."

"You know, Lil—Rosette, that's just business. It's nothing personal."

"Oh, it wasn't normal business." Rosette's voice rose. "We were beating you. We were taking your customers. So you used your influence to get our orders canceled, you got us kicked out of our space, you threatened our suppliers, you threatened us."

That put a different complexion on things. Marlee rested her head on the rough wooden door. "Look. I don't blame you for hating me. All that was certainly wrong. But I didn't know anything about it. I have a lot of things going on and can't oversee every aspect personally. It sounds like we treated you abominably, and if you let me go, I'll look into it and we can arrange some sort—"

"Ha!" There was a thump, and the door rattled. "Don't pretend you don't know what your people are doing. All your businesses work that way. And you can't give back what you took from us. But I can take from you. So just save your breath for your trial."

Marlee climbed to her feet and went to lie down, staring up into the gloom. Might as well wait for the next guard.

She tried to sleep, but the bed was hard, and the little rustlings in the dark were probably rats. She sat up and shook the glow wand, trying to chase shadows out of the corners. She wrapped her arms around her knees, and sat to wait.

CLORA

✖ ✖ ✖

CLORA HAD BEEN TO DIGRIZ'S building, pounded on the door, put a note into his box. She'd thought Marlee might've dropped Karina's key when she fell, so she'd returned to the scene and looked around, but there was nothing. If it'd ever been there, the police might have it, but she could hardly ask them. The pavement was marked with yellow grease chalk where perhaps they'd found some clues, but she couldn't interpret the marks.

Clora stopped in the high street for early tea at a cafe. She was getting to like Marlee's idea of a midday meal, but it was odd to be at a fancy place on her own. Going out with Marlee had been a game, being impostors together. Being an impostor alone was a different experience, intimidating, sitting there among the well-dressed crowd at the sidewalk tables. People who either wondered who she was, or if they knew who she was, what she knew about her missing mistress.

Clora poked at her oyster custard. She worried about Marlee, and felt guilty she hadn't managed to save her somehow. That she hadn't spotted the trap earlier, or insisted they take a guard, or made Marlee hold back while Clora went to the door alone.

Clora pushed the custard away, and put her head down on her arms. The truth was, she missed Marlee. It wasn't only that she felt responsible. When this whole thing started, she'd gone into it with an eye to her own advantage. But the woman's ridiculous ideas, her odd little jokes, her incredible ignorance.... Maybe it was just that Clora felt protective.

But Marlee could handle herself pretty well, cruising along with far more confidence and less fear than the situation called for. A weird mix, she was. A weird and confusing mix.

Looking down through the curly ironwork of the table, Clora could see a pair of polished shoes had stopped beside her table. She turned her head enough to look up with one eye.

It was a waiter in a dark suit, an empty tray held under his arm. "Are you well, miss?"

"Yes. Just thinking."

"Was your meal unsatisfactory?"

She sat up. "It was all right. I just wasn't that hungry." In fact, oyster custard wasn't her new favorite dish. She'd tried it because Lord Grah always ate it, but it was apparently too aristocratic a food for her.

"If miss would like to rest, we have a private room inside where one may lie down."

Stop scaring the other customers, in other words. "No, thanks, I have to go." She stood, took two coins out of her side purse and lay them on the table. No way would she use Marlee's credit today. She threaded her way out between the closely spaced tables.

She walked to Digriz's place—she'd given the horse to Jeyne to join the street patrols, figuring she could more easily take taxis to her destinations.

Her note was still in the mail drop, visible through the little glass pane. She left a second note saying she'd be at Marlee's apartment. On the way, she stopped at the guard station. There was lots of activity, everyone too busy to tell her anything, but no sense of any breakthroughs.

Two doors down, she passed under a gilt owl and paused, looking at the door it hung over. Marlee was a follower of Athene—well, the old Marlee, anyway, at least nominally—and it was Wiseday, Athene's day. Clora wasn't a follower, but an appeal on Marlee's behalf couldn't hurt, and she had nothing more useful to do.

The shrine was up a dark flight of stairs. The sun filtered in through a high, dirty window, lighting the face of a painted wooden statue of the goddess. An attendant in a chiton sat in a shadowed corner before a wall of bookshelves, and three other women read in comfortable chairs. Reading was a common activity for Athene's followers, though Marlee had always been more into the power and strategy aspects.

Clora approached the statue and bent, a petitioner. The statue's expression was remote, cold. Suddenly nervous, Clora fumbled a coin from her purse and dropped it into the slot on the edge of the short altar. She knelt and took a slip of paper from a box of blanks, picked up the pen which was secured to the slab with a thin chain, dipped it in ink.

The pen point hovered above the paper. Clora looked up again at the statue's unsmiling face. Had she been making an appeal to her own goddess, gentle Demeter, she would ask for compassion or mercy. But Athene was more interested in reason, justice and practicality. Athene was also most likely to grant what the petitioner asked for, rather than what she needed. A definite danger for those who failed to consider their requests.

She is innocent, Clora wrote at last. Help her to safety. She paused, trying to think of anything to add, but it was the best reason she could offer, and brevity was probably a virtue here. She dropped the slip into the brass bowl, watched it curl, darken, burst into flame, add its ashes to the pile. There was no answer, not that she'd expected one. The gods spoke rarely, and never yet to her.

As she neared the apartment, Clora looked again for the key, peering down into storm drains, even though she'd looked thoroughly that morning.

It wasn't on the stairway either. The door swung shut behind her, and she went up carpeted steps into the apartment.

Someone was knocking around in the kitchen, and Clora, suddenly hopeful, raced up the stairs. But it wasn't Marlee, it was some other woman, a foreigner with flat brown hair, stirring something on the stove. She looked up, and Clora recognized her as Jeyne's musician friend. Leesha? No, Alyssa.

Alyssa opened her mouth to speak, but at that moment the door from the hallway opened and Jeyne barreled out in a loosely tied robe. "That floodin' side-saddle has given me such a bruise. Ay, it's little Clora."

Clora had politely averted her eyes. "I'm sorry to intrude. I didn't know where else to go."

"Nonsense, you're welcome here. Just let me put some proper clothes on. Have you eaten?" Jeyne called back as he headed back down the hall.

"I'm not hungry." Clora stood in the kitchen door, squeezing one hand in the other.

Alyssa studied her. "Some calindale tea, then. That's soothing."

"Yes, all right. Thank you."

"My pleasure. We inappropriate liaisons have to stick together. Are you sure you won't eat anything? There's plenty. Your mother was here earlier making pizza. She went out for more ingredients."

Clora shook her head, and sat at the little table under the skylights.

By the time the tea was ready, Jeyne was dressed. He joined the women at the table, plunking down a plate with a mushroom-adorned wedge. "I can't stay. While it's in my head, when you see Marlee, her saddle's at Grimeldi's. I took it off after the first mile."

"If I see her."

A look passed between Jeyne and Alyssa. Alyssa rose. "I think I forgot something in the other room."

When she'd gone, Jeyne leaned forward. "We'll find her. Uncle Severn's going all out. If they... if she weren't still alive, the people who took her wouldn't keep quiet about it."

"I hope you're right."

"And something else I've been wanting to tell you. I've noticed... well, it seems to me Marlee's been different recently."

Clora's breath caught. "Different?"

"Yes, you know." Jeyne took a bite, and waved his slice at her. "Happier. Pleasant. I think you're a good influence on her."

"You think it's because of me." Fear gave way to amusement, both of which she hoped went unnoticed.

"Mind, I hardly got to talk to her. Just when we went out, and a half hour or so yesterday afternoon. But yes, I can't think what else it could be. You're important to her."

Yes, but not for the reason he thought.

"Anyway, don't sit here moping. Come back to the station and we'll find you something to do."

"I still think the best thing I can do is find Digriz. Where does he go during the day?"

Jeyne dabbed at his lips with a handkerchief. He stood, refolding it. "I rarely see him while the sun's up, but I'll write you a list."

MARLEE

✗ ✗ ✗ !

FAINT CONVERSATION WOKE MARLEE. SHE pushed the
blanket aside and moved quietly to the door, bending, putting her hand on
the chill floor to bring her ear near the slot.

"... need more people. And there's too much traffic. The plan was for
midnight." A woman's voice—Rosette?

"Change of plan." Was it the same man who'd commanded her
captors? "They've arrested Villy, and you know him, he'll talk. We have
an hour at most."

"What are we supposed to do with her? We can hardly walk her
through town."

"Frenkomerto's bringing the carriage. We have to get her to the old depot."

"And if they stop us and search us?"

"I've arranged a distraction. Open the door."

Marlee's mind raced. Should she jump him when he came in? If it was
the same man, he was big, and he'd be wary. If he knocked her out, she
might miss a chance to surprise him later.

She hurried back to her slab and sat. It was too dark for her to see the
features of the man who entered. Marlee's eyebrows rose when the lock
clicked home behind him. "Careful much?"

"Stand and turn around." He moved forward into the light, and Marlee
studied his features, making sure she would recognize him if she saw him
again. Fortyish, flat nose, thin lips, pointed chin....

"Turn!"

Marlee's hands were grabbed and pulled together, held firmly behind her while cord was looped several times around her wrists and pulled tight. He gripped her shoulders and turned her around to face him. His hand came up and clapped over her mouth, leaving something stuck to her face.

"Mphm!"

The man grinned coolly. "Magic tape. Made in your father's factory." He turned her toward the door and shoved. Her feet got tangled and she almost went down, stopped herself by bumping into the wall.

"She's secured. Open."

She was encouraged into the passage by a hand on her shoulder. Rosette—it was her—looked her over and nodded. She took a light rod from a wall sconce. "East tunnel?"

"That'll be fastest. You lead." The man also produced a light, and urged Marlee along with a hand on her back.

Marlee kept her head down, trying to look discouraged while scanning the floor ahead of her. Was this the way they'd carried her in?

After about thirty steps, her search was rewarded with a sliver of white against the dark floor. Rosette's shadow fell across it, but Marlee had marked the spot.

There'd be no second chance. Hoping she'd gauged the distance correctly, she stopped and started to turn around. As she'd expected, the man behind her shoved her forward. She let herself fall. Her knee hit the stone floor hard and she gasped in pain, landing hard on her shoulder since she couldn't use her hands to stop herself. The breath whooshed out of her, and she tried to keep it together as she rolled onto her back, fingers scrabbling on the rough floor.

"Get up!" The man loomed over her, and she kicked at him, using it as an excuse to shift farther back, searching a different patch of floor. The man's arm swung around and his hand caught her on the temple, knocking her head against the wall and making lights swim before her eyes. But her fingers had found the thing she'd seen, and she scraped it out of the groove between two stones, closing her fist around it. Thin, smooth, curved. Three grooves. She suppressed a smile.

"Up," he snarled, and lifted her with a hand under her arm.

Marlee's legs almost went out from under her again when she put weight on her knee. She whimpered, stumbled, still out of breath from her fall, but the man's rough hand held her up.

"She's hurt her knee," Rosette observed dispassionately. "If you don't want to carry her, best not knock her down."

"She can walk. And I'll give her worse than that if she delays us further."

She could walk, though pain shot up her leg with every step. She limped after Rosette, the man's regular footsteps behind helping hurry her along.

After about a century of this, they came to a set of steep metal steps which she simply couldn't manage. She sank down on the second step, tears clouding her vision, nose running freely onto her chin.

"Just pick her up," Rosette said. "She obviously can't do it, and we're almost there."

"Fine." Hands grabbed her around the waist and hoisted her up. Air huffed out of her as she landed on the man's broad shoulder. Soon they were up the stairs and through a doorway into a large, dark space. His boots raised echoes as he hurried forward. Marlee, unable to see ahead, watched his shadow on the wide wood planks.

Suddenly she was thrust forward, flailing, banging her elbow. She landed on a springy surface, and looked around. She'd been dropped on a carriage seat. The man climbed onto the facing seat, Rosette following to sit beside her.

"Go!" The man rapped on the wall behind his head. There was a rattle and a rumble, the clopping of hooves on wood floor, then on cobblestones, as the carriage jerked into motion.

"Easy there! Don't attract attention."

The carriage slowed. Marlee tried to see where they were, but the shades had been drawn tightly. The interior was arranged like the dynamo-powered carriages she'd been in, with a sliding panel in front to talk to the driver, but that was also closed.

She fingered the poisoned needle concealed in her palm, trying to figure out a way to use it. There were three of them and only one needle. She could probably stab Rosette from where she sat, hands still tied, but then they'd just take it away from her. And besides the fact that Rosette was probably the least dangerous of the three, Marlee had sympathy for her, and didn't want to poison her.

The others might have equally valid reasons to hate her, of course, but Marlee didn't know what they were. And as for the man who sat glowering across from her, she didn't care about his reasons. She had no qualms about stabbing him.

Marlee tucked the little sliver of bone under the back of her sash, and started trying to surreptitiously work her hands loose.

EDSGAR

XXXII

WHEN DIGRIZ'S NAME WAS CALLED on the street, he kept walking. Then at the call of "Hey! Hey, wait!" and running footsteps, he stopped and looked back, because anyone would.

It was Clora, looking confused. "Oh, I'm sorry sir. I mistook you for someone else."

Digriz shrugged, and started to turn away.

"But do you know him? He lives in your building." She pointed back up the street. "Foreign gentleman, brown hair, third floor? It's really important I find him."

Digriz had hoped to get away without giving her a chance to recognize his voice, but she might have information he'd need. He tried to make his voice especially raspy. "He was here. Said he'd be at the Saw Mill later."

"The Saw Mill?"

"A bar. Near the Gage building. Luck." Digriz nodded, and hurried off.

He turned the wrong way on purpose, and paused in a darkened doorway. This would teach him not to leave by the front door when in disguise. The one time he was in too big a hurry to sneak out the back, and he was even further delayed and nearly caught besides. Satisfied at last that the girl hadn't tried to follow him, he went one street over and doubled back.

The house he went to was small, a bit ramshackle, dwarfed by an apartment on one side and a shuttered chandlery on the other—driven out of business by the new chemical lights. Digriz took his mask from his pocket and slipped it on. The gate clapped shut behind him, and he noticed a shadow moving in a window.

Digriz raised his hand to knock, but before he could, there was a scrape of metal, and a blue eye peered out through the spy hole.

"Who's that?"

He pulled his hood back to let moonlight fall on his face. "The breeze."

There was a chuckle, and the door opened. Digriz entered and pushed it closed. The old man walked away into the back of the house. "You've been missing all the excitement. A nip against the chill?"

"Thanks." Hikurk's home brew was better as a cleaning agent than a beverage, and it wasn't all that chilly out, but the old man might be more forthcoming over a cup. "What did I miss?"

"Reodorid catched Severn Forossi's daughter. Means to put her on trial." Hikurk took down two small cups of crackled glass, and a clay jug from a corner cupboard. He shook the jug, listening, and took out a second. "Just him and his folk know where."

"Ah. That's something I'd like to see. Any idea how I could find them?"

"They's all hiding, owing to the city guard's rounding up everyone they can grab." Hikurk illustrated the roundup with a swoop of the jug, then popped the cork and poured a generous amount into his cup. "You best be careful, yourself. Figger they'll all meet up somewhere, but they laying low till then."

"Haven't the Forossis hired wizards?"

"Reodorid's got him a wizard too." Hikurk held out a cup.

Digriz set the cup on a high stool beside him. "The wizard must know where they're taking her, to lay on protections. Do you know where he is?"

"Nay, he's already gone there, wherever. Aren't you drinking, then?"

Digriz raised the cup, held his breath, and took a tiny sip. "Reodorid's being pretty careful."

"Eh, so what? Them guard'd be on him in a second if anyone knew his right name."

"Why? It's not like he'd take her to his house."

"No, but they wizards'd track him down. Don't suppose he can pay to hide all his folks, just the one."

"Nor does he need to, if the Seidos don't know who they are." But Digriz did know, having made it his business to find out. He took another small sip. "Ah well, I guess I'll miss the big event. Too bad."

"Peh. Who wants to go to a trial anyway? Deadly boring things. I'd know, I had three of 'em and not a one could I stay awake to the end."

Digriz smiled. "If it were my trial, I'd want to know how it came out."

"Oh, I never had no doubt on that score."

Digriz set the cup down. "I'd best get going. I have a few stops to make. I don't suppose you know where I could find a change of clothes at this hour."

Hikurk looked him up and down. "Those togs don't look too dirty to be going about in, but if you want a change, I got some boxes in the cellar as fell off a wagon, might be something your size."

CLORA

✕ ✕ ✕ ‡‡‡

LETTING HERSELF INTO THE APARTMENT, Clora called out, in case anyone above was in a state of undress. Her mother answered, "C'mon up, dearie!"

She was not in a mood to talk to ma. She could just leave, but she hadn't eaten since her failed attempt at lunch, and the apartment was full of enticing smells. She leaned her umbrella in the corner and climbed the stairs.

There were parts of three pizzas on a large flowered platter on the dining table. Clora pulled loose a wide slice covered in tiny green fishes, onion, and stringy cheese. There were no plates, so she folded it over, and went to the kitchen.

Her ma was at the counter, grinding something in a mortar. The oven was off, but the room was still oven-like. Elinora wiped her forehead with her sleeve. "I'm makin' desserts now. Thought they'd like a fry bread with sugar and ground kalli pods." She pointed with the pestle at a pile of the confections laid out on a cheesecloth.

"Sounds tasty." Clora took a large bite of pizza. It was no longer hot, but still good. The little salty fishes were intense, flavorful. She swallowed the bite quickly. "Any word about Marlee?"

"Nah. Jeyne pokes his head in now and again, and he'd have said." Elinora laid a floury hand on Clora's arm. "Are you much upset over this? You look troubled. You been crying?"

"Of course I'm worried about her."

Elinora gave her a sharp look. "About her, not about your position?"

"Aren't you? You've known her since she was a tiny child."

"Oh yah, I'm right fond of her, and hope like anything she's well, but she's a hard, hard woman. You bump up against her, you come away bruised. Don't get to thinking you'll be with her forever."

"It's not like that, ma."

"So you keep telling me, but I got eyes, is all I'm telling you. Now eat up, and have some tea and a little lie down. You look wore out."

Clora took another large bite, and left so she could sit, and to avoid having to talk any more. But before she reached the table, there was a pounding on the door. She went down enough stairs to look out the little window in the door. It was too dark to tell who it was, but she could see the outline of a large ladies' hat adorned with flowers.

"Who's down there?" Elinora yelled.

"I got it, ma!" Clora went down and turned the handle. A tall, black-skinned woman with high cheekbones and forehead, black hair done in spikes where it peeked out under the hat brim. "Miss Perridino." The visitor's voice was deep and smooth. "Where is your mistress?"

From the voice, Clora recognized her. "Chalula!" And she paused, confused. What was the singer doing here?

"I require to know."

Apparently Chalula hadn't seen today's newspaper. "Come... ah, come on up. She's not here."

Clora's mother appeared at the top of the stairs, moving aside as they came up. "Who is this, dear?"

"Uh, this is Chalula, don't know her whole name. We just met the other night. This is my ma, Elinora Perridino."

"Honored." Chalula bowed. "That is my full name."

"She's here looking for Marlee."

"How do you know Miss Marlee?"

"Ma! Don't pry."

"We are... acquainted. I expected her to visit my hotel, or at least a note. I decided to call. I thought perhaps she was... distracted." Chalula gave Clora a cool glance.

Elinora nodded. "She ain't heard, then. Miss Marlee has gone missing. That's why she don't write."

"Missing? Is she in danger?"

"Yes," Clora said. "She was kidnapped right in front of me. Right outside that door, in fact. All the city guard are out looking for her."

"They say it was anarchists," Elinora said with relish.

"Then we must find her. Come, we will go immediately."

"Clora's already been out all day and from the look of things, hasn't had time for a bite or a rest. If you want to help, go on down to the guard station and they'll likely give you something to do."

"No, ma, I can't stay. I'm going see a man who might know something. I'd intended just to stop and leave a note in case he came here while I was out looking for him."

"Wonderful," Chalula said. "I shall assist. Let us go."

"But I don't understand. The other night it seemed as if you and Marlee didn't know each other."

Chalula looked away, seemingly embarrassed. "Ah. This is, I suppose you would say, a game we play. She always comes to my opening night, and... so. I know her well, and wish to help."

"Then let's go. Your help is welcome. Can you find the Saw Mill?"

"The bar? Certainly. Though it's a rough place."

"Don't fret as to that," Elinora said. "If my girl's going out, I'll come too, with my rolling pin."

The Saw Mill was several blocks walk. The door was below street level, down a half flight of stairs. It was dim, packed, and noisy, and Clora and Chalula were easily the best-dressed people there. Clora stood on tiptoe in a vain attempt to see over the crowd.

Chalula looked around, too. "Whom do we seek?"

"Edsgar Digriz. He's a Dwillikan—"

"I know Eddie. And there he is." Chalula pushed her way through the room, the other two following.

The crowd was mostly around the entrance and the bar, where some contest was happening. Digriz was alone at a small corner table, his back to the wall. He was dressed unusually for him, in a loose orange-gold silk shirt with puffy sleeves and tight-fitting black trousers. He looked up as they approached.

"You!" Chalula boomed. "Where is she?"

There was a roar of triumph from the bar, and hoots from the audience. Digriz stood, beckoned them to follow, and led the way through a curtain in the back wall. His half-boots clopped on the wooden floor as they followed him down a short hallway. There was a fresh scrape on his right boot-heel, and Clora frowned at it.

Where had she seen a scrape like that recently?

"Just in here." Digriz ushered them into a small room with a round, felt-covered table and several chairs. This must be a back-room gambling den, such as Lord Grah was constantly bursting into in pursuit of some miscreant!

Chalula fixed him with her gaze. "I am told you know where Marlee has gotten herself to."

"You don't pick around the edge of the pie, do you? Sit, all. I don't know where she is, but I've asked around, and I think I know who has her."

Clora's heart raced. "Is she all right? Where is she? Let's go there."

"So far as I know, she's well. I visited the gentleman's home while he was out, and found this." Digriz opened his satchel and removed a glassine envelope containing a browned apple core. "I know a wiz—"

"You broke in?" Elinora stood with her back to the door, arms crossed.

"It seemed best. Unfortunately, at the moment I'm a little short—"

"If you know who has her," Chalula interrupted, "shall we not simply tell the city guard?"

"They'd want to know how I got the information, and I'd rather not say. Even if they believe me, they would respond in their usual bumbling way, going after her in force. From what I know of her captors, that would get her killed. I know someone who can walk right up to them without alarming them. I hear she's being moved, so it might be easier to break her free, if we hurry to catch her in transit."

Clora reached for the apple core. "You think a wizard can track him with this? They have a wizard of their own who's hiding them."

"I know. But hiding from the guard doesn't come cheap. They put a fog on Marlee, because they know the Forossis will trace her. But they can't afford to fog themselves, too, and why should they? They don't think anyone knows their real names."

Chalula rested her hand on the tabletop. "But you do. How?"

"I can't tell you. But what I can tell you is, owing to a temporary embarrassment of funds, I can't afford to hire a wizard."

Clora reached for the purse hanging at her waist. "How much would you need?"

Elinora had straightened up at this turn in the conversation, and she put a hand on Clora's shoulder. "We got to have a word in the hall."

"Ma, not right now."

"Right now, aye."

Clora rolled her eyes, and stood. "I'll be right back."

Elinora closed the door carefully and pulled her a few steps down the hall. "Don't you trust that man. You give him money, you'll never see him no more. I can smell it on him." She huffed. "You mark, that there is a knave."

"Marlee trusts him. And he needs her, she's how he makes his living. He wants her back too."

Elinora shook her head. "How can she do with the likes of him? She used to be a good girl, you wouldn't recall you was too young. Her floodin' family ruined her."

"Families are trouble," Clora said dryly. "Look, ma, I hear you, but I don't have any better ideas. And we have to hurry." Clora stepped around her mother.

"It's settled, then," Chalula was saying as Clora pushed the door open. "I arrange the carriage. You bring your wizard to my hotel and I pay the fee. How soon?"

"An hour, perhaps less. We should begin immediately." Digriz stood.

"Let me walk with you a little way," Clora said. "There's something else I have to ask you. Ma, you go with Chalula."

"Leave you alone with that man?"

"Just for a minute. It's not open to discussion. Go."

Clora took Digriz's arm, the silk cool under her hand, to stay with him as he pushed through the crowd and onto the street. The cold night air was wonderful after the close air of the bar. She took a deep breath.

Digriz looked around to make sure no-one was near. "What's the story?"

"Karina's key. She has to have it back by tomorrow morning, or she'll beat it out of me. Which may take a while, since I don't have it."

"All right, you don't have to over-dramatize. I'm done with it, and I'll see it's returned."

Clora stopped walking, forcing Digriz to stop also and turn to face her. "Wait. You have it? How could you possibly have it?" Could he have been working with the kidnappers?

"I found it where it was left for me. Ah." Digriz beckoned her on with his head, and walked on. "Where she must have dropped it during the struggle. I thought she'd just hired an incompetent courier."

That was a relief. He'd hardly admit he had the key if he'd gotten it from Marlee's abductors. "You finished what Marlee wanted done?"

"Yes, and the boy is safely home." He ran his fingers along his collar. "Smooth as silk."

"What boy?"

"What... oh. The boy we set out to rescue. I suppose she didn't tell you the whole plan."

"No, but you could, now it's done."

"Sorry, I shouldn't have said anything. That would be up to her." Digriz looked up at the street name posted on the building across the way. "This is where we part ways. I really must dash."

MARLEE

XXXIV

THEY'D BEEN RIDING FOR AT least two hours. The city noises had faded, and streetlights no longer cast streaks of light through the cracks around the shades. Rosette was asleep. The man sighed, and opened a shade to look out at the dark night.

Whenever he wasn't looking right at her, Marlee had been trying to get her hands loose. He'd tied her pretty tightly, looped three or four times around. She'd managed to get a finger under a loop, and tugged it a little larger. But that pulled the other loops tighter, cutting off circulation. So she had to stop working on it and wait to get the sensation back. Which of course undid all her progress. She'd tried three times.

Now that he was absorbed with the moonlit view, she tried again, hoping he'd continue to look away long enough to let her get a loop free. After a couple of minutes, her squirming earned her a sharp glance. She leaned forward, waggling her chin at him meaningfully. He reached out and brushed his fingers over the tape that covered her mouth. "What?"

"I can't get comfortable with my arms behind me like this."

"I don't need you to be comfortable. Anything else?"

"Yeah, I gotta pee."

"My, how delicate your upbringing must have been."

"You'd best stop pretty soon."

"It won't be long now." The man leaned forward and slapped the tape back over her mouth, then sat back, looking amused.

So, pretty soon they would arrive somewhere, and lock her in room, then more people would arrive, and her chance would be gone.

Marlee waited for him to look out the window again, then tried the ropes. Finally, just as her fingers were getting numb again, she managed to pull the loop over her knuckles, scraping the back of her hand with her nails in her eagerness to have it off.

She wiggled her fingers, feeling pins and needles. She must have let out some involuntary sound of relief, because the man glanced at her again.

She twisted her hands, trying not to move her shoulders, and hooked another loop. This one came off much more easily, and in another minute the rope fell onto the seat.

Marlee closed her eyes, visualizing how this would work. Her knee was still throbbing, and had stiffened up, so she couldn't count on outrunning anyone, though if she could somehow get into the driver's seat, the horses should outpace any pursuit.

She pulled the needle from under her sash, and ran her thumbnail along the grooves. Her heart raced. She wouldn't get a second chance. She took a deep breath, and let it out.

The man looked around as Marlee lunged forward. His eyes were wide in the moonlight, and his arm came up to block her, but too slow. The needle sank home near the base of his neck.

He roared, and shoved her away. Her hand whacked into the wall, and she dropped the needle. Someone grabbed her shoulder, probably Rosette. Marlee swung in the darkness, catching the girl a glancing blow on the head.

The man was making choking noises. Hoping the poison would deal with him, Marlee pulled her arm back and took more careful aim at Rosette, hitting her squarely on the nose with all her strength. The girl's head snapped back, thumping into the wall, and she slumped.

"Here, what's on in there?" the driver's voice called from outside.

Marlee swayed forward as the carriage slowed, brakes scraping. She dropped to the floor, groping in darkness for the dropped needle. Miraculously, she'd held onto the cap. There might be more poison in it, and if she could dip the needle in it, it might be enough to take out the driver, too. But her hand didn't seem to be working right.

The man thrashed around, fighting for breath, and whether by accident or by design, his foot jerked up, the toe of his boot striking Marlee soundly on the temple. She fell to the floor, dots flashing before her eyes. She twisted up onto her elbow, holding her arm out to block any more kicks.

The carriage rocked as the driver climbed down. Hearing something slide across the floor, she brought her hand down on it. The needle! Clumsily, she picked it up. What was wrong with her hand?

The door jerked open, and light flooded the carriage. The driver roared outrage and grabbed her ankle, dragging her toward the door.

Marlee braced her other foot against the door frame. Desperately, she jammed the needle into the cover, but missed, felt it prick her own finger, instantly burning. The driver now had hold of both feet, pulling. Marlee tried again, and the needle slipped into the cap.

She was afraid the driver would drag her out and let her head hit the road, but he pulled her only partway, the door frame digging into her back, then grabbed the front of her dress to haul her out, slamming her against the carriage. "What have you done?"

By way of answer, Marlee stabbed at him with the needle. He tried to dodge, but again it found its mark. He looked down at it, protruding from his shoulder. Again he slammed her against the carriage, then dropped her and stepped back, pulling the needle out and throwing it down.

Marlee lay on the ground beside the wheel, ears ringing, nauseated, every part of her body beginning to shriek pain at her. Her knee, from the driver yanking on the leg. Her hand, something in there grating sickeningly. Her other hand, a line of fire tracing up her arm from the pricked finger. Half a dozen other spots she hadn't noticed at the time.

Marlee blinked something out of her eyes to see the driver, looming over her. He swayed, and his hands went to his throat. He took a step back, choking, then staggered off the road, weeds rustling as he fell out of sight.

Marlee could hear him thrashing and choking for perhaps a minute, then there was silence except for frogs, and wind in trees, and bubbling breathing from inside the carriage. A horse nickered, and there was a metallic scrape.

Marlee lay there a while, knowing she had to get up but finding it impossible. She held up her right hand against the starry sky. Two fingers stuck out at a wrong angle, probably broken. With her other hand, she explored the tape over her mouth, but it didn't come off for her as it had for her captor.

Well, that wasn't her first priority, anyway. With her unbroken hand and an effort of will, she levered herself to a sitting position, then stood, wheezing, leaning on the door sill. Using the step below the door, she raised her butt onto the sill, got into the carriage and onto the seat.

The driver had dropped a light rod on the floor when he grabbed her leg. Now, it lit the interior from beneath. Rosette was slumped into the corner, looking tiny. Her chin and the front of her dress were covered in blood, and the bubbling breathing sound came from her.

The man didn't seem to be breathing. She grabbed his pale hair and pulled his limp body to the floor, paused to catch her breath, then planted her foot onto his bottom, trying to shove him out onto the road. This was harder than she'd expected, and she paused, gasping for breath. He hung partway out, so she got down on her knees, whimpering in pain, and lifted him up and forward by his sash until his weight pulled him to the ground.

Rosette was much lighter. Marlee dropped her onto the man's body. Sorry, she thought, as Rosette fell the last foot or so. She climbed out and dragged Rosette away a little, off the road to the edge of a gully. The driver must be down in there somewhere, but it was too dark to see, and she didn't care at this point. The other man's legs had ended up under the carriage, but Marlee was too exhausted to move him, and anyway, why bother? She felt around his waist and found a knife. She drew it, and cut a small slit in the tape, nicking her lip slightly, then used her fingers to tear the hole in the tough fabric wider.

It took four tries to get into the driver's seat, then she collapsed there, gasping, sobbing. She looked out over the four horses. One looked back, his gaze full of doubt. She unwound the reins from a post beside the seat and gave them a shake. "Get-uff." Her voice was muffled by the stiff tape.

The horses started walking and the carriage jerked forward an inch, scraped to a halt. The horse who'd looked at her before turned his head again, even more skeptical.

"Brake." She spotted a lever, twisted to reach it with her good hand, jerked it into a different position. "Go." She gave the reins a little snap.

The carriage started moving again, rocking a little as it bumped over the body in the road, then picking up a modest amount of speed.

The only problem was, it was headed the wrong way. She needed to go back to the city, not onward to wherever they'd been taking her. How could she turn the carriage around? The road was too narrow to make a U-turn, and pulling back on the reins just made the animals stop.

There was probably some way to do it, but she was too dizzy to figure it out. Her throat was closing up, the wheezing getting worse. She urged the horses on, and in a quarter-mile or so found a place where the ground was level and open. She steered off the road into a wide turn, bumping over the hummocky ground.

It was hard to concentrate on steering, and for a moment she lost track of what was going on, recalled to attention by the jab of pain when her hand slipped off her lap and hit the bench seat. She sat up, blinking back tears, and got the horses back onto the road, heading for home.

It was easier to breathe, she found, if she lay on her back on the hard seat, legs hanging over the edge. She kept loose hold on the reins and closed her eyes.

CLORA

XXXV

WHEN SHE CAUGHT UP WITH them, her mother and Chalula were walking and arguing. "How can he know who took her?" Elinora hurried to keep up with Chalula's long strides.

"I do not know, but if he lies, I will crush him."

Elinora clutched at Chalula's sleeve. "Don't you think the guard oughter deal with this?"

"To crush him? I would want to do that myself."

"No, to find Miss Marlee. There's a station just down there, see?"

Clora looked. There was a crowd of guards in front of the station. "Something's happening. See, here come more of them."

Chalula paused in the cross street. "Is it to do with Marlee?"

"Probably. I don't think Josip will let them deal with anything else until she's found. It must be a great time to be a criminal."

"Let us inquire." Chalula walked up behind an epauletted officer. "Pardon me, sir. Is there word of Miss Forossi?"

The man frowned at her. "Who asks?"

"This young lady is the missing woman's companion."

The officer's eyes flicked to Clora. "Sorry, miss, didn't see you at first. There's been a sighting in Lowertown. She ran down the street shouting and banging on windows, went into a shop to ask for help and ran out again, then several people in hooded robes caught her and took her away again. We're sending every available man to search buildings in that area."

"What variety of shop?" Chalula asked.

"Sorry?"

"What type of shop did she run into?"

"A smithy, I think."

"Which means what?"

"Iron-work," Clora said.

"Here!" The guard waved. "Pull up that carriage here. Stay in order, men, don't waste time. I'm sorry, miss, I have to go. If you wait here, we'll send word when we find her."

"Come." Chalula pulled Clora along. "We cannot wait."

Clora looked back at the crowd of officers. "But what if they find her?"

"Ridiculous! It is not her."

"You sure?" asked Elinora.

"She is in a store full of sharp metal... things, and she runs out again? She does not try to leave from the back? She does not take a weapon? Pfft."

Elinora nodded. "She's right. It don't sound like our Miss Marlee."

But it's not our Miss Marlee. Still, the new Marlee did seem to have the same instincts. "So people were supposed to think it was her. Why do that?"

"Did not Eddie say she was being moved?"

"Aye," Elinora said. "And every guard in town all busy with this."

"A ruse," Chalula agreed. "It supports Eddie's story."

Clora stepped sideways to avoid being run into by a bike messenger. This street predated the idea of sidewalks. "What if we're wrong? What if that really was her?"

Chalula shrugged. "Then the police will find her without our help. If not, though, there is nobody but us to save her. Come, there is much to prepare."

The River Inn was a three-story building of ancient tan brick, encrusted with eroded gargoyles and ornate balconies. Chalula grabbed a random porter on her way in, giving orders for a fast carriage, a picnic basket, and a selection of first aid supplies. She pressed several coins into the man's hand and aimed him toward the door behind the desk.

Chalula led them upstairs. "Do you two have weapons?"

"My rolling pin, eh."

"I took Marlee's spare pistol from her room." Clora's hand went to her sash.

"Little two-shooter?" Chalula paused in front of a door, reaching into her purse. "Can you use it?"

"I don't know, I've never tried."

"Pfft." Chalula opened the door. "Can you use a sword?"

"I could probably cut off my own foot."

"We'll hope that is not necessary." Chalula went around the room shaking up lights, then opened a trunk at the foot of the bed and threw things out onto the floor. "It may be best, if there is trouble, you just hand me bolts."

"Bolts?"

Chalula passed her a stiff leather cylinder with a shoulder strap. "It is, how do you say, fire bolts. Not just fire. Boom!"

"Exploding bolts." Clora held the cylinder farther from her body.

"Do not worry, the quiver is bespelled against, ah, exploding."

Clora gingerly opened the cover to reveal about twelve short arrows, fletched end upward, but their ends had no groove for a string. "That's a crossbow?" The device Chalula took from the trunk had a polished wooden stock like a crossbow, with an open groove on top, but there was no bow on it.

"It operates by magic." Chalula tapped an area of lighter colored wood behind the groove. "This is nether-ash."

Elinora pursed her lips. "That there must've cost a pretty penny."

Chalula shrugged. "I travel much. Highwaymen are cowards. A loud noise, the insides of their friend decorating the ground—they flee. It has paid for itself. Now, go out and close the door. I must change."

When Chalula joined them in the foyer, she was dressed for travel. A practical-looking split skirt in heavy tweed, padded jacket in the same material, calf-high leather boots. She eyed Clora critically. "I would offer you my second outfit, but it is much too large."

Clora fingered the soft material of her dress, eyeing Chalula's ensemble enviously. "There's no time anyway."

At that moment the street door opened and two people entered. One was a rotund woman in a black and silver wizard's cloak, laugh wrinkles around her eyes and a net of jet beads over her hair. The other, a stranger. Or, no, it was Digriz's neighbor, the pockmarked man. "You!"

He grinned. "Hello again, miss. I'm Lorezzo. Ready to go?" The man's voice was raspy. Perhaps he had a cold.

"Where is Eddie?" Chalula asked.

"He had something else to do."

"More important than this?"

"Related to this. Here's a note from him, explaining the situation. Is that our carriage in front?"

Clora took the note. Chalula scowled at Lorezzo, hefting her weapon. "If this is some game, I will crush you. Then I will crush Eddie."

"Really, we must hurry." Lorezzo held the door open.

"I ain't going with no strange man," Elinora muttered. "Prolly slit our throats as soon as look at us."

"I already have a trace on the man you're looking for." The wizard held out a small wooden box. "No telling how long it'll last."

Clora folded the note and passed it to Chalula. "Ma, I have to go. You can wait here."

Elinora shifted her bag further up her shoulder, and stuck her arm into it. "I'll come along to pertect you." She gave Lorezzo a hard look.

Lorezzo dismissed the driver the inn had supplied, and climbed into the driver's seat himself. The wizard sat beside him, and Clora crowded into the little remaining space, leaning forward to look past him at the magic box in the wizard's hands. It was hard to tell in the dark, but it looked like there was a glass top, with something suspended inside.

Clora leaned in to look. "Is that the apple core?"

"That's right. Turn right up here, young man."

"You didn't use the spell with the glass ball, where you paint symbols around the edge."

The wizard beamed at her. "What's your name?"

"Clora Perridino."

"I'm Mrs. Wellibom. That's a good spell, but you need something flammable from the subject and the ingredients are a bit dear. It's third law, of course, hence the glyphs. This is second law." She gestured with the box. "Simpler, but shorter range. Also, of course, when he finishes digesting the apple the connection is lost. Are you a student, dearie?"

"No, I just saw someone use the other spell earlier."

"Hm." Mrs. Wellibom reached into the black bag she'd set beside the bench, pulling out an illuminated clipboard with a map on it. She held the box beside the map. "Which way is north, now?"

Clora pointed. "The weather tower is northeast." The top of the tower was just visible over the Perlmite Dome, moonlit flags promising rain and cold on the morrow.

Mrs. Wellibom rotated the map, measured distances with her thumb. "He's on the Gevverton road."

"We just passed that turn." Lorezzo sounded annoyed.

"Good, then we don't have far to go back."

"Are you sure?"

"The rest of the apple is there. The man who ate it is likely to be near."

"Fine." Lorezzo reined the horses over.

Soon they were out of town, following the pool of glow from their headlamps. Trees arched overhead. Lorezzo clucked to the horses, and they picked up the pace a little more. Clora sat tensely, listening to the night, listening for threats. The hooves and breathing of the horses, creak of carriage springs, quiet voices from inside the cabin.

It was good to finally be doing something useful, but waiting was hard. "Can you tell how far he is?"

Mrs. Wellibom glanced up from her map. "If you know when he ate the apple. Maybe six to eight miles."

Unless he was going exceptionally slowly, it would be an hour or more before they might hope to catch him. "Can't we go any faster?"

"This is already faster than is safe," Lorezzo said. "If we hit a pothole we're like to break an axle."

Something touched Clora on the back, and she almost jumped from her seat. She twisted to see her mother, through the sliding panel behind the bench, holding out a plate. "You still ain't eat much."

The light was too dim to see what was on the plate, but she was suddenly achingly aware of how long it had been since her last, inadequate meal. She gladly took it, holding it level as she turned around.

Lorezzo glanced at the plate. "What do you have there?"

"My ma always brings food. Give me a second and I'll tell you." Clora bit and chewed. "Mm. Flatbread with a spicy kavvi spread, um, cress, hard-cooked egg, and, I guess, goose."

"Got any more?"

"Soon!" Elinora called out.

After eating, Clora held the reins to let Lorezzo have his. "Do you want me to watch the spell for a while?"

"Thank you, dearie, I'm fine." Mrs. Wellibom was bent over her map. "Did you notice the number on the last milepost?"

Lorezzo finished swallowing a bite of bread. "108."

She turned the map, held a ruler up to the sheet, consulting the box to adjust the angle. "I believe they've taken the side road on the left, just past mile 110."

"Right."

"Are we getting close?" Chalula said from the back. "We must discuss our plan."

Lorezzo wiped his mouth. "When I—ah, Eddie and I—searched Reodorid's house, we found two spell globes labeled Enervate. They're in my satchel."

"That's what they used on Marlee," Clora said.

"And it's what I'll use on them. When we get close, you all hide in the carriage. They don't expect trouble from me. I'll make sure they're all gathered around, and drop a globe. Then you come out and get us."

Elinora and Chalula's faces were in the opening behind the driver's bench. "You'll use the spell on yourself?" Elinora said.

"If there's nothing to duck behind. It's harmless enough, wears off in a few hours."

"Unless you brain yourself falling down," Mrs. Wellibom said.

"I'll make sure that doesn't happen to me or Marlee. As for the others, you'll have to kill them in any case."

"What!" Clora's hand came to her throat.

Elinora shook her head violently. "I don't hold with no murders. That ain't decent."

"I'm Marlee's spy in their organization. Such as it is. I can't let them go around telling everyone I rescued Marlee. It destroys my usefulness. And they'll be hanged anyway when the guard catches them."

"I have no worries about killing them," Chalula said. "I will do it if they are squeamish."

"Why don't we just wait and see what the setup is," Elinora said. "Maybe they don't have to see you. We might surprise 'em and be able to just hurl that spell at them."

"I concur," Chalula said. "And I will deal with any who escape."

For a time, there were only the sounds of their carriage, trees rolling past in the dim glow of their headlamps, then open land, grain fields on one side, a tidy orchard of short trees on the other.

Clora spotted a mile marker. "One ten," she announced.

Lorezzo looked at the wizard. "Any change?"

Mrs. Wellibom consulted her map. "They've slowed. Maybe stopped. Turn left up here."

The new road was narrower and bumpier. Clora held on to the bench as they rattled along.

There was a thump and a country oath from inside the cabin. "Where did you learn to drive, young man?"

"You think you can do better?"

"Blessed right!"

Clora put her hand on his sleeve. "Please don't fight."

There was silence for a time, until Mrs. Wellibom announced they were close. "They don't seem to be moving."

They rearranged themselves, Elinora on the driver's bench since she wouldn't be recognized, everyone else inside. Chalula covered the interior light and closed the front window to a slit, kneeling on the seat to peer out, scowling, loaded weapon in hand, like a fierce barbarian from the tales of Gergyon.

That last quarter mile did seem a bit smoother, whether from her ma's driving skill or because the road was better.

"Whoa then." The trap rolled to a halt, horses snorting and stamping. Those inside waited in silence, hearing Elinora climb down. "There's a person lying in the road," Chalula whispered.

Mrs. Wellibom was bent over her box. "We're right on top of them."

"Why, look," Elinora announced. "This man is dead, seems like." There was a rustle of dry grasses. "And here's two more in the ditch. One's a woman."

Clora's breath caught in her throat. Beside her, Chalula muttered something unintelligible.

"Hello! Anybody out there? There's folks as need help here!"

After a suitable interval with no response to Elinora's hail, Lorezzo reached for the door handle. He poked his head out and looked around, then climbed down, making no signal whether to follow. Chalula and Clora both headed for the door at the same time, and Clora let the other woman go first, preferring the exploding arrows in front of her than at her back.

Lorezzo knelt in the road, his fingers on the body's throat. Clora joined her mother beside the ditch, aiming a light down at two forms lying in a patch of flattened weeds. Her stomach unknotted a little. "It's not Marlee."

Lorezzo stood. "This one is dead. Still fairly warm. No obvious wound."

Chalula had gone a little way down the slope. "There is blood on the woman. What happened here? Did they fight each other?"

"Who knows? Check whether they're alive. We need someone—"

"Eh, look up there!" Elinora pointed. "There's a light ahead."

They all looked. There was a brighter patch, as of a light shining on the road from behind the trees, around the next bend. A shadow moved in that light.

"Back in the carriage," Lorezzo ordered, but Chalula was already striding ahead, weapon at the ready. Lorezzo swore, and started after her, his hand inside his jacket. Clora took out her little gun and followed.

She stopped behind the others, who stood looking at a carriage pulled up beside the road. Its headlamps shone on the backs of four horses, heads down, cropping the grass on the verge. One raised its head, blew, and shook itself, making the harness jingle.

Behind the headlamps, Clora could make out a figure lying on the driver's bench. She pointed it out.

"Right. Check inside." Lorezzo ran past the horses, grabbed the mount bar with one hand, and swung up, a glint of metal in his other hand.

The carriage door was on the far side, against the forest. Chalula started around, then paused as the lead horse on that side raised its head and looked her in the eye.

"I do not care for horses."

"Let me," Clora walked up confidently—horses needed to feel that you knew your business—and pushed the beast aside so she could edge past.

"Found her," Lorezzo called down. "Alive."

MARLEE

✖ ✖ ✖ Ⅵ

MARLEE FELT ROUGH, CHILL STONE against her bare arm. She was so tired, it took all her energy to pull in even a shallow breath. She opened her eyes. She lay against the side of a building, a protruding window sill about two stories up, and above that, a large halogen light in a metal bracket, unlit. She must be back on Earth. The wall was lit from the side by another light she couldn't see from where she lay, in the shadow of a shorter wall. She tried to sit up, but couldn't move. Distant voices, laughing—she tried to call out, but lacked the breath. She lay in something warm and sticky. "Over here," she mumbled. The wall swam out of focus, and she closed her eyes.

"She's having trouble breathing." The voice was almost familiar. She opened her eyes, didn't recognize the face. Fingers swept over her chin, and the stiff tape fell away.

"Digriz?" she whispered. It was his voice, but not his face. "Did you... get swapped too?" She raised her hand, meaning to touch the pockmarked cheek, but a jolt of pain stopped her. She gasped.

"Hsst. Shut up. I'm Lorezzo."

"Ow-w-w. My hand."

"What's the matter?" Another familiar voice, a woman, but she couldn't quite place it.

"Get the medicine kit. Go! Have you been poisoned?" The man—Lorezzo?—pushed her eyelid up, touched her neck.

"Stop it." She swatted his hand away as he tried to open her mouth. Took another breath. "Stuck myself." She raised her hand, wiggled the pricked finger.

He grabbed the hand, held a light to it. "Poison," he called down. "On a needle."

"She had some needles." It was Clora's voice now. Marlee turned her head to look. "Hid in her hair."

"Gods preserve. What poison?"

Clora shrugged.

"Three—three grooves," Marlee said.

"I don't know what that means." Lorezzo stood, picked her up under her arms and knees, and lowered her into Clora's arms. "She's having difficulty breathing. Needs a stimulant, I think."

Hurried footsteps, and a person ran into the light. A wooden case was set on the carriage footboard, glass rattling inside.

Marlee blinked at the woman who'd brought it. "Chalula?" Was she dreaming? A man who sounded like Digriz but apparently wasn't, that singer unexpectedly here, and her head was spinning.

"Do not speak, katan. Hoard your breaths."

As Chalula sorted through little bottles in the case, two other women came into the light. "Give 'er a Gurnish salt." Elinora! Stranger and stranger!

The other woman, in an embroidered cape that would've been nice for Halloween, pointed into the case. "This extract helps with breathing." But Lorezzo had already pulled out a different tiny bottle. He popped the cork out with his thumb, and held it under Marlee's nose.

For a moment, Marlee was convinced someone had sandpapered her sinuses. She jerked her head back, then doubled over, coughing, Clora holding her arm. Someone pounded her back, and she gasped. Her breath did seem to be coming a little easier, but when Lorezzo tried to give her another dose, she waved him off.

"Put her inside," Chalula said. "She must sit up."

Clora pulled her toward a carriage. "Can you stand?"

"I don't know. My knee—"

"She's had a right beating. Lookit her hand."

"Ma, you hold her. I'll get the horses."

Someone gripped her around the waist. Lorezzo took up her hand, holding her wrist firmly. "Tell me where it hurts when I press."

"Ow, ow! There! Come on, it's broken! Quit poking at it!"

"I think the fingers are just dislocated. What about here?"

"Leggo!"

"Allow me, young man." The woman in the embroidered cloak stepped up. "I'm Mrs. Wellibom. Let's get inside, and we'll have a look."

Clora had climbed up into the driver's seat and encouraged the horses back into the road. Marlee let herself be helped inside, into the seat she'd recently sat in as a prisoner. Mrs. Wellibom climbed in, and Chalula stood in the doorway, dividing her attention between them and the dark road behind.

Mrs. Wellibom clicked back the cover of the overhead light, and jabbed the button beside it several times to brighten it. "Let's have a look. Never fear, I won't touch it. Just your arm, here and here."

There was a tingle along her forearm, and the throbbing in her hand stopped. She let out a long breath she hadn't realized she was holding. Outside, hoofbeats and the jingle of harness announced the passage of the other wagon.

"Where are they going?"

Chalula was standing outside the open door. "Looking for a place to turn around."

"That only stops the hurt for a few minutes, so let's get on." Mrs. Wellibom held out a small bottle. "Drink this down."

"What is it?"

"For pain. Half now, half later."

The liquid was bitter, spreading icy numbness on her tongue. She washed it down with water from a larger bottle.

"Good. Now put your hands together, palm to palm." Mrs. Wellibom poured a little water into her own hand, dipped a finger in it, and used it to draw a complex figure on the back of Marlee's good hand. Another dip, and a quick sketch on the other hand. As she completed the figure, the dislocated fingers snapped back into line with the others, with a nauseating pop, but only a little pain.

"Don't move them. You!" Mrs. Wellibom waved to get Chalula's attention. "Help with these bandages."

Chalula gave a final look down the road before hopping in. Mrs. Wellibom bound three of Marlee's fingers together, adding enough layers to hold them straight. "If anything's broken, it's not bad and the spell will hold it until it heals. You probably don't need the bandages, but a physician will decide that. As for the knee, I can't tell what's wrong."

The other carriage pulled up again beside them, paused while Lorezzo and Clora talked, then rolled ahead. After a second, their carriage jerked into motion too. Clora turned. "We need to haul the bodies away from the road, in case their friends come along. We'll send the guard out for them later."

"Bodies?" Marlee's heart sank. "Are they really dead? All three?"

"One for sure. I left after that."

The carriages stopped together, and Marlee reached for the door handle.

"Katan." Chalula put a hand on her wrist. "Stay inside."

"I have to see." Marlee stood, climbed out one-handed, and limped around the carriage to where Lorezzo and Elinora stood beside the road, arguing.

"How could you not check?" Lorezzo said.

"Me go down in the ditch? These here are my good shoes. They looked all dead."

"Well evidently, the woman wasn't. If she saw me—"

"Down!" Chalula rushed up behind Marlee and shoved her. There was a sharp report, and glass shattered.

"Gun!" Lorezzo shouted. "Get to cover!"

Marlee scrambled behind the carriage. Everyone was running. There was a second shot. Chalula joined her behind the carriage, then took a quick peek out. The horses neighed and lunged forward, dragging the carriage a few inches against its brakes.

"I will crush this one." Chalula pointed her weapon up. "This will make her into pieces." She waited for another shot, then leapt out, lowering her gun.

"No!" Marlee lunged for Chalula's arm, knocking it aside. There was a roar, and the road was lit with flames.

"Are you insane?" Chalula was back behind the carriage. "You made me miss!"

"You mustn't kill her." Marlee raised her voice so everyone could hear. "Don't kill her! I, uh, I need her alive."

"What for?" Lorezzo yelled from behind the other carriage.

Marlee glanced his way, but couldn't see him behind the headlamp glare. "Because I said so. Rosette! Throw the gun out on the road. I swear we'll let you go free."

"Ha!" The voice came from somewhere among the thick trees across the road. "I know about your promises."

"Psst!" came Clora's voice from behind the other carriage. "Marlee, is my ma in there?"

Marlee checked, and found Mrs. Wellibom, sitting on the floor with all the seat cushions between herself and the shooter, eyes wide. "Not here. Rosette, we can negotiate this. What do you want?"

"All I want is for you to—" There was a cry.

Marlee waited a moment. "Rosette?"

A different voice answered. "I got 'er! Don't shoot, it's me." A figure walked out into the ember glow left by Chalula's weapon. Elinora, holding something long and straight in one hand. "Whacked 'er with my rolling pin."

"Is she all right?"

"Ma!" Clora rushed to the side of the road.

Elinora plunged into the ditch. "When you was a girl, I taught you, Miss Marlee, but I guess you forgot. When a person cracks the noggin of another as is trying to make holes in ya, first ya say, 'Thankee, Mrs. Perridino and are you hurt, and can I replace the shoes you ruint in the muddy ditch.'" She raised her arm to her daughter, who reached down to pull her out while Lorezzo leapt the ditch and vanished into the woods. Elinora straightened her skirts. "After that, is the time to ask if the assassin is hale. That's the rule."

Marlee grinned. "Sorry, Elli. Thank you for clobbering the assassin. Please let me buy you new shoes, and are you well?"

"Aye, thanks." Elinora brushed herself off and straightened her skirts. "I know just the shoes I fancy. Saw 'em in the window of Bergrits."

Marlee held out her arm to Clora for support, and they walked over to the ditch. Clora shone a light down onto the two still forms lying there.

They were obviously dead, the driver's face dark and contorted, hands still near his throat, and the man who'd tormented her lying curled on his side, eyes open and staring. Marlee started to feel sick, and turned away. "I have to sit down."

Inside the carriage, she put her head between her knees and gulped air until she was fairly sure she wouldn't throw up, then kept her head down, rocking slightly.

A hand brushed her back, softly. "Are you well, katan?"

"I—I need a minute."

"I shall fetch the wizard if you're unwell."

"No." Marlee sat up and grabbed Chalula's arm. "Don't leave."

"Of course."

"Is the girl alive?"

"Yes, but blows to the head are chancy."

"I never...." Marlee paused. This woman seemed to know her, despite having acted earlier like she didn't. So she couldn't confidently claim she'd never killed anyone before. "I hated having to do that." But that was untrue. Now she was horrified and guilty, but at the time, she'd stabbed the needle into her tormentor's neck with glee. She was a monster.

"All set in here, dearies?" Mrs. Wellibom was at the door. "The prisoner is secured, and Mr. Lorezzo says to lower the shades. If we pass any of the kidnappers' associates, they mustn't see you."

"Where's Clora? Is she riding with us?" Marlee wanted her there to deflect any questions from Chalula.

"She'll drive the other carriage. Anyway, it looks like you two want to be alone." Mrs. Wellibom winked and shut the door.

God, no, she didn't want to be alone with this woman. Chalula reached across Marlee to pull the shades down as the carriage jerked into motion. The scent she wore drifted up, roses and something resiny, and sweat, and something seemed to loosen and drift free in Marlee's head. She was dizzy from all the excitement, and maybe the drug she'd drunk finally taking hold.

When Chalula sat up again, she raised a hand to Marlee's cheek, and their eyes met, inches apart. Chalula moved in, and Marlee wanted, didn't want to push her away. Their lips brushed, and Marlee gave an involuntary moan as heat flashed down her body, stop, don't stop. She put her hand on Chalula's leg, the cloth rough under her fingers. Chalula chuckled, and her lips moved around to Marlee's neck. "This is wrong," Marlee whispered.

"What, have you not in a carriage?" Chalula sounded amused. "It can be done. But you must remember to be more quiet!" Chalula's hand swept up slowly from Marlee's waist, pausing to cup a breast before moving on to tug on the lacing at her throat. "Tell me if you hurt. I will be careful."

Marlee's hand came up, as if with a will of its own, pulling Chalula closer. Their lips met again, and Marlee left thinking behind for a time.

EDSGAR

XXXVII

AN ORANGE GLOW ON THE horizon suggested sunrise was near. Digriz looked back to make sure the other carriage was keeping up. Their prisoner was inside, out of sight, guarded by Clora's mother. Presumably with rolling pin in hand.

It wasn't certain whether the woman had gotten a good enough look at him, in the dark and from a distance, to know who he was. But he couldn't take that chance. If he had to abandon the Night Wind persona, it would put an end to their plans. There wasn't time to re-infiltrate the organization under a new disguise.

Marlee might mean to hold the woman for questioning. But he knew Lily—or Rosette, as Marlee had called her—a little, well enough to know she was just a follower. She didn't have any important secrets.

Still, Marlee didn't do things without good reason. Maybe Lily knew more than he thought.

Mrs. Wellibom had been hunched over her lighted clipboard, reading a folded-over newspaper which she shielded from the wind with her arm. Now she sat up and looked around. "Do you hear something?"

Digriz listened. "A whistle?"

"A guard whistle, isn't it?"

"Could it be?"

Far ahead, across the fields, a blue light flickered behind trees, then emerged into the open, followed by two others, brilliant and steady as they coasted along the road. The whistling grew louder, and another vehicle came in sight, with a pair of regular carriage lamps.

Digriz turned in his seat to signal Clora to pull over with him and wait for the procession to pass. But when the lead vehicle reached them, the rider slewed to a stop, boot scraping on dirt, one hand raised to balance the giant hoop wheel he rode in, dust settling on his leathers. The other two riders pulled up behind him, hands on their holstered weapons, the carriage still a way back.

So much for the idea of being unobtrusive. "Good evening, officers. Is there a problem?"

"We'll have to search these carriages, sir."

"Ah, I believe we do have what you're looking for. We were just bringing her home." He rapped the top of the carriage. "Ladies, come out please. There are people here who wish to speak with you."

The door opened, and Chalula stepped out, giving Marlee a hand down. The officer beamed his light in her face, and she raised her bandaged hand to block it.

"Miss Forossi, who are these people?"

Marlee lowered her hand, squinting at him. "They're my rescuers."

The officer looked suspiciously at the ragtag assembly. "If they're making you say that—"

"I assure you, nobody makes me say anything. See, that's my companion on the other carriage, and this is my friend Chalula."

The officer's eyes widened. He perhaps recognized the singer. "Still, you'd best ride with us."

The trailing carriage had arrived by this time, and more officers piled out into the road. A wizard climbed down from beside the driver. He hurried toward Marlee, holding a glass ball. "I'm still getting no reading. Are you sure it's not another decoy?"

"You're the expert," the officer said. "You tell us. Is this really her?"

The wizard took a pair of spectacles from a tunic pocket—spectacles that would easily see through Digriz's disguise. He twisted to busy himself with something on the opposite side of his carriage. "There's no magical disguise on her," the wizard said. Digriz heard the click of the spectacles being folded, and turned back to watch. "But there's a spell on these garments. That's what's been blocking me. I'll take them to analyze. We may be able to recognize the spell-work."

"But you were getting a direction before."

The wizard gave Marlee a clinical glance. "I imagine she took the dress off at some point."

If it were anyone else, Digriz would've sworn Marlee was blushing. Doubtless a trick of the light. "You can have the clothes later," she said. "I have nothing else to wear."

The officer again scrutinized them all, including Elinora, who hung out of the second carriage. "I'm sure these are your friends, miss, but my captain will insist we search these carriages, and we'll need names and statements from everyone."

Marlee looked back at the second carriage, and nodded to Elinora, who ducked inside. "If you must." She moved aside and let the officer into the carriage, while another couple of men crowded into the second vehicle.

"There's someone unconscious in here!"

Elinora had gotten out to stand in the road. "That there lady is with us. One a them bad men cracked her noggin."

Digriz could see the ropes with which Lily had been bound, tucked into the back of Elinora's sash. Making sure no officers were watching, he eased them out, then meandered behind the carriage to throw them into the equipment locker.

When they were finally sorted out again and on their way, guard officers drove both carriages and perched on top as lookouts, leaving the powered guard carriage to proceed on to recover the bodies.

Digriz rode inside with Elinora. "That was good thinking." He nodded at Lily, curled on the opposite seat. The wind shifted, blowing rain through the broken window onto Lily's face, and Digriz leaned across to pull the shade down.

"Seemed like the missus signaled me so. I figgered if she wanted to turn her over, she's still able."

"Yes. You left it up to her. That's what she likes." Digriz looked again at Lily. Had the pulse at her throat quickened? Did her eyelids flutter?

"Marlee doesn't intend to hurt her. She just wants to talk with her, then let her go." Lily probably wouldn't believe that—he didn't believe it himself. But it was worth a try.

Of course, if Lily was awake, she could hardly fail to recognize him now. Well, they'd just have to make sure she didn't get to talk to anyone for a few weeks. After that, it wouldn't matter.

MARLEE

XXXVIII

MARLEE WOKE STILL IN THE carriage, leaning against Clora's shoulder. Her mouth was dry and tasted awful, her head ached. It was daylight out, but gloomy, rain beating on the roof. She sat up and pinched the bridge of her nose. "Where are we?"

"A little way outside of town. We stopped for a change of horses while you slept."

Marlee fished out the little bottle Mrs. Wellibom had given her, and looked across at the wizard. "Is it time for more of this?"

Mrs. Wellibom set her newspaper aside. "Near enough." She passed Marlee the water.

Marlee slugged down the bitter liquid, then sipped water. "What is this stuff, anyway?"

"Coca extract."

A sip of water went down the wrong way, and Clora pounded her back until the coughing stopped. "Sorry." Marlee cleared her throat. "Coca, you say? As in *cocaine?*"

"That would be the term for dried concentrate, yes. A useful stimulant and anesthetic."

She was a killer, a lesbian and a druggie, all in the space of one night. "My mom would be so proud," she muttered.

"When did you last eat, dear?" Mrs. Wellibom leaned forward to touch her forehead.

"I don't know. A while. But I'm not hungry."

"That's the coca talking. You should eat."

"There's food in the other carriage," Clora stood, reaching for the front panel. "My ma will make a plate." She slid open the front panel, and asked the drenched driver to stop.

"Thanks. I also need to talk with Lorezzo for a minute. Will you have them send him up?"

"Um, all right. But you and I have to talk first." Clora looked pointedly at the other two women.

Mrs. Wellibom sighed and stood. Chalula scowled. "You know it rains severely."

Marlee touched Chalula's knee. "Please, ah, katan, just for a little while."

"Pah." Chalula stood. "I will tell Eddie to come, and bring food."

Clora waited for the door to close, then kept her voice low. "Lorezzo is really Digriz."

"I thought maybe so, but they look nothing like each other."

"It's magic. Don't you think the voices are alike too?"

"Well, yes. But are you sure?"

"They at least wear the same boots, with the exact same fresh scrape on the heel. I think he's spying on the anarchists."

"They're not anar—Never mind. Anything else?"

"Did you and Chalula really—"

"Anything besides that."

Clora paused to think. "I guess not."

There was a rap on the door. Digriz stood outside, hood up. Mrs. Wellibom was a few steps away, her newspaper serving as an improvised umbrella. Marlee motioned Lorezzo in.

"All right, Eddie. Here's the deal."

Lorezzo glanced at Clora.

"She knows," Marlee said. "Anything she asks, you can answer. Got it?" There, now she could get Clora to ask him for the details of the plan.

"Anything?" His eyes flicked to Clora again.

Oh, that. Well, she would call it off when she had a chance to talk with him alone. "Within reason. So here's the deal. Is Lily awake yet?"

"She's pretending not, but I think so."

"I need you to help her escape."

Digriz looked shocked. "You're letting her go?"

"Yes. And—"

"You realize what this'll do to our plan."

No idea. "I've considered that. But you can figure something out."

"How in Hades—"

Marlee held a hand up. "Think about it. We'll talk later."

"Wouldn't it be better to just hold her until after?"

"How? Where? You think Severn won't grab her the minute we roll in the gate? I guess you'd better escape too, come to think of it."

"I don't understand. If she's an agent of yours, she certainly had me fooled. Seemed like she really wanted to shoot you dead."

"You don't have to understand. Just do it. And give her a message from me. Say, I meant what I told her before. Despite how it looks, I really am on her side, and I want to do whatever I can to set things right for her family."

Digriz raised both eyebrows.

Marlee racked her brain for a decent rationalization. "Look." She leaned forward and ticked off points on her fingers. "If we kill her now, Severn will know we're hiding something. If we let them take her in, when she's questioned, she'll tell them about you. We don't want anyone knowing I have contacts among the anarchists, right? I need for her to escape, but to have a reason to keep quiet."

Digriz gave her a long, considering look. "That almost makes sense. I still don't see why I shouldn't help her escape and then kill her."

"It's not necessary. If she talks, it's her word against yours, right? Doesn't it look suspicious that she's the only survivor of the plot? And we've told the guards she was helping us. We can arrange for that to get out if we need to. If she's smart, she'll keep her mouth shut and lie low. Explain that to her."

There was a pounding on the door, Chalula demanding to be let in. Digriz leaned back. "It would help greatly in the escape if I had Elinora's co-operation."

Marlee looked at Clora. "Will she help?"

"If you ask her to."

Marlee got paper and pen from Clora. "By the way, I understand you didn't change your shoes when you changed your face. Careless, Eddie!"

Digriz blushed. "Sorry. I didn't have time to find other shoes." He took the note, tucked it in his breast pocket, gave them both a curt nod, and left. Chalula caught the door before it closed, and plopped onto the seat, dripping wet. Mrs. Wellibom followed, shook her cape out in the doorway, and passed Marlee a covered plate of food.

They rode past more farm fields and the occasional estate, then the streets of town. The rain stopped, and Marlee opened the panel and all the windows, keeping a nervous lookout. They paused at one point to talk with a guard patrol, who took off running. At any moment, they might gain an additional escort, complicating Digriz's escape.

Were some officers still concentrating on the search for the decoy, across town? At any rate, they still hadn't picked up any additional guards when a commotion broke out in the second carriage—yelling, thumps, glass smashing. Marlee turned to watch through the back window. Elinora leapt from the carriage and laid about with her rolling pin, slashing at air and shouting "Git 'em offa me!" Three officers tried to restrain her, and the attention of the rest was diverted. Marlee caught a glimpse of what might be Lily's yellow dress behind the crowd of officers, but she wasn't sure until a sergeant looked into the carriage and raised the alarm. When he issued orders to organize a pursuit, Marlee leaned out the door. "Sergeant! I say, sergeant!"

The officer looked at her anxiously.

"Call those men back! I'm afraid the anarchists will try again. I require all of you here to protect me."

"But, miss, they've escaped! This woman helped them."

"Call those men back immediately! I already told you, those are my friends. They didn't 'escape,' they left to take the girl to a... physician." She'd almost said "doctor." "She had a nasty knock on the head. Elinora, are you all right?"

"Sorry for the commotion, miss. There was a big spider on me. You know I can't abide them things."

"That's true, sergeant. She's always hated spiders. Now please, let's move on. I'm exhausted, and want to get home." She shut the door, and leaned back with a little smile.

WHEN THEY ARRIVED AT THE big house, a little group awaited Marlee by the drive. Her parents, Bylamar, Elga, and a maid holding the handles of a polished wooden wheelchair. Her knee was throbbing in time with her heartbeat—she really must've done a job on it—so she was glad of Chalula's help climbing down. Clora tried to take her other arm, but Tam crowded her out, clucking solicitously. She and Severn walked on either side of her as the maid wheeled her in through large, carven double doors.

"We've sent down for a physician," Tam said. "What did you do to your hand, dear?"

"I think I broke it on someone's face."

Tam grimaced, but Severn just snorted. "I hear you did for two of those bastards. Good girl. Too bad you didn't leave anyone to question, but never mind, we'll track down the others. Can you describe any of them?"

Tam set her hand on Marlee's shoulder. "Severn, dear, she's had a hard time. Let her rest a few hours."

"Just gives them more time to escape." But he didn't press further, for which Marlee was grateful. She didn't feel especially tired, though that might be the cocaine. But she might cry if she had to discuss recent events with anyone who would compliment her for the massacre. She slumped a little, closed her eyes, and let herself be wheeled away.

Soon she was parked in a ground floor sitting room, waiting for the physician with Severn and Elga. Severn sat, then stood, started to pace, then excused himself, saying he had business to attend to.

"Where did Chalula go?"

Elga sat in the chair Severn had vacated. "The singer? I thanked her and sent her off with that nice lieutenant. He wants to talk with you later. We should send her a fine present, don't you think?"

Marlee was taken aback. "Don't do that." She hardly knew Chalula, but it appeared the relationship was based on play, not commerce. Offering a reward might offend her. This family seemed to have a habit of turning every relationship into a business transaction or a contest. Could that be why Marlee kept Chalula a secret, why she pretended every meeting was their first? Why risk spoiling things by allowing any change? "I'll, um, take care of it."

How unhappy, how desperately lonely, Marlee must have been. And how undeserving of Chalula's loyalty.

Digriz, on the other hand, would certainly expect monetary recognition for his role in the rescue. That, she'd see to. Clora too, perhaps.

"I've missed our regular tea. Do you have time for us today? Little Josip likes to see his auntie, and, well, I thought you might want to talk."

Auntie? Was Elga her sister? No, that's right, sister-in-law, Petro's wife. The women who married into the family, Tam and Elga, might actually have been raised with a little human decency. "I'd really like that."

Bylamar, standing quietly near the door, cleared his throat. "We're quite a bit behind—"

"And we'll get further behind. I've had, had a...." She didn't want to admit she felt shattered, all ragged bleeding edges. Elga's kindness was the last straw, and the tears wouldn't hold back much longer. But she didn't want Bylamar to report her weakness to Severn. "I need some time alone. Bylamar, just take care of things. I'll sign whatever needs signing, tomorrow. Now go, everyone, please."

CLORA

✕ ✕ ✕ ✕ ✕

CLORA FOUND A YOUNG OFFICER bouncing around just inside the door. The lieutenant, he said, had set him to wait for the dress the kidnappers had put on Marlee.

Clora knew Marlee would be happy to be rid of the garment. She'd complained about its smell and scratchiness. "I'll go up and pick out something else for her to wear."

When she returned with the clean clothes, she found Miss Yrenn waiting at the door, holding her hands out for the folded pile. "Your assistance won't be needed."

So Clora found herself at liberty, and wandered restlessly through the house. Though it was late, breakfast was still laid on the buffet in the front parlor. The room was empty, fortunately, so she loaded a plate with cheese and cold meats, feeling like a thief though she was perfectly entitled to do so. She made a cup of tea to take out onto the veranda, overlooking the river.

She sipped her tea, watching fog roll over the water. It was a little cool for comfort, with clouds massing in the south, but for now it was at least sunny, and the view excellent. She could get used to this way of life.

There was a clatter inside the room—she turned to look. Severn was at the buffet, emptying the chocolate pot into his cup. He saw her, and actually almost smiled. It seemed her role in Marlee's rescue had won her some points.

Not that her position was in any way secure, if Marlee should fall. She needed to learn what Digriz was up to, and why, and she meant to demand full details from him when next they met, now she'd been given that authority.

"There you are." Footsteps came up behind her, and Clora turned again. Karina, standing, staring coldly down. "Do you have something for me?"

Now what? Ah yes, the key. "Haven't you got it back yet? I told Marlee you needed it, and she said she'd arranged for its return."

"No, I haven't got it, and I need it now. I'm already late."

Clora shrugged. "You can ask her yourself." Sorry, Marlee. "But first check whether you've received any packages." Digriz wouldn't have brought it himself, but he'd had enough time to send it before they left town the night before.

"This is not the sort of thing to entrust to a courier. But I'll inquire." She turned away, took a half step and turned back. "You're not fooling anyone, you know."

Clora went cold. "I don't know what you mean."

"This whole supposed rescue. The entire police force out looking for her and you just happen to be the one to find her. As I thought, obviously she arranged it all. Everyone else will realize that soon enough."

Clora repressed a grin. With all the real secrets she and Marlee had, Karina had come up with something completely false. "Her friend Digriz found the clue. We would've given it to the police, but they were all off chasing some phantom and we didn't think it could wait."

"And just how did he find this clue? Awfully convenient. And then those other people who assisted in the rescue. I expect the police will be very interested to hear what they have to say for themselves. Oh wait, I hear they ran off! And the kidnappers conveniently died." Karina sniffed. "That must have come as a rude shock to them, but it's what you can expect when you deal with that woman. Well, maybe you weren't in on it. I imagine she could've fooled you easily."

Clora didn't answer. New Marlee hadn't arranged her own kidnapping, but could old Marlee have done it? Why would she?

Karina must have sensed her uncertainty. She gave a thin smile. "You wouldn't put it past her, I see. Well, I'd love to stay and chat longer, but, you know. Things to do."

MARLEE

JEYNE ARRIVED IN A GREAT bustle of apologies for being away
for her return. He'd gone to fetch the physician personally.

The physician, Welk, was a small, round, older man whose curls were
cemented to his temples with gleaming oil. He gave a quick professional
smile and a head bob, and went right to work. He opened his bag, removed
a device with two glass plates, and stuck her bandaged hand into the gap
between them.

"Amateur work, but it will do. The bandage can come off, but take care
while it heals. What else have we got?"

Marlee pointed to her knee, and Welk pulled up a chair and
unceremoniously raised the hem of her skirt and two layers of underwear.
Jeyne, who'd been pacing nervously near the door, politely looked away,
then circled the room to pull up a chair beside her. "I was so relieved to
hear you'd been found. There was such confusion, the police doing house
searches in the Rookery and Grubb Street all night, three reports that you'd
been sighted there, then here you come from a totally different direction."

"Were you out all night looking for me?"

"Oh, that's nothing. You know me, if I'm in bed by dawn my friends
worry I might be ill. I'll rest later. If Jennet allows it."

"How's it going with the restaurant?"

"We have a location, and Jennet is arranging things. That girl is a force, I
tell you, absolutely priceless. You must thank Digriz for recommending her,

if you see him first. Absolutely could not do it without her. Don't tell her I said so, of course. She's running down the things we'll need, and we should have a budget for you in a couple of days. Elinora's also excellent, so thank you for sending her."

"I meant to tell you, you need little shakers of dried hot pepper flakes."

Jeyne reached into an inner pocket for a small, thin notepad in a gold-chased cover. "Interesting idea. Anything else?"

She should introduce him to the concept of take away boxes and delivery, if she was around long enough. But none of the local restaurants seemed to get that. Maybe one revolution at a time was enough. Anyway, it would take a while to reach the point where they could cook enough to feed more people than could sit in the restaurant. "Elinora's still not interested in working there?"

"We're planning to engage a chef. And Alyssa's band has agreed to perform."

"A chef? A band? You don't want to get too fancy. Try to keep the cost down. The recipe is simple."

"We're looking to serve University students, right? They're mostly of good family. They'll expect a chef and entertainment."

They discussed the restaurant while Welk prodded her knee, examined it with scope and spell, and finally packed it in green goop, wrapped in a stretchy bandage. He set the tub of goop on a side table. "Stay off it for a week or so, and change the ointment daily. If you're in much pain, a spoonful of this, not more than twice daily. You might well not need it."

Marlee hefted the little brown bottle. "Coca?"

"Poppy. It might make you sleepy. Mix it with water if you prefer. Don't take coca or other stimulants at the same time."

"So what's wrong with my knee?"

"Don't you worry, just do as I said and you'll be fine in a week."

Inside Marlee, something snapped. She beckoned Welk closer, and he took a step forward, smiling genially.

Marlee grabbed his satin neck-cloth and pulled him closer. His smile vanished. "Do you treat all your patients like idiots? Or just the women?"

"Urk."

"Did they tell you I killed two men last night? I'm a little unhappy about it, and I don't have a lot of patience left. I'd kind of like to know what's going on with my knee. How about it?"

"Er, the knee cap is bruised and might have a small fracture. I cast a binding on it, in case. Two strained ligaments."

"See, that wasn't so difficult." She started to release him, then had a thought and grabbed on again. "Say. What causes scurvy?"

"What, er, what?"

"It's a disease sailors get, where—"

"Yes, I know what it is, but you don't have—"

"Does it seem wise to interrupt me? What causes it?"

"It's uncertain. Most likely, tainted meat."

Marlee released him. "You can go. Someone out there will pay you."

By the time Jeyne returned from seeing Welk to the door, Marlee was thoroughly miserable. "I'm sorry you had to see that. I just lost it."

"I found it entertaining."

"I just want to go to my room now."

Jenye walked behind her. "I'll push. Would you like to switch rooms, though, to avoid stairs?"

Marlee thought of her secret closet, full of items yet to be investigated. "I need to be in my own place."

Jeyne nodded. "I'd be pretty shaken, too. Familiar things will be a comfort for your state of mind."

Jeyne, she decided, must have been adopted. He pushed her into the hallway, where she found another little reception committee, this time consisting of Clora, Bylamar, and a policeman with silver bars on his tunic—not a familiar face. About thirty, medium height, burly, fit. Just the sort of man she'd have found attractive, in her old life. Not unlike Bobby, in fact. He made a curt little bow.

"Did you need something? I've already talked to the officer who brought me home."

He showed none of the deference of the other officers. "You know I'm not here about the kidnapping. You failed to keep our appointment."

"I've been... tied up. Perhaps you heard."

He seemed unamused. "Our appointment three days ago. Mr. Josip strongly suggests you co-operate with my investigation." He gestured at Bylamar, without taking his eyes off of her. "I understand you've cleared your calendar for today, so perhaps we can talk now."

Panic! This must be about Benin. How could she answer questions without revealing her ignorance? And how would old Marlee have reacted to this request?

All this flashed through her mind in a moment—too brief, she hoped, to be noticed. Could she do this now? She was so close to breaking. But she probably couldn't get away with putting this man off again.

She closed her eyes for a moment, pushed the tiredness and despair down and away. "I suppose now is convenient. In here." She gestured to the door she'd just come out of. "Clora, I'm starving. Something breakfast-like?"

Clora nodded and left, while the policeman rolled her into the sitting room. He pulled up a chair, and took a battered leather-bound notebook from a large pocket on his kilt, flipping through the pages. "Let's go over the events of that day once more."

"Oh, let's not. Seriously, in the times we've talked about this, have my answers changed?"

"Even so, let's review the situation briefly. Before sitting down to tea, you'd been all around the garden and the part of the path your uncle was riding on."

Thank goodness she'd had Clora go out and interview people. "Of course. We were playing a game on the lawn that took us under that tree." She'd forgotten the name of the game, but he must already know. From Clora's description, it'd sounded similar to croquet. "My family plays for blood. The balls can end up anywhere."

"Where else on the property did you go, before your uncle's... accident?"

She didn't know, of course. She looked him in the eye, trying to read him. "I get the impression you have some particular place in mind I failed to mention before. Why don't you just ask about that?"

"I understand you were in the stables shortly after your arrival. What were you doing there?"

"I don't recall visiting the stables then, though anyone who knows me can tell you it's a place I'm likely to go. If I was there, it would be for the usual reasons—to say hello to the horses, see how they're being treated. Who told you I was there?"

"We don't disclose that."

"Because if it was that stable-boy, Un-something, I meant to tell you he tried to extort money from my companion to keep quiet about some story he had about me. He must've improved the story after he told it to her, because at that time he only said I'd been in the stables after the accident. He also told her I'd given him an exorbitant tip to clean the horse thoroughly."

"Did you ask him to clean the horse?"

"I don't know, I was a little distracted by the recent gruesome death. Probably. The horse was sweaty and agitated, and brushing helps with both of those. I didn't pay him to do it, though. It's his job. He's already being paid for it."

"He showed me the coin."

"He showed you a coin. I don't expect it had my picture on it."

"Why did you bother to tell him how to do his job?"

What would old Marlee have said? There was a knock at the door and Clora entered without waiting, carrying a tray which she set on a small table near them. "Tea, Captain Gerounni?" He shook his head.

Marlee gave silent thanks to Clora for that clue. "Captain, I don't like people much. Horses, I like. They aren't bright, but they're sensitive and direct. They don't lie, they don't cheat. I don't like to see them mistreated or neglected. If I'd decided to kill my uncle, I'd've tried to do it without upsetting a horse. Now, while I have something to eat, ask Clora about her conversation with that boy. And then ask yourself why he waited so long to come forward." Marlee reached for a cup and the chocolate pot.

Gerounni gave her a long look, then turned to Clora. "Yes, miss. That's another reason I'm here. The people at the house told my man you'd stopped in. I'd like to hear all about your visit, starting with why you went."

Clora gave Marlee a glance, then pulled up a chair. "Miss Marlee knew you suspected her, so she sent me to find out what really happened. My cousin works there, and we thought I might be able to get more from the servants than what your men could."

"And did you find anything new?"

"I don't know what's new to you, but I'll tell you what they said." And she did so, while Marlee ate crumbly cheese, purple pickled vegetables, a hard-cooked egg, and small meatballs with a mint sauce. "I can't say for sure it was an accident," Clora concluded. "But if not, I don't see how it was done."

"If I knew that...."

Marlee set her plate aside with a clunk. "Look, captain, I get it. I mean, I think I understand where you're coming from. You believe in justice, and you're good at your job. You're not well paid, but your work is important. I think it's important. And you see people like me getting away with all sort of sh—things, and we're untouchable. If the dead man hadn't been a Forossi, Grandpa Josip would've written a note to your boss's boss's boss, and you'd've been told to back off. You'd love a chance to cart me off to jail, and frankly, I might deserve to be there. But in this case, you're barking up the wrong tree."

"I'm... *barking?*"

"What I'm saying is, if Benin was killed, I didn't do it. Yes, he and I had our issues. But I'm hardly the only one. Do you see this?" Marlee gestured with her cup, a dollop of cocoa escaping over the edge. "Oops. This is a poison-detecting cup. Several of us have sets of these dishes. We play for keeps, and expect people might try to kill us. It's a rotten way to live, frankly. In fact, Benin's death was the last straw for me."

"Wait. A straw?"

"It's a, an Aakol figure of speech. It pushed me over the edge. I'm tired of this. I want to have more friends than enemies from now on. I'm sorry I missed our appointment. I was off rethinking my life. Talking with my kidnappers was also a wake-up call. They have legitimate grievances. I want to start doing more good than harm."

Gerounni looked a little dazed. He slowly closed the cover of his notebook. "Well. This is a side of you I hadn't seen before. Assuming you're sincere. Miles away from your attitude the last time we spoke, which I might best describe as arrogantly defiant."

"The difference is I've decided I can trust you to keep this to yourself. If other members of my family had any notion that I was no longer willing to fight dirty, I'd lose everything. I need time to free assets from their control, and to help some of my relatives who also want something better. I'm setting up my cousin Jeyne in his own business, to free him from his father, and I've hired a psychist to help another cousin—you probably already heard about that, too. One of my nearest and dearest kidnapped her and drove her mad. I think. It's pathetic that I can't even narrow down the list of likely suspects to three."

"I'm familiar with the case," Gerounni said. "I was told to conclude she went mad and wandered off on her own."

"I'm sorry. You must've hated that."

Gerounni stood, putting the notebook back into his pocket. "Well. You've given me much to consider. Or, as you might say, a bone to gnaw on. I expect you to be available if I need to talk with you again."

"Of course. Are you telling me not to leave town?"

Clora spoke up. "Bylamar's arranged for us to see Neidra tomorrow morning. That's in Lar Quayno, a few hours by train."

"Very well. Thank you for keeping me advised of your whereabouts."

After the door closed behind him, both women were silent for a time. "Whoosh!" Clora said at last. "That was brilliant! I think you really moved him. Despite calling him a hound."

"I'm shaking. It helped that it was about ninety percent true. Thank you for his name and rank. It was getting awkward, not knowing what to call him."

"He has lovely calves. I do assert, I thoroughly approve of police uniforms."

"Why are you going around noticing men's calves? I thought you were sweet on Digriz."

Clora grinned. "I am, a little. But it hasn't made me blind. Now, about your figures of speech...."

Marlee held up a hand. "I know, I made some mistakes. Make a list and talk to me later, okay? I'm at the end of my... I can't talk to anyone else for a while. Help me upstairs, will you?"

EDSGAR

LILY WAS SKEPTICAL.

"Of course she's on our side." Digriz hit hard on his most persuasive point. "Why else would she let you go? It would've been far less trouble for her to just let the police have you."

Indeed, it was such a good point that he was starting to convince himself. Why did Marlee let this woman go? Not out of kindness, presumably, but while her explanation in the carriage had made a sort of sense at the time, it seemed weak now.

But then, he was used to being out of his depth in Marlee's plans. Her position was that just enough information to do his job, was more than she'd really like him to have. There was just some factor of which he was not aware. Lily was a minor player in the movement, so he'd had no reason to try to dig up her real identity. But Marlee knew her in a different context, had called her Rosette.

It could simply be that she was of important family, the daughter of someone Marlee wanted to avoid antagonizing. It wasn't unheard of for children of privilege, motivated by guilt, to oppose the system that had enriched them.

Anyway, she didn't seem to need professional medical attention. By necessity, Digriz had become something of an expert at evaluating what could be safely let heal on its own, and what needed the help of a physician, who might drop a word to the Seidos afterwards. He'd straightened her thoroughly broken nose himself. Her head still hurt, understandable after being knocked out twice. But she didn't have any nausea or dizziness, and her mind was still sharp enough to put up a good argument. He left her at a rebel safe house, suggesting she lie low and promising to check back in a day to see whether she developed any concerning symptoms.

Since the police would be looking for him, he would've taken his own advice and hidden too, except the face they sought wasn't his real face. He ducked into the first business he saw with public conveniences and enough early customers so he wouldn't stand out, and emerged a new man. Now, he could go home and sleep until night.

But at his home, someone waited on the stoop. A robust young man with rough features, a long scar across his forehead. Tanni, known to his acquaintances as "the Fist". Still dressed in country style, he must've come straight from the train station after doing the job Digriz had given him. Digriz unlocked the building door and let him in without speaking.

He studied the man covertly as they climbed the stairs to his apartment. Tanni was nervous, fidgety. Of course, he would've just committed a crime that could get him sent away for a few years, but that was nothing new to him. Digriz, too, began to feel uneasy. He'd chosen Tanni for the job mainly for his speed and ability to pass for Ovid from a distance. Tanni's brain, however, was of lesser quality than his legs and those eponymous fists, and he was apt to place over-reliance on the latter. Maybe he'd not been such a good choice, after all.

Digriz let them into his apartment and gestured to a chair, but Tanni went to look out the window, before stalking back. "It's done. I'll be wanting my pay."

"Wait here." Digriz went into his bedchamber and shut the door. He took seven thin gold coins from a cache in the hollow center of a bedpost, screwed the top back on, and returned to the main room, jingling the coins. "I'll need a report, of course."

Tanni's eyes fixed on the hand containing the coins. "What do you mean? I did like you said."

"Which was...?"

"Took my rifle to the King's Wood in Wesford afore dawn, took down a deer, started to skin it with that knife you give me, run off when a warden spotted me."

The man was a pathetic liar. "You left the knife?"

"Sure, like you said."

"You didn't touch it with bare skin?"

Tanni took a pair of supple leather gloves from his pocket. "Not a bit."

"You didn't leave anything else?"

"Nah."

"You weren't seen well enough to identify?"

"Nah, he won't... nah."

A chill went down Digriz's spine. "He won't be talking?"

"There was two of 'em." Tanni sounded aggrieved. "Ran into one and he wouldn't let go, so I had ta."

The idiot had murdered a King's Warden. No wonder he was anxious. A deer was no big deal. They'd be glad to receive a tip of the culprit's identity, but they wouldn't work too hard to find him. This was a different matter. "Leave town." Digriz handed over the money. "Now. Don't come back. And don't be seen leaving here. Use the back stair."

His guest gone, Digriz sank into the elegant little chair near his dark, shell-inlay side table. He put his head into his hands. How big a problem was this? A letter to the authorities now would see Ovid hanged rather than jailed, but that would still serve as a threat to keep Clora in line. He'd chosen Wesford, because it was far enough from Ovid's home to be well out of range of a tracing spell cast on his knife. They might try the spell from other locations, but a few castings would use up the trace, and they'd want to save enough to confirm identity if they ever had any suspects. Ovid was pretty safe unless that letter were sent. It certainly wasn't in Tanni's best interest to say anything.

No, from a practical standpoint they were all right. But it didn't feel all right. In the eighteen months he'd been working for Marlee, he'd caused his share of misery. But this was the first time, as far as he knew, that any of his activities had led directly to someone's death. When he talked with Marlee, he tried to match her ruthlessness, but the few times a killing would've neatly solved a problem, he'd gone out of his way to find another answer. Now that it'd finally happened, he felt chill and empty.

Before he met Marlee, he'd been in a bad way. Hip deep in gaming debts from before he'd learned how to play well, he'd been regaining lost ground, but too slowly to ever achieve his goal of returning home wealthier than his father. He'd been at a friend's Haloia party when he met her, and they'd immediately "clicked"—not in a romantic way. He'd seen she was feared, respected, got what she wanted, and she, he supposed, had liked his hunger and his cleverness. There had grown up between them a certain amount of trust and even affection of a sort.

How would crossing this bridge affect things, as far as he himself was concerned? These little tasks she set him had been a risky game, a constant challenge and adventure. It seemed much more serious now.

He sat up and sighed. Well, it would've come to this anyway in a couple of weeks. He couldn't pretend he hadn't been on this road already. But he hadn't guessed how he'd feel about it.

This would have to be the end. He'd finish setting things in motion to solve the Josip problem. After all, he wouldn't be conducting the mayhem himself. The payday from that would clear his debts, with a good bit left over. Not enough to meet his original goal, but enough to go home.

MARLEE

MARLEE LAY ON HER BED, STILL dressed. She'd asked the maid to draw her a bath, which turned out to involve twenty minutes of running back and forth with pots of hot water. Her apartment in town had hot running water, but the plumbing in the big house was old.

When the maid announced the bath was ready, she got the girl's help to undress. She propped a leg on the tub to keep the bandage dry, and soaked until the water grew cool. She went back to bed, but the bath hadn't relaxed her as much as she'd hoped. After a few minutes she stood, limped to her secret closet, and for a while just looked over the contents. There was a little stack of books, which she dropped on her bed on her way to the door.

The maid who'd helped her before was still standing outside. "I want Clora." Marlee shut the door without waiting for an answer.

Unfortunately, there was no journal. A slim book, The Stronghold by Min Fipp, about military strategy, a book of diseases of the horse—no obvious reason to hide this, but a close examination revealed no secrets—*Application of Natural Force*—apparently a magic text, and a catalog of poisons in two volumes.

The door handle scraped, and Marlee threw the covers over her books. It was just Clora, though. "Lock the door, and come over here."

"What have you got there?"

"You can have this one." Marlee handed over the magic textbook.

"Ooh! Thank you! What's this, poisons?"

"Looks well used, doesn't it? Notes in the margin, dog-ears." Marlee flipped through volume two, which fell open at a page marked with a strip of ribbon.

"Deekree fish venom. That sounds familiar." The entry listed symptoms, antidotes—give purgatives and hope for the best—properties—colorless, nearly tasteless—and a table showing fatal dosages based on body weight. Symptoms, for a small dose—nausea, headache, vivid dreams or hallucinations, sensation of cold in the extremities, strong sour coppery aftertaste hours later.

Clora crowded next to her to look at the page. "So was she planning to use it on someone, or did she think she was being poisoned?"

Where had she heard of this stuff before? Ah! "Marlee asked Dr. Rob about this poison. She thought someone was feeding her some, and he said the dishes would've caught it."

Clora looked over the entry. "But these are some of the same symptoms as kokoleaba."

Marlee was getting excited. "She was having those symptoms, then, and tried to find a poison that matched! Someone gave her kokoleaba for a while, before it finally worked. But how can that be? She was so careful, with the special dishes. How could someone dose her again and again without getting caught?"

Clora shrugged. "Maybe she depended too much on the dishes. Kokoleaba isn't a poison, after all."

Marlee closed her eyes. It wasn't a poison. Didn't harm the body. Didn't trigger the alarm. But it cast the mind loose to wander and maybe never come back. Someone who thought their dishes were enough protection might not realize the threat until too late. Hadn't.

"And whoever's been giving it to her, they don't know it worked." Marlee felt nauseated thinking about it. "They're still doing it!"

"What, you mean you've had more of it since you arrived?"

"It must be! I thought it was because it took a few days to wear off, but I had those symptoms stronger in the rebels' jail, and that was what, six days after my arrival? No, while I was here, someone slipped me more of the stuff!" She slammed the book shut. "Where did you get my food, this morning?"

"I had the kitchen make up a tray."

"They knew it was for me."

"Of course."

So she might already have had a dose today. "Well, I don't care. Maybe it'll send me home."

Silence. Marlee looked up. Clora looked away.

Oh. "Listen, Clora, I'll make sure you're taken care of. I'll set it up with Bylamar today. I'll just give you a bunch of money, and you'll be fine."

"I don't... it's not that. I mean, I wouldn't turn it down, because Ma would skin me. But I don't... want you to go."

There was a silence of another sort. Marlee was suddenly acutely conscious that they were alone, on her bed, with the door locked. But first, Clora didn't mean it that way, and second, she's a girl, and third, for God's sake she's sixteen, and fourth, dammit she's a girl. "I, I would miss you too. But, you know, my family. My boyfriend."

"Yeah." Clora smiled crookedly. "Don't say boyfriend. Nobody says that."

"Then what?"

"It depends what you mean by it. Fiancé? Suitor? Beau? Friend?"

"More than a friend, but those others sound too formal. We're not engaged. It's, you know. Casual."

"Like you and Chalula."

"Yeah—no! There's no me and Chalula."

"I don't think she knows that."

"Oh God. I mean, gods." Marlee lay back and put a pillow over her face. "I'm so screwed up. I'm a giant wrecking ball in other people's lives."

Clora made no answer.

"How long before I have to go have tea with Elga?"

"About an hour. You don't have to go. Some weeks you skip it."

"No, I said I would, and I actually want to. She seems nice, and I need something normal, for a change."

"Isn't it hard to talk with people who know you, though? I don't think I could do it. What if she asks questions and you don't know the answer?"

"There's a fine art to answering a question with a question. I got a lot of practice, growing up."

SHE WAS DREAMING AGAIN, OR astral projecting, or whatever the hell it was—vague, blobby, like when she'd seen Bobby. It was daytime, outside, in a grassy field. Trees flashed into focus, an airplane. Her mother's face. She tried to hold onto that, expand the borders of clarity. There was her father, too. Walking together. Suddenly they were closer, standing, looking down past Marlee.

Mom had her hand hooked around his elbow. And she was wearing her wedding ring. Wow! Were they back together? Had he ditched the bimbo? His hand covered hers—a ring there, too. Another skip, and they were farther away again, walking toward her. Skip, and they were standing. She heard her mother's voice. "... like she's here." Skip. "... like she's...." Skip. "It feels like...."

I am here! Over here, dammit!

What were they looking at? When Marlee tried to turn and look, the world wheeled around her, dizzying. Stop! She could see just a corner of slab of gray marble, polished on one surface, rough on another. Several smooth pebbles rested on the rough surface.

Not mine! That can't be me! But who else could bring them both here? She tried to back away to see more, but the world just spun again, dissolved into fog. "... like she's..." her mother said again, and then her eyes were open, dawn light coming in through the window.

Marlee rolled from the bed, retching, pain stabbing at her head. The sour copper taste was strong, burning her sinuses. She stumbled into the bathroom and crouched over the toilet, thinking she might throw up.

"Oh, god." She must've gotten an extra large dose of whatever it was. Was someone getting impatient?

The door to the hallway opened. "Miss?" It was the older servant woman, sounding tentative.

"I'm all right. Get Clora."

"Yes, miss."

She hung over the toilet until Clora was beside her, a hand on Marlee's back. "Gods, are you ill? Or is it the drug?"

"Drug."

"From breakfast yesterday? Almost a whole day?"

"I guess. I don't see how I could've had any after that." Marlee closed her eyes and swallowed. "I was really careful."

"Certainly not from dinner." Clora had taken the carriage into town to pick something up from a random restaurant. "Did you have anything at tea?"

"Just tea with a little cream. I poured, and Elga had hers from the same pot and cream pitcher. Help me back to bed. I'm a little dizzy."

Clora pulled her up. "Then it had to be someone who made your breakfast. We'll tell your grandfather and he'll sure enough find out who it was, who they're working for."

"No, we can't." Marlee lay back on the bed and put her arm over her eyes. "I can't risk anyone wondering whether the drug affected me. They might start putting things together. Something weird I said, or the time I had no idea what they were talking about then pretended I was kidding, or we passed in the hall and I didn't seem to know them. If anyone tests me, I'm dead meat. Man, it feels like someone's pounding nails into my head. Little ones, but still."

"You could have some of your poppy medicine."

"Yes, please. How long before our train?"

Clora's footsteps went toward the bathroom. "We leave here in about an hour. You're still going?" Pipes clanked as she turned on the faucet.

"Of course. I need to talk to Harrick, and it'll get me the hell out of here before anyone has a chance to sneak me more drugs. We can buy food in the station, right?"

"Yes. How much of this do I use? Never mind, the label says. Here, sit up and drink this. Did you have a vision this time, too?"

The vision. Physical discomfort had distracted her from it, but now she remembered. Panic rose in her throat. A little water went down the wrong way, and she set the glass aside, coughing.

"It wasn't—" She coughed again. "Wasn't a true vision, I think. All fuzzy."

"Is that how you can tell which are real?"

"How the—cough—should I know?" Now other visions or dreams hovered vaguely at the edge of recollection. Had she seen Bobby driving his car in a snowstorm? Her old room at home? Her spirit might've been wandering all night, with only the last bit clearly remembered. "This one couldn't be real."

"Oh?" Clora paused. "All right then. Can I send in Miss Yrenn? She'll need time to do you up for the trip, and even for you, they won't hold the train."

"In ten minutes. No, five." Marlee suddenly didn't want time to sit around and reflect. She should be up and doing. "She can come now."

THE TRAIN STATION WAS HUGE. confusing. The central dome was full of stairs, scattered with filigree-enclosed glass columns filled with bubbling liquid—functional, or just decorative? There were kiosks selling newspapers, tobacco and various intoxicants, food stalls, a seller of hats, cloaks, and umbrellas....

Marlee had no idea how to find their platform, so it was fortunate she was being wheeled about by Clora, with a gang of four burly guards to push the crowds aside for them. Marlee pretended to be engrossed in a financial report, leaving Bylamar to lead the way.

He led them to an elevator, just large enough for three plus the operator, a skinny teenage boy in a blue-and-silver suit with sleeves a little too short to cover his knobby wrists. As they rose, the guards kept pace with them on the stairs that curved around the elevator shaft. Marlee looked through the latticed sides at the bustle below.

"Is there a book stall in here?" she asked Bylamar.

Bylamar had pulled out his own sheaf of papers for the ride up. He looked up, pursed his lips. "I believe not. There are newsstands, of course. Did you want something to read?"

She was half-sorry she'd said anything. It had really been just to cover her nervousness. "No, I just think it might do a good business. Don't passengers want something entertaining to read on the train? Not news?"

"I would get a gazette, for the serials." Clora pushed Marlee out of the elevator, their escort re-forming around them. "Books are too expensive to buy on a whim."

"That's another thing," Marlee said. "There are more people who can read these days, but not so many who can afford books. Someone should publish small, cheap books. They could start by reprinting some popular serials, complete."

Bylamar looked unconvinced, but shrugged. "Shall I look for a small publisher you could acquire? One whose editions are already on the cheaper side, perhaps? They might be less resistant to such a change."

Hell, why not? It's not like it was her money, anyway. "Sure. Let's see what's out there."

Bylamar took a note, then looked up at the signs around them. "There's our track." He steered them through an archway, to a platform with waiting train, and to the last car before the caboose, past an armed guard who opened the door for them and stood aside.

Bylamar had said they'd use the "family car," but she hadn't known what to expect. From the outside it looked like the others, but on the inside, it must be much cushier than the rest of the train—a long room in pale blue velvet, polished wood, and brass. The seating consisted of a few undersized armchairs and a chaise. Doors at either end led to other rooms which must be smaller, perhaps a bedroom and restroom. Dr. Harrick was already in the car, standing behind a compact bar, mixing himself a drink from bottles ranged behind it on narrow glass-fronted shelves. He looked up at them and nodded.

"It seems you've made yourself at home." Bylamar's voice had a touch of frost.

"Which is fine!" Marlee signaled Clora to push her to the chaise. "I don't suppose you can make a Pepper Mill."

"Hmm." Harrick studied the shelves. "There's no Indellia, but I might manage an approximation."

Clora gave her a look. "Isn't it a little early in the day?"

"I've never understood why people say that. It's not when you start, it's whether you can stop. I just want the one, I assure you." She needed it to nerve herself for what she was about to do. "Do your best."

Clora consulted her watch pin. "There's just time for me to run out and get us some food. Did you see something you'd like?"

Two guards had followed them in—Rojais, and one she didn't know. "I can do that, miss," said Rojais.

And who knew if any of the guards had been bribed to drug her? Though she'd hate to think that of Rojais, better to be safe. "Clora knows how I like things. Did I smell frying meat as we passed the spear statue?"

"That's the nukilonas stand," Harrick said. "Probably not wholesome, but tasty. Madam, your drink."

Marlee took a sip and nodded. A little sweeter than they made it at the Crooked Dog, but it would do.

Everyone else had breakfasted, so when Clora returned, it was with food and beverages for just the two of them. She dragged up a small table and chair next to the chaise and spread their food out just as the train started moving. Nukilonas turned out to be a sloppy mixture of ham, tiny beans, lots of melted cheese, sauteed vegetables, and a great deal of bright orange spice on top. Clora used a thick green chip to mix the spice in, and scooped up a bite, washing it down with cold tea.

From her position on the chaise, Marlee had an excellent window view as they rumbled out into daylight. She'd watched trains taking to the elevated tracks from her balcony, so she knew what to expect. She put out a hand to stop her food from sliding off the table as the car slanted toward the sky.

Making up for her skipped breakfast gave her an excuse to watch the scenery and not talk, until they were on the outskirts of town. She washed down the last eye-watering bite with the last of her drink, and settled back. Bylamar looked up from a typewritten document he was making notes on. "Ready to work?"

"You are so cute." She turned to Clora. "He's like a little dog who sees a squirrel."

"Everyone's a dog these days, it seems."

"Bylamar, I'm sorry, but I have to talk with Dr. Harrick now, in private. If all you gentlemen could just retire to another room, I'd appreciate it."

Rojais stirred from his position on the wall. He looked around the carriage, swaying slightly to maintain balance. "I suppose you're safe enough in here."

"If anyone leaps up twenty feet from the ground and tries to pry a window open, I'll call out. Clora, please stay."

While the others filed out, Marlee bowed her head, hands clasped on her lap. Harrick could only be so much help to her while he didn't have full understanding of the situation, while he thought the goal was to fetch Neidra back rather than sending Marlee home. It was a risk, but to help her further, he had to know the truth.

"Well." Harrick dragged over another chair, and set his glass on their little table. "You want to prepare me for the patient? No, wait, let me guess. You're the patient." He smiled genially.

Marlee gaped at him.

His smile vanished. "What, really? It was a jest. People are always coming to me about 'my friend's' problems. You can't be in earnest."

"No, really. I'm from another world. I don't know what became of the original Marlee."

Harrick looked at them both, with an air of mixed suspicion and condescension. Then his eyes roved the luxurious car. "You seem to have managed pretty well, for a stranger to this world."

"Clora helped. I meant to say this has to stay completely secret, but you caught me by surprise."

"Rest easy. All my clients' concerns are held in confidence. So this trip is a ruse? You don't want me to examine your cousin?"

"As long as we're there, you should still try to help her. She didn't deserve what happened. As far as I know."

"As you wish. I would have to interview her anyway, to support your subterfuge. But now, regarding your case." Harrick looked her over, curiously. "We've already discussed alternate explanations—"

"I know, and I know just because memories seem real to me, doesn't make them true. But I've been testing, the way you said. I told my father's chemist about a way to improve rub—I mean, elastrin, and that worked. And I made pizza, which was tasty. And I know the real cause of scurvy, which apparently people here don't."

"What's pizza?"

Marlee described it. "It's so good that my cousin's starting a restaurant."

"Still, any cook might concoct a new dish. And you can't have had time to test your theory about scurvy—it might be wrong. All we have at the moment is a lucky guess about the elastrin." He held up a hand to forestall Marlee's response. "I know. You'll want to proceed on the assumption that you're correct. I have, as you asked, researched the matter of how one might communicate back with one's, er, home world, or call or send back a roving spirit. I've read what few papers I thought might bear on the subject, and written to other researchers—via air mail. Regrettably, as I supposed, nobody is even sure that what you describe can happen, and there were no suggestions for how to reach out to a particular person or a particular world. I can continue to look into it, but I've exhausted the list of reputable experts in the subject on Tambor, so it would require designing experiments, finding volunteers... a protracted matter. There's a good archive at the Royal University that I mean to visit. One could, of course, inquire abroad, but the rest of the world hasn't mastered scientific methods of inquiry."

Marlee was beginning to suspect she'd asked the wrong person. "What about disreputable experts?"

"Sorry?"

"You said you'd consulted the reputable experts. Might there be someone who, though not up to your standard of scientific excellence, still knows something useful?"

"I wouldn't be doing you a favor to steer you to mystics and witchy women."

"Yes you would though. I'm fairly desperate here. The hell with your experiments. Who else at least has some experience with this sort of thing?"

Harrick snorted. "If you go by unsubstantiated claims, you might as well just talk with the Haka San when you see her at court. She's supposedly visited many worlds."

"Sorry, the...."

"That religious leader from someplace in Tassicor. She's fashionable at the moment, been doing a tour of noble houses. The Queen likes her, so she's enjoyed the largess of the royal court for the last month or so, according to the papers. I don't imagine she'll leave before the prince's birthday. So many new wealthy people to meet."

Clora had been just sitting back watching, but now she spoke up, hotly. "I don't think you should say things like that about the Queen. She's devoted to Hera, and would never adopt some foreign religion."

Harrick waved a hand. "No, of course not. The old religion is the family's basis of power. The Haka San is just exotic and entertaining. Next it'll be hats with bird cages on them, or some such foolishness."

Clora's eyes narrowed, and Marlee hurriedly spoke up to avoid a fight and stay on topic. "I have some new information since we last spoke. We think someone is continuing to slip me kokoleaba."

Harrick's eyebrows twitched. He regarded her with new interest. "How was it administered?"

"It must be in my food, somehow. We haven't caught them."

"It's prepared as an infusion from the leaves of a plant. Pale orange liquid, fairly tasteless, and it doesn't take much. Not the most common, but it's a good one to dose someone unawares."

"So we know something about this person," Clora said. "Don't we? They had to have had access to a set of poison detecting dishes, to make sure they wouldn't light up for this drug. And they had to know about these drugs and choose the right one."

Marlee shrugged. "Anyone can read a book."

"Yes, but you have to know about the book first."

"It's not a secret," Harrick said. "Just obscure. Any third-year in psychology would've heard of these experiments."

"Who in my family would spend three years studying something with no connection to business?"

"That, I couldn't say. I would, however, like a full relating of your experiences since, er, arriving here, particularly your visions."

Marlee hesitated, looked at Clora, whom she still hadn't told about last night's dream. "Well... all right. But I'll need at least one more of these." She pushed her empty glass toward him.

By the time she finished talking, Harrick was tapping steepled fingers against his lips. "I'm not sure I understand the setting of that last vision."

"I think it was a cemetery."

He looked her in the eye. "You saw your parents visiting a grave site."

Marlee slugged down the rest of her drink, gazed into the glass. "I don't know. Maybe."

"You believe it was yours."

"I don't know that."

"Well." Harrick sat back. "These visions are often confusing. When experiencing other worlds without the benefit of your sensory organs, it's hard to judge the accuracy of any impressions you take away, how much comes from your memory or expectations."

"I wasn't expecting *that.*"

"No? Because I suggested it to you as a probability when we first met."

Marlee glared at him. "Has anyone ever told you that your bedside manner sucks?"

"I'm not sure what that means, but I gather you're unhappy with my frankness. I thought you were the sort of person who'd appreciate it."

"I'll work on my appreciation skills."

"Mhm. You woke with a strong sour taste this morning?"

"Sour, bitter. Nasty."

"At about seven," Clora added.

"Then you must have been dosed after eleven yesterday morning."

"It could only have been with yesterday's breakfast," Marlee said. "That was maybe half past nine."

Harrick glanced at Clora.

Marlee snorted. "Yes, she bought me dinner last night, but we're being careful now. She served it up herself. If she wants to ruin me she only has to denounce me. Plus, she knows the drug already worked, so why bother giving me more?"

"This tea you had with your sister, then."

"I didn't eat anything, I poured, and we drank from the same pot and cream pitcher. She's my sister-in-law, not my sister, by the way."

"People usually just say sister, anyway," Clora said. "But how do we know Elga didn't get a dose at the tea? I haven't talked with her this morning, did you?"

"Good point. We'll have to check with her when we get back." Marlee set her glass down with a thunk. "If she's not a mindless shell by then."

CLORA

✕⌐⌐⌐

CLORA AND BYLAMAR WAITED IN the office of the sanatorium director, while Harrick and Marlee followed the director and one of the facility's psychists to see Neidra. A surly older woman in a pale blue uniform brought in a tray of head cheese, jams, and crispbreads. Bylamar fixed himself a plate and drew a chair over to a window, taking his little lap desk out of his satchel.

Clora had picked up another serial at a stop along the way, but it was hard to be interested in the fictional mystery story while in the middle of so many real mysteries. She wandered over to the other window, looking out at the grounds, where a group of patients was exercising under the direction of another blue-uniformed staffer.

Could old Marlee really have killed Benin? Could anyone have? Nobody had suggested how, but there was a horse involved, and Marlee did know horses.

And, what was the plan Digriz was working on, to get Marlee out from under suspicion for the killing? How did he use Karina's key? He knew a lot about the rebels. Could old Marlee have set up her own kidnapping? But if so, why did they treat her like a real prisoner?

And what about the boy, Karina's secret? The obvious assumption was that he was her son. Hard for a woman to keep secret, but not an impossibility for someone who could easily afford to take an extended holiday, or a months-long business trip to the colonies. Say he was her son—hers, and who else's? Why the big secret? She wouldn't be the first woman in that situation, and could certainly afford to raise him alone. Though in her family, perhaps, that mistake might be a setback in their jockeying for position, a sign of weakness.

And of course, the big question—who was drugging Marlee? Clora liked her own theory that it had to be someone with a set of dishes to test, but they were the likeliest suspects anyway. There must be eight or nine of those sets—Josip, all his children, and a few grandchildren.

Clora looked at Bylamar, scribbling a letter with a new-fangled mechanical pen and pencil combinations. Envy—but then, she could easily afford one of those for herself, now. She smiled.

She served herself crispbread and plum jam, and leaned against the wall near Bylamar, watching his pen fly. He must know everyone in the family pretty well. Perhaps she could make some headway on at least one of the mysteries on her list.

After a moment, Bylamar must've felt her eyes on him. He finished a paragraph and looked up at her, eyebrows raised. Clora swallowed the bite she was chewing. "I was just wondering. Who in the family knows medicine? Marlee's thinking about some deal involving drugs, and she wants confidential advice."

Bylamar's sour expression said what he thought about Marlee's running business ideas by a former housemaid. "She hasn't mentioned this opportunity to me."

"I guess she will, if it turns out to be anything. Who could she ask?"

Bylamar pursed his lips. "None of the principals. But her father must have some employees in his laboratory who could help. Or, for that matter, the *shouk* she brought with her today."

"I think she wants to keep it in the family for now. It might be kind of a big deal."

"Why not just ask Elga? She sees her practically every day anyway. Isn't she close enough family?"

"She would know?"

"I'd think so. She took her green in medicine and psychology, and did post-degree work at the University here for a year or so before marrying Petro."

"Oh."

Bylamar gestured to his letter in progress. "Anything else?"

"No. No, that's plenty. Thanks."

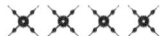

"ELGA? BUT SHE WAS ONE of, like, the three decent people in the whole family!" Marlee kept her voice down, though the rumble of the train would probably frustrate any eavesdroppers anyway.

For the return trip, the men had been banished to the main room. Clora sat beside Marlee on the narrow lower pallet of the sleeping compartment, leaning against the wall. The train's vibration came through the wall's padding. "You thought she was that pleasant? She never said a word to me at the family tea."

"Compared to some, that was pleasant."

"You have a point." Clora was touched—she'd thought Marlee too busy with the Aakol to notice. "But she doesn't have a set of those dishes, does she?"

"No, but she has access to Petro's." Marlee reached across her for the bag of toasted chestnuts they'd bought at the station. "She deliberately dosed herself as well as me. That's pretty dangerous."

"Maybe not for her. Leave me some of those, you pig. Dr. Harrick said it's dangerous if you're untrained, but she's trained. Maybe she tried them at University."

"But why? That's what I don't get. She doesn't play the family power games. All she cares about is the baby. What'd I ever do to her?"

Clora took the dark-stained bag and dumped the last few nuts into her hand. "The other Marlee might know."

"That's the story of my life. Elga's probably perfectly justified."

"So wuf—" Clora swallowed. "What will you do about it?"

"I don't know. She's got someone in the kitchen helping her, because I got dosed on Thursday even though I didn't have tea with her then. Let's go back to the apartment. No, wait. Gramps won't let me."

"Gramps?" Clora had never imagined she'd hear the Forossi patriarch referred to in that way.

"He's keeping me close until that detective decides whether I'm guilty. He's like—I'm sorry, I have to say it—like a dog who has hold of one end of a rope."

Clora smiled. "The way to get a dog to let go is to drop your end."

"Yeah, I don't think that'll work in this case. So I have to think what to do about Elga. And I want a nap. I didn't sleep well, plus it's a good excuse to avoid Bylamar." Marlee reached out her hand, then drew back. "Thanks for figuring it out. Nice work."

She looked so unhappy that Clora resisted the urge to correct the use of the word "nice"—again—and instead impulsively reached out to give her hand a squeeze. "Dr. Harrick is just guessing. I'm sure the Haka San will be able to help."

"Great, we're off to see the wizard."

"She's not a wizard." Clora stood and pulled a knitted blanket from a niche in the wall. "Come then, lie down."

She closed the door softly behind her. The train had moved into a storm, rain beating against the side, swaying slightly in the wind. Though it was only about fourteen, it was nearly dark outside, and someone had switched on the lights. These were blue, ran off the train's dynamos, and didn't need shaking. Probably the next thing people would be wanting in their houses.

Bylamar was in a corner, working as usual. Two guards hunched over the small table, playing cards with a tattered pack, and Dr. Harrick was back at the bar, concocting something in a small glass from several open bottles. Clora leaned against the bar to watch.

Harrick nodded. He took a small sip, and added a dash from an opaque white bottle. "Can I make you something?"

"I only have a little wine sometimes." Two weeks ago she would've said beer. Clora looked around. Bylamar was settled at the far end of the car, close to Marlee's door if she should call. "Marlee says you didn't let her sit in when you interviewed Neidra."

"No. I could see I wouldn't get anything out of her with Marlee present. Definite fear there."

"Fear of Marlee? Could Marlee have, have caused her condition?"

"I couldn't discuss the details of the case."

"But Marlee's paying you."

"Even so. What's said in a consultation is private." He paused. "I can say, since she clearly recognized Marlee, Neidra hasn't been switched with someone from a different plane."

It was frustrating to know no more than this, but Clora had to admit it was mainly curiosity that drove her. It seemed unlikely to have a bearing on Marlee's current problems. "Do you think you can help her?"

"Perhaps. Some things, only time can aid. I'll consult further with the facility's director by post, come out again from time to time if your mistress wishes to pursue it."

Clora glanced at the guards, still absorbed in their game, and spoke quietly. "I worry about your other patient. She seems discouraged."

"I'm sorry I had no better news for her. But she'll ultimately be happiest if she accepts facts. If she really is from elsewhere—still much in question—it's quite clear there's no going back."

"But you could at least help her get a message to her family."

"I'm willing to try. It's a fascinating case, an excellent opportunity for study. I hope that she'll eventually permit me to write up my findings for the Society."

"So you're going next to look at those archives?"

"Your mistress instructed me to set off immediately. By the time you arrive, I'll have had enough of a look around to give a preliminary report."

"What, we're to meet you there?"

"You're going there anyway. The Royal University is, of course, in the capital, so we'll meet in Paroona."

MARLEE

XLIV

THE STORM WAS STILL GOING strong, wind whistling around the corners of the carriage. As it rolled through the gate of the big house, the two fresh guards who'd met them at the station jumped from their outside seats to check in at the little brick guard station. When the carriage reached the portico, the wind was so strong that the rain blew in beneath it. A tall manservant ran out with a huge umbrella to help them into the house.

Marlee stood shaking water from her skirts just inside the hallway. "Is Elga here?"

The servant folded the umbrella and set it in a canister by the door. "I believe Miss Elga is in her chambers."

"And Petro?"

"Not yet returned from the city, I believe, miss."

"Perfect." She started to give her handbag to Clora, then changed her mind. It contained her little pistol. She didn't plan to use it, but it never hurt to have it handy. "I'll see you in my room in a bit."

Marlee let herself into Elga's rooms unannounced. Rain drummed on the tall windows, and the room was dark except for a work light at the table where Elga sat, the same table where they'd had tea earlier.

Marlee wasn't sure what her own face was showing, but whatever it was made Elga look alarmed for a bare instant before that expression smoothed away into mild surprise, as if she were just wondering why Marlee had decided to show up suddenly.

The table was taken up with a partitioned tray containing glass beads, spools of wire and little tools. A half-finished necklace rested in a groove along the edge. "Don't let me disturb you. I only came for this." Marlee detoured around the table to get to the sideboard, picking up the tea container. It was from somewhere in Tassicor, maybe, a lightweight lacquered wooden cylinder painted with a thorny tree and bird in silhouette. She'd seen a similar thing in an import shop. "This is where you keep the kokoleaba, right?"

Elga should never attempt any plots. The fear on her face was plain to read. "I don't know what you're talking about."

She could offer to brew a cup for little Josip, asleep in a hammock in the corner. But it wasn't really necessary. "This is such a pathetic plot, I assume my brother doesn't know about it, or he'd have put a stop to it. It ends now. Tell your helper in the kitchen to quit. By which I mean, quit their job and get as far away from here as possible. I hope you paid them well."

"What will you do?" Elga couldn't keep a tremor out of her voice.

"Right now, nothing. I don't care to annoy Petro at the moment." Marlee raised the tea container. "But if I have even the smallest problem from you again, I'll take this to Josip and we'll have it tested. It'll be easy to figure out where you got the stuff. It's not like they sell it on the street corners."

"From what I hear, Josip's likely to kill you himself." A note of defiance.

"He might, but I'm pretty sure he wouldn't like anyone else trying." Marlee took a few steps toward the door, then turned back. "I'm disappointed in you."

And she was. As she walked back to her chambers, it was hard to fight back tears. She'd gone in with a fine head of steam, to scare Elga into backing off permanently. But now her anger turned against old Marlee, for whatever she'd done to back Elga into a corner. Wishing she dared ask why. Wishing she believed Elga could keep a secret well enough to be let in on hers.

With the weather and onset of evening, she'd expected her room to be dark, but when she opened her door, every light in the room was lit, with a few extra floor lamps added, and the middle was taken up by a long table strewn with clothing, which Clora, seated on the bed, was flipping through.

There was also a dress standing on a wire mannequin. The dress was spectacular. Golden silk in folds and folds, with swirling patterns of amber beads across the front, around the low neckline, down the sleeves. Miss Yrenn's head poked out from behind it. "Good! I am just arranging it. You must try it on. I believe it's acceptable."

"Acceptable" was inadequate. It was magnificent, almost too lovely to consider wearing. Though Marlee was pretty sure she could bring herself to do it.

Two other dresses, less elaborate, had been laid across the tables—one in smoky brown velvet, and another of silk, ruby red shading into black. There was also a sharp-looking riding outfit, a variety of jackets and blouses, and the usual ridiculous profusion of undergarments.

Were they packing all her things for the trip right now? They weren't leaving for another three days. Back on Earth, she'd never started packing more than four hours before a trip. But then, this world's Marlee had backup plans for her backup plans. Of course she'd want to make sure everything was ready well in advance.

Marlee stood behind the wire dress mannequin to look into her large mirror. A good color for her. "I suppose it will do."

Miss Yrenn grinned. "You cannot fool old Yrenn. You love it. You see I was right to insist on garnets."

Eek, these irregularly-shaped beads were gemstones? How much had this cost? Weren't garnets supposed to be red? "Is this everything for the trip? I want my new Boraggan style outfit."

Miss Yrenn frowned. "I saw that. Unsuitable for court. Trashy metal disks all jangling. One does not wear, er, noisy pantaloons for the King."

"I'm sure I won't be with him the whole time. We're bringing it."

Miss Yrenn tsked, and gave Clora a significant look, but took the despised garment from the wardrobe. Clora meanwhile rummaged through the gilt-lacquered cabinet across the room, piling more items on the bed.

Marlee walked around the bed to get out of their way. Two large trunks stood open on the floor, and an openwork rack near the wall for hanging things.

"We try these on now." Miss Yrenn picked up the brown dress. "To see whether adjustments are required. In the morning, we look at the colors again in proper light, to be certain. But they are good. Here, girl, help your mistress undress."

The new dresses all fit perfectly, and Yrenn finally left. Marlee plopped her butt onto the bed and looked over the items piled there. Besides the various layers of clothing, her gun case was there, and a travel kit of toiletries including a clever folding hair brush, a flat box which turned out to be a portable desk with little fitted compartments for various accessories and stacks of stationery. There was also a mesh bag of the lint-padded sticks that were this world's dismaying best answer to the tampon. With luck, she'd get home before she had the embarrassment of having to ask Clora what exactly she was supposed to do with them. "Will all this really fit in the trunks?"

Clora looked around from rooting through a drawer. "Oh, I'll make it fit, with room to spare. What happened with Elga?"

"We have an understanding."

"So it was her? But why?"

"I don't know. It doesn't matter. It comes down to I'm evil, and she's scared of me."

EDSGAR

XLV

DIGRIZ PAUSED IN THE THE doorway, as usual, scanning the taproom for anyone he knew. And he did see someone, a gentleman who'd helped him sell a few things he'd acquired by irregular means, at his usual corner table, facing the door as always.

The fence saw him, too, and gave a little headshake. Digriz paused for not a second, taking a quick look at who else was in the room as he backed into the entryway and outside, grabbing his rain cloak from the peg as he passed.

The burly fellow of upright bearing with a large half-full glass of beer gone totally flat, that was probably a policeman, nursing one drink for hours while waiting for a regular to come in. It would take him a few seconds to follow Digriz onto the street, especially if the patrons, few of whom had any love for the law, contrived to insert a few chairs into his path.

Digriz took off for the farther corner, crossing the street diagonally. He had just time to make it, and didn't care whether the few people about saw him running. If the officer had to choose a direction to give chase, he'd probably try a nearer corner first. Once out of sight, Digriz slowed to a rapid walk to quiet his steps. A giant boot hung above a shop door a few paces ahead—a good place to get off the street.

The establishment sold factory-made shoes, not bespoke. This was fortunate, since he didn't want someone bustling right over to help. Unfortunately, it also had a huge display window, making him easily visible from the street. He turned away from the window and squatted to examine a lower shelf of lady's boots, with the new clip fastenings instead of buttons.

The sole clerk on duty set his newspaper and pipe aside and came to stand behind Digriz. He was an older man, wizened and thin, wispy haired. "May I assist?"

Polite, but not anxious. Probably the owner, or the owner's father, happy to make a sale but with no cause to fear for his job.

Digriz fingered an ankle boot in practical red leather. "I'm considering a gift for a lady."

The old man sized him up, assessing the fit and quality of his garments. "That there shelf are thirty centimes a pair. Will the lady come in to be fitted?"

"Ah, good point." Seeing the shoes had reminded him of Clora's mother, who was owed a pair by Marlee. She deserved an appreciation for her help in managing his escape, and even if Marlee delivered on her promise, in his experience few women, regardless of age or circumstances, felt they already had enough shoes. He looked up at the shopkeeper. "Perhaps I could bring her tomorrow."

A movement outside the window drew his eye, a broad shoulder, a head turning to survey the street. Digriz turned back to the shelf, moving to put the shopkeeper between himself and the window, pretending to examine a different pair.

There was a soft sound of fabric brushing against fabric as the old man turned to look at the street. Digriz tensed, wondering whether he'd have to push him aside and run for it.

The old man cleared his throat. "You and your lady friend are, of course, welcome any time we're open. However, we have a special deal available, which might interest you. Today only, the use of our back door, which leads to a small inner courtyard opening to the next street over, is only ten centimes."

Digriz grinned, and fished a coin from his purse, laying it on the shelf.

"Just through that doorway, turn left and go straight back. Thank you for your business, sir, and Hephaestus bless you." He moved over to the window, rearranging the display, while Digriz nipped out. The arrangements in the rear were as promised, and he lost no time in putting steps between himself and the officer.

Why were they looking for him? They would certainly want to question the fictional Lorezzo about Marlee's rescue, now two days past. But he now wore his own face, which shouldn't be wanted in connection with anything.

Unless, of course, someone had mentioned him. Three people knew of his involvement—Elinora, Chalula, and Clora. Marlee would surely have cautioned them to silence, but with the possible exception of Chalula, they were unschooled in deception, and the police might have gotten his name from them. It had been a risk, but one he'd had no choice about.

Or, Tanni the Fist might've been arrested for killing the warden, and given the police Digriz's name in a misguided attempt to save his own skin. This chilling thought brought him to a momentary halt. Tanni should've been hundreds of miles away by now, but the man wasn't noted for following good advice.

If Tanni, it would be best to drop everything and head back to his native land immediately. But if they just wanted to question him about his role in Marlee's rescue, he would be all right eventually. He could say he knew a lot of people—quite true—and that the mysterious Lorezzo was among them. Lorezzo had bragged to him that he knew everyone in the rebel underground and what they were doing, so when they took Marlee, naturally he went right to this fellow and offered him a large reward—for which he expected to be reimbursed—to go rescue her. Of course, he had no idea where to find the mysterious Lorezzo now.

The police would be unhappy about that. Though they could prove nothing against Digriz, it might be several days before he was freed. But those, unfortunately, were days he urgently needed for other purposes.

He needed to get off the street. It wasn't certain how wide a net the police had cast for him, but a pale, long-haired foreigner stood out in this city. He had a choice of two faces, and while both were sought by the police, the visage of Lorezzo, the Night Wind, had been specifically designed to be unmemorable, with a description matching a large swath of the population. It was probably the lesser risk.

Too bad he couldn't just create a new face. It took weeks of practice before a mirror to get it right, and until it was "worn in," it would have an inexplicable creepy quality which drew attention, especially the attention of police, who were trained to spot them. Even reviving an old out-of-practice face would take longer than he had to spare.

Applying a disguise spell was unfortunately much more difficult than removing it, requiring privacy, decent light, and a mirror. The safe house he'd left Lily at would have those, and wasn't far. Lily hadn't been there when he returned yesterday. If she'd returned, well, he'd deal with that if he had to.

He'd been most careful to avoid connecting these two parts of his life, so at the proper time the Night Wind could simply vanish permanently with no evidence connecting him. Approaching the safe house in his own skin made his hair stand, magnified every noise.

The door was down a brick passage that let onto multiple dwellings, chosen because it was easy to see whether there was anyone else in the passage or watching it, in which case one could simply move on. There was no-one, and Digriz quickly entered the combination to unlock the door. He slipped inside and closed it softly, pausing to listen.

The place seemed abandoned. He moved quickly down the hallway, into the bathroom. He shut and locked this door, and breathed easier. In case there was anyone here, now they would only find a closed bathroom door, from which would eventually emerge the Night Wind, who had every right to be there.

THE NIGHT WIND HAD ACCESS to certain resources which Edsgar Digriz did not. A few policemen were members of the movement, and it was one of these Digriz tracked down on his regular foot patrol that evening, a young man walking along jauntily, truncheon bobbing at his side. The officer glanced at him curiously when Digriz came up beside him. Digriz gave the current recognition signal, and the officer gave the countersign and looked at him curiously. "I don't know you."

"That's to the good, I think."

"We was asked to keep sharp for someone looks like you. You were in on that thing with the Forossi woman, eh?"

"Yes. We lost two people, but I managed to rescue one of our sisters."

"The story was kind of mixed up. I heard you helped rescue the bitch."

"What a fantasy! No, I heard about the whole thing late. My source told me the Seidos knew where she was being taken. I went to warn them, and got there barely ahead of the police. I and another were captured, and the Forossi woman wanted to take us back for her own people to question. Fortunately, we escaped."

The officer shuddered. "I shouldn't like to answer questions for that lot."

"Exactly. We shouldn't talk too long. Act like you're giving me directions."

The officer pointed up the street. "What you want, then?"

"Were you asked to look for a tall pale-skinned foreigner, also?"

"Aye, and tell Sergeant Dettrick if we saw him. Wanted for questioning."

"Is Dettrick on the Forossi thing?"

"Aye."

Elinora or Chalula must have mentioned him to the detective. "Anything else happening?"

"Nothing out of the normal. Couple break-ins, drunks fighting, as they will do. Oh, we picked up Tanni the Fist for a killing. Reckon he'll swing for it this time."

Digriz found it hard to breathe for a moment. "Oh? What's the story there? Don't forget you're giving directions."

"Ay, right." The officer pointed again, mimed turning right. "About what you'd expect. Had a huge bender, got in a brawl, stabbed some poor soul with a piece of glass, I think it was, and had the crap luck to hit an artery. Cut up his own hand pretty awful, too. I saw him when they brought him in."

No mention of the game warden, a small relief. Still, given what Tanni knew, Digriz would much rather he be far away, anyway.

"Funny thing is, Tanni hired an advocate. Not a fancy one, but still. Don't know where he got the coin, but whomever he took it from ain't complained yet, so the desk officer said look for more deaders."

"All right, that doesn't sound like any concern of ours. What about the shooting the other night? Someone tried to kill Marlee Forossi?"

"Huh. With all the ruckus since, I nigh forgot about that. I don't know if they got any leads. They wouldn't be telling me. Did we do that?"

"Better you don't know."

"Too bad they missed, is all."

"Thanks, brother." Digriz raised his voice a little. "So it's this way, right on Milk Street, left on Seventh, at the sign of the rooster?"

"You can't miss it, sir." The officer touched his chin in farewell and went on his way.

So. Things weren't as bad as he'd feared. Still, he couldn't go home, since it was probably being watched. Inconvenient, since operations were in a sensitive state. He'd have to tell Marlee to use an alternate contact method if she needed to reach him. Fortunately, this was easy enough to do. He looked at his watch. If he could find a stationer in the next ten minutes, he could make the last post.

CLORA

XLVI

CLORA BLINKED SLEEP-DEPRIVED EYES and pushed her book aside. She stood, feeling a little creaky, and sneaked around her Ma's bed to look outside at the brightening sky. Though she couldn't see it from this side, the sun was up, lighting the tall stack of the laboratory building and its plume of green smoke.

The two-volume set on magic Marlee had bought from Fillerner's turned out to cover much the same ground as the book from her secret cupboard—using many more words to do it. Still, she'd gone through both volumes in one long sitting, gleaning a few scraps of new information.

She'd been hoping for something more along the lines of a how-to manual, but both works had been heavy on theory, the few specific spells just by way of illustrating a general principle.

Did she dare try any of it? It was clear she had a lot to learn before she could do anything of significance. The mathematics was far beyond what she'd been taught at the King's School, and spells seemed to rely a lot on languages nobody had spoken for centuries—partly, she gathered, to help the practitioner into the right mindset by being different from any language they might use for regular communication, but also, she suspected, as deliberate obfuscation, to make it all look more complicated than it was. There was a lot to know, and it required a weird way of thinking about things, to see the connections and consequences. But she could follow the examples, once she got the hang of the mental trick involved.

So, could she try a simple spell? It was a little silly and over-proud of her to suppose it could really be as easy as it appeared, but a couple of example spells in the first book looked reasonable—possible to fail, but not dangerous if they did.

Approaching the book casually, as if she could sneak up on it, she flipped to the page she'd chosen. The spell diagram was done using Worrian pictograms, a good language for beginners since meaning tied in with the appearance of the symbols. She re-read the description on the facing page.

The practitioner in the example was age forty, three months, twenty days—a hint she'd have to adjust for her own age, but how? This was something she was apparently supposed to already know. She licked her lips, and reached across the table for paper and pencil.

CLORA'S ARMS WERE FULL, SO SHE pushed down the handle to Marlee's room with her elbow and leaned against the door to open it. The room was empty, but through the balcony doors she could see someone's shadow, so she hurried out to share her news, but stopped short in the doorway—Marlee had company.

"I don't know what you're complaining about." Marlee's back was to the door. "You've got your key back, your boy is safe, and I promise never to use him against you again. A deal's a deal."

The other person at the table, Karina, gave Clora a look of pure poison. She stood, her movements abrupt, and carefully pushed her chair in. She nodded at Clora—a short, sharp nod—and pushed past into the bedroom.

Marlee grimaced. The door to the hallway slammed. "Oops. I didn't see you come in."

"I should've called out."

"Still, no harm done. You already knew about that stuff."

Clora pushed aside the clutter of dishes at the other end of the table, and set her things down. "Yes, but I've been real careful to not let Miss Karina know I knew."

"Oh. Not so good, then. Still, she can't do anything about it."

Not, Clora thought, so long as you're around.

"What is all this stuff you've got? You look like hell, by the way. Were you up all night?"

"I'll nap later. I want to show you something. And don't say looks like hell. If you want to compliment my appearance, you can say I look like cat-kill." Clora laid out her materials—three glasses, a blank sheet of paper, green chalk, and charcoal. She touched the glasses in turn. "Salt. Water. Salty water." Or was it? She took a little sip from the third glass, then switched the last two. "Watch, and marvel."

Marlee sat back and grinned. "Nothing up your sleeve?"

Clora looked at her sleeves. "Um. Arms? Why?"

"Never mind. Proceed."

Clora closed her eyes, picturing the symbols. Meaning and intention. Symbol is substance. She opened her eyes, took the chalk and drew, first the curvy enclosing shape, then the symbols, focusing in until they were all she saw. Meaning and intention. She placed the salt water in the center of the diagram, picked up the charcoal, and scraped a dusting into the glass with her fingernail. A little charcoal dust into the other two glasses, too. Then she raised the glass of water and the glass containing a little mound of salt, and clinked them together.

Instantly, the salty water turned cloudy, then a snowfall of tiny crystals settled to the bottom, leaving it clear again.

"Wow. That will be so useful at court. I can't tell you how pleased I am that you spent a day and a half learning that before our trip, which starts tomorrow, by the way."

"You have to admit it's pretty...." Clora looked carefully at Marlee. "You're not really upset, are you? It's hard to tell sometimes."

Marlee sighed. "No, I'm just stressed. There's no point in you sitting around watching me read all day just to answer the occasional question. I made a list." Marlee stood, and went inside.

"Aren't you supposed to spare that knee?"

"It's a lot better. And yes, your trick is pretty amazing. That sort of thing doesn't work back home."

"Magic works differently there?"

"Magic doesn't work at all there." Marlee returned with two pieces of paper. "Some folks claim it does, but none of them can demonstrate it like you just did. I think they're fooling themselves."

"That's so odd. Do you have something else instead of magic?"

"Nothing you would want. Did you have breakfast? I'll go ask them to bring you something while you look that over."

Clora scanned the list. "I don't have answers to most of these. I've never been to court."

"Then we'll have to hope I seem eccentric rather than ignorant. Be right back."

The second paper wasn't a continuation of Marlee's list, but a flimsy post-office foldover, addressed to Marlee and blank on the inside but for a single word, periann, and a bunch of numerals. Everything was written in block letters. Thinking of messages written in invisible ink, she tilted it into the sun, but there was no suggestion of any other marks.

"I don't know what that's about." Marlee sat. "I had such a backlog, I didn't see when it arrived."

Clora pointed out the postmark. "This morning. Did you ask Bylamar?"

"No, how could I? I don't see a quarter of the mail that's addressed to me. If this got through his filter, there must be a reason."

"A periann is a kind of hawk."

"It must be a codeword, probably from Digriz. I wrote asking him to drop by."

"Well, he won't. The police are looking for him. The sergeant, the one with a face like a sheep, kept asking me questions about him."

"Why do they want him? I told the others not to mention him. You didn't say anything to the police, did you?"

"No, I said Lorezzo approached us and claimed to know where you were." Clora paused, experiencing a sinking sensation. "Oh. Cruft. It's my fault. Karina was after me to explain it, saying you'd set up the kidnapping yourself, and I got flustered. I said he found out where you were."

Marlee set a cup down sharply on its saucer, breathed out heavily.

"I'm sorry! She's scary!"

Marlee shut her eyes for a moment. "Well, it's done. If anyone asks you about it, deny it. It's too bad, though. I wanted him to explain the whole plot to you, so you could explain it to me."

"I'll try to find him. I have to go out anyway, so I'll stop by his place." Clora handed the note back, and picked up the list. "Now. Let's see which of these I can answer."

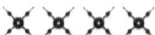

IT WAS LIKE HALOIA, ONLY with better presents. Clora had commandeered a steamless carriage and driver. Even drawing Kraik as her driver, and her mother insisting on coming along, didn't eclipse her joy. She was making the rounds of the stores.

During their brief stay in the apartment, Marlee had taken Clora to be measured and to order scandalously expensive clothing, knowing the trip to the capital was coming. Now, with their departure imminent, Clora was picking those garments up. At each store, she tried things on, and any final adjustments were done on the spot, while Ma commented, asked questions, scrutinized the buttons and the stitching, and generally made herself annoying and embarrassing.

It didn't matter. Resting beside Clora on the car seat was a tall stack of boxes of things made just for her, much finer than she'd ever expected to own, wrapped in colorful store papers.

Even Ma was well satisfied with the haul. "You'll look real pretty at court. You know how to behave, there, and do credit to your Ma?"

Clora patted her mother's knee. "Don't you worry. Just this morning I had a long chat with Miss Yrenn. She's been there many times, and she answered all my questions." Which conveniently included most of Marlee's list, as well.

The carriage came to a stop, and Ma leaned over to look out the window. "What now? More hats?"

"Not hats. Books." Kraik was supposed to come around and open the door for her, but experience had taught her not to wait for that. Clora reached for the handle. "Want to come in?"

"Books?" Ma sniffed. "I don't think so."

"I might be a bit, and they bring you wine and cheese and things while you wait."

Ma stood. "Just to keep you company, then. I tell you, though, them hats you got is too small. You should have something grander."

"I know a professor who has interesting ideas for hats. You should talk."

CLORA'S FINAL STOP WAS DIGRIZ'S apartment building. She left her mother in the carriage. There was no answer when she pounded on his door, so she went back down to the entryway, maneuvering around a wide youth lounging on the stairs. She looked through the window of Digriz's mail drop. There were several envelopes, and she couldn't tell whether Marlee's note was among them. "Don't you ever pick up your mail?" She slipped her own note into the slot.

When she stood, the wide youth was standing beside her. He rattled a candy against his teeth. "You lookin' fer Mister Die Griz?"

"Do you know where he is?"

"Naw. I want im too. I was told off to wait here. If you see im, give im this?" The lad took a small stack of cards from his shirt pocket and thumbed one off to hand her. "The man ud like to talk with him about his pal Tanni."

It was too dark in the entry to read the card. Clora dropped it into her purse. "If you see him, tell him..." She didn't want to leave a name. "Never mind." If Digriz came here, he'd pick up his mail anyway.

The boy shrugged, scratched his nose, and resumed his post on the stairs.

EDSGAR

XLVII

HE PAUSED BEFORE THE CLOSED bedroom door. He didn't want
an outcry, as might occur if the occupant decided there was an intruder in
the house. On the other hand, he also wanted the fellow in a reasonably
good mood. Waking up with a hand clamped over one's mouth and someone hissing, "Be quiet," he had found, rarely put someone in a co-operative
frame of mind. So he raised his fist and knocked, softly. Then when there
was no response, a little harder.

The snoring within stopped. "Wha—Who's that?"

"Edsgar Digriz. You sent for me, so come out and talk."

There was a pause. "What are you doing in my house? I do have a door
chime. And business hours, for that matter."

"I apologize. I mean you no harm, but I couldn't come in the front door,
or in daylight. I'm quite sure your place is being watched. Your back door
was unlocked, so I came in." This last was technically true, in that the door
was unlocked once he had picked the lock. He hadn't wanted to pound on
it and risk disturbing any neighbors, or their dogs.

"Go down to my office, then. I'll just be a moment."

"No lights, if you please." Digriz carefully descended the darkened
staircase, and found a room with a pedestal desk and a few armchairs. He
took a chair within the moonlight beaming through the front window, and
in a short time, the advocate came in, standing in the dark and presumably
looking at him. Digriz did his best to look harmless.

The advocate stayed in the doorway, still in darkness. "Why do you believe the police are watching my house?"

"I heard from three separate people that you were looking for me. I'm sure the police heard, also, and they too, want to speak to me. I don't know why you didn't just buy space on the front page of the newspaper."

He came further into the room, and sat in another chair, half in darkness. He was a small man, middle-aged, sharp-looking, with protruding eyes and a goatee that did little to disguise his lack of a chin. "You're not easy to find."

"Ordinarily, I make myself available to all, but the police believe I had a role in the rescue of Miss Forossi, and they wish to thank me down at the station. I'm a humble man, and do not desire public acclamation. Moreover, it isn't convenient to my schedule at present. Still, I try to help where I can, so when I heard you urgently desired to speak with me, of course I came. It's about Tanni Keddar, I gather."

"Yes. I represent him in the matter of his recent arrest."

"I'm a bit puzzled. Tanni and I are mere acquaintances, and since I have no knowledge of the incident, I couldn't provide any useful testimony."

"Mr. Keddar thinks you can make these charges go away. He tells me you have friends in high places."

Digriz raised an eyebrow. "I have a wide and... varied social circle, but nobody I could impose on to such an extent. And I certainly don't possess the funds myself, nor am owed sufficient favors, to influence the outcome of a capital case. Moreover, I barely know your client. Why should I exert myself?"

"Mr. Keddar said I should remind you of a job of work he did for you recently. Should he be sentenced to die, he means to relate the particulars to the authorities."

That's what Digriz had been afraid of. They couldn't hang Tanni twice, so once sentenced for the other crime, he'd have nothing to lose by confessing all. He gave a show of thinking it over. "I have no idea what your client is referring to."

"He didn't provide details, but he seemed to assume you'd know what he was talking about."

"And I'm surprised you would be a party to extortion. Is bribing officials a usual legal tactic for you?"

"I don't believe I mentioned bribery. That was your interpretation. I'm quite sure Mr. Keddar simply expected you to convince the Crown Prosecutor that death was too harsh a sentence for a simple mishap arising from high spirits and an excess of... celebration. I'm sorry you view this as extortion. It's simply that, if he is to die, Mr. Keddar has certain things he'd want to get off his conscience."

"Or perhaps, in desperation, he's fabricated some tale and involved you in his slanders. Well. Many of my dealings are of a confidential nature. However fictional, I wouldn't care for the attention his story would bring. And I do think the punishment is over harsh." Digriz stood, picking up his gloves from the chair arm. "Tell him I'll do what I can for him, but I can promise nothing."

The advocate also stood. "We must all do what we can, and greatly hope it will be enough. I'll see you out the back." He led the way down the hallway. "It's odd. I felt quite certain I'd locked that door."

"Funny how one's mind can play tricks. By the way, I'd get a better lock if I were you. I recommend Kobos."

Digriz recrossed the neighbor's yard, avoiding a rosebush with which he'd had a dispute before, and walked several blocks before seeing a cab. He rode to Veterans' Park, and walked down its shadowed paths to the fountain in the center, which was shut off for the night. He sat on a particular bench, leaned forward and felt around under the seat.

His fingers found a fine thread. He tugged it free, and brought out the rolled-up paper tied to it. Without unrolling it, he could tell it was the same one he'd left, but he opened it anyway to see whether a reply had been added, using a tiny glow stick from his waistcoat pocket to read it.

Just his original coded message giving time and place for a meeting. A meeting she'd missed. She must be finding it hard to get out. Undoubtedly, after that strange rescue, she was under scrutiny. Inconvenient, but there'd been no choice. Getting killed would've put an even greater crimp in her plans.

So, was the plan still on? Another incident involving the rebels so soon, might be too risky when suspicions were already aroused. Now he had a second urgent reason to talk with her—the matter of Tanni. But she'd be leaving early the next day. He tucked the note into his pocket. He'd have to assume the plan was unchanged for now, and try to reach her at court.

MARLEE

XLVIII

THE FAMILY WENT TO THE dirigible mast in ones and twos, to make a less obvious and less tempting target for potential bomb-throwers. Marlee and Josip arrived near the end, cutting ahead of a long line of waiting passengers for other flights. They received glares, but no explosives.

The cage had seating for twenty people, but they and the guards had it to themselves. It jerked into motion, and Marlee sat abruptly, grabbing an armrest. Her knee gave a twinge, and she flexed it.

The openwork sides gave an excellent view of the city, in the gaps between diagonal girders, as it rose, and rose. Marlee swallowed. She'd had no problem with heights in her previous life. In fact, she'd been bungee jumping and enjoyed the high dive. But she was having a problem now. The mast swayed slightly, but unmistakably, in the brisk wind, and Marlee's head spun—her heart raced.

Rationally, it had to be perfectly safe. Thousands of people rode the damned thing every day. She opened her eyes, looked up. The other cage rushed down toward them. She closed her eyes. At least the floor was opaque.

The cage halted near the top, and Josip walked briskly out, cane sounding on the metal floor. He looked back at her, and she swallowed and stood.

The guards didn't accompany them onto the ring-shaped platform, which unfortunately was not opaque. The wind shifted slightly, and the outer wall moved, oiled rollers trundling a few inches along a track at the edge of the floor.

"Just a little way now." Josip sounded impatient. "If you flew more often, you'd get accustomed to it, and it wouldn't be a problem."

"If I didn't do it at all, it wouldn't be a problem either."

Josip snorted, and ducked through an opening in the outer wall, clattering along a suspended walkway with walls of flexible fencing, like chain-link. The dirigible waited beyond, white with a blue stripe, the catwalk leading to a gondola the size of a large house, snugged up beneath the huge gasbag. It seemed an impossible distance to the other end of the catwalk.

"Coming?"

Taking a deep breath, Marlee hurried along the catwalk, catching up with Josip as he reached its end. As a crewman reached out to help him aboard, Marlee distracted herself from looking down by looking at the wall of the gondola. Disturbingly, it seemed to be made of wicker. She'd overheard someone in the station mention the "basket" of the ship, but she hadn't realized it was meant quite so literally.

It was still a better choice than standing out here in the cutting wind, though. When the crew member reached out for her, she gladly let herself be pulled through the hatch. The wall was about two and a half inches thick, and the wind didn't blow through it as she'd expected. The flooring was also wicker, heavily coated with a clear varnish, but felt firm enough. The vessel did, however, creak as the wind changed, shifting on its mooring, and Marlee put a hand on the wall for support.

The crewman was a slight olive-skinned man with fine, springy black hair lightly touched with gray. His white uniform suited him exceedingly well. "Your trunks are already in your rooms." He led them down a curving passage with frequent round windows showing glimpses of city and bay. Marlee stayed close to the opposite wall. "Miss Forossi, you're in cabin seventeen. It has a good view, as you prefer."

Josip laughed. "Who told you that?"

The crewman looked confused. "Um, thin woman, with a pointy nose? Was I misinformed?"

"Karina," Marlee said. "Very droll."

"We could make a change, miss, if you like. There are several empty cabins this trip."

If Josip hadn't been there, she would've gladly accepted. "It'll be fine, I'm sure. Thanks."

"Very well, and you're in nineteen, sir. The mandatory safety briefing is in ten minutes in the dining area, right through here. Until then, and after, there are drinks and snacks in the bar."

Marlee looked into the bar, where most of the family was standing in little groups, and wandered around the craft for a few minutes, finding her cabin and the bathrooms. The vessel was busy with last-minute preparations for departure, several crew members hurrying past in the corridors, carrying bundles, boxes or clipboards.

When Marlee entered the dining area, Clora waved her over to the empty chair beside her. "I never been on one of these before. Isn't it a wonder?"

"It's certainly memorable. How long is this trip again?"

"Two thousand miles in just a day and bit, depending on wind."

"Wouldn't a train be faster?"

"No, and this can go straight there." Clora flipped through a little brochure and opened it to a map page with routes shown in dashed lines. "We just fly over the mountains and the wastes, see?"

Marlee took the brochure and flipped through, noting floor plans and schedules, until the crewman she'd met earlier blew a whistle. People filtered in from the bar, filling seats at the little round tables. Finally, a woman entered wearing a crew uniform with extra gold braid and bars on the sleeve. She stood in the doorway, looking around the room. She was a foreigner, light skinned and brown haired, with a long, homely, horse-like face. "Honored guests. I'm Captain Henneria Bosh. Welcome aboard the Sweet Venture."

Most of the Forossi clan weren't paying close attention. A few looked up, then went back to their books, newspapers, or letters. Marlee tried to look like she'd heard it all before. Clora stared at the captain with interest.

"You may have noticed that smoking, or combustion of any kind, isn't possible on this craft. We apologize for the inconvenience. The ensorcellment is for your safety, since the gas that gives us lift is highly flammable."

The gasbag was filled with hydrogen? Another thing to add to her list of worries. It's nice there was a spell preventing them from doing a Hindenburg, but Marlee didn't place a lot of faith in magic. The captain went on, drawing their attention to booklets on each table. She held up a chart to point out exits, requesting they not be used except in emergency since the first step was a long one. "In case you do need to make a precipitate exit, there are fifteen parachutes in lockers here." She tapped the chart.

Marlee looked around the room. There were more than fifteen passengers, and she'd seen at least three crew members. And since the Forossis had pre-empted the whole vessel, it was less than half full. Well. Hopefully the parachutes wouldn't be needed.

"I suggest you consult the booklet to acquaint yourself with the procedure for using the parachutes." Henneria's dry tone suggested she'd fall to the floor in amazement if anyone actually did this. "Please do not throw yourselves or each other, or any objects you wish to dispose of, out of the airship. Instead, use the receptacles which are placed at intervals in the corridors. Bear in mind, if someone sues us because their cow got killed by a falling shoe, you own the line, so it's your money."

"I like this woman," Marlee murmured to Clora.

"There's a change to the meal schedule shown in the booklet. Since we have fewer passengers than usual, there's only one seating for each meal, at eight and six. If you want hot food at other times, you may prepare it yourselves. Instructions are posted beside the stove."

How did the stove work without flame? Clora was flipping through the booklet, perhaps also curious. The captain made a few more announcements about the bar, toilets and the like, thanked her audience, and paused for questions.

Clora waved her hand. "When do we get underway?"

"When I return to the control room. After the horn sounds, there may be a small bump. If there's anything else you need, any crew member can assist you. I wish you a good journey."

A few people stood, Clora among them. "Come on, I want to see our cabin."

"Our?"

"I asked them to put us together. That's all right, isn't it?"

"I suppose." Marlee followed her into the corridor. "Where's the captain from? I like her accent. I wash you a goot churney," she exaggerated.

"Ruddigor, but I don't know what country. Gazland, maybe, since she's fair."

A horn sounded, and Marlee braced herself against the stairway wall. There was a little lurch, a pause, then a gentle hum, barely audible, a vibration in the wall.

"We're off!" Clora picked up the pace. "That's the dynamos. Hurry!"

Marlee followed at a slower pace, to find her at a large, curved, outward-tilted window in their cabin. The mast was receding, gas bag looming above.

"I love this view. I can see straight down."

"Please don't lean on that. You're making me dizzy." Marlee looked around the small, tidy space. Situated at the end of the gondola, the cabin was wedge-shaped, with two low bunks. Her two trunks were strapped underneath one bunk, precisely fitting the space. Clora's single trunk, though much older, was the same size as hers. There must be a standard. "We should've gotten you a new trunk. That one's pretty beat-up."

"Oh, no, it's fine. Josip gave it to me. He doesn't like to throw out old things. Like that wheelchair you were using, I'm pretty sure was your grandma's once."

"Not so loud, okay? These walls are pretty thin."

"Sorry. I want to look around. Did you see on the map there's a spiral stair all the way to the top?"

"I saw. It's in a section marked 'crew only,' as I recall."

"But you're an owner. I'm pretty sure you want me to inspect the whole craft for you."

Marlee was getting a headache, and Clora's enthusiasm made it worse. "I would like that. It should take several hours. Before you go, do you see how to get into my trunks? I want a book."

"The bunk just lifts up, I think."

It did hinge up, securing into place with a hook, and the trunks had been placed so they could be opened without being pulled out. Clora opened hers also to change into clothing more suitable for negotiating maintenance corridors. She paused halfway through changing, to look into Marlee's trunk. "What's that?"

Marlee hefted the container Clora pointed at. "Tea."

"That's Elga's. Is that what she dosed you with? Why did you bring it?"

"In case I need it." Marlee shifted some underwear to look for her book.

"You brought those scarves too?"

Marlee looked up again. "I thought you were leaving."

"Yes, but those were in the secret closet."

"They were, but I can't think why, unless she just ran out of room in the bureau." Marlee picked up one with gray-green patches, and tugged it free of the jade ring that bound it. "This will go nicely with the velvet, I think, and see, they each have a matching ring."

"It's pretty, but...."

Marlee threw the scarf and ring back in. She took up her book, and closed the chest. She didn't really want to discuss it. She just felt more secure somehow with the scarves along, and irritated that she couldn't give a good reason. She pulled down the bunk and sat, her back to the gently swaying scenery. "Close the door on your way out."

WHEN THEY DOCKED IN PAROONA, Marlee hung back from exiting the airship, so the whole party was already on the platform by the time she crossed the catwalk. They were surrounded by several nearly identical guards in red uniforms with gold trim—royal house colors. Black-haired and brown-skinned, they looked like Spaniards.

As she'd intended, the welcoming committee's attention was taken up by the others, relieving her of the need to recognize anyone. Aside from the guards, there were three strangers who, through eavesdropping, she gathered were Duchess Jumori, her husband, and—from his silence and sober dress—an assistant of some kind.

The Duke was a small, plump man with slicked-back black hair and a formidable mustache, wearing a blue uniform encrusted with medals. Sea admiral, or air? The Duchess, slightly taller, wore a dress fluffed out in the bosom and behind, with a tasteful amount of jewelry.

The elevator cage was a little smaller than the one in Corilan, but had no seating, so there was just room for the whole party at once. Marlee ended up near Severn, who introduced her to the Duchess.

"My dear." The Duchess touched Marlee's arm. "Your recent ordeal is the talk of the court. Quite shocking. The rebels are more troublesome where you are. I attribute it to your mixed population. You get folk from all over, don't you?"

"It's a big seaport."

"The pale races, I believe, tend to irrationality and truculence. Haven't you found it so?"

The woman was starting to annoy her. "Your Grace." She had meant to suggest by her tone of voice that she wouldn't mind if the conversation ended, but Josip was nearby watching, looking a little surprised. She should probably make more of an effort to be pleasant. "Perhaps. I haven't especially noticed."

"Everyone will want to hear about your adventure, I'm sure. So brave, to dispatch your captors."

That wasn't bravery, she wanted to say. That was desperation. Someone would grieve for those men, and hate her for killing them. She forced a smile. "Thank you. I don't know if I'm ready to talk about it."

The Duchess touched her arm again. "Of course. Most harrowing, I imagine. I do love your gown, by the by. One doesn't wear one's best for travel, of course, but this is quite the mode."

It was one of the three made especially for this trip, the red silk. Marlee smiled again and wondered what the punishment was for smashing a Duchess in the face. She might wear her jingly Boraggan outfit to court, after all. Nobody had to know it was originally intended as pajamas.

She managed to make more small talk, until safely loaded into a carriage with Clora and her parents for the trip to the royal compound. Clora, too, was in a new outfit, a trim light yellow wool with silk ribbons.

"I'm glad the style has moved away from hoops," Severn said. "With three of you in here, I wouldn't have room to breathe."

Tam hung on the window to look at the city as they passed, pointing out stores and museums she'd like to visit. Unlike the dark rectangular brick and timber buildings of home, the houses here were mostly stucco or adobe, painted in light colors, with curved walls and domed roofs. Stacked in rows on the hilly terrain, in bright sunshine, the place looked like a pile of pastel mints.

Severn started out reading a report, but soon set the papers in his lap and leaned back, glaring at the scenery. "It's a Gods-cursed waste of time. What use are titles? Will it make us a single centime? No, on the contrary, it's costing a fortune." He transferred the glare to Marlee. "I blame you for this."

"I'm innocent."

Severn snorted. "You think I don't know who put these ideas in Josip's head?"

"Josip makes his own decisions."

Tam patted her husband's knee. "There, dear, it'll be most diverting. There's the ball tonight, and you do look so well in a swart. All the ladies will be jealous. It may be unfashionable to dance with one's own husband, but still I require to have you as partner for at least a quarter of the time. Then court—I've never been to a swearing-in, you know. The clothes will be quite a sight."

"I'm of a mind to skip the whole thing. Perhaps I can move my business appointments forward and go home a day early."

Because of her reading, Marlee could speak with authority on this subject. "You could skip the ball, though that would be unkind to Mother. But since you're to be Count-heir, you have to be sworn in too."

"I suppose you would know. That was to be Benin's job. Curse him for bashing in his fool head."

This caused an uncomfortable silence.

"Very well, then. I'll attend the ball. But I don't promise to stay past the first interval."

"Thank you, dear." Tam pointed. "Oh, look, the Exhibition Center! We must find time to ride about inside while we're here. Did you know there are 200,000 panes of glass?"

"If we do even half the things you've already mentioned, I'll need to stay an extra week."

"And why should you not? Nobody else is hurrying home at the earliest possible moment."

"Josip and Petro are. It's a busy time at home. Cargoes arriving nearly every day. After I deal with our business here, they'll want me to join them as soon as I may."

"Nonsense. They have matters covered, and you have people for that anyway." Tam looked at Marlee for support. "How often do we get to travel together, after all? There's more to life than business."

"If you leave her here," Marlee pointed out, "she'll just have to visit all the shops without you."

"And I thought the title was expensive." But he smiled. "We'll see."

The party re-assembled on the grounds of the royal compound, which contained a crumbling stone castle atop the highest hill in town, and several buildings in the same pastel stucco as the town, though larger and taller than most. They were met by a calm elderly woman, dressed soberly but well, who gave them a vague, reserved smile. "Welcome, all. I'm Mistress Sessae Druze, the hostess assigned to your party. The reception is about to begin, so I won't detain you long.

"First, weapons are prohibited in the royal compound, so if you're carrying any, please turn them over to a guard as you pass to the inner court. They'll give you a receipt. You can pick them up at the gate anytime you go out into the city. Ceremonial blades are permitted if you allow the guards to peace-bond them. Please don't forget to turn over those weapons, because the dogs will detect them.

"Those of you who've been notified that we have space for you in the compound, we'll also remove any armaments from your luggage. Your quarters are in the east wing of the palace." She pointed to a large pink building looming over the inner wall. "Use that entrance. Any servant can show you to your room. For those who've arranged lodgings in town, there are generally carriages waiting here. If not, there are always cabs to be found outside the gates. I'm sorry we couldn't accommodate more of you here, but because of the war, there are many persons receiving honors this year."

Clora pulled Marlee a little aside and whispered excitedly. "Are you staying here?"

"I don't know. I hope not. A hotel full of strangers sounds good to me."

"Listen, if I'm a guest in the palace, my ma will expire from joy and amazement."

"You want her to expire?"

"Excuse me, are you Miss Marlee Forossi?" Mistress Druze wielded a clipboard at her. "Mister Josip asked we make room for you in the palace. Will your companion remain with you?"

"Yes," Clora said. "Yes, yes. I'm her dresser."

"O—sure, yes." The others were being led away by a tall, liveried manservant. "I guess they're going to the reception. Let's go, I could eat a horse." Noting Mistress Druze's shocked expression, she added, "Not that I would expect to find one there."

The gates through the inner wall were guarded by pairs of red-uniformed men. One held the leash to a dog who eyed Marlee fixedly as she walked up, until she drew out her little pistol and passed it over. The guard tucked it in a satchel, made a note on his tablet, ripped off the half the sheet, handed it to her, and gestured her on.

The guests trailed through the grounds to a pavilion on the lawn. There, about two hundred strangers milled around, a string trio played in a little alcove, and waiters carried trays of beverages and small fried or pickled things. Half the people there were smoking pipes of some sweet herb she didn't recognize, and many were perfumed to the hilt. Even though the outer walls were punctuated by many open arches, Marlee found the atmosphere a bit thick, and hung around the edges.

She picked up a beverage as a waiter sailed past, and tried to get one of each different food, to see what she might want more of. So she had a glass in one hand and a greasy overstuffed napkin in the other when Josip spoke behind her. "Your Majesties, may I present my granddaughter, Marlee."

Marlee quickly swallowed what she was chewing and turned, smiling, making a quick curtsy which almost sent her staggering when her knee complained. The king blinked at her. He wore no signs of office, just a good tunic and kilt and a little striped cap. A long cigarette dangled from his hand. "Pleased." Boozy breath wafted from him.

The queen, holding his arm, looked Marlee over critically and gave a pointy little smile. Beside her stood a lanky boy of about fifteen, with pimples and a downcast eye. The prince, whose birthday celebration was to be held in two days. He was the youngest of three, Marlee recalled, his elder brother now serving as a general overseas, and a sister married to some bigshot in Ruddigor. The prince looked up at her and gave a quick, uncertain smile. His eye drifted down to her low-cut dress front, then he looked away, blushing. "I hear you play quadge."

Was he talking to her? "Do I? Ah, I mean, I'm a bit rusty. I mean, out of practice."

The king seemed to awaken a bit. "Rusty, hah! Picturesque manner of speech you have. Perhaps you'll give the boy a game, this afternoon. Nobody here is good enough to challenge him."

Sensing someone hovering at her shoulder, Marlee turned to look. Clora cocked her head urgently at the royal trio. "Oh, sorry. Your Majesties, this is my companion, Miss Perridino."

Clora made a deep curtsy. "Your M-majesties. Um, honored. Miss Marlee did... has hurt her knee. But I play."

The queen's nostrils flared. "Were you injured in your recent mishap? Disturbing, how bold these people are getting. But our man in Corilan assures me he'll have their leaders rounded up soon." She looked at Clora. "You play well, Miss Perridino?"

"I used to win a lot of games back home, Majesty."

The prince looked up, smiling shyly at Clora. "At three, then? If you're not busy."

"Three is fine, your Highness."

"Call me Drexi, please, if we're to be playing together."

The queen glanced sharply at the prince. Clora was looking only at him, and didn't appear to notice. "C-Clora."

"Well. Until then." The queen took the arm of the king, whose attention had wandered to somewhere in the middle distance, and moved on to the next group of people, the prince trailing.

Josip watched them go, then looked around to make sure nobody else was near. "So. Assessment?"

He'd asked this question every time they met with anyone in the way of business. The first time, she'd answered automatically. Apparently it had been a habit between them. Marlee took a few seconds to think. "The king is a drunk, and hates his job. The queen is a bully. She probably runs things. The prince has no real friends, because his mother drives them off."

Clora stood aghast. "You can't say that sort of thing!"

"Clora, they're only people."

"They're the chosen of the gods!"

"Then the gods have rotten taste."

"I'm not listening to this." Clora turned and walked away.

Josip smiled. "Your companion is well chosen, I must say. Was this your idea all along?"

"I'm sure I don't know what you're talking about." Marlee assumed air of fake innocence, meanwhile wondering what he was talking about.

"Do take whatever opportunities present themselves to put her in the prince's way. I know you have better sense than to be obvious about it."

"Of course."

Josip patted her shoulder. "I'm surprised to find you taking such a practical view. I always thought your passion for the nobility was a weakness, but you seem to be thinking clearly."

"Well... thanks."

"Now if you'll excuse me, I see Baron Biebstal over there. There's that matter of whaling rights I wanted to discuss with him."

"Good idea." Marlee watched him make a bee-line for a hairy man in a brocade jacket, and fanned herself, and thought. What good was it supposed to do them if Clora got friendly with the prince? He'd never marry a former housemaid. Even if he did, that would benefit Clora, not the Forossis.

Where was Clora, anyway? Marlee should probably apologize to her for dissing the royals. The pavilion was getting more crowded by the minute, and Marlee couldn't spot her. She wandered, listening to bits of conversations, grabbing a few more fish pastries to sustain her in her search.

She spotted Clora at last near the front of a little crowd of mostly women, surrounding a slight orange-skinned woman draped in undyed linen, bare-armed, sari-style. Her graying black hair was pulled back with a silver band, and she otherwise wore no jewelry. The simplicity of her attire stood out among the silks and velvets, gold trim and pearls, of this assembly.

"Trivial?" the orange woman looked around the group, her eyes a startling pale blue, dark-edged. "The world rests on the point of a needle. No action is trivial if done with a whole purpose." Her gaze stopped on Marlee, heavy eyebrows rising. "We have a visitor from afar."

Everybody looked at her. Marlee's stomach tightened, but she forced a laugh. "I believe a lot of people here are from out of town."

"Out of town." The woman looked amused. "Yes. I'd like to hear about your home."

"I don't have time now. I just came to collect my friend."

"Later then. But tell me who you are."

"Marlee Forossi."

The woman gave a little bow. "I'm the Haka San. May we speak later?"

The foreign mystic Dr. Harrick had mentioned. What was that knowing look about? Why did she want to talk? "Sure. Clora, come on. You have an appointment in half an hour, remember?"

Clora pushed through the group to follow Marlee away. "I actually have an hour. I didn't want to leave just yet."

"It's an excuse to get away from the woman's questions. Why does she want to know about my home?"

"You could've said you had appointment instead of dragging me away. She's pretty interesting."

"I thought you considered her a blasphemer."

"She's not talking about religion. It's about living big."

"Living big?"

"Paying attention, figuring out what's most important and doing that. Not giving in to fear."

"I'm surprised the queen likes her, then. I think she wants people to fear her."

"You exchanged two sentences with the queen, and you think you know her." Clora shaded her eyes with her fan as they left the pavilion.

Marlee pointed down a paved path, coral and shells embedded in concrete, glittering in the sun. "Let's go find our room, and figure out what you'll wear for this game with the prince."

MARLEE WALKED DOWN TO THE playing field with Clora. Quadge looked similar to tennis. The net was much higher, the court narrower, outlined by a perfectly straight edge of lawn. There was no-one there when they arrived, ten minutes early. Clora had been too impatient to wait in the room.

There was a rack of large paddle-gloves beside the court. While Clora tried on a few, Marlee took a ball from a nearby basket. Something bouncy covered with layers of string, covered with canvas. "These must wear out pretty quick."

Clora waved a paddle experimentally, then exchanged it for another. "The cover doesn't stay on long, but you can still use it without. In fact, we only ever got to use old ones without covers."

Marlee gave the ball a squeeze. "With the new elastrin, we can make better balls than this."

Clora took the ball and walked across the court, bouncing it on the hard clay surface. Marlee sat on a small wrought-iron bench to watch her practice against the smooth adobe wall on the other side. Clora had changed into a light cotton print dress with much fewer than the usual number of layers of undergarments—practical for running around in the hot sun, and it also showed her figure nicely. Marlee looked away, embarrassed. The prince would probably appreciate it also.

And here came the prince, a few minutes early himself. Marlee started to stand, but he motioned her down and gave a tiny bow as he passed, strolling to the rack and picking up a paddle. He glanced at Clora, who didn't seem to have noticed him yet. "Your friend. What kind of family is she from?"

"Your Highness..." It hardly seemed likely the prince would associate with Clora if he knew her to be a former housemaid. On the other hand, it might be unwise to tell a direct lie. "I've known her all her life. She grew up on a horse ranch, near my country house." On the same property, in fact.

"Her family raises horses?"

Marlee noticed a guard standing just inside the entrance to the enclosed court, who must have come with the prince. "Her brother does. Her mother is, ah, advising me in a business I'm starting."

Clora came hurrying over. "Your highness. I'm sorry, I didn't see you."

"Do call me Drexi."

"I couldn't possibly."

"Suit yourself, but we're all friends here, in my view." He hefted a paddle.

"I see you've started without me, but if you don't object, I'd like a few volleys to warm up."

"Of course... Drexi." Clora blushed, and nearly ran away to the center of her side.

The high net made for a slower game than Marlee was used to, with a lot of lobs. Probably necessary, since a ball coming in at a shallow angle wouldn't bounce high enough to hit. Still, there was a fair bit of running and jumping. There was some rule Marlee didn't understand, about when one was supposed to let the ball bounce before hitting it.

Clora seemed to be holding back at first, but then an easy shot came her way and she spiked it at the prince's feet. He gave a big grin, and after that, she didn't spare him.

"May I join you?"

Marlee started, turning to see who had snuck up on her. "Haka San." A woman who'd easily seen through her most dangerous secret. On the other hand, evidently no fool. She slid to the end of the bench.

The Haka San sat, sighing, and extended sandaled feet, working her ankles. "Too much stone in this place. Happy feet, to have a rest." She looked at Marlee with those startling blue eyes, smiling. "I've asked about you."

"I didn't think you were here because you couldn't find any other bench on the property."

"Yes, I sought you. I come to learn." She leaned closer. She didn't use perfume, and smelled of sweat and an unfamiliar, resinous spice. "Tell me of your home."

"Corilan? It's a big sea-port. Spices, coffee, olsan wood...."

The Haka San waved this away. "Not home of this body. Home of your mind."

Marlee gave her a long, considering look. "How can you tell?"

"I cannot well explain. I have spent long and long learning to see. I travel, myself, in these realms, and know others who do. It is an uncommon faring, though, that brings you here to stay."

Marlee looked down. "I don't want to stay. I came here by accident."

"Rare accident. You are but the third I know. First on this side of the world."

"How does it happen? How did I end up here? What is this place, actually?"

"Your world, this world...." She held up both hands, index fingers bent around each other. "Near together, for a little. These are the worlds we can visit, those that twine close. The mind in this body—" She touched Marlee's hand. "—There was an affinity, a likeness, to that other. This flesh was a good home, a match for your spirit."

"We are nothing alike. She was a horrible person. All we have in common is our name."

"A name is much. Names have power. It creates a resonance which might have drawn you together. But there is more. To keep you...." She paused. "I do not wish to argue. It happened, one cannot argue that. It seems you do not like her, but I urge kindness in your judgments, if only because life is kinder to those who forgive."

Marlee stifled the urge to tell her to save the self-help lectures for her followers. She needed this woman. "I want to go home. Can you help me find the way back? Can you tell me whether there is... is a body to go back to?"

The Haka San hesitated. A ball landed on the grass at her feet, and she absently bent to pick it up, threw it back out without looking. "There is a tricky word there, when you talk about two different worlds."

"Which word is tricky?"

"Is." She paused again. "I don't know if I can well explain. But you have been in this world some considerable time."

"Two weeks."

The Haka San's eyebrows rose. "Not so long as I thought. The worlds may still be near enough to reach."

"I had a vision of home a few days ago. A dream."

"You already know how to open your mind to the worlds, but you ask questions that make no sense. How do you imagine a return?"

"However I got here, I'd go back the same way. But I don't know how to control it. Someone was drugging me without my knowledge."

"Ah. Very dangerous, indeed. Do you have the drug?"

"Yes."

"And you want to know what became of the body that grew this mind."

"Yes, and to go back."

"We must discuss more, what you mean by that. But if you wish to learn what befell in the other world, I can help. You need no help finding it, it seems. But you do not know how to hold your purpose while you wander. That is difficult. If you take the drug, I can follow, then guide you if need be."

"Is that safe?"

"For me, yes. For you, not entirely. Can you be calm and take direction?"

"Yes. I want to do it."

The Haka San ran her hand over her chin. "You decided quickly."

"I always do. Will you help? I can pay."

The Haka San smiled. Her teeth were white and even. "I don't collect coins. For my aid, you must tell me about your home." She shifted on the bench, giving the impression of intending to stay for a while. "Tell me how your people live."

CLORA

XLIX

THE OLD MARLEE MIGHT POSSIBLY have been easier to deal with. This one had to be talked out of attending the ball in her pajamas, and didn't seem to particularly care which dress she wore, forcing Clora to do all the worrying.

"I like the smoky velvet. Can't I just wear that to the dance and the party? Those garnets look heavy and stiff."

"Miss Yrenn was most specific." Clora held up the yellow gown. "This is for the ball. That's where everybody wears their fanciest gear. This dress, this hat, these shoes."

"I hope I won't be expected to dance. Really I don't want to go at all."

Clora sighed. "Miss Marlee would never miss a royal ball unless she was this near to dying. And it would look funny for me to go alone. And I will go. So stop complaining and put this on. With your knee, you don't have to dance. But you have to be there."

"Yeah, you're right. If I don't go I'll just sit around worrying about tonight."

Their room in the palace wasn't large to start with, and was crowded with the bed, their three trunks, and a lot of heavy furniture. Clora shifted a table to make space, and helped Marlee step into her underthings and the heavy, garnet-encrusted gown.

As Clora started on the straps and buttons, Marlee smoothed the fabric. "Do you think I've lost weight?"

Clora didn't look up. "If that means, are you thinner, then no, not that

I can see. I don't know why you make such a deal of it, in any case. You're healthy, attractive enough, and rich besides. The only reason men don't chase after you, is that they're afraid."

"As they should be." Marlee bent over her open trunk, reaching down.

"Stay still. I'm tying this."

"I think the red and gold scarf would go well."

"Miss Yrenn—"

"Isn't here. Hand it over."

Clora handed it over. "You'll be too hot."

"Look." Marlee tucked the weighted ends into her bosom, patted the scarf into shape. "Not bad, is it?" She put on the ring that had bound the scarf.

"It's beautiful. Now stand straight. I'm getting to understand why Miss Yrenn is so cross all the time."

"Hey, I just remembered something I wanted to ask you. They're so worried about weapons here, why don't they do a fireproofing spell, like on the airship? Then nobody could fire a gun."

"I don't know." Clora picked up Marlee's hat, a gauzy thing encrusted with yet more gems. What sort of spell would that have to be? She positioned the hat, stepped back to view the effect, reached up to adjust it slightly. "Actually, maybe I do know. It's probably an air-fire spell." She jabbed in two long hatpins. "If you ground it, it'll leak off in no time. That must be why the end of the boarding bridge on the dirigibles is wood instead of metal."

"So if the building were up on stilts? No, never mind. People could still shoot into it from outside, and you couldn't shoot back."

"Shoes. Sit. I can't help noticing how you're always thinking about how to kill people."

"That's unfair." Marlee stuck out a stockinged foot. "If people kept trying to kill you, you'd notice that stuff, too."

Clora shoved on a short yellow kid boot, and reached for the button hook. "It's a good point. Still...."

"All right, fine. I'm not just looking out for danger. I think about ways to hurt other people. Maybe it's a leftover from old Marlee, but it's in me now, it's me."

Clora took up Marlee's other foot, then just held it and looked into her face. "You're not her. I know her, and you aren't like her."

"But I don't feel like I'm really me, either. I'm not always in control, and it scares me. The Haka San thinks I'm just like her."

"She said that?"

"She's too polite to say it in so many words."

"But you don't really want to hurt people."

"Like hell I don't. I could've killed that drunk the other night. I constantly want to slap the stupid servants."

"You don't, though."

"No. But is it because I'm decent? Or because it would be a bad idea?"

Clora reached for the other boot. "I don't think Marlee used to worry about trying to be decent. So you're different in that way. Quit picking at those beads. You'll tear 'em loose."

Marlee closed her eyes. "I just want to go home and be me again. I wasn't perfect. I was far from perfect. I was undisciplined and thoughtless and selfish and probably a couple of other things I haven't figured out yet. But murder wasn't in my life." She leaned forward and took Clora's hands, her hands cold. "I would miss you. But I can't live like this. If I can go back, I have to."

Clora pulled her hands away and finished the last couple of buttons, her fingers trembling. She felt cold herself, despite the stuffy room. It wasn't just a question of missing Marlee, not anymore. Marlee didn't seem to realize the fix Clora would be in without her. Karina would consider Clora a loose end to be cleaned up. She knew too many secrets.

But she couldn't expect Marlee to stay for her sake. Give up her life, her love, her family? Clora had thrust herself into this situation, unasked. She'd seen an opportunity and taken it, not thinking about the dangers, and that was hardly Marlee's fault.

No, best to just prepare to flee if the worst happened. Tomorrow morning, she'd go to the train station and buy an open ticket to carry everywhere. It was just as well she hadn't yet opened a bank account, instead carrying cash in the bottom of her trunk. Not that there was much left, even at the higher rate of pay. One's expenses, it seemed, quickly rose to match one's income. Marlee had talked of settling a sum on her, but hadn't yet.

Fortunately, it seemed unlikely Marlee could return home. But it would be best to be ready.

"So," Marlee said. "What are you wearing?"

HERE ARE THE DIFFERENCES BETWEEN a country dance and a royal ball.

At a country dance, all the dancers mingled. Here, there was an upper set and a lower set. The latter, larger, less glittery group, included Clora. It was strange to see the attire of the lower set and realize she might now consider herself superior to some of them. Everyone receiving honors had brought along family, including many poor relations.

At a country dance, women usually outnumbered men by about four to three. Because of the press, it was hard to be certain of numbers here, but Clora had a male partner for every dance she chose to dance. However, they weren't more clever, nor less likely to step on one's toes, than the boys back home, and they were on average much older.

The musicians here were polished, but they should play faster. Perhaps the slow music was because many of the outfits—or costumes—of the upper set were fragile.

A country dance didn't include food. Usually, the only refreshments available were of the liquid sort. Here, buffet tables lined one wall, crowded with tiny glasses and small complicated dishes. Little meat pastries, small disks of a blue-veined cheese with orange-colored jam on them, berry tarts, brown blobs with a powdery surface.... It all looked interesting, but she'd rather dance than eat.

She'd expected a polished stone floor, like much of the royal compound. But someone here must be serious about their dancing, because the floor was varnished wood with bounce to it. Was there a spell involved, or was it just somehow constructed that way? A barn floor did not compare.

The band leader announced a segyre—an even slower than usual dance, in which her partner was likely to hold her close and try to put his hand on her bottom. Clora excused herself to check on Marlee.

As companion, it was her duty to do so, she told herself. It had nothing to do with any hope the prince would notice her on the upper side of the room and ask her to dance, since that was clearly ridiculous. In fact, there he was, leading toward the dance floor a woman at least twice his age, whose dress seemed to be made of thin strips of silver cloth. Fashions here were certainly more revealing than back home.

Marlee was on the side, at a set of tables mostly occupied by those too old or too drunk to dance. The fellow sitting with her was Torvig, Baron Bellado—Karina's husband—talking and gesturing to her while she nodded absently and scanned the room. She spotted Clora and smiled. Torvig followed her gaze, and waved Clora over.

Clora moved a chair from an adjacent table and sat, setting down a little plate she'd picked up from the buffet.

"I'm glad you could join us," Torvig said. "We didn't get to talk at the tea, and I've wanted to meet you, but you two have been a bit busy of late."

Clora smiled. "There has been a lot of excitement." She'd always been fond of the pudgy Baron. For a lord, he was unusually chatty and friendly to servants. "We've met before, as it happens."

"I've seen you in the offing, I suppose, running about the hallways with stacks of linen."

"No, before that, at Marlee's ranch. You gave me a sweet."

"Did I? I'm sorry I don't recall. How forward of me, I must say. Most improper. I hope you rebuked me."

"Not at all. This was about six years ago, and I was glad to have it."

"Ah, that does put a different complexion on the matter. Anyway, I'm glad you spared a moment for the old and infirm."

"Oh, sir, you're not so old."

Marlee smirked. "Distinguished, I would say."

"That's kind, but actually I place myself in the other category. Gout, you know. A terrible thing."

Marlee leaned in confidentially. "I hear wine causes it."

Torvig gave a start. "Do you say so? Well, that is a terrible dilemma." He gestured at the plate, which contained a blue cheese. "I haven't examined the spread. Is there any real food, or just tarts and fancies?"

"Mostly fancies. I thought Marlee might like this."

Torvig pulled out a pince-nez on a gold chain and examined the plate. "Looks like an honest enough cheese if you scrape off the marmalade."

"Have it," Marlee said. "I don't think I can eat."

Torvig pulled the plate toward himself. "My girl, it was lovely to meet you, and I hope we can have a proper chat soon. But I can see from the way you look about that you want to get back to the dancing. I'm doing my best to keep your mistress diverted by telling her all about my dogs, and the servers are here to see she lacks for nothing."

Clora stood, gave a little curtsey, and stopped by the buffet on her way back for something to sustain her efforts. She scanned the offerings doubtfully, hoping for something familiar.

"Try the pickled quail eggs," someone said from behind her.

She turned to look, heart pounding. "Your hi—um, Drexi. They're purple."

"It's wholesome. The color comes from a flavorful herb."

Clora picked up a plate, but held it uncertainly. She didn't want to chew in front of the prince. She looked away, trying to think of something to talk about. The segyre was still playing. "What happened to your partner?"

"Her garment suffered a misfortune, and she had to retire. I wasn't disappointed, since she seemed to want to talk only about the condition of the roads in her province, a subject on which I have no influence and even less interest."

"You didn't cause, um...."

The prince laughed. "I plead innocence, though I can't deny I'd've been tempted had I thought of it. A gentleman trod on it, and it tore. A pity I can't ask you onto the floor. You'd be more entertaining than any of these folk."

"This dress would look so plain there."

"No dress looks plain with...." The prince paused and cleared his throat, looking at the floor. "Unfortunately, my mother would have words on the subject. But I will see you at the kites tomorrow."

"Of—of course." Clora gave a little bob and hurried away.

MARLEE

"A KITE? WHY?" MARLEE WALKED over to the window again and looked out at the moonlit grounds.

"There's kite flying tomorrow. The prince asked if I would be there."

Marlee let the curtain drop. "You're going home in a few days and when will you ever see him again? Why bother?"

"Because he's the prince."

Marlee sat on the bed and rubbed her knee. "I don't suppose I can have some poppy syrup."

"The Haka San told you not to drink. I'd guess she doesn't want you to take poppy neither. If you'd rest your leg, like the physician said...."

Marlee waved a hand. "Yes, all right. I'll be good. You can ask them to hunt up a cane for me, if I'm still here tomorrow. But what's the big problem about the kite? Go buy one. I'm sure there's a store in town."

"I want a special one. They'll have a hundred fancy kites, boxes and animals and pinwheels. I want him... I want to be noticed."

"Him? Eddie will be disappointed. So fickle."

"Marlee!"

"What are you saying? You want me to 'invent' a new kind of kite for you?"

"Could you?"

Marlee shifted on the bed, trying to get comfortable. "I'm no kite expert. I could do you a cross with two sticks, but that's probably not the kind of attention you want."

"Oh."

"Just buy one tomorrow. Help yourself from my purse, what do I care? Get a big one. And would you hand me my book?"

Clora tossed the book onto the bed beside Marlee. "Don't you go to sleep yet. The Haka San said—"

"I heard her." Marlee picked up the book, *Practice of Trade* by G. Adolfini, and opened it to the place she'd marked the night before. Her bookmark was the booklet from the airship, folded open to the parachute page. She smiled at the optimistic drawing of a passenger floating safely to the ground under a huge dome of fabric. She set the booklet aside—it might be entertaining, but the book was necessary.

She managed to struggle through a chapter before there was a quiet knock at the door. Marlee put the book down with relief, while Clora ran to let the visitor in.

The Haka San stepped in, looked around, and sat, looking like a child in a big, dark wooden chair. Her feet swung an inch above the floor. She looked at Marlee for a few seconds. "You are ready."

"Let's do it."

"What am I to do?" Clora asked.

The Haka San pulled her feet up to sit cross-legged. "Observe."

"Looking for what?"

"Just observe." The Haka San touched her forehead. "What happens, happens inside. If I ask for anything, be ready, and if we say anything, remind us of it later."

Clora got a notepad and pen from her trunk, and set it on the table beside her chair.

The Haka San looked intently at Marlee. "To begin, I must tell you a lie, but it is a useful lie. You must try to believe it, to help you make sense of what you see."

"Why are you telling me it's a lie? Don't you think it's easier to believe if you didn't say that?"

"Because, if you cannot perceive in my way, you must give up trying, and perceive in your way. I cannot tell you a truth, because the truth is too large and strange to know. I can only tell you the lie I have found most useful."

"All right, go ahead."

"The world is a long, thin, crinkly noodle." The Haka San brought her hands together, then drew them apart, fingers pinched to draw out an imaginary strand. "This end is the past, this end the future. All the worlds are in the great bowl, jumbled together." She dropped the imaginary noodle in a large imaginary bowl, and tossed the contents with her hands. "There are other things as well, but they are best avoided. Most will not harm you, but they are not useful for us."

"Skip the meatballs, got it."

"It may happen that two noodles cross each other. They may touch again elsewhere, but the life of a person is as nothing to the life of a world. So, as concerns us, they meet only once, for a period of weeks or at most months."

"All right."

"But the noodles are very crinkly. Their crossing is... complex. This is why your visions seem out of order. Some are later in your world, and others earlier."

Marlee sat up straighter. "Wait, wait. I thought those were memories. You're saying I was actually there? When I dreamed about being in class and not knowing the answer to a question, I was really there?"

"It's not always easy to separate memory from vision, but yes, probably."

A small hope bloomed in Marlee's heart. "Did I change the past? I dreamed I didn't know the answer, but I told myself the answer, I pushed the answer into my head. Then when I woke up, I remembered giving that answer in class. Did I change what had already happened?"

The Haka San hesitated. "That's the kind of question that makes the noodle bowl a lie. You can say you changed what already happened. Or you can say you came to understand how you knew the answer before learning it. Both are a kind of truth. This is why I said happenings involving two worlds are difficult."

"Try to make it simple. If I find the right place in my, my world noodle, can I push my past self to not do whatever caused my... accident? Can I undo all this?"

Another hesitation. "To answer this, I must tell a different lie, which I am not so sure of. A world is not a noodle. It's a branch of a tree, on which we sit. You can reach out to a nearby branch and shake it, if you have the strength. Maybe that moves your branch a little, too. This is like your answer in school. A little shake that shakes you too. But you seek to reach behind you and, and, cut off your own branch."

"You're saying it can't be done?"

"I say it was not done. If you do this, you never came here, so who is here to give you the warning?"

"Yes, I get it. It's a paradox. But what happens if I try?"

The Haka San shrugged. "There is much I do not know. Time, I think, is the biggest lie of all. What is to come is as real, or as unreal, as what has already passed. The future feels like it can be changed, only because we don't know what is to come. The past seems like it can't be changed, only because we remember it so. Neither is entirely true, I believe. Perhaps if you find the right moment in your own world, you can push the world in a different path, one where your body lives. Or you could say, you cause to sprout a new branch. But to push, you must have a place to push from."

Marlee looked at Clora. "Are you making sense of that?"

Clora had picked up her notebook. She riffled the corners of the pages, a soft sound. "Maybe. You can make little changes and then it's as if it was always that way. But if you make a change so big that you wouldn't be here to do it, then you're really just creating a new branch with a different you, but you're still stuck on the old branch." She looked at the Haka San. "Right?"

A shrug. "It's a lie. The history of this mind...."

"I think that means it's close enough," Marlee said. "So if I create a new branch, can I go there?"

The Haka San rubbed her knuckle over her chin, looking frustrated. "I don't know how you are using this word, go. You will be right here, in the bed. Seeing. Maybe touching. Not going."

"Look." Marlee was getting a little frustrated herself. "I was there, now I'm here. I went from there to here. If I create a new branch where I don't die, I want to go there."

"Again, this wish makes no sense. It is as if you wished to be the moon. If you don't die, you are there." She flipped her hand. "If you do die, you are there, also here."

"I don't understand you. Clora, do you get it?"

Clora shook her head. "We should first just learn what happened, for sure, on your world. Then maybe the Haka San can think of what to do about it."

The Haka San threw her hands up. "I will think to make sense of your question. For now, yes, let us proceed."

"All right." Marlee took a deep breath. "What do I do?"

"Sleep, and await me in your dreams. I have no more words."

Marlee covered the light, and lay back, but she was too keyed up to sleep. There was someone talking in the courtyard, a laugh. The buzz of a fly. The covers smelled of dust.

The Haka San's chair creaked a little as she shifted her weight.

What did Josip think her brilliant plan was, regarding Clora and the prince? It's not like they could marry, or anything. She was too warm. There was a twinge from her knee.

A low, droning noise began, across the room. Was the Haka San humming? The note drifted into a tune, slow and soothing. Marlee breathed in, breathed out, listened, watching the lights behind her eyelids, imagining them as strands, twisting, winding, separating....

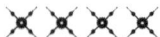

SHE HAD A VIEW OUT over the garage roof, to a baseball diamond in the park down the street. There was a night game, shouts and the crack of a bat drifting in through the window. She turned, seeing the rectangle painted by the lights shining in through the window, but not her own shadow in it. The closet was open, and mostly empty, clothes taken out and laid on the bed and over a chair, things shoved randomly into open boxes. Her pen cup, a mug from Nome, Alaska, lay on the floor near the desk, pens strewn beside it.

What is this place?

"My room at home."

Are you on the bed?

"That's my mom." Marlee moved to the bed. Her mother lay on her side, curled up, partly on top of two blouses. She was dressed in sweats. Marlee wanted to sit next to her, touch her. She imagined reaching out, pushing her mother's hair back from her face... and stopped when she realized she'd envisioned a brown, short-fingered hand.

Step out of this. See as I see.

Marlee felt a tug, and the scene receded, collapsing to a point of light, and the point was on a string, the string one of many that twisted around her. The celestial noodle bowl. She turned to see who had spoken to her. There was supposed to be someone with her, wasn't there?

What else can you touch from here?

A curl of light drifted near. Marlee looked at it, thought of approaching— and it enveloped her. She lay on her back, a book over her face, warmth under her, sun beating down, gritty sand between her toes.

"Marlee, look, girl, Wayne's going up!"

She sat up, looked for her hat. Her friend Miko pointed out over the water. Miko must have sharp eyes, to be sure the distant speck on the back of the boat was Wayne. Must be the eyes of love, or at least the eyes of lust. "I still think you should've gone with him. They can do two at a time, you could ride together."

Miko snorted. A gust of wind came up, and Marlee held her hat. A second later, the distant boat jumped forward, a rainbow-striped canopy billowing out behind it. Miko had her phone out, recording video. The people in the boat reeled out the canopy, lifting Wayne, if it was him, to join two others already aloft from other boats.

I would enjoy that.

Marlee found herself back in the tangle of worlds. "I know, right? It's great. I did it twice." She reached for another thread, and darkness and silence wrapped around her. For a long time she lay, just breathing, the world at a distance, muffled. Her throat was raw, but the pain didn't really bother her. Was she supposed to be doing something?

You cannot remain here.

Marlee tried to look for the speaker, but couldn't move, couldn't speak.

Come. Someone took her hand—or no, nobody touched her, but there was a pull. She lay there for a time, feeling that pull. Then coldness dashed into her face, and she sat up, coughing out water.

Clora stood over her, empty glass in hand. "She said to wake you."

Marlee wiped water from her face. "Next time you could say, 'Hey, wake up,' instead."

"I tried that. I couldn't tell if you were breathing, and I was scared."

Marlee looked over at the Haka San, whose eyes were closed, legs still crossed under her, slowly exhaling. "What time is it?"

"About four."

The Haka San opened her eyes. "No more of this for you. Until you can guide yourself. You were nearly lost."

What had that period of dark waiting been? Had she been in a hospital, in a coma? She shivered, pulling the covers around herself. She could've been stuck there until she died—again, apparently—and then what? "May I have more water? In the glass, this time."

The Haka San stood, stretched, then folded smoothly forward, head touching knees, then up again and back, back, hands on hips. Showoff.

Marlee took the glass Clora handed her, and tried to wash the bitter taste out of her mouth. "So now what? When can we try again?"

The Haka San bent gracefully to the right. "When you learn to remain apart. You went too deep, forgot the goal. You may lose yourself."

"Can you teach me today?"

Bending, to the left. "It is a discipline. You can learn in perhaps four months."

"That'll be too late!"

"That is so." The Haka San straightened, swayed. "I must consider other ways. We will speak again." She nodded, turned and left.

"Great." Marlee set the glass down. "Well, it wasn't a total loss. At least I have an idea for your kite."

EDSGAR

"WHERE ARE YOU GOING?"

Digriz, hand on the door latch, looked back at Imealde. Her hair was an odd shape from her pillow, a little stiff from the black hair dye they'd both used before leaving home, the better to blend in. "I thought you were still asleep."

"Who can sleep with all the racket you make? For that matter, who can sleep anyway?"

Digriz tried not to show what he was thinking—that he'd brought the wrong person along. Too nervous, too suspicious, that was Imealde. Too bad she was the only rebel with airship experience who wasn't a spy. "You should sleep. You'll need to look alert when the time comes."

Imealde paced to the window, looking out through the gap between the curtains and cracking her knuckles. "I'm ready."

"Don't be ready now. It's your constant readiness that's driving me onto the street. Be ready on Saturday."

"You shouldn't show yourself unnecessarily."

"On the contrary, I'm here to show myself so you can remain hidden. I mustn't be a suspicious recluse. Besides, I have to pick up a few things, such as food. And meet my contact so we'll know when to move. You stay quiet and count the lilies on the wallpaper or something. And don't stomp around. You're supposed to be sick." Before she could respond, he ducked out into the hallway and downstairs. The faded runner on the staircase frayed where it was tacked to the blackwood planks, shifting under his feet. Someone would break their neck on this stair.

The clerk looked up as he came into the lobby, the same stooped woman who'd greeted them last night. "Mister Odelbehr. Is your wife any better?"

"No, unfortunately. I have to go downtown. Can you recommend a decent apothecary?"

"Try the Willow. Poor dear. What's the matter with her?"

"Nothing contagious. Kalavisae disease, runs in the family. She gets these attacks, but she'll be right in a few days. Too bad, she was looking forward to seeing the capital. The Willow, you say?"

"Yes, so called because it's on Willow Street at King's Way."

Digriz nodded thanks and left, dodging an Aakol who was entering. Though it was early, the city was already showing promise of an uncomfortably hot day. Digriz paused for a jilberry ice. Vapor streamed down the zinc sides of the cart as the vendor popped the cover open for a chunk of blue ice, dropping it onto the platform of the shaver and pumping the lever with his foot.

Digriz ate slowly as he wandered downtown, keeping an eye out for Marlee. He'd sent her an encrypted note at the palace asking for a meeting. This was counter to his instructions, but matters had been left in such a state of uncertainty that he really must.

He could, of course, just carry on with the plan if he didn't hear from her. But after all was done, he wasn't to contact her for weeks. By then, Tanni's trial would be long over. A brief conversation now, before she might be under any especially intense scrutiny, was essential.

Not knowing Paroona well, and having no specific meeting places arranged between them, he'd just asked her to come to the Fish Market. This was so called for historical reasons, since fish was no longer sold there. Now it was the domain of artisans and importers. He wandered at random, looking into the better quality stores and stalls. The market was much larger than he expected, and he feared it might take quite a while, but in fact he'd been at it only a quarter hour when he heard a familiar voice from the next row of stalls. He backed up a few steps and stood on tip-toe to look over a tall pile of fabric rolls.

"These colors are right, except the yellow is too pale. I'm making a rainbow, it oughta be bright."

Digriz ducked around the end of the table and walked up beside Clora, pretending to be interested in a hanging sheaf of swatches. Clora, watching the stall owner root through a tall crate of smaller rolls, moved aside for him without really looking.

"Pretend you don't know me," Digriz mumbled.

Clora turned. "I don't... holy Artemis, it's you. What've you done to your hair?"

"Hush, we're strangers. I must speak to your mistress."

"And she wants to speak to you. Hold a moment and I'll take you." She turned to the fabric vendor. "Yes, that one. How much for all these?"

The vendor looked at the collection on the table, five narrow rolls of brilliant silk. "Four crowns."

"What?" Digriz said. "Nonsense! She'll give you two."

The vendor's eyebrows came down. "Sar, the miss here is shopping." She looked at Clora. "Finest quality. Here, feel it."

Digriz persisted. "Two of those rolls are barely scraps. Who else can you sell those tiny pieces to?"

Clora turned to him, looking exasperated. "Do I know you, sir?"

Digriz opened his mouth, then shut it and shrugged. Clora turned back to the vendor and in a few minutes, secured the five rolls for two and seven. While she counted out the coins, the vendor wrapped the rolls in a large sheet of paper she pulled from under the table.

"Now, sar, can I help you?"

Digriz didn't pause to answer. Clora, with her light hair, was easy to follow amid the black-haired locals. Digriz trailed her to a wagon whose fold-out shelves displayed a selection of weapons. Naturally, where else would one find Marlee? She leaned on a carved cane of gnarled wood, testing the balance of a slim dagger with her other hand. She looked up at Clora, and showed no surprise at spotting him. "Lorezzo. What do you think of this?" She flipped the knife, catching the tip to hand it over hilt-first.

The balance was good, the handle tightly wrapped in braided wire to improve grip. He breathed on the blade. The edge was folded, but not many times. He handed it back. "Not bad, but not as good as some you already own."

"Yeah." She set the knife back on its stand. "There's a cafe advertising chocolate over there. Come along and let's talk. Clora, you too."

Digriz hurried after her. "Have you gone insane? You mean to sit where anyone can see us?"

"Yes. Things have changed. You'll tell me where things stand, and I'll tell you what to do next."

Relief was mixed with apprehension. Maybe she'd decided to not destroy the airship after all. Still, he'd rather not ruin his cover identity. He might still need it. But then, Marlee was calling the shots, and it was unlikely anyone who knew him as the Night Wind would be within a thousand miles of here—excepting Imealde. He fell behind so at least they weren't walking together.

Marlee took a seat at a sidewalk table whose surface was quickly drying, now the sun had touched it. The restaurant must have just opened, for no other tables were occupied.

Clora went in to find a server, Marlee leaned her cane against a chair, and Digriz pulled up another. "We have a problem—"

Marlee held up a hand. "Wait for Clora. You can update her on the whole plan."

"This is about her brother."

Marlee glanced at the door. "What about him? I told you to cancel that."

"I received your note too late. And I'm afraid my man exceeded his instructions. He ended up killing a man."

"What?" Marlee half rose, looked again at the cafe door, and sat, looking as if she'd been hit in the gut.

What was this? He hadn't expected such a reaction at this point in the story. What was another body to her? Yet she seemed even sicker about it than he'd been. "It's all right," he assured her. "He got away, and we can still wrap this onto Ovid if we need to."

"That's not the...." She closed her eyes, took a breath. "Oh god... gods. I need a minute."

What could be the matter? "There's more, but she's coming back."

"Then let's talk about our other... business." Marlee looked up at Clora, apparently calm again. "We're just about to hear the status of our... operation."

Clora handed her a hand-written menu card. "Best wait. They'll be out any second. I already asked for a pot of chocolate. The pastries look good."

"Get thee behind me," Marlee muttered. She looked over the card, then passed it to Digriz.

The menu had an Ijolais theme— trifolds, pack tarts, edible flowers in honey. A girl in a lace-trimmed chiton came out with the chocolate on a tray, setting heavy cups before them. Marlee stopped the girl from pouring. "I'll do that."

"I want some of everything," Clora said. "We came out without breakfast."

"I'm pretty hungry, too," Digriz said.

The waitress pointed at the menu. "I could bring a large collation for the table. That may be enough for all."

"Fine." Marlee set down the menu. "I give up. Let's have that. And more chocolate. And some sugar."

"Sugar?" The girl seemed uncertain.

"For the chocolate."

"One doesn't use sugar in chocolate."

"If one is me, one does."

The girl looked uncertain for a moment, then seemed to come to a decision. "Miss, I'm sorry, we have no sugar."

"What? Your cooks must use a barrel of it every day. You say you're out?"

Digriz, smiling, leaned forward. "I can solve this. I'd like coffee."

"Yes, sir."

"You'll bring sugar for the coffee."

"Naturally."

"And a little cream. Thank you. I think that'll be all."

Marlee stared at the girl's retreating back. "Unbelievable."

"Sugar in chocolate is a bit odd, you must admit."

"I have a feeling it'll catch on." Marlee poured for Clora. "Now, tell all. For Clora's benefit, start at the beginning and lay out the whole plan."

MARLEE

DIGRIZ LOOKED AROUND, THEN LEANED in. "Briefly, the plan is to blow up the *Pride of Fools*—the airship Josip will use for his return trip to Corilan—somewhere over the wastes."

Clora's eyes widened, her jaw dropped, her hand came up to grip the collar of her dress, fabric bunched in her fist. "But that's horrible! All those people!"

Marlee shook her head. "Don't worry. We certainly won't do that. It's off."

Digriz's shoulders visibly relaxed. He took a deep breath. "Good." He looked at Clora. "Why are you looking at me like that? It was her plan."

"But how could you even do that?"

"I needed the money. It was my way out of debt and out of town. Which, incidentally...."

Marlee waved a hand. "Don't worry, you'll still get paid. It's not your fault I changed my mind."

Clora shook her head. "I don't just mean how could you bring yourself to do it, I mean how is it possible? There's a spell on them to prevent explosions. And how do you know which ship? They wouldn't even tell us."

"I gave Karina's key to a sharphair. He worked the thinking machine to figure out which ship. We planned to sneak someone aboard, ground out the spell, then set the bomb."

Clora set down her cup. "And blow themselves up too?"

"She would parachute out."

"Over the wastes?"

"Right at the edge. The timer would set off the explosion forty minutes later. Not that she wouldn't've been willing to blow herself up too, if necessary. These people are really dedicated."

"What people?"

"Why, the rebels, of course. The anarcho-democrats. I infiltrated their organization and suggested various, um, projects to them. The Forossis are a prominent symbol of the injustices they're fighting. It wasn't hard to convince them to act against the family."

"Wait, so Marlee really did arrange her own abduction?"

"Horrors, no! Far too dangerous. Someone might've taken it into their head to kill her right away. No, I encouraged them to paint slogans on walls, burn down a warehouse... I did convince someone to take a couple of shots at her on the street, though."

Marlee barely stopped herself from gasping. Clora did gasp. *"You* did that?"

"She suggested it. With the lookahead potion her guards take, she knew she wouldn't be hit. It gets her sympathy, and I had to work them up to the big project. So even though it wasn't planned, the abduction worked out nicely. When she got away, it made everyone all the more furious and determined to get her and her family."

"By blowing up her airship."

"Yes. Well, they don't know she never flies, which is her plausible reason for not being aboard at the time. I understand you did arrive by airship this time, though. How did that come about?"

"Grandfather is keeping me under his thumb."

Digriz seemed about to object. Marlee held up a hand. "That's not why I'm calling it off. It's complicated."

Digriz shrugged. "It's your show."

Clora leaned forward to ask something, but Marlee, seeing the waitress returning with food, signaled silence. The girl deftly managed a tray on one hand, and a tall wire rack in the other. The rack's shelves held three plates of descending size, crowded with pastries and little sausages.

To spare herself a lecture about the proper treatment of chocolate, Marlee waited until the girl walked away before appropriating Digriz's sugar dish.

She'd been using the time to think, seen the big objection to the plan and how to answer it... and decided that would be a good chance to prove she wasn't totally ignorant of her own plan. In case he'd started to wonder. She poured chocolate onto the sugar in her cup. "Of course, there's the minor problem that I'd be going home to a city where hundreds of people were still out for my blood, but that's easily dealt with. Eddie knows the names of all the movement's leaders by now."

Digriz dropped the tiniest amount of cream into his coffee. "Exactly. One little anonymous note to the Seidos, or rather a fairly long note, and problem solved. That part of the plan, I suppose, is still on." He laughed. "Unless, of course, you mean to wipe the slate, and become a friend of the people."

Marlee forced herself to laugh, too. "We'll see. Don't send that note yet. Talk to me after we get home."

"You're the boss."

"Yes. Yes, I am. Say, Clora, if you're to finish that kite early enough to try it before the event, you'd best get to sewing."

Clora finished swallowing a mouthful which appeared to consist of approximately half of a large jam tart. "I've got three maids to help. They were glad to take hand in a surprise for the prince."

"Even so, best not delay. If the design needs any changes, we don't have a lot of time for them."

"True." Clora threw four small pastries into a cloth napkin, drained her cup, and stood. "You'll manage without me all right?"

"Certainly. I have to see whether our friend at the University has any news for me, but I'll be back in time for the field test."

"See you, then." Clora hurried away, making off with the cafe's napkin. She was adapting well to privilege.

Marlee dragged the tower of pastries toward herself and looked over the remaining choices. "So. There's more, you said. About Ovid."

"Ah. Right." Digriz shifted in his chair, and set his coffee cup down with a click. He stared at the cup. "Well. The gentleman who did this work for me, as I said, escaped cleanly. Unfortunately, however, the man he killed is a royal game warden." Digriz looked up, apparently expecting a reaction.

"Ah."

"Exactly. Also, he has since had a disagreement with the forces of order, in a different matter. He's incarcerated, and not expected to live." He hunted around for a knife, and started cutting a yellow tart into bite-sized pieces.

Marlee watched, tearing a little bun to pieces with her fingers and not eating any of it. She wished she could tell herself this was a bad dream, from which she could awaken. Asking Digriz to do this project had been a horrible mistake. He had to know she'd been drunk at the time, so he should've confirmed it before going ahead. And she should've known better, even drunk—but she hadn't known Clora as well then as she did now.

And now someone was dead, and she bore some responsibility for that. Well, to be honest, more than a little responsibility. When she gave Digriz that task, she already knew what methods Marlee typically employed, what sorts of people she would've hired to carry them out. She'd deluded herself into thinking he was a decent person, just because he behaved pleasantly.

And because it was convenient for her to think so. He'd been taking care of the Josip problem. She should've known it wasn't anything as benign as trying to destroy evidence or find the real killer. No, that wasn't the way Marlee and her minions "took care" of things.

She realized, with a sick feeling, how neatly and coldly she'd set things up. Whatever horrible thing Digriz had been planning, when he carried it out, she'd have been able to tell herself she had no idea. That was old Marlee's way of operating, and she'd fallen right into it.

But no. That wasn't right either. Old Marlee never hid behind ignorance. She'd planned the whole horrible scheme with the airship. She was ruthless, and made no bones about it. This, this cowardice, was all herself. She'd been afraid of Josip, so she carefully didn't let herself think too hard about what Digriz was up to.

Digriz finished cutting up his tart, and looked up. Marlee quickly schooled her face to a neutral expression while scrambling to recall what he'd been talking about, and to come up with a Marlee-like response. His hireling in prison, right. "So what concern is that of ours?"

"Normally, none. However, he sent word that should he be sentenced to death, he would reveal the little job he did for me. He doesn't know who I'm working for, but he figures—or perhaps just hopes—I have enough influence to save him."

Marlee didn't have to fake anger this time. "So he's blackmailing us."

"In the circumstances, one can hardly blame him. What does he have to lose? And normally, it would just be my problem to deal with. I understand how our deal works, and wouldn't expect you to rescue me. But our connection is known now. The fellow doesn't know what this is about, but he knows enough that it might come back to you. Even if not, you could never use the manufactured evidence against Ovid."

"Clora must never know about this."

"I thought you might feel that way. Once it's public, she'd be furious and at the same time, you'd no longer have anything to hold over her. Fortunately, it should be fairly simple to deal with, for you anyway. A word in the right ear, a few crowns judiciously applied—I know you've done it before. You don't need to free him. Just reduce the sentence to transportation. He won't be happy, but he won't talk, and it gets him out of town, which is a benefit."

Transportation? What kind of punishment was *that?* "That... seems reasonable."

"Of course, you might instead... well, but I think this way is best."

Might instead have him killed trying to escape, Marlee assumed he meant. "So do I." She emptied her plateful of torn-up bread scraps onto the street, causing a riot among the crowd of pigeons who'd gathered to watch them eat. She took a bite from a fresh bun. "So. How long do I have to take care of this? And what's the fellow's name?"

"He won't come to trial before the end of next week." Digriz reached into a jacket pocket. "I've written out the details."

EDSGAR

IT TOOK DIGRIZ FAR TOO long to notice he was being followed. The relief of learning the bombing was canceled had made him relax his vigilance. He spotted the blue-garbed figure reflected in a shop window, and realized it had been behind him for several blocks. Probably since the post office, in fact. Hopefully, if the gods were kind, not from the cafe.

He swore under his breath. He'd made too many turns in his route for this to be a coincidence. Especially since the young man was trying to keep other people between them. He looked vaguely familiar. Was it someone he'd met since his arrival, or had he been followed all the way from Corilan?

Digriz had been headed toward the inn, but now took a different turn. He dropped a parcel, to have an excuse to turn around and covertly scan as he bent to pick it up.

Either the lad was on his own, or any others were doing a better job of blending in. It was simple enough to elude a lone tracker—but he really needed to know who it was.

He let himself be followed for another block, and still didn't spot anyone else. Rounding the next corner, he hurried ahead, took a crushed velvet cap from his pocket and jammed it onto his head. He walked casually back the way he'd come, slouching, head bent to shade his face. As he walked, he twisted a ring to point inward.

The tracker rounded the corner and scanned the street. But of course, he was looking for someone far ahead and walking away. Digriz was able to walk right up before the man's eyes went wide with recognition.

"I wouldn't." Digriz grabbed the tracker just above the elbow. "That point pressing into your arm? A little scratch, and you'll die a most painful death." There was, of course, no poison on the ring—who would be foolish enough to wear such a thing? But Digriz's tone was deadly convincing.

"I'll scream."

Hearing the voice, recognition finally clicked. "Lily? What are you doing here?"

"Let go. You don't want the police any more than I do."

Digriz released her. "Why are you following me?"

"Why do you think? I don't trust you out of my sight. If you try to get away, I'll make a fuss."

"How did you...?" They were already getting curious glances from passers-by. "Never mind. We can't talk here. Let's go to my rooms."

They walked in silence. Digriz took a circuitous route to the inn, being extra vigilant but spotting nothing else suspicious.

The same woman was still behind the desk. Didn't she ever sleep? "No messages, Mister Odelbehr." She glanced curiously at Lily. "You found the apothecary with no trouble?"

"Yes, no problem there. This is my wife's cousin who lives here in town, come to check on her."

"I hope he can also stay and see to her while you're about your business in town. You were gone so long, sir, I worried about her. I had breakfast sent up hours ago."

"I thank you for your care. Excuse us, please, we must go up."

Imealde was seated facing the door, legs crossed, one foot swinging. When Digriz entered, she raised a finger at him, but whatever she meant to say went unsaid when Lily followed him into the room.

Digriz closed the door. "I don't know whether you two have met. Imealde, Lily. Lily's with us."

Imealde stood. "Wait, this is a woman? Oh, I see. But this isn't part of the plan. This place was to be known only to us two."

"Apparently she followed me from the post office. How she knew which post office to wait at, or even that we were in town at all, I haven't yet had an opportunity to ask."

"I'll tell you," Lily said. "When I went to my cell meeting, the others were complaining because Marlee escaped justice. But someone said, never mind, the Night Wind will end her in a few days. So after the meeting, I took him aside to learn the particulars."

"And he told you?" Digriz scowled. "Who was this? This loose talk will bring us down."

"He didn't tell me. But when I insisted I had an urgent warning for you, he agreed to forward a letter."

"Ah." Digriz reached into his tunic. "This letter?"

"Yes."

He unfolded the paper. "It appears to be in code. I thought Imealde might understand it."

"Those are just random symbols. They match this." Lily pulled a second note from her waistcoat.

Digriz fingered the neatly torn edge of the paper he held. He could see it now. These were two halves of a larger sheet. The torn edges were highly relevant to each other, and with identical text on the two pages, it would've been easy—and inexpensive—to lay a tracking spell on one half. Ingenious. He cleared his throat. "That explains how, but as to why?"

"You know very well why." Lily turned to Imealde. "I don't know what your plan is, exactly, but if you thought you were here to execute Marlee, I regret to inform you this man is in cahoots with her. He helped rescue her from us, just the other day."

Digriz's heart beat quickly, but he kept his voice steady. "I most certainly did not! What a fantasy! What are you talking about?" Was that enough puzzlement? Not too much outrage?

"She didn't defeat our people on her own. This man was among a party who aided her."

Digriz carefully didn't look at Imealde to gauge her reaction. He needed to seem surprised—not defensive, not as if he were pleading his case to her. "This is news to me. Who's spreading these rumors? Probably the Seidos, trying to discredit me. Let me confront my accuser."

Lily paused. Digriz waited, tense. Would she claim herself an eyewitness, be forced to relate the incredible tale of her release, and explain why she'd said nothing for days? Or would she back down?

"I... can't reveal my source. But I know it to be reliable."

"Oh, right, then, I'm convinced." Digriz extended his arms. "Lock me in irons!"

Lily turned to Imealde. "I don't expect you to just take my word for it. But I mean to stay to make certain he doesn't sabotage the plan. Whatever it is."

Digriz gave a skeptical snort. "Or perhaps you mean to make sure it fails."

Imealde looked from one to the other of them, sucking air through her teeth. "For that, she could've just sent word to the Seidos. No, I think she's sincere. She is also, I hope, mistaken. Nobody else was supposed to know where we were hiding, but now she's here, there's no reason she shouldn't stay and help."

Digriz carefully refrained from grinding his teeth. This didn't seem quite the right time to announce that the bombing was canceled. He shrugged. "As you like. But she needn't know the details before their time. I don't trust her."

MARLEE

LIV

MARLEE HAD EXPECTED THE ROYAL University to have corners and columns and things, to have brick and gravitas. But it was mostly like the rest of the city—pastel colors, rounded corners and roofs, round and six-sided windows.

The library building was huge, sitting in the hot sun like a giant peach. Inside, it was cool and quiet. Her cane echoed on clay tiles, which reflected diffuse light from the big glass-paned doors. A thin older woman with pointy features, standing behind a long counter, looked up as she entered, then resumed reading. When Marlee reached the counter, the clerk closed the book with a bit of a snap, and looked at her expectantly and a bit impatiently.

"Doctor Harrick, please."

The clerk slid a binder to herself, and opened it to a page marked with a ribbon, running her finger down the pages. She was dressed in light linen robes, like most people Marlee had seen on campus. This one had a row of small embroidered patches on the front, just below the left shoulder. A star, a spiral, a cat, a quill maybe? And a little campfire. University merit badges. This woman wasn't just a clerk.

"Rabbit seven." The woman shut the binder and reached for her book.

There were several archways in the pale plaster walls, but only three had labels above them—Literature, Natural Philosophy, and Theosophy. No rabbit. "Where might that be?"

The woman gave a little sigh. "I'd better show you." Tucking the book under her arm, she walked around the counter toward an unlabeled opening, briskly.

Marlee, with her cane, didn't try to match her pace. The woman paused at the base of a spiral staircase, then when Marlee arrived, started climbing, leaving Marlee to follow as she would.

By this means, they came eventually to a narrow room lined on both sides with study carrels, ending at a big round window that painted the room in light. The students didn't look up as they passed.

"Sedon, you have a visitor."

Harrick's head appeared above the wall of the end carrel. "Thank you, Doctor Zebaroon. She's expected."

Zebaroon gave a short little bow and left. Harrick stepped out, rolling his shoulders, and picked up a canvas satchel from the desk. "I've reserved a meeting room."

"Super." Marlee followed him back out to the hallway. "You address her as doctor, but she calls you by your first name?"

"She was my Classics instructor. She's only ever used my title once, at my graduation ceremony."

"She doesn't seem happy to be working at the front desk."

"No." Harrick pointed her down a side corridor. "The student whose duty it is, failed to show up this morning, I believe. Having received a few of her critiques myself, I'd advise him not to return. Did you converse with the Haka San?"

"We talked."

"I'm curious for your impressions."

"She definitely knows some things, but she's hard to understand. I think her brain's been warped by too much spirit travel."

"That can happen. Perhaps I should try to interview her while I'm here." He opened the door to a small interior room. Light rods were mounted in a single long holder on the wall. Harrick grabbed a handle on the end of the rack and shook it vigorously to brighten them. "She has no structure or method, I'm sure, but perhaps there are insights to be gleaned. In here."

Marlee pulled out a chair and gratefully sat. "What do you have for me?"

Harrick pulled papers out of his bag and dropped them onto the table. "I did find one item of interest. It helped that I now know what problem I'm actually trying to solve." He flipped through pages of handwritten notes. "Most of this isn't directly relevant. People have been experimenting with these drugs for decades, but the experience is so subjective and varied, it's hard to draw conclusions. No documented case quite like yours, but! About sixty-five years ago there was a Doctor Zgany Rice, a Kwedonni, working with a system that's no longer used, involving harmonic tunings."

"Are we talking soul travel here, or music?"

"A little of both. In this technique, each world has a characteristic chord, which changes over time...."

Marlee held up a hand. "Skipping ahead to the part I care about...."

"Um." Harrick looked down at his papers. "Yes. Rice was dying. In the spirit of scientific inquiry, he decided to try to project his spirit permanently into another world, where his students could confirm the success of the endeavor by signs they had arranged."

"He tried to put himself into someone else's body."

"Yes. Most unethical, of course. He tried for some time without success, but finally they made contact with a world whose inhabitants were particularly susceptible to outside influence, and his students claim he managed to take one over."

The ethical aspects weren't Marlee's highest concern. "You mean that really worked?"

"It was in dispute. The students' logs were the subject of great debate. I don't know whether I've mentioned it, but spirit travel is confusing. Your visions are unusually clear, probably because of your spirit's affinity to its world of origin. For others, things are vague, subject to interpretation, and events may seem to occur out of sequence. It's believed this occurs when you connect with someone's memory rather than with ongoing events."

"The Haka San has a different theory about that, but go on."

"The logs record the subject giving the arranged signals several times during the student observations, and this continued intermittently until contact with the other world was lost. Of course, other researchers claimed the students were just seeing what they expected to see. The finding was widely disregarded, and I certainly can't swear it's correct. But I thought it would be of interest."

Marlee pulled over a bound stack, a copy of the logs. "It is of interest. What happened to Doctor Rice after they lost contact?"

"He never awakened, though his body lived another two months. You might assume this means he managed to remain in the other world, or that he was simply lost, as sometimes occurs even with the most experienced travelers. Naturally, there wasn't a rush of other scholars trying to reproduce his results."

"Not even others nearing death?"

"Not given the theological concerns. The god Hades has promised we live on after death in his land, but can he claim our souls from a different world? Or would that world's pantheon have charge of them, or would they simply be lost? Some researchers took recourse to divination to answer that, but didn't receive consistent answers."

Marlee gave him a look. "Seriously?"

"Seriously, what?"

"All you supposed scientists believe that silly religion?"

Harrick sat up straighter, frowning. "There are well-documented acts of the gods every year. They speak to many people. Theomancy is a recognized branch of magical studies! Why, Apollo was sighted by dozens of people in Port Daparine last summer."

"Doing miracles?"

"Eating a meat pie, actually, but that's hardly the point—"

"Fine, whatever. Don't get your shorts in a bundle. The gods are real. What I care about is, nobody's tried to do this again?"

"I'm unsure. I plan to learn what I can about his students, if you agree. If anyone pursued this further, it would likely be they."

"And you think I might be able to do it? This expert failed a bunch of times, right?"

"The chance of success seems remote. On one side of the coin, your soul may have a special connection to its world of origin. On the other, it depends on having a compatible body to return to, which may prove difficult."

Unless she could return to a point in time before whatever happened to her. "If I could, would I remember my time here?"

"Who can say? Doctor Rice remembered the signals he'd arranged with his students. But the results are hard to predict. At any rate, this is what I've found so far. Shall I continue looking?"

"Yes, of course. Does this stuff explain his technique? I'll look it over." Marlee squared up the papers and stood. "If you find anything interesting, send me a note at the palace."

MARLEE OPENED THE DOOR TO find her things spread out across the bed, hanging over chair backs, piled on the floor. Clora was bent over one of Marlee's trunks, stationery box in one hand and empty pistol case in the other. She looked first embarrassed, then defiant. "Where is it?"

"Where is *what?*"

"Don't act innocent. You know very well. The Haka San said not to try again."

"Oh, the kokoleaba? I got rid of it. Too dangerous." This was, of course, a lie.

"I don't believe you. You hid it so I couldn't get rid of it."

Marlee threw a couple of books onto the bed so she could sit in a chair. "You planned to throw it away without asking? Well. Lucky for you I didn't want it. I don't like people messing with my things. I assume your taking time to rifle through my trunks, means the kite is ready to test."

"I already tried it. It folded up in the middle."

"Show me, maybe I can fix it."

"I already did. I couldn't afford to wait for you. It works now."

"Nice!" And kind of amazing. Clora had hidden talents.

Clora threw what she was holding back into the trunk. "It's almost time for the garden party. Where were you? It didn't take that long to talk with Dr. Harrick."

"Sitting. Feeding pigeons. Thinking."

"Well, think about what you're wearing to the party."

Marlee stretched out her legs, massaging her knee. "Is something the matter? You seem cross."

"I'm... I'm incensed. You and your nasty minion. Plotting to kill dozens of people. Your own family!"

"Hey, not so loud. It wasn't my plan." Even to her own ears, it sounded weak. "All right, I could've tried harder to find out what it was."

Clora stopped pacing and sat on the bed. "It's not you I'm angry at. It's just... I really liked Eddie. I was so stupid! I should've known he was a villain. He's too smooth!"

"He seemed relieved not to have to go through with it."

"He never had to. He always had a choice."

Marlee started to answer, then shrugged. There was no purpose in defending Digriz, and anyway she felt ambivalent too. She liked him. And Marlee, the master of manipulation, had pushed him. He wouldn't have been evil—well, as evil—on his own. But he'd been weak enough to let himself be dragged into it. "Well. Forget him, then. Focus on the prince."

Clora looked up, startled. "What do you mean, focus on him? He's a prince."

"He's a boy. I can tell he likes you."

"He's only being pleasant. When I go home, he'll forget all about me."

"I'm telling you—"

"It doesn't matter if he likes me. He isn't free to do as he pleases, so nothing can come of it. I'll have a good story to tell back home, is all."

Marlee smiled. "What kind of story?"

"I know what you're thinking, but I'm not that sort of girl. Regardless of what your family—and my mother—assume about me."

Marlee waved her hands. "Okay, okay! I'm dropping it. What shall we wear for our memorable afternoon of innocent kite-flying?"

MARLEE HAD BROUGHT ALONG MORE dresses than just the new ones. Miss Yrenn deemed some of her existing wardrobe acceptable for less formal occasions. Judging this to be one such, Marlee chose for comfort. Though the wind had picked up, the day was growing increasingly hot, so she wore only one layer of undergarments and dispensed with the corset. Many women in the court didn't wear them.

A large crowd had already assembled on the lawn by the time they arrived. There were perhaps fifty kites, ranging from elaborate to ridiculously elaborate. The king's kite was already flying, pinwheels spinning, long streamers trailing. Groups holding other kites stood watching while three men in palace livery held up one of the simpler kites, a red silk dragon with yellow flames and a long tail. Prince Drexi, standing beside his father, held the string. A gust of wind came along, the servants launched the kite in unison, and it soared into the sky. Drexi laughed and ran back a few steps to give it a boost, but with the stiff breeze and so large a kite, it was unnecessary. In a moment he was leaning back to keep from being pulled across the field.

The moment the royals' kites were up, other crews hurried out, spreading across the field, each team sending a runner to carry a roll of string to the kite's waiting owner. Marlee spotted her brother, with a colorful box kite, and Karina flying a rotating helix.

"We should start now."

Marlee held her back. "Not yet. You want to make an entrance."

The field was in minor chaos. There were some collisions, and one eagle-shaped kite escaped to drift over the town. After a few minutes, they were sorted out enough that the folk flying them were able to mill around and converse.

"Now," Marlee said. She walked up to Petro, while Clora hurried down the field, trailing a cord to which Marlee held the roll. Petro looked up at her and nodded. "Sister."

"Brother. We haven't had a chance to talk much recently."

He cocked his head. "Why start now? Do you want something?"

"On the contrary, I have something for you. You're in charge of passenger airships, I think."

He took a second to answer. "Yes.... Why?"

She pointed at Clora, who had reached the end of the field and stood poised, a small crumpled bundle between her hands.

Petro looked. "Your kite looks rather tiny."

Some spectators and participants had noticed the only one-person kite crew. When the wind picked up, Marlee gestured. Clora spread her arms wide, colors streaming out between them, and ducked under the rainbow kite as it caught the wind. It shot upward, tugging hard on the cord. Clora shaded her eyes to watch it ascend, then started running toward Marlee.

"It hasn't got any sticks." Marlee handed the reel of string to Clora as she pelted up, breathing hard. "I'm thinking to sell them in the capital. Have you seen how many kite shops there are around here?"

"Clever! And demonstrating it at a court event causes a lot of notice."

Marlee turned to see who'd spoken. Josip and Severn walked up. "Many people are watching," Josip continued. "Well done."

Severn looked across the field. "The prince seems interested. Though I'm not certain it's the kite he's interested in."

Marlee turned to Clora as she arrived, out of breath. "Why don't you go talk with him?"

Clora looked at the prince, a line appearing between her eyebrows. "I can't just walk up to him."

"Nonsense, of course you can."

"He seems to be signaling you, in fact," Severn said. "You must go."

"Marlee, you come too. I won't know what to say."

"I'm sure he doesn't want me there." Marlee handed her the roll. "Tell him it's a present for him, if he likes it. Or offer to trade."

"All right." Looking up to navigate the forest of strings, Clora backed toward the prince.

"Good move," Josip said. "Have you found a local manufacturer?"

"Not yet. It's brand new as of this morning."

Josip turned to Severn. "What about your contacts here? Any clothing or kite factories?"

"I'll ask around." Severn looked at Marlee. "Where did you come across this?"

"Clora invented it. She's amazingly clever."

"So there's no letter of patent. We'll have to apply immediately, now that everyone has seen it."

Marlee suspected the patent wouldn't be in Clora's name. "I promised her thirty percent of the profits. We have a contract."

Petro snorted. "You're going soft in the head, sister. We could've had it for nothing."

"Thirty does seem awfully generous," Severn said.

"Perhaps so, but A, I like her, and B, she has lots of other valuable ideas, if we treat her well. Speaking of which, if we make a larger version, it'll work as a parachute. Clora says. It'll be smaller and cheaper than the ones in our passenger airships, so we can carry enough for all the passengers."

Petro quirked an eyebrow. "Or we can continue to carry the legally mandated number, and use the extra space for something else."

Marlee gripped the head of her cane a little tighter, and forced a smile. "Or that, of course."

"I'll have the pointy-heads try it out with some volunteers." Severn touched her arm. "Look, the prince took the kite."

"Ah," Josip said. "Excellent. 'As flown by the royal family.' We'll need a name for it."

"Parasail. Because of the parachute thing." Noticing Clora walking back, smiling, Marlee started off to meet her. She had to hear the news about her thirty percent contract, and her new career as an inventor, before she talked with anyone else.

TITLES AND HONORS WAS TO be a sober event. Following Miss Yrenn's instructions, Clora laid out the smoky velvet and simple silver jewelry. Marlee stepped into a corset and let Clora tie it, every bit as tightly as Miss Yrenn had. This dress wouldn't fit otherwise. Once the final button was secured, Marlee stood before the mirror appreciating the effect.

It looked great on her. She could stand to lose, say, fifteen pounds, but good tailoring made the most of what she had. Once she got back into her own body, she should upgrade her style of dress. Jeans and button shirts were easy, but she could do much better with a little effort.

She looked around for her pistols, remembered again that the guards at the front gate had them, and picked up her cane instead. "Coming?"

Clora looked longingly at the setup she'd been working with the last couple of hours—lit candle, box of metal filings, glass of water, fat book of magic, and a partially completed diagram on a large sheet of paper. Several crumpled papers also cluttered the table.

"Come on. The prince will be there."

"Must you go on about the prince?"

"What magic are you trying to do here, anyway?"

"Make a flame burn underwater."

"Oh, I know that one." Marlee picked up the glass and held it above the candle. "Abracadabra!"

"You're the funniest person ever." Clora took the glass and blew out the candle.

"Anyway, I might need your help."

"I know. I'll didn't say I wouldn't come. Here, undo me."

Marlee reached for Clora's buttons. "If your mother could see your lack of enthusiasm for a royal event, she'd disown you."

"I won't be able to answer your questions during the ceremony, you know. I can't stand in the section for the families. I'll be in back, with whoever wanders in off the street."

"That may be so, but you'll look fabulous." Marlee looked again in the mirror. Something was still missing. "Hand me a scarf and ring, will you? The brown one."

Clora passed her the scarf. "I'm only saying I hope you already know your part."

"Miss Yrenn made certain of that. Not to worry, I have nothing to say. I'm not in line for the title." Marlee adjusted the hips of her dress.

"Pretty nearly, though! It's Josip, then Severn, then Petro, so if not for Petro, it'd be you."

"Thank the gods there's Petro, then." Marlee picked up the dress Clora had picked out for herself, pale blue with straight lines, trimmed in blue feathers. She stooped for Clora to step into it, then paused and stood again.

Clora, who'd raised a foot, straightened. "What? You've got an odd look on you."

"It matters what order people die in. For the succession, I mean."

"What do you mean?"

"Josip will be a Count. When he dies, Benin would've been Count next, then it'd go to his kids."

Clora tipped her head. "Livestock can't hold titles."

"His children, I mean. He had a daughter, right?"

"Yes, Netille, but she's just a child."

"She would be Countess after him, then her ki—children, if she had any. Severn probably never would get the title."

"I suppose...."

Marlee didn't pause. "But Benin died first, so Netille is out of the running. Now it's Severn, then Petro, then little Josip. But if Petro dies before Severn, little Josip is out, too. Then I'm next in line after Severn. Right? Did I understand how that works?"

"That sounds right."

"And who was to be on the airship, going back? Just Josip and Petro and maybe Elga and the baby. Everybody else plans to stay here longer. If it crashes...."

"Severn becomes Count and you're Count-heir." Clora sat on the bed. "Would she do all this just for a title?"

"You know her better than I do. You tell me."

Clora grimaced. "I don't know. I thought she'd just marry a noble. The gods know there are enough poor ones, willing to marry for money."

Marlee sat beside her, making the bed bounce. "And not have the title herself? Just be Lady Whatever to some poor man, without any power?"

Clora shrugged. "You have a point. That might not be enough. But I thought she was killing Josip to get away with Benin."

"Maybe it's a twofer."

"A what?"

"I mean, maybe she had two reasons for it, that plus the title. Marlee was efficient. We have a saying, two birds with one stone. She could slay a whole flock."

"But you—I mean she, didn't kill Benin, did she? Yes, that fits with her plan to make your da Count-heir, but it seems impossible."

"This makes me think she must've done it, somehow. If anyone could think of a sneaky way to pull it off, she could. And what do you want to bet she was lining up meetings here for Severn weeks in advance, to make sure he didn't fly back with Josip?"

"Because if Josip and Severn die at the same time, Freddan gets the title, not you. How horribly devious. Do you think she meant to end Severn too, later?"

"I don't know. Judging by her journals, she seemed fond of him. She might have been satisfied with Count-heir for the present."

Clora shook herself. "Well, fortunately, whatever the plan was, it's not happening now. I assume you don't care whether you get to be Countess?"

"I'd prefer to stay out of the spotlight, thanks anyway." Marlee glanced at the clock on the mantel. "Oh gosh, we'd best be going."

EDSGAR

IMEALDE SLAMMED HER CUP ONTO the table. "What do you mean, it's *off?*"

"It won't work." Digriz held up the encrypted message he'd written to himself and then decoded. "See for yourself. They've got wind of the plan somehow, and they're not flying back. I don't know how they'll travel instead."

Lily grabbed the paper. "Who sent this? I don't believe it."

"You know I can't tell you who it's from. What if you're a spy?"

"What if *you're* a spy? If they know, it's because you told them."

Digriz sighed. "In that case, why would I warn you? I'd let it go ahead, so they could arrest you in flame, as they say."

Lily walked to the window of their room, tapping the paper against her thigh as she looked down at the street. She still wore her boy clothing—she'd come without luggage. "We can't come all this way and do nothing, while that bastard takes a title and goes home in glory to the people he oppresses."

"It's too late to arrange anything now. We'll have to figure something out at home."

Imealde poured herself more of the sweet orange wine Lily had brought from the market. "That's pathetic. Blowing up the airship, that makes a statement. You said it yourself, Night. It's not just about justice. It's about the message."

Digriz took a tiny sip of his wine. It was just as appalling as he'd feared. He set his cup down. "True. But what's to do? If you knew the weeks of machinations I went through to learn that canny rat's travel plans. We don't know where he'll be, to plan an attack. Even if there were time to put something together, the local movement doesn't know us. We'd have to do it all ourselves."

Lily was still at the window, looking out at the Commerce Building clock tower. "I know where he is right now, though. He's getting ready to be made a Count. I know where he'll be tomorrow evening, too. Where they'll all be. At the idiot prince's birthday revel."

Imealde blew out derisively. "Nowhere are they more careful than the royal court. We won't get close to them there."

"The royal guards protect the royal family. Their guests have to fend for themselves, and without their usual guards. Honestly, I don't know why you didn't plan it that way from the start. An attack in the royal court is so much more dramatic than an airship burning where no-one can see it."

Digriz raised an eyebrow. "Mainly it was about not getting killed in the process. Also, good luck getting a weapon in there."

Lily turned to face them. "Getting away isn't necessary for me. And you might be surprised what I can make into a weapon."

Digriz shrugged. "Go watch the ceremony tonight, then. I believe the party's to be held in the same hall. If you see a way to do it, I have no objection to your dying for the cause. Just let us know so we can be well away by the time they catch and interrogate you." And so he could get a warning to Marlee. It seemed unlikely Lily could think of anything she could carry out so quickly, but if she came up with something, Marlee could decide how best to make use of it.

CLORA

CLORA ARRIVED EARLY AT THE Ocean Court to secure an advantageous view. The palace staff were still dragging open the huge shutters of four large arches rounding the far end of the long wood-floored room. The arches framed the area where the royals would stand, opposite the bleachers for the public. Both the palace-side door she entered through, and the as yet unopened underground passage to the street, were already guarded by men and dogs, eying all comers with suspicion.

There were a few people Clora recognized from other events, already crowding the rail. Hangers-on and relatives of those who would be let onto the main floor for the ceremony. She found a spot midway up, with a decent view of the proceedings, and took from her beaded bag the gazette she'd bought in town.

She'd have preferred the magic textbook to read while waiting, but it was too bulky to carry around. This magazine had two serial stories in it, unfortunately not the same ones she'd been following back home. She would miss an installment of Lord Grah, which nobody here seemed to publish, and she hadn't thought to ask anyone to save a copy for her. Marlee's idea of collecting the finished stories into cheap volumes had real merit.

This paper had a serial with an intriguing heroine, though, an Athenic priestess named Sharlotta who went around in disguise, avenging crimes. That seemed worth reading, even starting with part five.

Caught up in the narrative, she paid little attention to the opening of the public gate and people filling the stands, until a whiff of littchi-spice drew her attention to the vendors circulating through the crowd with trays of sugared fry-bread, roasted nuts, and wax-paper cones of warm beer and fruit juice. Clora put away her gazette and waved at a vendor, passing over a coin for a grease-stained bag of crisp fry-bread.

The families to be honored were filing onto the main floor now, and Clora took note of their outfits, knowing her mother would expect a full description. There were no vendors down there, but servers carrying trays of dainties.

"I've never seen such a lot of frippery in one place." The murmur was right behind her, clearly intended for her ear only. Startled, she turned, to find Digriz's pink face grinning down at her.

"Oh, it's you." She turned away.

"Does it seem to have gotten colder in here suddenly?"

"What do you want? And what happened to your disguise?"

"Sometimes the best disguise is no disguise. I don't much mind if the family sees me now, but there's someone else present who knows my other face. If you look, ever so casually, across the room and midway back, on the top tier, you might spy our mutual friend, Lily. She's dyed her hair dark and dressed in a man's brown trade suit with a yellow band, but perhaps you'll recognize her from our little adventure on the road."

Clora scanned the crowd, trying to seem as though she were looking for a friend, and found the person Digriz meant. Was that really Lily? She'd only ever seen the woman unconscious, and hadn't tried to memorize her features. But yes, it could be her. "What is she doing here?"

Digriz helped himself to a crisp from her bag. "Looking for ways to cause trouble. Being of a suspicious nature, she came to make certain I didn't sabotage the bomb plot. As you might suppose, she didn't receive the news of its cancellation gladly, so she'd like to find some other mayhem to commit."

"There are a lot of people who'd like to cause trouble for the Forossis. Do we need to worry about her especially?"

"I don't know her well, but she seems fairly ingenious, and has no regard for her own safety, so there may be a threat. I'd like to know why she feels so strongly about it. Do you happen to know who she is? Marlee calls her Rosette."

"Yeah, Marlee knows her. The last name is Val-something."

"Valutin?"

"That was it." Clora shifted her bag of crisps away from Digriz's reaching fingers, then changed her mind and pushed it into his hand, wiping her greasy fingers on her skirt. She didn't really like them anyway. "You know something about her?"

"I know what she has against the family. Still no idea why Marlee let her live, though. She's clever and dangerous. Tell Marlee to have an eye out for her. I don't know who she'll go after first." Digriz crumpled the now-empty bag, and gave her an ironic little salute. "I'll be in touch when I learn her plan."

MARLEE

LVII

MARLEE HALF DOZED. SHE WAS too warm, but she had her arm around someone, snuggled together, and the comfort of bare flesh against hers was too pleasant to make moving worth while.

She drifted into consciousness again, and saw past the other's head the big numbers of a digital clock, glowing dimly red. 3:20. She did sit up then. Across the room her roommate's bed lay empty, unmade as usual. The person in her bed—Bobby, of course—muttered something and burrowed more deeply into the pillow.

She looked down at his tousled dark hair, his mouth half open. Her own long-fingered hand rested on the blanket, pasty pale in the streetlight through the window. She wanted to reach out and brush that hair, but she wasn't in charge, or not entirely, so her hand stayed put.

Wake him up. Tell him not to let you go to that party. She wasn't sure she'd remember any resolve she reached in this state, but Bobby would certainly remember, if she told him, if she made sure he knew it was important.

She reached tentatively toward Bobby's shoulder, but the idea didn't make sense to the Marlee of this time—she hadn't been invited to the party yet. The conflicting mess of her thoughts, other's thoughts, made her awareness slip, and she lost some time, found herself standing at the window, breath fogging the glass, gazing melancholy at the park across the street. Her eyes refocused on her reflection in the glass, thin white face, long nose. A detached feeling of half-familiarity, as if this were an almost stranger, someone she'd known once. She spun away again, resurfaced an unknown time later. She'd pulled the blankets down to expose Bobby's bare shoulder, trailing her long hair over him as she straddled him, kissing his shoulder. His breath caught, and he twisted onto his back, eyes still shut. She ran her hand over the thin black hairs on his chest, brushing a nipple.

His eyes opened then, shadowed. Still half asleep, he freed a hand from under the covers to rest on her thigh. A shiver rushed up her back. "More," she said.

"So soon?" He shut his eyes, pretending to sleep.

"Don't tease." She ground against him, feeling hardness growing through the covers. "You're ready."

Tell him now. No party!

But this Marlee had other priorities. She hitched herself up off the covers and pushed them aside, her hand running down his side and along the inside of his thigh. He groaned and reached for her.

Dammit! She pushed again, trying for control, but bounced off hard passion, blurred, slipped away, whirling dizzily through blobs and streaks of light, feeling wrapped, trapped. She kicked, freeing herself from her covers, and woke to darkness, a sharp coppery taste, the beginnings of a headache. She badly needed to pee.

She sat up, memory returning. This was her room in the palace, much darker than the dorm room had been. A few stars shone through the wavery window glass. Clora breathed softly, on her cot across the room.

Marlee stood and groped for her robe, wrapping it over the silk slip she'd worn to bed, and left as quietly as she could, walking a few doors down the green-lit hallway to the bathroom she shared with other nearby rooms.

Her business there concluded, she didn't leave immediately. She splashed a little water on her face, and drank a little from her cupped hands held under the faucet. The headache was starting to fade. Maybe she was becoming acclimated to that horrible stuff. It had been challenging to sneak away from Clora long enough to brew a cup from her hidden stash.

The bathroom had its own dim light, and a full-length mirror on the door. She pulled her slip off overhead, the cool fabric slithering over her back. She let it drop to the floor, and stood before the mirror, staring at the landscape of her spirit's home. The round face, shadowed in the green light, under the short, light hair. Short neck, heavy breasts with dark aureoles. Round tummy, wide hips. Another little patch of white between her legs. A negative image of her real self, a reversal. She was a little pigeon-toed, her short feet splayed out on the shiny wood floor.

Her dream, vision, or whatever, of desire, had left her wanting that same completion. But Bobby wasn't here, and anyway, the memory that came to her now wasn't of Bobby, but of the time in the carriage with Chalula, crammed together on the narrow seat, the scent of her, the brush of skin against skin....

She turned away from the mirror, embarrassed. She hadn't been herself then, fresh from the trauma of her captivity, the fear for her life, the desperate struggle. The killings. She'd been distraught, lost, appalled at herself. Weak. It wouldn't happen again.

She'd tried not to think of it, since, but she couldn't forget. Chalula had started at her neck, nipped her gently. Had worked her way down, slowly, touching her....

Marlee shivered, grabbed up the slip and pulled it back on, donned the robe and tied the sash tightly. She unbolted the door and started back toward her room. But no, she didn't want to be in there with Clora, while feeling this need. Sleep was out of the question. What she really needed was a strong drink. But she had none in the room, and waking the palace servants at four or whatever the hell time it was, smacked just a little too much of desperation.

She walked on toward the stairway, meaning to walk it off in the courtyard. But midway down, she met an ascending light, with her brother's face behind it. He seemed surprised to see her, but moved aside without comment. She started to walk around him, then stopped, giving him a searching look.

Petro held the light stick up, the better to see her. "What? Do I have a smut on my face?"

"Couldn't you sleep either?"

"I could sleep, indeed, but I have a pile of orders that must post in the morning." He raised his other hand, which held a plate of some little sea creatures, covered in a dark sauce. "If you're restless, come help me, and share this. The kitchen gave me about three times what I wanted."

"Okay. I mean, certainly." She followed him back up. "I don't suppose you have any alcohol in your room."

"None of your fine vintages, but I have a flask of the very fire of the hills, from South Ruddigor."

"That will do nicely."

His room was two doors down from hers... his suite, she corrected herself, noticing a door partway open on the wall opposite his desk. He saw her looking, and motioned for quiet. "Elga and the child are asleep." He set the plate on the desk, just outside a circle of light cast by a floor lamp. He opened a drawer to pull out a flat bottle holding about a pint of amber liquid, and two small silver-chased glasses. He filled each glass about halfway, then gestured to her to choose.

The liquor tasted smoky, tracing fire down her gullet. The potent vapors swirled up into her sinuses. She let her breath out in a whoosh.

Petro grinned at her. "Little sips. It goes well with these." He picked up a little creature from the plate, held it by its tail while scraping it out of its shell with his teeth, then took a tiny sip from his own glass.

Marlee tried one. The sauce was peppery, and the creature tasted a bit like a shrimp, though its segmented shell was wider and flatter. Call it a shrimp, close enough.

She looked around. This was a much nicer room than hers. It probably wasn't intended as a slight, though—he'd just arranged for it in advance instead of being tucked into an available corner at the last minute. She looked him in the eye. "We never talk."

Petro considered. "I wouldn't say that. We seldom agree."

"I don't mean about business. Just about... stuff. Life."

Petro's eyebrows lifted, and he looked at her for a long moment. Her heart beat a little faster. Was this a mistake? She just felt so isolated, always having to look over her shoulder. Clora seemed like a friend, but she still wasn't sure Clora wouldn't sell her out if she got scared, or found it to her advantage. And Elga... that betrayal had left her hurting, feeling alone.

"I'm trying to discern what your tack is here."

"You're my brother." She tried to think of a way to say it that wouldn't seem like weakness, like fear of competition. "We're stronger if we have each other's back. I mean, if we work together instead of against each other."

Petro ate a shrimp, took another sip. "What is it specifically you want my help with?"

"Nothing specifically. I just want peace in the family."

"That seems odd coming from you. Elga has just been warning me against you. She seems convinced you mean to have me in an early grave. Just between us, since we're trusting each other now, do you know how Uncle Benin met his end?"

"I believe it was an accident. Just between us, why does she think I want you dead?"

"She didn't say. It may have just been some evilly considering look she caught you casting in my direction. She's perceptive, and I usually trust her impressions." A sip. "If I had to guess, I'd say you wanted my position, and my future title."

"If you think I want a job that requires me to stay up half the night scribbling on papers, you're delusional."

"I'm what?"

"Badly mistaken. I hate detail stuff. You're welcome to it. As for the title, I don't care about that. Anymore."

"Really."

"Really. I already have power, don't I? I have lots of money. What do I care whether people have to call me Your Grace or whatever the h— whatever they call Countesses." She ate a shrimp, fiercely, and took a larger sip of the very fire of the hills than was advisable. Her eyes watered, and she wiped them on her sleeve. "Whoo. You know, I've met the royalty here, and I went out with a Duke the other week, and I was distinctly unimpressed by any of them. If this is what passes for nobility, I'd just as soon not be one. The prince isn't bad, but the others are just a waste of space. Oh, and Uncle Torvig is all right. Earls are probably less stuck up than the rest.

"Anyway, keep your job and title. I just want to work on my projects, the kites and things. Clora is a genius, so many excellent ideas, I have a long list of new things we can make."

"How do you mean, she is a genius?"

Jesus, she should just stop talking before she got into serious trouble. "I mean she's clever. Gifted by the gods. We can make a lot of money from her ideas."

"She *has* a genius."

"Sure, right. That's why I made her my companion. I want to keep her close. So what do you say to a truce?"

"I'll give it a thought. Meanwhile, if you truly want to work together, here." He picked up the top half of a pile of papers bearing his untidy scrawl, and gave to her, along with a pad of blank order forms and a fountain pen. He shifted the light to illuminate more desk surface. "If you can't make out my notes, ask."

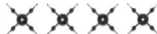

THE CIRCULAR GARDEN WAS A maze, sandy paths winding between sparse, prickly hedges to little clearings with benches and statues. Marlee seated herself on a boulder beside a small artificial waterfall, set her travel desk on her lap, and took a moment to look around. In an hour or so, it would be unpleasantly hot, but now the sun had just peeked above the palace wall, chasing away the night chill and lighting the tops of the shrubs. Little brown birds darted between the rough-barked branches, picking for seeds among clusters of small, tough-looking leaves.

Marlee opened the desk and pulled out the document she'd started the day before, a sheaf of, so far, seven pages, kept in an envelope addressed to Clora. She flipped through it to remind herself what she'd got so far. Tested a pen in the margin.

The problem with inventing things, is you need to know how they work and how to build them. As nice as it would be to invent radio, for instance, she only vaguely knew the principles, and had no idea how to construct tubes and circuits.

So she'd been coming up with ideas for things that had been simple but popular back home, mostly entertaining rather than useful. Her last entry, for instance—goggles for dogs. Weak. Likely a total flop. Magic 8 Ball, though, that was a good one. Nutella, probably a winner.

She had enough toys. Next, something genuinely useful. She'd already written the plans for the paper clip—on page two, after attaching it to page one with a straight pin. What other inconveniences had she noticed about life here? Mainly the stupid clothing. She flipped to the last sheet, and after a moment's thought wrote Zipper. She leaned in to draw a scaled-up picture of her best guess of what a zipper looked like inside. Severn's engineers could figure out the details.

While she was drawing a brassiere, there was a scuff on the path. She flipped the paper face down.

"It's morning." The Haka San, squinting against the sun.

"As usual for this time of day." How had the woman found her? And why? They didn't have an appointment.

The Haka San looked at her with a faint frown. "I told you of the danger, but you try it anyway."

No hope of hiding anything from this irritating woman. "I have to get home if I can."

"Home is a funny notion." She seated herself on a boulder beside Marlee. "I think perhaps we used the wrong lies to discuss this before."

"You have better lies?"

"You talk of traveling, of sending your mind to another place. But you could also say, you have been here all along. You were born here."

"This body has been here, but I arrived two weeks ago."

"This notion of I is a useful illusion usually, but now it blocks your thinking. Without a body, there is no you."

"Sure there is. There's whatever flew over here when my body died, or whatever happened to it." It was possible to think more calmly about that, since there was a chance to undo it. "My soul. Whatever it is that survives after death."

The Haka San drew in air through her teeth. "Another difficult word—*after.*"

"I know what it means."

"Do you?" The Haka San kicked her feet a couple times, then bent to pull a loose thread from the hem of her robe, to hang from her fingers. "Here is your life. It begins. It ends. Even if there is nothing after the end, the thread still is. Here is the moment you first took a step, here where you broke your arm, here where you wed. They do not go away."

"It's all still there in the noodle bowl, you mean."

"That is a wrong way to say it, but there is no right way. Time is the biggest lie of all. Things happen, before, now, after, but those are only places on your thread. They mean nothing when there are many threads." She pulled another strand from her hem and wadded the two together in her palm. "What in one thread is before a place in the other one?"

"I kind of get that. But what does this have to do with my spirit traveling between the threads?"

"Nothing travels. Your mind, your soul, is not something you can rip out from your body. Do you not know people whose bodies are ill or old, and so whose minds do not work well? Your spirit, your mind, is not a thing. It's something your body does. This body." The Haka San poked Marlee's arm, emphatically. "The mind has altered, but this has been your only home."

"No, it's like after I d-died or whatever, I came here and took the body the old Marlee left vacant. The psychist who's looking into this for me says that's what must've happened."

The Haka San shrugged, indifferent. "I only say what I think is true. I'm sure this man who spent many years to have a piece of paper, knows better than an old woman."

"So how did I get here, according to you? I don't see how your way makes sense."

"All the drugs that let you perceive other worlds, they also make your mind like, I don't have a word, like soft clay."

"Impressionable? Malleable?"

"Just so. You must be cautious. Most often, when the inner eye is opened, you see a little of what is hidden. But out there is," the Haka San gestured widely, "everything. Sometimes, it all pours in at once, most terrible. If trained, usually you can squat, hold tight, let it pass over you. But if you didn't learn to do this, you lose yourself in the flood. When it ends, you, your body, it reaches for a familiar thing. If your luck is good, you find yourself again. If your luck is bad, the flood washes you away, and your family feeds you with a spoon while you learn to walk and talk and wipe yourself. Or if your luck is strange, perhaps you find nearby someone like yourself, and grab on. Fierce, desperate, lost, you embrace it into the soft clay. So you become that person."

Marlee took a moment to digest this. "You think I'm not really Marlee Feldman, I'm just a copy of her."

"Now there is another tricky word."

"What's tricky about—never mind. Explain this, then." Marlee recounted Dr. Rice's experiment. "His students kept in touch with him in his new body," she finished, "until that world was too far to reach."

The Haka San had pursed her lips while listening. She tapped her fingers on her knees. "This was an evil thing to try."

"Well, yes, it was hard luck for the person whose body he took over, and I'm sorry for them, but think what it means."

"What does it mean? All it shows is his mind could turn that other to his purpose. Could they see something leave him and go there? Measure it with their scales? Could they show his mind remained in that other place beyond where the threads part?"

The woman was really starting to annoy Marlee. "Well, you can interpret it the way you like."

The Haka San spread her hands. "Indeed, who can know anything with certainty? But may I say more?"

"If you must."

"Marlee Forossi had everything she could want, but I do not think she was happy."

Where was this going? "Probably not."

"How much, when the storm took her, did she want to find herself again? Did she prefer to be someone else?" The Haka San looked closely at Marlee, who didn't respond. "Marlee Feldman had a good life, too. Your world has many wonders. Was she content?"

"I don't know. I think I was pretty happy. I liked it well enough to want it back."

"Enough to destroy the mind in that body, take it for yourself? As evil Doctor Rice perhaps did?"

"That's not how it is! I'm the same person! I'm not taking it from someone else."

"Is that how she would see it? The Marlee of that other place?" The Haka San's voice was a little clipped. "Are you so much like her? Think of the things you've done here. Clora has told me of your activities, the restaurant, your escape, the other businesses you are starting. Marlee of Corilan is bold. Marlee of Cleve Land, much less so. What has she achieved?"

Marlee forced herself to relax her tight grip on the portable desk. "It's easy to accomplish things when you have lots of money to hire people to do the actual work."

"And yet, many in this court who could easily afford such employees, are still useless. You bear her memories, but you and she are not so alike."

"I know who I am. It's the situation that's different, not me."

"You will do as you like, of course. From what I hear, you always have." The Haka San stood and brushed herself off. "Much as you might think you have improved." With a little bow, she started to walk off, then turned back for a final word. "If you are unhappy where you are, and you go somewhere else, your unhappiness travels with you. You are just the stories you tell yourself about yourself. If you want to be different, change the story. Not the place."

EDSGAR

IT WAS A BIT OF a dilemma. Since the authorities were now supposedly on the alert for them, they should leave town. But these stone-headed women were unwilling to go. Lily and Imealde had vanished in the early dawn, looking for materials for some secret plan. When he woke, at a more civilized hour, he'd found their note directing him—him, the Night Wind!—to have breakfast ready on their return.

Ah well. He needed a peek at their plans, so he should go along for now. Once Lily was in the custody of the palace guards, Imealde would be more amenable to going home.

As he entered from the street, the innkeeper looked up from counting a stack of linens to return his cheery wave. She wasn't in a talkative mood this morning, thankfully. Climbing the stairs, he tucked his basket under his arm to dig out the key, but the room door was open.

"About time," Imealde said. "What did you bring?"

Lily had spread her things out across the whole table, so Digriz set his burden on the window seat. "Smoked billfish, a freshly baked kirazza, gessi curd, and an assortment of fruit. If you're determined to commit mayhem today, you should eat hearty. Keep your strength up."

Imealde wrinked her nose in disgust. "Did you have to get that appalling curd again?"

"If you try it, you'll find it goes wonderfully with the fish, but there's also a quantity of goat cheese left from yesterday. Is there tea?"

Imealde was already picking up the kettle from the room's built-in gas ring. "I'll pour. You serve."

Lily cleared space on the table, which mostly involved tossing an ornate silver tray onto the bed. Presumably the tray was plated rather than pure, because neither of them had much money. The rest of the clutter, pushed aside, left ample room to set out plates and utensils.

Digriz drew his knife to attack the kirazza. "What's the tray for?"

"Beheading our oppressors."

He flashed the knife at her. "Something with an edge to it is perhaps more practical for the purpose."

"It'll have plenty of edge once I'm done."

Now that he knew her identity, Digriz had been trying to recall what he'd heard about Lily. He'd helped Marlee drive her family out of business, but he hadn't been involved with the planning—just been asked to divert a shipment here, threaten a supplier there. He had a vague idea what their factory had been making. Little devices, something to do with the war.

Judging by the collection of clamps, blades, mysterious little disks, and other apparatus on the table, topped by a pair of goggles, Lily must have been directly involved in the creation of these devices. Digriz served her a portion of smoked fish. "I'd think the weapon detection charms they use at the palace entrances, would notice a sharp-edged tray."

"No doubt. But I don't mean to sharpen the edge. I'll sharpen the middle, instead."

Digriz paused, a large spoonful of curd suspended over his plate. "You'll sharpen...."

Lily flashed him a tight little smile. "I'll cut it in half down the center, at an angle to give me two razor edges. Each half will even have a handle." She reached across to touch a handle of the tray. "And then I'll have someone weld it back together. Magical merge weld. You'll barely see the seam."

Digriz sat. "But once welded, they will no longer cut."

"As it happens, we had a problem at my—a factory where I used to work. Some of our welds weren't holding. They tracked it to a welder who was missing a step in his ritual. I know which step."

Imealde came to the table with the plate holding yesterday's cheese, and three cups of steaming tea. "Thank you. So you mean to do a bad weld on purpose?"

Lily drew her cup and plate to herself. "It'll hold just long enough."

Digriz had a sip of tea. "Still, a tray is an odd thing to bring to a royal event. Assuming you can procure an invitation."

"Certain attendees don't require an invitation, and are expected to bear trays."

Digriz laughed. "Surely the guards know all the palace staff."

Imealde picked up Digriz's knife from the table, and started slicing cheese. "For a big event like this, they hire extra staff from an agency in town. We also know who supplies their uniforms. Not to worry, she'll get in."

Digriz spread curd on his kirezza, and topped it with a slice of fish. Perfection. "It seems you've thought of everything. I'm only sorry I won't get to see it. How may I assist?"

Lily crunched into her kirezza, leaning over her plate to contain the crumbs. "There's a certain amount of buying and bribing yet to do. Mm." She wiped the corner of her mouth with her thumb. "We thought we could borrow your purse."

"I'd love to help fund this worthy endeavor, but you may find my purse rather light at the moment. Where shall we go first?" He'd actually prefer not to tag along with them, since that would make it easier to stop by the palace to warn Marlee. But one had to make a show of willingness.

"You'll be here, resting." Imealde reached out, laying her hand over his wrist as he reached for his teacup. "You've had enough tea, I think. We don't want you to come to harm. We simply don't trust you."

Digriz looked at the cup, with mounting alarm. "What have you done?"

"Not to worry. You'll just have a little nap. It's a funny drug. You don't notice a thing until you try to move quickly, and then... oops, yes, like that! Grab his other arm, Lily. Let's get him onto the bed."

MARLEE

LIX

TIME TO ROLL OUT THE big guns. Marlee stood before the mirror, watching while Clora adjusted and smoothed the yellow dress. Evening sunlight through the window made the garnets flash as she shifted her shoulders.

"Hold still, will you?" Clora tugged at an underskirt that had bunched up in back, then walked around examining Marlee critically from all angles.

"Do I pass?"

"Miss Yrenn might call it satisfactory."

"I'll want the red and orange scarf."

"Miss Yrenn would not approve of your making adjustments to the costume she so carefully planned. Besides, you'll already be too hot in all these clothes."

"It's so sheer, it's not really for warmth. I just feel better wearing it. And you have to admit this could use a touch of color. A bit too much yellow."

"Well, you're in charge."

"I am." Marlee picked up the scarf, enjoying its slick feel as she pulled it from its ring. "Shall we?"

The courtyard was already in shadow. They passed servants in pale blue, lighting the tall lamps along the path. They still mostly used gas lighting in the palace, from tradition perhaps. As the sky darkened, she and Clora wandered from island to island of soft, flickering yellow. Something was in bloom, pale spears of tiny white flowers.

Clora drew in a deep breath of the scent. "I could get to like living here. It never freezes, even in the dead of winter."

"I like seasons." Marlee paused near the end of the outer wall, where a wall was no longer needed because of the protection afforded by a sheer cliff face overlooking the sea. She leaned on the pitted metal rail to watch the last sliver of sun sink below the waves. "Good place to come for a break from winter, though."

Clora stepped up beside her, and they watched together for a while.

"It's the same moon," Marlee observed. "Isn't that odd?"

"Same as your home? Why shouldn't it be?"

"Our continents are all different. Maybe the moon is too, a little. It's not like I memorized it."

They listened to the waves crashing below. Clora ran her fingers over the railing. "I well know you didn't throw that drug out."

"No?"

"No. And I'm not happy with you lying about it."

"Since I knew you didn't believe me, I don't really consider it a lie."

"More like a way to not talk about it."

"It worked for a day, anyway." Marlee turned her back to the sea, leaning back against the rail, and looked around to make sure no-one was nearby.

"Would you at least not use it unless the Haka San is there?"

"She and I aren't speaking just now, I suspect."

"If you ask her, I think she'll come sit with you. But couldn't you just stay here?"

"Fighting my crazy relatives every day? Wondering what happened to my—to Bobby? With my parents thinking I'm dead?"

Clora was quiet for a time. "Do you miss Bobby much?"

Marlee turned and started walking away from the cliff. "I don't want to miss the party."

"We're still early."

"I've got to check for a message from Eddie."

"Do you really think Lily will attack the party? Couldn't you just alert the guards?"

Her party shoes had thin soles, and weren't great on the shell path. "Ow.

I don't know. If she does try, I'd like to stop her myself, quietly, so she doesn't get arrested. What would they do to her?"

"You mean, how would she be executed? It depends who—"

"Never mind, that's what I needed to know. I don't want it to come to that. If Eddie can tell me exactly what she has in mind, maybe I can intercept her without anyone noticing."

The palace halls were busy with servants, excited guests, and drably dressed functionaries hurrying on single-minded errands. Marlee pulled in her skirts to avoid getting them caught on anything, and they made their way to the message center near the main gates. This was a small, overheated room where three clerks worked, surrounded by a tall enclosure with hundreds of labeled cubbies. Marlee dodged aside for a running page girl, and nipped inside before anyone else could block the doorway. She leaned over, placing her hands on the counter where various other people stood. "Anything for Marlee Forossi?"

The nearest clerk looked up, sweaty and exasperated, and glanced at the other people waiting nearby. Judging that Marlee was the biggest wheel among those present, he shot his chair back to scan a column of boxes. He pulled an envelope out of one.

Clora caught up to her then, and Marlee had a sudden urge to mischief. "While you're back there, if there's anything for Karina, Lady Bellado, here she is." She put her arm around Clora's shoulders.

The clerk nodded absently, reached into a different box in the same column and pulled out three envelopes, which he dropped in front of Clora before turning to the elderly gentleman beside her.

Marlee scooped up all the envelopes, turned, and dragged Clora back to the hallway.

"What are you doing?" Clora struggled to keep up as Marlee pushed her way back through the bustle. "You can't read Karina's mail! She'll kill you. Actually, she'll kill me, if that clerk remembers me."

"Read her mail? Certainly not, that would be wrong. Ooh, these two look like invitations. Gold ink." Marlee flipped the envelopes, but didn't recognize the seals. "No, I'm just picking them up for her. She'll get them, eventually. Maybe next week."

The address on Marlee's letter hadn't been written by Digriz. She'd hadn't seen enough of his handwriting to be sure of recognizing it, but she did know this hand, having read much of it the day before. Why would Doctor Harrick write to her so soon after their meeting? As they headed back, Marlee watched for any unoccupied room where she could stop to read it, but found nothing until they were back under the stars in the cool night air. There, she sat on a bench under a gas lamp and broke the seal.

Clora sat beside her. "Well, does he say what Lily intends?"

"Eh? Oh, no, this isn't from Eddie." Marlee re-folded the letter and tapped the edge against her palm. Should she tell Clora about the contents? She wasn't exactly on board with the going-home project. "I need to send a clacker. Do you have paper and pen?"

"You won't tell me what it says?"

"I have to answer right away, then I'll tell you later. Do you have paper?"

"I have better than that." Clora opened the clasp of the beaded bag at her waist, and pulled out a yellow clacker form and a thick pencil.

"Seriously?" Marlee took the form and laid it on the smooth stone bench. "How do you have this?"

"Bylamar's been instructing me on my duties as companion, which include carrying various necessary supplies."

"Clever Bylamar." Marlee licked the pencil tip, copied the return address from the letter, and wrote in the message space, "Yes, as soon as possible. Sample much preferred. Leaving for air port at 1650 tomorrow." She wrote her name, and folded the form. "Can you run this back to the message room?"

Clora opened the paper and glanced at it.

"I'd do it myself, but my knee hurts."

Clora stood. "You don't need to make excuses. You're the boss, after all." She started walking away. "It's up to you whether you tell me anything." Teenagers on all worlds apparently evolved passive-aggressive tendencies independently.

Marlee opened the letter and re-read it in the flickering light.

Esteemed Client,

    In the course of my researches on Doctor Rice, I ran across letters from a former student of his, one Vergentus Cloot, who retired early from academe, under some vague disgrace. The correspondence, addressed to the editor of the Royal Society's Journal on Psychical and Theological Sciences, described further experiments of his, following up on his mentor's work. There are few details, since these were just inquiries whether the journal would consider a paper on the subject, which they apparently declined to do, perhaps owing to aforementioned disgrace and the controversial nature of the research. He claims to have formulated, and refined through experiment, a combination of ingredients which allows the spirit traveler greater focus, and more influence on the inhabitants of other worlds.

I mean to take train this night to his last known address. He is quite elderly, of course, if he still lives, but I hope to learn from him or his surviving relatives, any details I might about his work. I am interested on my own account as well.

As we discussed, I doubt its utility for your intended use, but it may be helpful in conveying messages. If you wish, I will try to obtain the formula, or a sample, of his potion. Please reply to the address below before nine, or thereafter to Central Delivery, Pagentil Bay.

Respectfully, etc,
Sedon Harrick, PSD

How far was Pagentil Bay? Might he be able to return with the new drug before her departure tomorrow evening? She'd use kokoleaba again tonight, since it was what she had—indeed, she'd already taken her dose in mid-afternoon. But the way she'd slid off the hard surface of her past self's mind, the night before—perhaps with the new drug, she could break through and stay.

Marlee folded the letter, and considered. It had been incautious of Harrick to write her so openly, but he probably didn't realize how insecure the palace message center was. To be fair, when there weren't hundreds of extra people on the premises and frantic last-second party preparation underway, they were probably more careful to identify people picking up mail, but still. If he continued to work for her, they'd have to create a code or something.

Marlee looked at the letter once more, committing the names firmly to memory. Then she stood on the bench and reached up to raise the glass cover of the gas lamp, holding the paper into the flame. This was one note she couldn't afford to risk anyone seeing.

MARLEE DIDN'T USUALLY LIKE TO arrive at a party early, but there was no telling when Lily might show, and the fewer people there were around when Marlee spotted her, the better. She took a seat at the tables, again using her injured knee as an excuse. Though in truth, it pained her, and she regretted leaving her cane in the room.

The room had been reconfigured after yesterday's titles ceremony. The stands were gone, leaving a huge expanse of pale polished wood. A few other early arrivals were dancing at the far end, near the giant doors that stood open to the night, but the musicians hadn't really gotten going yet.

The royals weren't expected for at least another half hour. But, as Marlee's eye roamed the room, checking every face for Lily's features, someone stepped out of the shadow of an archway. His costume glittered with silver braid on a red jacket—Prince Drexi. His eyes roamed the room, spotted her, and he walked around the edge of the dance floor, giving perfunctory bows to the surprised partygoers who dipped before him. He grabbed a little cup of fizzy golden liquid from a passing server, and approached Marlee's table.

"Pray do not rise. May I join you?"

"Of course, your, er, highness. Congratulations on your birthday." Was that the right thing to say? She had a crazy urge to sing the Happy Birthday song, but not only was it a stupid song that she hated, but it would come out in English if she tried. "Please sit."

He pulled out a chair and slumped into it, every inch the disgruntled teen. "I despise parties. And my costume itches. I wish my brother would come home."

"You must miss him terribly."

"Not really, but when he's here I don't have to parade before the people as much. Well, there's one bright spot, at least. Tonight I get to dance with whoever I floodin' well please. Speaking of which, where's Miss Clora?"

"Running an errand for me." She'd been dispatched to the message center to check for anything from Digriz, bearing a note of authorization from Marlee, in case the clerks had gotten more careful. "She won't be long, I assure you."

Marlee ate a pickle from her plate. She had a question which might display ignorance, but after all she was from the provinces, an excuse for not knowing everything about how things were done in the capital. "It may be presumptuous, but...."

"Please, go ahead." His tone carried a hint of a suggestion that everyone else did.

"I've known Clora's mother since I was little, and Clora herself since she was born. I feel responsible for her. So I think I should ask, er, what are your intentions toward her? Your highness."

The prince snorted. "She's the first person in the longest time whom I've talked with for ten minutes straight, who hasn't asked me for anything. Well, aside from fetching the occasional stray ball. It's hard to have friends in my position."

"So you don't mean, to, um...?"

"Bed her? Come, Miss Forossi, you do know I'm sixteen years old. I'd love to. But she seems a modest girl. I won't press her."

"You're right, she's very moral."

"It's not like there aren't women willing if I chose to avail myself. I just don't care for their motives. No doubt I'll be married off to some princess or carazan before long, though. It's my duty."

With any luck, his older brother wouldn't return from the war. This boy seemed likely to make a better monarch than any other member of his family. How had he managed to grow up decent, with such parents? She raised her glass to him. "Here's hoping it's someone you like."

"My thanks. And see, here comes Miss Clora now. If you do not require her for anything else?"

"She's all yours."

Clora hurried up, blushing, and dropped into a curtsy. "Your highness...."

"Drexi."

Clora's flush deepened. "Drexi, I wish you joy of the day."

"If you will do me the honor to tread the boards with me, Clora, my joy is assured."

"Oh! C-can you?"

"Tonight, I can."

Clora looked at Marlee, pleading.

"No letter?"

"No."

Marlee made a shooing motion. "Keep an eye out."

As they moved off together, Marlee took another look around for Lily, didn't see her, but spotted Josip looking at her from across the room. He glanced at the Prince and Clora, raised an eyebrow, and gave a satisfied smirk. The old bastard.

Soon enough, the room began to fill with the brightly costumed elite of the kingdom, and Uncle Torvig joined her at the table. "We meet again, my dear." He plopped down a plate of pepper biscuits and fried squid. "Have some, if you like."

"Thanks. How's the gout?"

"A bit better. If biscuits are bad for it, by the way, I'd prefer not to know. Are you enjoying the party?"

If she had to spend the whole of it on guard for Lily, it would be the worst party of her life. The stress of it was giving her a headache, and the growing crowd was obstructing her view of the entrances, especially from her sitting position. If that damned girl didn't show soon, she'd have to alert the guards. And then think of a way to explain how she knew. And then look like an idiot if she never did show up after all.

She realized Torvig was awaiting an answer. "Oh, yes. The clothes are amazing." Torvig himself, in a flatteringly tailored outfit of blue satin with white piping studded with tiny red gems, was among the most restrained of the gathering.

Clora whirled past in the arms of a tall blue man with abundant black mustaches. She'd had at least a couple of dances with Drexi, but Marlee could no longer spot the prince's red coat among the colorful throng. He must have ducked out to make his official entrance with his family.

And indeed, at that moment, the music paused, and a deep thrumming note blown on conch shells announced the royal party. The crowd turned as one toward where the royals were to enter. Marlee stood, looking around. If Lily was here, this would be her moment to strike.

Most people this far from the action were on tiptoe, trying to see over the crowd. One person, however, a bald waiter Marlee had halfway noticed a couple of times earlier, was staring in a different direction.

Marlee followed his gaze. The man was looking at Josip, who stood sipping a narrow glass of red wine, unconcerned with the royal hoopla.

Marlee's gaze snapped back to the waiter, who now was stooping, setting his tray on the floor and stepping on the edge. Was it? It was! The shaved head had fooled her, but now she could recognize the features. And Lily now noticed Marlee looking at her, because she looked right back at Marlee, with an evil grin. Then she stood, a gleaming half-circle of metal in each hand, and lunged toward unsuspecting Josip.

Crap! She was too far away, even had she been in any condition to run. "Stop her!" Marlee screamed, pointing, and heads turned, but nobody would understand what was going on in time. Josip's head snapped around, and his eyes widened as the attacker shoved aside a large woman who was in the way, but he had nowhere to run.

And then Marlee's hand went, on its own accord, to the scarf around her neck. She grabbed one end, whipped it free, whirled it once by a weighted end, and let fly.

Lily saw the scarf coming and started away from it, but it had caught the air and slowed, falling short.

Then Marlee's other hand shot out, the hand with the matching red-orange ring, and the scarf echoed that motion, flapping across the remaining distance to wrap itself around Lily's face. Marlee snapped her hand down and around, and Lily was dragged to the ground, clawing at the fabric, while her improvised weapons clattered across the floor. A moment more, and two royal guards were on her, flipping her to apply an arm lock. "Safe!" one shouted, nevertheless looking around for any other possible attackers.

Josip had sunk to the floor, hand on his heart. A gentleman in a costume of diamonds and circles offered a hand, and Josip climbed to his feet, dusting himself off and quickly regaining his composure. He walked over to the little group standing around his attacker, and Marlee stepped out to join him, heart still pounding.

"Make way!" someone shouted. The crowd parted to let through the royal trio, queen at the fore. The little grouping around the prisoner dissolved, save for Josip, the guards, and Marlee, just arriving.

"What happened here?" the Queen asked.

One guard was just unwrapping the scarf from Lily's head. "Wha—? This is a *woman!*"

"It appears he... er, she, was after me." Josip bowed to the queen. "Most sorry for the commotion, Your Majesties."

The Queen knelt to pick up a half-tray, and tested its edge with her thumb. She glared at the guards. "How did she get in? How did this get by you?"

A guard with more metal on her uniform, presumably their captain, had just pushed her way through the crowd, and it was she who answered. "The spells evidently didn't pick it up. Be assured, ma'am, we'll learn why and correct the problem immediately."

"We'll expect a detailed report in the morning. And what is this?" She pointed to the scarf dangling from a guard's hand.

Marlee raised a hand. "That's mine. I, uh, threw it in her face to distract her."

The guard handed it back to her, as the other hoisted Lily to her feet. "Good aim. How did you know it was a woman?"

"Um?"

"You yelled, stop her."

"Oh. I recognized her. A former business rival..." Whose life we ruined. Who had legitimate cause to murder us. "... who holds a grudge because she couldn't manage to compete."

Josip looked more closely at Lily. "Valutin!"

"Count." Her voice dripped venom. "I missed, but I'm not alone. Your days are numbered." She glared at Marlee. "Yours too."

The King ambled over to look at her. "Your prisoner, then, I believe, Count. Unless you'd prefer to have our people question her?"

"If you wouldn't mind, Your Majesty," Josip said. "We didn't bring the necessary personnel or equipment from home. But I would hurry. She displays signs of grevaxtin poisoning, presumably self-administered."

The guard captain grabbed Lily's hand to look at her fingernails, and swore. "Hustle," she told the guards. "Room three." They marched the prisoner away, and the captain pointed to a page who stood among the watching crowd. "You, girl. Have the physician on duty meet us there. Run! Sire, if I may?"

The king waved dismissal, and the captain hurried off with the tray halves. The king didn't watch her go, but clapped for attention, walking toward the musicians. The crowd, and Josip, followed.

With the wall of spectators breaking up, Clora finally pushed through, mumbling apologies. She took Marlee's arm. "I couldn't see what happened. Are you all right?"

"I'm not sure. I mean, I'm not hurt. But I couldn't save her. I couldn't even tell her I was sorry."

"It's not your fault."

The King had stepped up onto a low platform with the musicians, to be visible to all the gathering. "My friends, we regret this unpleasantness, but refuse to let it spoil our evening. Come here, my boy." Drexi joined him on the platform, and the king laid a hand on his shoulder, wobbling slightly. "My youngest son is legally a man today, and a fine man he is. Studious, serious, a little boring perhaps, but responsible for fewer of my gray hairs than any of my other children. He does his duties to the people diligently, and his duties to the gods devotedly, and I know they all value his service. We gather tonight to honor him." He patted Drexi's shoulder heavily. "A big cheer for my boy."

Marlee and Clora joined in the shouting and finger-snapping, then the king told the musicians to play something lively, her cue to return to her table, to be out of the way of the dancers.

"Do you need me?" Clora asked.

Karina was just leading Torvig onto the dance floor, but Marlee wouldn't be alone, since her grandfather stood beside the table. "No, it looks like grandpa wants a private chat anyway. Go have fun."

Josip waited for her to sit first. "So. Her Majesty would be dismayed to know that not one but two people smuggled weapons past her guards."

Marlee touched the scarf at her neck. "This one is hardly lethal."

"I suppose not. Thank you for the timely assistance. A pity she won't live long enough for us to learn who she's been plotting with."

The rush of action was fading. Marlee's headache was returning with a vengeance. She looked around for a server, but they all seemed to have vanished. In fact, the last one was being escorted out by a guard. Of course, they must be checking there were no more imposters, maybe asking questions about how Lily had gotten in.

She rested her forehead on the heel of her hand. "Grandfather, would you get me a glass of water or something? I'm feeling shaky."

"Certainly." The chair scraped, and she was alone again.

Poor Lily! There was no way for Marlee to have saved her, even if she'd spotted her much earlier. But despite Clora's reassurance, she did feel guilty about it. If only she'd done something sooner! She could've written a letter. Gone to see her.

And been shot for her trouble, probably. Nobody named Valutin would've been interested in anything she had to say.

Had she done the wrong thing in stopping her? If Lily had managed to kill Josip, she would at least have died happy, and the horrible old man probably deserved it many times over. Marlee had been intent on stopping the attack, to save Lily. By the time Lily was rushing at her intended victim, it was too late. There was no way to stop her quietly then. But there hadn't been time to think about that. She'd meant to stop Lily, and she had.

Something clunked down on the table, and she opened her eyes. As Josip settled back into his chair, she reached for the small tumbler, but he held up his hand. "Have a care. It's not water. Thought you could use something stronger."

Marlee took a small sip of the clear liquid. Vodka, or something similar, with a hint of bitter citrus. Smooth. She took a bigger sip.

Josip pushed a small enameled case across the table, and she gave him a questioning look.

"Willow bark. You look like you need it."

She opened the box, took out a gray-flecked pill. Should she be taking drinks and pills from this man, though? Well, why not? If he wanted her dead, there was no need for subterfuge or for causing commotion at a royal event. She washed the pill down with a big slug of vodka, then belatedly remembered alcohol and kokoleaba weren't a good mix. She pushed the glass away. "Thanks. That'll help." She cleared her throat. "So. You don't think she was working alone."

"Why poison herself, if she had nobody to protect? No, she's probably with the anarchists. It's their style, don't you think? They like to make a big show." Josip had brought a drink for himself, too, a glass of wine to replace the one he'd dropped during the attack. He gave her a measuring look as he sipped it.

He was always sitting there passing judgment on her. It was seriously annoying. "What?"

"It might've been more convenient for you if she'd succeeded. After all, the matter of Benin is still unresolved."

"Yeah, I thought of that."

"Before or after intervening?"

Marlee reached for her glass, then remembered. She set her hands in her lap. "Since I didn't kill him, I'm not worried."

"Hmph. Well, again, thanks." Josip levered himself to his feet. "I should go congratulate the Prince. Will you come?"

"He and I already had a friendly little chat. We're like that." Marlee held up two fingers together.

"Like what?"

"We're close. Buddies. It's been a fun party, but maybe enough excitement for one night, so I believe I'll turn in early. Give him my regards."

Josip shrugged, and levered himself upright. "Then I wish you good dreams. Our carriage will be ready just after tea tomorrow. Be on it."

Would Harrick be back by then? "I'd rather stay on for a few days."

"No." He wandered off, looking for the Prince. Marlee waited a minute more before standing.

Clora spotted her, and excused herself from a dance with a rotund officer to run after her. "You're leaving?"

"Yes, but you stay. The more dances you can get in with the Prince, the happier Josip will be."

Clora smiled. Her reasons for wanting to stay had little to do with pleasing Josip. Marlee gave her a gentle push back toward the dancing, and went out into the night.

WHEN THE KNOCK CAME. MARLEE ignored it. Clora would just let herself in, and she couldn't think of anyone else she was interested in talking to, and she was well into the trashy romance novel she'd found in Clora's trunk. After it became clear the visitor wasn't giving up, though, she sighed, set the book aside, and put on her robe.

It was the Haka San, looking irritatingly serene as usual.

"Yes?"

"May I enter?"

Marlee stood aside and the woman brushed by. "I thought you weren't talking to me."

"Your friend sent me. She worries about you." The Haka San looked around at the floor. "Was there an accident?"

Marlee used her foot to brush aside a few pearl buttons, which rolled under the bed. "I had to undress myself."

"Are you journeying tonight?"

"Why do you ask?"

Without asking, the Haka San took the armchair, glancing at the book on the side table. "I will stay to guide you."

"Don't you mean, to prevent my escape?"

"What you desire will only destroy you."

"Really? Because the way you were talking before, it sounded like you thought my plan was possible, only wrong."

"Very well. It could destroy not only you, but also an innocent. Fortunately for her, you cannot do it, but you may still come to harm as you try."

Would the woman interfere, if Marlee had a chance to flee back to

Earth? Maybe. On the other hand, she'd so far had no luck even getting noticed by anyone back home, much less taking over their body. Her body. She needed to stay focused, to remember what she was there for. Maybe she could learn how to do that tonight.

"Stay if you like. But I'm not sleepy yet, so hand me my book." Marlee flopped onto the bed and riffled through the book, looking for her place. "I'm sure I'll be at least an hour, if you want to go back to the party."

"It didn't suit me. There was no place of quiet to talk in."

To hold court in, she meant. "Well, don't sit there staring at me."

"I'll use the time for contemplation."

Napping by any other name... "Fine, but contemplate in a different direction, if you don't mind."

EDSGAR

THE DOOR OPENED QUIETLY, AND someone slipped in, briefly illuminated by the light from the hallway. Digriz snorted through his nose and struggled against his bonds, but made no more progress than he had for the last two hours.

She loomed over him. "If you call out, I'll have to wallop you over the head with this baton. I really don't want to. I believe you're true to the cause. I'm just not certain." She rolled his head to the side and removed the gag.

Digriz spit out the damp rag that had been stuffed behind it. "Imealde, this is insane! Untie me!"

"Not just yet, I think."

A while earlier, the clock in the Hephaestus temple had tolled three. "Why not? Everything must be over by now. What happened to Lily?" His voice was rough, mouth dry and filthy tasting.

"Here." Imealde held a glass to his lips, and he took a long drink of water, then bumped the rim away with his chin.

Imealde set the glass down. "There's been no word, so I believe she failed. She never expected to escape, but there should at least be whispers, if she succeeded in killing the monster Josip. Don't worry, they can't make her betray us. She took poison."

So Marlee hadn't been the main target, at least. Though no doubt Lily would've finished off as many other members of the family as possible, after dealing with the new Count. "I honor her sacrifice for our freedom. So that it's not in vain, release me, and let's get out of town."

"We made an arrangement, she and I. We decided if they questioned her about the airship plot, she would give them an address where her co-conspirators were hiding. If they didn't ask about the airship, she'd give them a different address. Calm down, they're the addresses of empty buildings."

"What was the point of that?"

"I just came back from checking those places. If they'd raided the first one, we'd be on our way to the train station now. But the second one's being watched. I assume they've been inside, but of course I didn't go close enough to check. So it seems they don't really know about the airship plan. What do you make of that?"

Digriz stared at her dark outline, his mind racing. "Ah. Well! Good work! It means I'll have a sharp-edged conversation with the person who sent me that letter."

"If such a person even exists. It raises the question of why they would warn us, rather than warning the Seidos about us."

"You know what the politics of our organization are like. Gotsgill is probably behind this. When we destroy the tyrants, he wants to be on top. He doesn't want me to have this victory. But he doesn't want us dead, either."

"It's that likelihood which keeps you breathing."

"Really, why would I go to all this trouble only to drop it and go home? Whose agenda does that serve?"

"That consideration, also, contributes to your survival."

"Free me, then, and we'll move forward with the plan, since we are not expected, after all."

"You've arranged everything so nicely, I believe I can complete the plan alone. That way, I don't have to worry about whether to trust you."

"But who will seal you into the crate?"

"Lily was most ingenious. She concocted a way I can do that myself."

"It seems you've thought of everything. Well, if you feel you must leave me tied up, I can't fault your logic. But you must release me for a minute, so I can relieve myself."

"Must I?"

"Of course. Then, you may tie me up again."

"It would be most unpleasant for you to soil the bedclothes."

"It would indeed."

"Unpleasant, but not fatal. Whereas, releasing you might be fatal for me."

It would be pleasant to kill her, but not necessary. He could easily render her unconscious. "My word of honor, madam—"

"Is not enough to sway me in this matter. Now, before I put the gag on, will you have more water?"

"In the circumstances, the less I drink, the better."

"Truly? I've paid a fellow to drop by this evening and free you, but you'll get terribly thirsty meanwhile." She held up the glass. "A few more sips?"

"I will abide."

"As you wish." Imealde's hand moved to his mouth. "Open up."

Digriz glared at her in the darkness.

"Come, now, my man. I can open it myself after I club you."

Digriz sighed, and opened his mouth. The same saliva-damp rag was stuffed back into it, then the sash replaced around his chin and tightly retied.

"Those cargo hands start their pickups pretty early, so I'd best be going now." Imealde patted his head. "If all goes well, I'll see you in Corilan and we'll laugh about this. Well, I'll laugh, at least. I'll buy you several drinks for your inconvenience, and it will be a fair story to tell for years to come."

The door opened and closed again, and he was alone. He twisted furiously, but it was no use. The flooding women had secured him most unconventionally, perhaps through inexperience, but with Lily's engineer's eye to guard against his escape. They'd stripped him to his undergarments, so all his tools were across the room. They'd tied his feet together, and his arms and wrists to his sides, with loops to prevent him bringing his hands together. Then they'd wrapped him tightly in layers of sheets, with more ropes around the outside to hold it on snugly and attach him to the bed.

Digriz had managed to loosen the sheets around his thighs enough to get one hand awkwardly twisted around, to pick at the sheets with his fingernails. He'd picked through one layer, with who knew how many to go, and his fingers were already sore. Once he got through, he'd try to find knots to untie. He couldn't be sure in the darkness, but feared they'd had the sense to place the rope ends out of his reach. Still, getting a hand into open air would be a start.

It was, at least, something to distract him from the growing pressure in his bladder.

MARLEE

LXI

THIS VISION HAD THE FOGGY, jumpy quality Marlee associated with events that she, her body back home, wasn't present to witness. She was looking at a pale disk on a dark background. She focused, and the disk developed a frosty texture with a starburst in the center, inside a shiny ring. It was illuminated briefly as the car passed a streetlight, and she saw the dome light of a car. Of Bobby's car, a restored 1970-something Chevy Camaro.

She drifted up to look forward, between the seats. Outside was just whirling blobs of light, but the orange glow of the dashboard was sharp, as was the outline of Bobby's crewcut and protruding ears. Another outline was in the passenger seat, shorter, hair pulled back in a brushy ponytail, moving animatedly, talking with her hands.

Who was with him? And could she get sound on this thing?

Is this your friend?

Wait, was there someone else here? Oh, yeah, the Haka San. Marlee felt drifty, unfocused. *That's Bobby. I don't know this chick.*

There was a jump. Still in the car, but no longer traveling. The outdoors steadied for a moment, lights spread out before and below. She recognized the view from up on the bluff, overlooking town. The unknown chick's head rested on Bobby's shoulder, which Marlee knew took deliberate effort because of the big divider between the seats. Why are you letting her do that? And what is she doing with her hands? Maybe nothing, she couldn't see.

They were sitting still, or maybe time was just being funny again. But Bobby didn't bring girls up there just to admire the view. The last time she'd been there with him, she'd spent more time looking at that dome light than the city lights. *How can I tell when this is?*

She couldn't see her guide, but got an impression of a shrug.

Look about you.

The scene was starting to slip. She got another glimpse out a side window. No snow on the ground, leafy branches against the sky. *Could it be after winter? The next year?* But she already knew, could imagine the dry tone of the answer the Haka San didn't bother to make. Bobby had replaced her very quickly.

Well, who was she kidding? Any number of girls would be happy to console Bobby for his loss, and he wasn't the type to mope around. If she were on the spot, he wouldn't stray, but he wouldn't see the point of loyalty to someone who wasn't around to appreciate it. She *would* get him back, she vowed as the scene dissolved. She'd get him back before she ever lost him.

Threads spun past, and she reached out, grabbed one. This scene, too, had the unreal quality of not being present in person. It was painted in flat cartoon cutouts. She was at a bar, a heavy, uneven countertop. Across the room, past thick arches of unpainted brick, windows looked out over a sunlit pedestrian street, where a mix of European tourists and hippies wandered past. She recognized the place from a visit with her father a couple of years back. The weird little pot-infused freetown in Copenhagen was his favorite break between business meetings. She'd been of legal drinking age in Denmark at the time, but nobody'd been checking IDs there in any case.

She looked around and found him on the next stool over, staring over the bar at an antique sign advertising crackers that probably hadn't been sold in fifty years. He had an empty tumbler before him, and a bowl of peanuts. She maneuvered herself in front of him, trying to make him see her, but his flat gaze passed right through.

Dad, I'm here.

Her invisible companion loomed beside her. *Be where he is.*

Marlee twisted, tried to imagine herself sitting on the stool her father occupied. Settled down, felt the wooden countertop under her hands, worn smooth from decades of other hands. The glass was no longer even a little cold. There was a whiff of something frying, children shouting from the street.

I'm here. No, too non-specific. *It's Marlee. I'm okay.*

He picked up a napkin, took a pen from his shirt pocket, started drawing. He didn't seem to have heard her, but for whatever reason, he was thinking of her, because he drew her face. The old one, of course. Their attic contained sketches and paintings he'd done in college, and he was really pretty good. He should've been doing that instead of tax law. A few more lines added the features of her mother, beside her.

He sighed, folded the napkin, tore it once.

Marlee remembered the vision she'd had of her mother, stopped in the middle of cleaning out her room to curl up on the bed. *Go home. Lisbet needs you. Tell her not to worry about me. Tell her... I'm sorry.*

The flat outlines were going solid color, wavering. Her last chance, perhaps ever, to get a message across. She pushed it hard. *I'm coming home.*

And then she was out, whirling, colors flashing around her.

Return now, someone thought at her. Was there someone else with her? Wasn't there something else she was supposed to be doing? She had to find herself in all this mess.

Enough. She felt herself yanked, twisted around, shoved. She sat up in darkness, gasping, clutching at the bedclothes, head spinning, nose running.

What time was it? She had to get back to sleep, try again. She groped for the bedside light and shook it just enough to read the clock. Almost four, and Clora wasn't back yet. Must be quite a party.

The Haka San was still there, a dark shape slumped in the armchair. Shouldn't she be awake, too, if she was jerking others back into consciousness, ruining their chances?

Marlee climbed out of bed and went to check on her. She was breathing heavily, apparently asleep. Marlee shook her shoulder, but she didn't wake.

"Right," Marlee muttered. "Extreme measures." The water pitcher near the window was about half full. She poured half of that over the somnolent mystic, then tilted the woman's head back to direct the rest of it right in her face.

The Haka San heaved up, coughing, grabbing at Marlee's nightdress. She said a word in a foreign language, probably impolite, and lurched forward, staggering past Marlee to lean over the bed.

"Wake up."

The Haka San glared at her for a moment, before her usual calm expression snapped back like a mask. Marlee smirked.

"You were nearly lost." The Haka San stood, bunching up her robe to wring water out of it. "*I* was nearly lost, and I know what I'm about. And you can see what good it did. He didn't hear you. You risk us both for nothing."

"I'm not making you stay." Should she tell the Haka San about the possible new, stronger drug? Given her opposition to the whole project, she wasn't likely to make any useful suggestions. At least tomorrow night she'd be on the airship, far away from any well-meaning interference.

Marlee wished she'd left herself some water to wash the taste from her mouth. There was no hint of dawn, but she wasn't sleepy anymore. "Maybe there's breakfast available at this hour." She tilted her head at the door. "Perhaps you'll step out to let me change?"

The Haka San left without a word. Marlee chose her Boraggan jangly pajamas. The other outfit she could put on without assistance was her riding clothes, a silly thing to walk through the palace in. When she stepped out, the Haka San was gone. Well, fine. It's not like they had anything new to say to each other.

IT WAS A MUCH SMALLER and surlier crowd boarding the airmast elevator this time—Marlee, Josip, Petro, Elga and the baby, Karina, and their assorted hangers-on. The staff looked alert, but the family were all, in varying degrees, the worse for wear, except for Elga and herself. Few people had left the party before five.

She still wore her jangly duds. Petro raised an eyebrow, then looked around. "Where's your little genius? You're not leaving the child here on her own?"

The cage jerked into motion, and Marlee grabbed a post, heart already racing at the thought of riding up the swaying mast. "She's running an errand for me. I saw something in a store earlier that I just realized I needed. Don't worry, she won't miss the flight."

Clora had been sent to meet the last possible train that might bring Harrick back with the new drug. He'd neither shown up, nor sent word. What was the dratted man up to? The place he'd gone was only a couple of hours away, plenty of time to go, get the drug and return. She would've gone herself, for whatever incentive she could contribute, but Josip had made it pretty clear she wasn't going anywhere without him.

There was, at least, one thing Harrick and the Haka San agreed on—she didn't have unlimited time to pull this off. At any moment, Earth might go out of range forever. Every day, every hour was a strain.

Marlee moved to the edge of the cage, forcing herself to watch the city growing smaller below her, and fought down fear. At least on this trip, she'd made sure to get a cabin without a window. She looked up at the airship, a different one than their trip out, larger, painted in angular blue and black interlocking patterns. A dark opening in the bottom of the gondola was in use for loading cargo, a cable reeling in a large crate. As it reached the opening, crew leaned out with poles to guide it in. The sight gave her shivers every time.

They drew even with the platform, clanked to a stop, and a crewman pulled back the door. Then they had to wait while a couple of his colleagues finished wrestling a trunk down the gangway.

This airship was as clean and well-maintained as the first, but had a more utilitarian look. No niches with vases of fake flowers, no artwork. It was a cargo ship, with a few passenger cabins as an afterthought. With so few flying back, there was no need to take up a whole ship that could carry paying passengers. The captain greeted them himself, a burly, worried looking man in a neat but faded uniform, soft from many washings, the rank bars on the collar slightly tarnished. "Your gear will be aboard directly, sirs." He peered down the gangway to gauge the height of the remaining stack. "We're scheduled to detach in forty minutes. I must see to the loading. The steward will provide anything you require." He pointed to a short, thin woman whose uniform was slightly more shabby than his. She bowed.

Marlee didn't require anything. She just wanted to be in her cabin, away from people. She'd wanted to go into town again, use her little remaining time to see a few sights she'd heard about. But she couldn't leave in case Harrick should arrive. That made her so snappish that Clora had refused to hang out with her. She'd gone off somewhere to sleep or practice spells or something, while Marlee wandered around the gardens, checking in periodically with the people at the gates to make sure they knew where she could be found.

Then finally she'd had to go in to pack up her things, only to find Clora had done it, so she fussed at Clora for putting away the book she wanted. Clora had opened Marlee's trunk, taken out the book, which was at the top, dropped it on the table, and gone out without a word, leaving Marlee furious and embarrassed.

Well, she'd make it up to her. She'd added four more top-notch inventions to her list, and stuck the document in Clora's trunk, so she'd be sure to find it when she unpacked. That should ensure her future. Karina might still want to kill her, but wouldn't as long as Clora could make the family big money. Assuming, of course, Marlee wasn't around to provide the protection herself.

EDSGAR

DIGRIZ SPOTTED CLORA FROM TWO blocks away, in front of
the air port building. She didn't walk in, however, but paced back and forth
near the entrance. He quickened his pace, hoping to catch her before she
made up her mind to go inside. But before he got near, she reached some
resolve, and passed between the guards standing at the entrance.

Digriz couldn't do the same. The two large men regarded him with
suspicion as he approached with a genial smile, and one moved to block
him. "This mast is in use by a private party."

"I'm well aware." The nearest guard tensed as Digriz reached into his
tunic. Last night's attack must have them on edge. Moving slowly, Digriz
withdrew a letter and extended it to the guard. "I merely have some
information for Miss Marlee, which she requested."

The guard stared at the letter for a moment before taking it, and at
Digriz's hand. "Someone tie you up?"

Digriz rubbed the raw skin on his wrist. "My lady friend likes rough play."

"Hmph." Without taking his eyes away from the visitor, the guard
reached back to knock on the door frame. After a few seconds, a squarish
woman poked her head out, and the guard handed the message back to her.

She pulled a lorgnette from her bosom to look at the envelope, then
looked over them at Digriz. "Will you expect a reply?"

"No." He had no intention of standing around while people inside
decided whether he should be detained. "But she particularly requested

this, so please make certain she receives it." He turned and left, trying to walk purposefully but not in a special hurry.

By the time he'd freed himself, and gotten cleaned up, he knew time was short. There was no point in going to the palace, and while he could tell which mast the airship would leave from by simply reading the name from the ship's side, there was little chance he could catch up with Marlee before she boarded. Given the previous night's incident, letters might be intercepted.

So, he'd used a simple cipher Marlee had shown him to quickly encrypt an innocuous message. Then he'd carefully, slightly thickened or lengthened the ends of certain strokes of the characters, to encrypt the real message. He could only send a few words this way, but the phrase "bomber on board" should suffice, and was all he had time for anyway.

He strolled toward the market. Had he done the right thing? He could've written a plain warning to the ship's captain, or to old Josip. That would be more certain. But no, Marlee would certainly want to choose how to handle it. If it suited her to raise the alarm, she could, but if she preferred to quietly dispose of the problem, she doubtless had the means to do that also. She would be unhappy about his failure to stop the plot from getting so far, but overall, no harm done.

In two hours, he could catch an evening train for Corilan. Meanwhile, it was perfect weather for an icy drink.

MARLEE

L ✕ ┆┆┆

MARLEE WAITED NEAR THE BOARDING door, ready to try to order the crew to delay departure, but it turned out not to be necessary. Clora arrived just after the last armload of small cargo. She gave Marlee a cool glance and sailed past, following signs to the tiny combined passenger lounge and dining hall.

How was Marlee to interpret that? Had the girl gotten the damn drug or not? Marlee hurried after, but couldn't ask because Petro and Elga were seated at a wicker table, sharing a newspaper.

Petro looked up, and gestured at the untidy stack of newsprint on the table. "Join us, if you like."

"Thanks, I will." Clora sat with them, and flipped through the stack. "Is there anything cold to drink? I've been running all over town, and I'm parched."

Elga leaned back to pull a bell cord, and within two minutes Clora was perusing the war news over a glass of mint tea. Marlee sat at the one other table, trying to appear calm.

"Here's a description of the party." Elga smoothed the paper down. "Too bad you missed so much of it, sister. It was quite the event."

Petro looked over his own paper. "I skimmed it. No mention of the would-be assassin, I noticed."

Elga was poring over the columns. "No, they don't care to cast abroad the fact someone snuck through their security. The Information Office would never approve. But there is a mention of you, Clora dear."

"Is there?" Clora almost squeaked, setting aside the Mechanics section of the paper to lean over the article with Elga.

"Not by name, but see here? 'This reporter observed, that a young country lady of no particular birth but considerable charms, attired in dusty rose silk with a sufficiency of bows, had several dances with His Highness over the course of the night.' That is you, I believe?"

"Mother will be pleased. But I'm a little surprised they printed that, since his mother was none too pleased."

"It's good press," Petro said. "Every girl can put herself in Clora's place, in their dreams. Let the common people think the Prince isn't proud."

"He *isn't* proud," Marlee said. "I like him."

"How did they know I'm from the country?"

Petro and Elga exchanged an amused glance over Clora's head, those supercilious assholes. But she was also jealous. Her brother and father weren't nice people—ruthless would be a kind description. But they'd made good marriages. They had a rapport with their wives that she'd never observed in her own parents—nor found for herself.

Marlee stood abruptly. "I'm going to stroll around. Clora, I'd like your help with something when you have a moment."

Halfway down the hallway, the departure bell rang, and Marlee braced herself against the wall through the slight lurch and gentle swaying of departure. Another few seconds, and the hum of engines came through the walls.

There wasn't much place to stroll in the tiny passenger section, but nobody challenged her passing under the "Crew Only" sign to wander the larger part of the ship. She walked past large storage rooms where crew were busy with last minute sorting and strapping down of cargo. Better to finish that before launch, she'd have thought, but no doubt they had their reasons.

Down a set of stairs, past more cargo space, crew quarters, a kitchen, tiny offices. She passed a cross-hallway lined with square wicker cubbies stuffed with parachutes. Then she came to an open space with large windows around three sides. Three people sat at control boards, and the captain stood by a polished wood steering wheel and set of levers, listening to a small, earnest young woman talk about trim and balance. He frowned at Marlee, then ignored her to attend to the report.

"Well done," he said at last. The small woman smiled, pivoted, and left, and the captain turned to Marlee. "May I help you?"

She could pretend to be doing an owner inspection, but he might try to explain things to her, and pretending to listen sounded like too much work. "Just aimlessly wandering. Please carry on."

"Don't wander too near the controls, if you please. Nothing is locked down until we're properly underway."

"Understood. Just enjoying the view."

It was a pleasant view, of city giving way to larger, scattered homes and farm fields, a glittering lake, puffy white clouds. Distant blue mountains. She could almost ignore the expanse of empty air inches beneath her feet.

Of course, if she stayed here, Clora wouldn't know where to find her. So she returned the way she'd come, and met Clora coming down the stairs as she was going up.

"There you are. Do you have something for me?"

"I have." Clora walked slowly down the steps, Marlee backing up so they could meet on level floor. Clora looked around.

"Nobody will hear us here, if you keep your voice down."

Clora withdrew a small brown box from her side-purse. "I debated whether to give you this, or throw it away."

"You made the right choice." Marlee opened the box, to find a small vial of green crystals and a folded piece of paper in tiny handwriting, Harrick's.

"I hope I can convince you not to use it, though. It's so dangerous...."

"If you check your trunk, I've put something in there to guarantee your value to the family. You don't have to fear Karina after I'm gone."

"That's not really the point, or at least not all of it... wait. You hid something in my trunk?"

"A document."

"I went to the cabin to look for you, and Josip is in there, searching it."

"*What?* You didn't think you should lead with that information?"

"I didn't think there was anything for him to find."

Marlee ran down the hallway and stuck the little box in beside a parachute in the nearest row, back out of sight, to not have it on her in case she was searched. Then she hurried to her cabin.

Josip wasn't searching when Marlee arrived. He was seated on Clora's bunk, with Marlee's bunk raised to let the trunks under it stand open. Her things were scattered around. The shallow wooden case containing her scarves was open on the bunk beside him, and beside the bloodstained section of tree branch.

Josip looked up at her with sad eyes. Picked up a scarf, the gray-green one, and laid it across the log. It was a good match for the gray bark and green moss growing on it. "So."

Marlee stood in the doorway, thunderstruck. "Grandfather, I swear...."

"Don't. No more lies." He shoved the scarf and matching ring into his pocket. "I'm surprised you kept it. You must've been certain no-one would figure it out. Of course, that ruse with the stable-boy was inspired. You had us all looking at the horse. And no trace of magic at the scene, since you'd removed the enchanted item." He stood, moving slowly. Looking old, broken. "I'd so hoped I was wrong."

Marlee moved aside to let him leave, hardly tracking, seeing Elga stopped in the corridor, little Josip over her shoulder. Marlee pulled the door closed, and sank onto Clora's bunk, a pit yawning open inside her.

Then the door opened again and Clora slipped in. "I had to wait until they were gone... gods, Marlee, what's the matter?"

"Oh, Clora," she whispered. "I did it. I killed Benin."

"How... no, never mind how. That wasn't you."

"Wasn't it? Then who was it? What am I? Shit, it doesn't matter. Josip will kill me for it anyway. Someone has to pay."

"Maybe it's time to tell them, then. If he knew the person he wants to punish is already gone...."

"Sure, that doesn't sound a bit like a wild-assed excuse to keep from being executed. How could I prove it? And what would they do with me if they did believe it?" She crossed her arms over her stomach. "Oh, Clora, I'm scared."

Clora moved closer, put an arm around Marlee's shoulders, and held her silently for a few minutes, rocking slowly from side to side.

"I guess it's time to try your escape." Clora stood. "I saw where you hid it. I'll be right back."

While Clora was gone, Marlee picked up her things and crammed them into the trunk any old way, then lowered the bunk. This revealed a letter, poking from the gap between mattress and wall. Probably it'd been placed on the bed, and slid down when Josip flung it open. She broke the seal and had a look, but it was in code. She didn't know how to decode any of her own codes, unfortunately, though Bylamar always decoded the ones he knew how, before giving them to her. Bylamar wasn't on this trip, though, so she'd do what she always did with the ones she couldn't read—hope it was nothing too important.

Probably just a reminder from Digriz about his minion who needed rescuing from justice—and she'd already told Bylamar to deal with that.

Nothing, at any rate, to compare with her current problem.

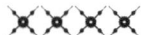

THE NEW DRUG IS BRIGHT, diamond-sharp. Other worlds twine around, the bends upon bends where they brush. Her home, her two homes, where she is and where she wants to go. Her fingers brush the few strands in reach, and there's the feel of sunshine on skin, scent of bread toasting, flashes of vision.

There. She finds herself, mind busy, typing. She bashes her way into the thread, sees with her old eyes. She's in her dorm room, at her computer, working at that damn Econ final project. It's a third of her grade for the course, and needs to be pretty near perfect to eke out a B overall. She's stiff from sitting too long, has a bit of a headache, and is starting to hate the subject.

The experience is weird, hard-edged but dreamlike. She's in the chair at the computer, feeling the keys click, her neck crick, but at the same time drifting alongside. The drug shows her the mind of her other self, sparks and lines and stacks of memories, hovering around her head. She tries to settle into the chair with her other self, and the sensations grow more real, though she still feels like she's surrounding the body rather than inhabiting it.

Time for a break. Other her is on a roll and doesn't want to stop typing, but Marlee focuses on her discomforts. She saves the document, stands, stretches.

The instructions for the drug had been vague on how to actually move into a new body—understandable, since no-one had actually done it and then been able to report back. Dr. Rice's student hadn't dared try, but, *You need a mirror,* Harrick had written. There was one on the closet door. She walked over to look into it.

It doesn't make sense for a mind to have a reflection, of course. She supposes, like all the Haka San's lies, the mirror is a metaphor to guide her perception. She can see other Marlee's mind in the glass, and her own, in her ghostly self, clutching and surrounding the body. Her mind is hard, faceted. Durable. If she mushed it against the fuzzy, blobby mind of other her, it would win.

Dominate, crush, destroy.

But that's my body. I have the right.

Do I? Who am I?

It was hard to compare her drug-tempered mind to the shifting softness of the other Marlee. But they weren't as identical as she'd thought. She had a sense of what the different parts were, and when she looked closely at any part, it ramified, grew more complex.

She explored. Other Marlee, deciding it was too discouraging to stare in the mirror at her incipient zits and too-long nose, went down the hall to the vending machines for a snack.

If she took over, would she really be moving in? Or destroying another mind to make a copy of herself, the original escaping execution only by erasing itself first?

The Haka San's voice rang in her mind. *If you steal this body, who have you become?*

The woman was a nag even when she wasn't anywhere nearby.

Marlee sat before the computer again, setting her potato chip bag on the Formica desk surface. Oh, bliss, potato chips. She should invent those.

Marlee made herself not feel like resuming work on the paper, which wasn't difficult in the least. Closed that document. Closed her eyes.

She couldn't do it. Other Marlee didn't deserve to be demolished. But perhaps she could be saved.

It wouldn't make sense to resolve to not go to a party she hadn't been invited to. Such a nonsensical decision might not stick. Other Marlee needed her mind changed in subtle ways, but her unpracticed fumbling might shred the delicate structures of mind.

The Haka San's remembered voice wove through her mind. *You are the stories you tell yourself about yourself. Tell a different story.*

Marlee hesitated a moment more, then opened her eyes, raised her hands, started a new document. *ABOUT ME,* she typed.

• *I don't really like Economics. I could find something I actually love to do.*

And she riffled through her memories, found Clora sitting with her magic text late at night, surrounded by crumpled papers. Found her gleefully demonstrating how to separate salt from water. And gently, she tapped these memories into the mind before her. In this Marlee's mind, found the sad image of an attic full of her father's paintings and brought it to the fore.

• *I deserve better than Bobby. Someone it would really hurt to lose, who would grieve if he lost me. Real love doesn't come without risk.*

And she found the memory of Tam and Severn teasing each other during the carriage ride to the palace. Of Petro and Elga exchanging a secret look of amusement. Of the way Jeyne looked at Alyssa when he thought no-one was watching.

• *My dad loves me and misses me. The divorce wasn't about me. It was about him, and he may be regretting it now.*

Which went with a memory of him in that hippie bar, drawing pictures of his ex-family on a napkin. Other Marlee would think she'd invented these memories, but they would still be there, still have an effect. She hoped.

• *I need to drink less. Instead of hiding from my unhappiness, I could learn to be happy.*

That was the key one, the life-saving one, but she didn't have a positive memory to reinforce it. Only lying in shadow near a tall wall, cold creeping in on her, unable to move. Perhaps those were her last conscious moments. But the connection wasn't clear, it wasn't persuasive.

She had to do one more thing, to make sure.

She printed the document, saved, closed. The next step would be resisted, so she had to be sneaky. She moved the mouse to the new document, meaning to drag it to a new location, but forgot to press the mouse button to pick it up, until the pointer was over a different document, *"Econ Final Project."* Which she dragged until she could accidentally drop it onto the Shredder program, which security-conscious Bobby had insisted she install.

PERMANENTLY DESTROY
ECON FINAL PROJECT?

"What? No!" Marlee moved the mouse to the "No" button, but her other hand had leapt up in alarm, coming down with the index finger on the "Y" key.

The computer speakers emitted a mechanical grinding noise, and the paper was gone. Marlee leapt up from her seat with a wail of dismay. "No! I said no!" And she leapt for her phone to call Bobby, knowing there was no way to recover it—that was the whole purpose of the Shredder program. But she had to try.

My work here is done. Marlee let the thread drop away. No way the poor girl could go to a party in two days' time now. She'd need every spare minute to recreate her paper. Plus, it had given definite evil satisfaction to destroy the hateful document. Blue-glowing world lines swirled around her, and she let herself be drawn back... home.

SHE WOKE TO FIND CLORA leaning over her, looking concerned, then relieved. "You scared me," Clora whispered. "You stopped breathing four times. I told you that was too big a dose."

"How long was I gone?"

Clora glanced at her watch. "About an hour. The instructions say drink a lot of water, and move around, and we can try again in four more hours."

Marlee shook her head. "I'm done. Water sounds good, though." She was limp, wrung-out.

Clora poured a glass from their pitcher. "What do you mean, you're done? What will you do about Josip?"

Marlee's hand shook as she took the glass. "I don't know. Wait to see what he does."

Clora paced the floor, wicker creaking beneath the rug. "You *know* what he'll do."

Marlee swallowed water. Shrugged. "It's out of my hands. It didn't work." A lie. Clora was a good person, one who could understand how the price of escape could be too high, even to avoid death. Marlee just didn't have the energy for that discussion now. She forced herself to stand, swung her arms. "Let's walk around and get this stuff out of my system."

Clora was quiet, despondent, as they walked the night-dimmed passages. Marlee's step felt lighter—a burden had dropped away. But she respected her friend's mood, and refrained from chatter. They made the round of the top level, encountering a few night shift crew doing cleaning or repairs.

The wheel in the control room was locked down with a strap, on a fixed heading, and the boards were all covered, except for one manned by a sleepy-looking woman who straightened when they entered. The land was pitch black under a splendid sweep of stars. Far ahead, blinking lights showed another airship on the same route. "Are we over the wasteland?" Marlee asked.

The crew woman looked around. "Not yet. This is desert, so some things live here. Another hour should bring us over the wastes."

"Not a good place to have engine trouble."

"Not to worry, ma'am. The winds are prevailing inland at this altitude, and we can change altitude if we need to. So long as we have buoyancy, we'll get back over habitable land before long."

Marlee shut up and looked at the stars. There was Orion, but nothing else looked familiar. Not that she would know. No doubt if the moon was the same, the stars were too.

By unspoken assent, after a few minutes, they retraced their steps. But when they reached the cross-corridor where the parachutes were stored, Clora fell back.

Marlee turned to look at her. Clora was staring at the parachute bins. "Something's wrong."

Marlee looked—ten cubbies, but only nine parachutes. "I'm sure it was here before."

"Yes. Did someone jump out?" Clora looked around more closely, especially at the hatches to the outdoors at either end of the corridor.

A thin, dark line ran from the top of the port-side hatch, up the wall to a metal pipe. A braided metal wire. "Would this be the sort of thing someone would use to drain off the anti-combustion spell?"

Clora rushed over, examined the wire, and tugged on handles to try to open the hatch. Marlee pulled her away. "Let's assume it is. I think we have a bomber aboard. I guess Eddie couldn't stop them." It was almost amusing. How many different ways would this world try to kill her? It seemed excessive.

Clora didn't see the humor of the situation. "Gods preserve us," she whispered, then pounded down the corridor toward the crew quarters, shouting, "Wake up! Emergency!"

The crew came pouring out in their nightclothes, blocking the corridor. "Make way!" The captain pushed his way through. He wore a pale blue nightdress with smiling suns on it. "What's the issue here?"

Marlee pointed out the wire. "If that's hanging all the way to the ground, it's draining your fire protection."

The captain swore, looked around, and found a crewman still dressed for work. "Your knife," he demanded, and used the proffered blade to saw through the wire. It parted with a twang, the loose end vanishing out the hatch. "Anyone got a lighter?"

A smoker among the crew left to fetch his.

"We think someone's trying to blow us up," Clora said.

"No floodin' joke! Think anyone would bother with this just to warm their floodin' tea?"

There was a scratch, and the crew member with the lighter held up the flame for all to see.

"Cruft. Right, you lot, get dressed. Roust everybody. Teenie, Houck, break out the hand lights and weapons. Search every corner, starting in the envelope. Wake the passengers too, they can help look. If you've lost your safety shoes, go barefoot. Check whether anyone is missing. You people," he growled at Marlee. "I swear."

"I don't think it's a passenger." Marlee felt oddly detached, but her brain was working at full speed. "My family hire people if they need this sort of thing done, and they would hardly blow up a flight they're on." Having done the hiring herself in this case, she felt pretty sure of this point. "And by the way, there's a parachute missing, but he might still be aboard. The bomb certainly is. Probably best we land before we get to the wastes."

"Muddy ducks! I'll see to that." He ran for the control room.

"Wait!" Clora ran after him. "I don't think landing is smart. If we get too low, we can't use the parachutes. They need at least two hundred feet...."

A crewman walked by with a crate full of crossbows, and Marlee grabbed one, hoping she knew how to use it. There was a tube of quarrels hanging from the shaft, and she slid one into the groove. Wooden tips. To avoid striking sparks from any metal they might hit? Aiming at the outside wall to prevent accidents, she cranked it, locked it. There, not so hard. She'd prefer her little pistols, but hot lead and hydrogen were maybe not a good combination.

Whatever safety shoes were, Marlee was probably not wearing them. She lifted her skirts to unbutton and slip her shoes off, stuffed her stockings inside, and left them in the corridor, following a group of crew members. She wasn't sure she'd recognize all the crew, but if she saw someone wearing a parachute, she was prepared to make a pincushion of them. Sympathy for their cause was one thing, but anyone willing to kill innocents would get no quarter from her.

THE ENVELOPE WAS COMPLETELY DARK, but sounded huge and empty. Wind drummed on the outer fabric layer. Crew members swarmed around her, following catwalks along the floor, their lights showing flashes of each other, curved outer ribbing, open staircases, triangular support beams, and a series of white gasbags, surprisingly far above. The gasbags filled maybe only half the available space. No doubt Clora could explain why, if she were here.

Her knee, and the staircases and catwalks whose builders had considered handrails a frivolity, helped her decide to be among the contingent that stayed on the floor. She hurried after a man headed aft, who aimed his light into the gaps between the cylindrical gasbags. If anyone was there, they should be visible through the mesh surfaces of the steps and landings. Impossible to tell from far off whether there was a tidy little bomb tucked away somewhere, but other groups were climbing each stair, walking each catwalk. Meanwhile, they might get lucky and spot something from down here. Marlee kept her finger near the crossbow trigger.

The floor was starting to curve up noticeably, when there was a shout from the other side. "Hoy! Aft of number twelve, four levels up!" The man with the light hurried ahead to shine it into the gap, and Marlee limped after him. The bright beam showed a frightened-looking face peering over the edge of a landing, and Marlee let fly, hearing the twang of another crossbow at the same time. One quarrel splintered on the bottom of the landing, and the other vanished into the dark. She adjusted her aim upward and reloaded, in case she got another chance.

"Stay away, or I'll blow it now!" A woman's voice, sounding terrified. With multiple lights now shining on the underside of the landing, she was plainly visible through the mesh. A crossbow quarrel passed through the mesh, but was deflected, missed her. "I mean it!" she screamed.

"Hold!" Josip hurried up. "Let me talk with her. Take that light off her. She can't see a damn thing, and that's bound to make her nervous." He raised his voice. "Just one light on her! The rest on the catwalks alongside!"

There were some confused voices, but someone else shouted, "Do it!" and the beams moved.

"All right. You can see nobody's sneaking up on you. What is it you want?"

"Lights off while I climb! A clear path to the top, or you all die!"

Josip had stepped up beside Marlee, craning his head back. "I'm thinking her plan is we all die, anyway," Marlee said.

"Of course. If she planned to use a parachute, she must have a timer on the device. If she sets it to half a minute and drops it on a bag before she jumps off, we have no hope of reaching it in time."

"Well? I'm counting to twenty!"

Josip cupped his hands around his mouth. "One moment while we consider your request." He turned to Marlee. "Bows are too risky. If we just injure her, she'll set it off. Any ideas for a clean kill?"

"Five!"

"I'm thinking!" Marlee hissed. If only she would stick her damn head over the edge again. At least five people had crossbows aimed.

"We need a guarantee," Josip shouted. "Drop the timer first, and you can go." She'd never agree, but he was buying time. There had to be a way.

"Ten!"

Marlee grabbed Josip's sleeve. "Tell me you have my scarf and ring in your pocket, still." It was just the sort of morbid thing he would do, to carry it everywhere until justice had been administered. "Also something heavy."

Josip stared at her, face unreadable in the darkness. Then he reached into his hip pocket and stuffed something into her hand. She closed her fingers around it, felt the ring through the sheer fabric, the pull of the weights. Carefully, to avoid dropping the ring, she pulled the scarf loose, wrapped it around what Josip was offering in his other hand, a cold, heavy, round-cornered shape.

"Fifteen!"

Could she do this, now that she was thinking about it? At the Prince's party, it had come automatically, and this was by no means an easy shot. How did the ring actually work? She jammed the ring on. "Get ready to rush her."

"Seventeen!"

She had to stop thinking and just do it. She allowed herself a rush of panic, to clear her head of doubts. Grabbed the scarf by the ends, swung it around twice, perpendicular to the floor, as hard as she could, and let fly.

The scarf shot up, through the cone of light, up... almost high enough, and into darkness. Guessing at its location, Marlee squeezed her fingers together, gestured, and the scarf fluttered back up into the light, to land on the platform.

"Eight—*oy!*"

The bomber's face was visible through the mesh. Marlee made another desperate lunge, and the scarf flew up, enveloping the bomber's head. A twist of the wrist tightened it, while Josip yelled, "Go, go!"

Feet pounded up the steps. With a muffled screech, the bomber groped around. She rose to her knees, and two crossbows twanged, finally seeing clear shots. Marlee couldn't tell whether they hit, but the woman was still reaching for something, so Marlee jerked her hand savagely to the side...

...and the woman fell, screaming all the way down, to land with a hideous crunch.

Silence. Then one set of footsteps continued, hurrying up the stairs. Lights shone at the base of the stairs, and Marlee turned away, not wanting to see. She jerked at the ring hard until it came free, stuffed it back into Josip's pocket, and left. If she headed straight for the dim light from the stairwell, she'd remain on the walkway. And in the darkness, nobody could see her cry.

BY THE TIME THE SITUATION was resolved, the captain had vented too much hydrogen to clear the mountains, so they paused to pick up a few people who'd used parachutes to leave the flight early, and headed back to the capital, only long enough to get everybody on a train bound for home. It was a long trip, through empty territory.

Josip was already in the observation car when Marlee arrived. Her two guards joined his two at the bottom of the spiral stairs. She ascended into the dome and sat, looking at him expectantly.

He scowled back at her. "Yes, what?"

"You sent for me."

"No, you asked me to meet you here."

"Actually, I invited you both." Clora's head rose through the opening. Once through, she shoved the sliding cover shut with her foot, and pulled up another chair.

"You invited me?" Josip's expression was thunderous.

"You two have to settle this. If you don't make an announcement, someone's likely to do something stupid. And it's not fair to Marlee to leave her in suspense."

"Not fair? She murdered my son."

Marlee looked out at passing desert, biting her lip.

Clora leaned forward earnestly. "And that's unforgivable. Of course. But it makes you look weak to leave things open. If you're dispensing your own justice, you have to go ahead and do it. Now, I think I know what's making it hard for you. You have a code. It's biscuit for biscuit, right? She saved your life, when it was to her disadvantage to do so. You owe her. In fact, she saved you twice, and your daughter, grandson, and his son. And an expensive airship."

Josip stiffened. "I believe she was saving herself then."

Clora frowned at him, then looked at Marlee. "You can step in any time."

"It sounds better coming from you."

Clora shrugged, and turned back to Josip. "All right. Look. She found that wire. She could've grabbed a couple of parachutes, made me put one on, and jumped. That would've been much safer than trying to stop the bomber."

"And she'd have died of thirst in the desert."

"Petro thought it was safer to jump. That's why he insisted that Elga and the older servants do it. That's a well traveled route. While we were in the air, there wasn't a single occasion I couldn't look out a window and see at least one other airship. Someone would've noticed the fireball and come to look for survivors. Two times, all she had to do was not stand in the way, and she would've been safe from your vengeance. And if she'd let the airship blow up, there in one easy boom goes everybody standing between her and a title. You know how she feels about titles."

Josip's lips were pressed tightly together. He looked at Marlee. "Did you put her up to this?"

"No, but I'm curious to see where she's going."

Clora sat back. "I don't have a plan beyond that. I want you two to find an answer."

Josip snorted, and addressed Marlee. "I can't simply let you get away with it. Let the others think I'm fine with them killing each other provided they make themselves sufficiently useful afterward? Faugh. The family would be extinct in two years."

Marlee looked at him closely. This time he was the one who looked away. It sounded like he'd rather not have her killed. "Why do you think I did it?"

"You could answer that, if you chose."

"But I want to know what you think."

"Apart from the obvious, we know he was blackmailing you about something. You managed to destroy whatever evidence he was holding, so we don't know what it was, but that's what made us take another look at the case."

What to say? The obvious rejoinder was that the person who'd taught her, taught them all, to be so ruthless, was sitting across the table from her. But that was an excuse.

"Do I have the right of it?" Josip demanded.

She looked down at the table, tracing a circle with her finger. Looked up. "That's probably close enough. In fact, my memories of that time are a little... muddled." Absent, she didn't say. "And of course you're right there have to be consequences."

"What would you suggest?"

"I would suggest... what everyone in this family hates more than death. Losing. Disgrace. Loss of status."

"You're saying I should—"

"Fire me. Disown me. Have me removed from the succession for Count. Banish me from your, your Countdom or whatever you call it."

"And that would be goodbye forever, then."

Once again, a hint of regret? She put her hand over his. "I'd miss you too, you black-hearted old villain."

He pulled his hand away, but not quickly. Clasped his hands on the table and stared down. Here was a man who hadn't a friend in the world—only minions and rivals. He looked at her, eyes bleak. "I'll arrange it. Be ready to leave in a week's time. Now, please go."

CHALULA

LXIV

SAILING WASN'T THE FASTEST WAY to get around, but it was the most pleasant. Two weeks of open water and sun had baked the chilly fogs of Ruddigor from Chalula's bones, and new places awaited. Now, a stop in the capital to fortify herself with fine food and scented baths, before making further forays into the hinterlands. And to fill her purse, of course. They brewed excellent warming beverages on the misty isles, and they had a fine appreciation for music, but not much coin with which to show it.

As the ship glided in to dock, she leapt off, waving to the crew who jumped off with her to tie ropes. They'd had a proper farewell while waiting their turn at the dock, and now she must run. An exciting storm had delayed them a few days, and her booking agent would be worried, poor man.

Indeed, she found the little fellow waiting on the busy dock, looking anxious until he spotted her. He hurried over, pulling a sheaf of papers from his satchel.

"You do not need to meet me. I would go to your office."

He grimaced. "Not right off, knowing you! There's no time to delay. Your first performance is tonight." He handed the papers over.

Chalula fingered the little coil of wire that held them together. "What is this?"

"It's called a Feldman clip—and it is *such* an improvement over straight pins! Anyway, please go check the place over, so they know the show is on for tonight."

Chalula examined the top sheet. "Campus Pizza?"

"A restaurant opening. They serve a new dish that's got popular in Corilan. Guess someone decided to try it here."

"Campus means it is in the University?" The eateries on campus were all small, and mostly dingy.

"Not in, near. Don't worry, it's solid. Go look it over, and I'll send your luggage to your hotel. You're staying at the Towers."

The address wasn't too far to walk, and she was ready to stretch her legs. Fine as it might be to ride with the wind and spray in your face, it was also fine to walk in a straight line for more than eight paces.

She found it without a problem—a large, glass-fronted place which had obviously been a restaurant before. She dodged around a sign-painter's ladder, and entered.

The place was large and open. The bare brick walls were decorated with quaint antique opera posters of the previous century, and old equipment and uniforms of University boating teams. The acoustics were probably adequate.

A tall, pale man was out among the tables, directing the placement of some mechanical object on the ceiling. Chalula stopped, amazed. "Eddie?"

Digriz seemed unsurprised to see her. "Good deal! You made it. One fewer thing driving me mad. The stage is over there, see? Tell these fellows anything you need. This one will work the lights during the show. Love to talk, but I've got to see about a missing cheese delivery."

"But why are you here?"

"I own the place. Half of it. Now, really, must run. Head on back to the kitchen. Everybody else is there."

Everybody else? She only knew the man as Marlee's shadow. Was Marlee here, too? She wove through the tables to the swinging door in back, then paused.

Did she want to see Marlee? Their last time together had been bewildering. Marlee was eager enough in the carriage, but at other times seemed embarrassed by her, and had not called on her afterward.

Their unspoken understanding had always been that Marlee was in control of the relationship. Every goodbye was the end, and she would never know if there was to be more, until the next time Marlee came to her.

And she'd thought she was satisfied. But their last parting hadn't had any kind of recognition of the relationship, just a lack of further contact. And this, after she'd ridden to the rescue. Chalula felt slighted. Used.

Well. If Marlee had any notion that she could treat Chalula badly, then send for her like a servant and pretend nothing was wrong, she would learn otherwise. But Chalula was a professional, and would do the show she was hired for. She reached for the door, but just then it flew open and a short, plump woman backed out with a tray full of little glass shakers.

The woman stopped and craned her head back, and Chalula was surprised—and this time, delighted—to see another familiar face. "Elinora! My comrade in arms!"

"Barbarian lady!" Elinora set her tray on the nearest table, wiped her hands on her canvas apron, and grabbed Chalula's sleeve. "Come, come!" And led her into the back, past the area where a few kitchen workers were chopping vegetables and minding large pots, to a corner where a few people were sitting at a round table.

She knew them all. The zoukis player from the Crooked Dog, whose name she didn't recall. Jeyne, who stood to greet her. The girl Clora, a little taller than at their last meeting and more self-possessed, wearing austere scholars' robes. And Marlee, casually dressed, looking up at her with a lazy grin.

Jeyne grabbed Chalula's hand in both of his. "Welcome! We were worried about you. Sit and have a glass with us. You've met my fiancée, Alyssa."

"I remember her. Will you play tonight?"

"I'll open, and accompany you if you like."

"I do like." She looked at Clora as she sat. "You are at the University now?" The girl's shoulder bore two round badges, a flame and a right triangle.

Clora nodded, flushed. "That's right. Magic and engineering. I won a Royal Scholarship."

"I congratulate you." Chalula's gaze drifted to the last person at the table. If Marlee was expecting her to continue their game, she would be disappointed. "And you, of course, I know. Are you the other owner of this place? I like to know who I am working for."

Marlee did look disappointed, and Chalula was the tiniest bit sorry. Her tone of voice had perhaps been colder than it needed to be. "No," Marlee said. "My former cousin, over there, sent for you. But when I heard you were coming, of course I wanted to see you."

Chalula looked at Jeyne, then back at Marlee. "What does this mean, *former?* He is no longer your cousin? It makes no sense."

"That's right! My family threw me out."

Her tragic words were so at odds with her cheerful tone, Chalula was still not completely certain she'd understood correctly. "What happens after that?"

"I'm on my own. Footloose and fancy free. Jeyne and I are no longer cousins, nor business partners, but still friends. Please don't tell his father, though."

"And you wanted to see me? Why?"

Marlee looked around at the others.

"Oh!" Jeyne leapt to his feet. "There's still much to do! I think my rest time is over. Alyssa, dear, could I get your advice about something? Over there?"

Clora also stood. "I have an examination to prepare for, but we'll talk again, won't we? I want to hear about everywhere you've been."

"Of course."

"Can I bring you something to eat?" Elinora asked.

"A cold drink, only."

"Miss Marlee's drinking a lemon-lime soda. It's her own recipe. Want to try one?"

"If you mix it with berry brandy."

"I'll see it done." Elinora flapped her apron and bustled off.

Marlee, after a moment, looked up from a close examination of her fizzy glass. "To start with, thank you for your help rescuing me. I never got a chance... well, that's not true. I could have thanked you properly at the time. My head was mixed up. I was afraid. Not of you, of what it meant about me, that I wanted to be with you. That's why I didn't try to see you again. I'm sorry."

It took a moment to parse that. If Marlee wanted to be with her, why wouldn't she? She'd never been shy before. "You were most puzzling. Unlike yourself."

"Yes, I'd changed. I'll tell all about it later. No secrets. Right now, though, I just want to apologize, and ask if we can start over."

Chalula laughed. "We start over every time!"

"N-No, not like that. I don't mean pretend there's no history."

"Then I do not know what you mean."

Marlee sighed. "It's really hard to explain until you hear the whole story. In important ways, I'm not the same person you knew. But I want to find out what we can be to each other."

"Why do you think this is what I want?"

"I am assuming kind of a lot. But here's something about me that hasn't changed—I'm a deal maker. If there's anything we want from each other, I'll find it. If not, at least I tried."

Elinora nipped in to leave an icy glass, flitting away again. Chalula looked into Marlee's eyes, and found things there she'd never found before. Kindness, and hope, and apprehension. And, perhaps, the promise of an end to goodbyes.

"Well. It does not hurt to talk. Already I know a few things I would like. Let us... discuss, after the show."